A HEXCRAFT NOVEL

By Invocation Only

PATRICK THOMAS

PADWOLF PUBLISHING INC.
WWW.PADWOLF.COM
www.facebook.com/Padwolf

WWW.PATTHOMAS.NET
WWW.MURPHYS-LORE.COM
www.facebook.com/PatrickThomasAuthor

BY INVOCATION ONLY
a Hexcraft™ novel
© 2018 Patrick Thomas

Book edited by John L. French
Cover Art by Patrick Thomas and Roy Mauritsen
Cover Design by Roy Mauritsen

10-digit ISBN 1-890096-75-X, 13 digit ISBN 978-1-890096-75-5
Printed in the USA
First Printing

The Dark Mother Superior pulled a fresh human heart from beneath her robe and thrust her knife into it. The heart had to be fresh, probably still warm. They must have taken it right before coming here. Fairness be screwed. They were not getting away with a death sacrifice on my watch and thanks to my being asked to help the kid, they were fair game. They were going down. Way down.

"Dark Lord, join us, we beseech thee!" they screamed in unison.

"Idiots!" I shouted. My companions stood stunned, as they realized what the red fleshy piece of meat she held in her hand was. "All they needed was another drop of blood. The fools didn't have to kill anyone."

"It looks like they wanted to," Gary said, watching the smiles of ecstasy on the dark nuns' faces. A claw the size of a horse broke through the barrier. The sheer enormity of it caused Gary to stumble back. I caught him before he could trip.

"Careful. You fall out and the ward won't let you back in. Watch where you step. You erase that line and we're all dead," I said, but Gary was trembling too much to pay attention. A second, then a third claw appeared, followed by a head with only one clear feature; a pair of jaws that would make a Great White Shark drool with envy. All the teeth were pointed incisors, each the size of a man.

"Incoming!" I screamed over the din.

The claws seemed to be reaching for us. Gary screamed and stumbled again. This time, I was not fast enough to catch him. Landing on his hands and knees, he looked up at the Manglar, like a deer in the headlights. Sensing his opportunity, the Manglar struggled to pull himself through onto the mortal plane faster. His bulk already took up most of the stage and, with a mighty effort, the Manglar hurled himself at the paralyzed Gary. Before he could get fully airborne I was already moving.

"*Stay*," I invoked at Sister Anna, who was preparing to throw herself in front of the boy, throwing away her own life. It wouldn't have been a fair trade. I hated to use magic on her, but to keep her safe she needed to be in the circle. Otherwise, I couldn't protect both of them. I managed to reach Gary first, which gave me about a two-second head start. Before I landed my chalk was out. Ignoring the jaws hurling toward me, I managed to complete a second circle a nanosecond before the Mangler could devour Gary. It bounced off like it had struck a steel wall.

"VERY QUICK, MR. HEX, BUT ALL IN VAIN. I WILL HAVE THE BOY!" the Manglar belched, waving twenty sets of claws in the air.

"Don't think so, Cazz," I answered.

"I WILL GIVE YOU ANYTHING YOU DESIRE – JUST GIVE ME THE MAN CHILD TO DEVOUR!"

"D…devour?!" Gary stuttered.

"Yes. If he can't get you to join him, he can still absorb your power by eating you," I whispered to Gary. "Sorry, Cazz. Snack bar's closed. We both know you have nothing I want."

"FINE. I AM ON EARTH NOW. IF YOU DO NOT FEED THAT TENDER MORSEL TO ME, I WILL CARVE A PATH OF DESTRUCTION SUCH AS THIS TINY WORLD HAS NEVER SEEN!" Cazz bragged, standing up so his enormous head brushed the ceiling of the theater.

"Wrong again. This time, you're on my turf," I growled. "Let me show you how we do things in New York.

This one's for Diane too
for inspiring Hex's curse

"I'm only trying to help."
-Hex, cursed magi

Catherine's neighbors heard her screams and did nothing. Repeatedly. Even across the city, her cries were deafening to me, yet somehow the New Yorkers around her were able to pretend not to hear or care about the battered woman who lived in their midst.

Too many live by a credo that allows them to ignore those in need and do nothing. People don't want to get involved. It's too much trouble. Too dangerous. True enough, but if people sit by and do nothing the bad guys win.

I was done sitting. I would have stepped up sooner except for my damn curse. It's not sentient, but sometimes it feels like it gets off on making me do nothing but wait. It's a special kind of torture. The sad part is that it's so damn simple to get around. Somebody just has to ask for my help.

My curse was inflicted on me because of my many gifts. One is the ability to read a situation or person. I now knew about William's years of abuse toward his wife. I can see how he broke her spirit and body. I see things that no sane man wants to see because they've already happened and there's nothing that can be done to change them.

I was going to make sure they didn't happen again. Catherine's nightly beating began earlier. The poor woman didn't even try to defend herself, the past having long ago convinced her that she couldn't do anything to stop it and that anything she tried would only make her pain worse in the end.

Catherine whimpered and begged for William to stop. Her husband didn't care. Her pleas would have had more effect on the kitchen sink.

What's even more depressing is that Catherine doesn't realize that she's allowing all this to happen. She could have stopped it at any time by leaving but fear kept her in line. A social worker would call it co-dependency, but that's not what it is.

It's black magic, dark and evil. William is a total amateur with no idea of what he was doing. The scumbag had no skill, not even one iota of technique. He was just a brute with an affinity for power. William was able to channel his own anger, mix it with his wife's pain and suffering to weave a submission spell. To further deepen his hold, William would take his wife against her will which added tantric ritual to his dark magics.

Most people can do magic. Rarely is there the flash or fireworks from movies or TV. Things seldom fly around the room. The biggest part of magic is head games. One has to convince the universe that they can do something out of the ordinary. The universe is often easier to convince than others or even one's self. Belief is the mixing bowl which holds all the other ingredients. Stir in will or ritual and you end up with a spell. When most people do magic they don't even realize it and give the credit to luck or positive thinking.

Tantric magic takes the mystic head games to another level. Emotions are power in those rituals. A spellcaster concentrates on a goal, picturing it as the point of climax is reached. The release of sexual energy is channeled into magic which sole purpose is to bring about that goal, whether it's good, evil or somewhere in between.

When William had intercourse with his wife, with or without her consent, he obsessed on her domination and it strengthened his control over her.

In some ways, I'm just like the neighbors because I block out suffering. It's the only way to keep my sanity because I can't usually help. But tonight I heard Catherine's cries and I flashed on her history of agony and abuse. Tonight's horror show was worse than ever before. It was so bad that Catherine did something she had never dared before. She cried out for more than mercy.

"Please somebody, anybody, help me!"

It was barely a whisper, but my magic let me hear that wonderful act of rebellion.

And with that, I was invited to step in and step up.

The miles between us became nothing as I body slid to the street outside of her building. Sliding's dangerous as hell, but a real rush. Basically, I phase out from the world then surf using natural forces like gravity or the Earth's movement through space to travel almost instantly.

I stood and got my bearings. Usually takes a moment. Picture riding the wildest roller coaster ever as it is launched spinning into space and you'll understand why.

The couple's normal looking window glared bright in the night. This part was never easy – my last chance to back out. Graywalking style is hardly without dangers. There were mundane things to worry about like falling off the fire escape if I went up that way. William could have a gun and blow my brains out or I could be arrested.

Whimping out is always the smarter option. Sticking my nose into dangerous situations is how I ended up cursed in the first place. Still, most of the time there is nobody but me that's going to help and I've been in spots where I could have used help and help never came. Still, it never hurts for me to review the risks because I have a habit of being too cocky.

No fire escape needed tonight. The front door of the building was open, but the inner door was locked. No need for magic when hitting every call button on the wall ensures that sooner or later, someone was bound to buzz me in. Sooner won the day.

I sprinted up the seven flights of stairs to their apartment. With each flight, the screams got louder and my legs moved faster.

There aren't a lot of folks who graywalk. There's Jack Wisp, the grandmaster of us all. Known in legend as the Will O' The Wisp or Jack O' Lantern, he'll take on Host and Horde to protect an innocent. Not that all graywalkers are human. Occasionally you'll get a guardian angel, at least one of the ones who'll actually step in and help their charges. Unfortunately, those are few and far between these days. Most guardian angels have gone over to the side of bureaucracy, following the rules of the Host-Horde Accord to the detriment of those entrusted to their care.

The dark sides have been winning for a long time now. People keep allowing them to triumph, making the mistake of thinking there's nothing they can do to change it, so most don't even try. It makes me want to bang my head into a wall. Even tried it once, but all I ended up with was a headache and a dent in the sheetrock.

The apartment door was locked. I did a reading and didn't pick up on any weapons, but all the raw emotion being slung around clouded up the ether, so I might have missed something. It's impossible to prepare for all the possibilities and risk is one of the spices of life. The deadbolt wasn't on, so with one swift snap-kick, I busted open the door, praying William the bastard didn't have a shotgun.

No firearms in sight, but what was made my eyes and heart sore. Catherine was laid out on the floor, battered and bleeding. Her left eye was swollen shut and her husband loomed over her like some horror show monster.

William was balding. His breath stank of onions and beer mixed with tobacco. Two days of stubble covered his chin. An undershirt, sadly and ironically known as a wife beater, was plastered to his body with sweat he worked up beating his wife. It was a yellow color that may at one point actually have been white. His gut lopped over the belt of his half undone pants. Scumbag was laughing in evil ecstasy but that stopped when he saw me.

"Who the hell are you?" William growled, his fist stopping in mid-punch, inches away from connecting with Catherine's swollen eye yet again.

"Avon calling. I have those fragrances you ordered," I said as I stepped closer to him.

"What the hell is this, some sort of joke?"

"No, not a joke, unless you mean you," I said.

William was confused by my home invasion. "You a cop?"

"You wish, William." I grabbed his hand and pulled him off her.

The scumbag was dumbfounded, staring at my hand like he couldn't understand what it had done.

"You touched me!"

"You're observant for a scumbag." I made sure I smiled. Nothing ticked off his kind like smiling at them. Made him feel like I was mocking him. Which I was, but I had the added intent of making him angry, which with luck would make him sloppy.

William's reaction was as pitiful as it was predictable. He swung at me. Still smiling, I ducked. The punch missed so he tried again. This time I hit him with a hex I cast while in contact with his punching hand. I combined it with a two finger Aikido move that added to his force.

"*Flip*," I ordered. William lifted off the floor and spun around, landing flat and hard on his back. The impact jarred his spine and knocked the wind out of him. It was nowhere near enough to take him out. William was still riding the power wave created by his domination spell over his wife.

Worse, I just embarrassed him in front of Catherine. He realized instinctively that he couldn't allow me to go unpunished or he'd lose his power over her.

Too late. The process had already begun. A realization smacked Catherine upside her head. Her crappy husband wasn't all powerful. Part of her fear died a quick and quiet death then and there. Ignoring the pain that racked her body and the blood that covered it, Catherine pulled herself up into a sitting position so she could have a better view. Her body language remained meek, but her pupils had grown wide in the watching.

William stumbled but got to his feet. "Get the hell out of my apartment before I call the cops."

"Call away," I said. "Pity your phone doesn't work."

William didn't believe me so he picked up the receiver. No dial tone on his landline. Enjoying his confusion, I gave him a wink. Being the big man that he was, William slammed the receiver down in the cradle.

"Oooh. Do you work out? Because if you do, you should fire your personal trainer because you just look fat and stupid. Not that the stupid part is the trainer's fault," I said. The idiot didn't realize that the phone still worked. I was just blocking him from using it. Just more head games, this time on my part. These games required will and finesse. William had will, but mine was stronger. In terms of finesse, an ant would have a better chance against an elephant than William had against me.

Painfully aware he was losing, William searched the kitchen, desperate for a weapon. William and his kind preferred dealing with the weak and meek. When faced with an opponent in an equal or greater weight class, the Williams of the world are cowards at heart. That doesn't mean that they'll always run away. Cornered animals are still dangerous. Stumbling toward a drawer in the kitchen, William struggled to remain defiant. Slowly and calmly, I followed him.

His search bore fruit or rather hand tools. William found and pulled out a hammer. Weapon in hand, William felt powerful again, not realizing that feelings are often illusions about what is really happening.

"If I had a hammer..." I sang.

He mustn't have liked my voice because he started smacking the hammer over and over into his palm. "Idiot, I'm going to hurt you."

"You really think so, don't you? Amazing. What color is the sky in your world? *Bad Aim.*"

I almost felt sorry for him at this point so I let him swing the hammer once. The hex I threw at him messed with coordination. The tool missed me but managed to smash William's right knee. The pain made him jump then trip landing on his face.

I'm not embarrassed to admit I enjoyed that. Hoping for more entertainment, I let William get up. His next attack was a roundhouse swing that would have taken my head off if it had connected. No danger of that with him lacking basic motor skills. Without my head to stop it, the hammer's momentum carried it in an arc that ended with William managing to bash in his own skull.

His destructive dance continued its downward spiral for five more swings. With each blow, he lost his power and raised a welt on himself. With every miss, his wife gained back a piece of what she had lost until William was on his knees and Catherine was standing tall. Looking down at the sad figure before me, I felt no pity. I'd been dealing with his kind ever since I was a child and had yet to see one of them show any remorse in their lifetimes. William was no different.

Catherine was frozen no longer. One tentative step was followed by another as she advanced toward William. The abused woman was still uncertain as to what had happened, but Catherine realized she was winning back her freedom with each step, shattering the last remnants of William's spell. Her journey ended when she stood over her husband. He looked up, his eyes open wide and flushed with tears.

Catherine had never seen him cry before and she enjoyed it.

"Please, honey, help me," he begged, lurching himself unsteadily to his feet. With those simple words, his hold on her was completely broken. Catherine looked down and no longer saw an overlord. That vision had been replaced with that of a pitiful man. Their marriage had been the biggest mistake of Catherine's life, but in that instant, she knew she could correct it.

Catherine reached for his face with a tender touch that savagely transformed into a slap. William was stunned. For a moment, the fury of the slave master had returned. Problem was, his anger didn't cower Catherine any longer. William was clueless on how to deal with that. Catherine wasn't. A kick to the groin brought William whimpering to his knees. Catherine followed it up with a knee to his chin, which knocked him from his knees to his back.

"Bastard," Catherine snapped. "I'm leaving you. If you ever touch me again, I'll gladly cut your balls off and feed them to a dog."

William lay on the floor sobbing and she stood savoring the moment. Calmly, Catherine walked into the bedroom, took out a suitcase and filled it up with a few necessities. That done, she picked the bag up and walked to the door. Pausing only for a moment's glance back, Catherine marched out of the apartment without so much as a goodbye. I followed her.

I stopped at the door and peered back at the broken man on the floor. "If now's not a good time, I can come back later with your order. Thank you very much for your business. Bye now." I shut the door, trying not to enjoy the feeling of smug satisfaction I had and failing happily.

Catherine had stopped at the elevator door to look at me. Disheveled hair complimented her make-up, which was running down her face. Catherine's right eye was black and blue, swollen to the point where she could barely see out of it. Despite it all, she was smiling and that made her a beautiful sight.

She whispered two words. "Thank you."

I smiled back. "You're welcome. It was my pleasure."

A *bing* signaled the arrival of the elevator. We moved past the sliding doors. Catherine carried her bag. I didn't offer to help. That action would be counter-productive to the independence we both had just fought for.

"What happens now?" she asked, as the reality of survival outside of William's sadistic protection began to sink in.

"I don't know," I answered. I had no desire for her to lose any of her newfound freedom by entrusting it to me. "Do you have any friends or family you can stay with?"

"No," she said. "Momma disowned me when I married that bum and he picked us up and moved us across the country. He never let me go out. I really don't have any friends in New York."

"I have a friend who might be able to help you," I said. "But first we have to stop off and get you something."

"What?" she asked.

"Protection," I said.

Catherine squinted and pulled her head slightly back. "Look, I'm not interested in getting involved in a sexual relationship with anyone, even for a place to stay."

"No, I wasn't talking about condoms. I meant a different type of protection. What we need to get you is a cross."

"Blood is thicker than a lot of things."
   -Hex, cursed magí

Our feet felt the rhythm vibrating through the sidewalk long before our ears could hear them. Our travels had landed us down in the Village, outside a trendy little club called Plasma. The line stretched out the door and down the block. The bulk of the crowd was dressed in various shades and styles of black. A handful had dyed their hair the color of night with neon highlights and worked to make their skin as pale as possible by avoiding any contact with the fireball we call the sun.

Eighty percent of them were what I call blood groupies. Others might say they were vamp wannabes. They'd read the books, they'd seen the movies. Now they wanted to live the life. At least that way, they'd have a life. Yeah, I was harsh, but these idiots had no idea what they were wishing for.

Plasma was packed. Most of the folks on the line had a better chance of getting a tan than getting in. Catherine and I strolled right past them to the front of the line. The children of the night gave us dirty looks, a few even made some harsh comments questioning our parentage. As I turned my head and glared, the crowd became very still. If there were any locust or crickets in Manhattan, we would've been able to hear them quite clearly. Curse or no curse, I can still be damn intimidating when I want to.

Tending the velvet rope that led to the club was a very large black man. Shoulder to shoulder, he was as wide as most doors. The guy's name was Barber and he had arms that would do tree trunks proud. It wasn't that he had the definition of a bodybuilder. He didn't. His physique was the type someone got from a cocktail of hard work and good genetics. Add the basketball sized head, which he kept clean shaven and you had one damn intimidating bouncer, especially to the average club-goer. Had me beat easily in the intimidation department. When he saw me coming, he did a double take then rolled his eyes.

"Mr. Hex to see Layla," I said with a grin. Barber knew very well who I was and who I was probably here to see.

Barber was the head bouncer. Barber's over two centuries old and one of most dangerous undead around. Barber didn't take kindly to being pushed by anybody. Those who dared hurt an innocent or break a rule regretted it. In extreme cases, the offender could end up being found in an alley somewhere with two pinholes in their neck, lacking some vital crimson bodily fluids. Barber was a traditionalist and still often went for the jugular. Most modern bloodsuckers get more creative in their choice of arteries and veins to conceal their activities from a public weaned on the films that were the descendants of Dracula movies. The only time these vamps sparkled was when they cooked in the sunlight.

Barber nodded and took the rope off its hook to let us in.

"Thanks," I said with a smile. Barber gave me a soft glare. He accuses me of being obnoxious, but I had stopped resenting it awhile back. I have never figured out if Barber actually likes me, but I've been a fill-in bouncer at Plasma enough times to know he trusted me to watch his back. He would never let anything happen to Layla or Plasma, which meant as a close friend of Layla's, I could count on him to watch my back. Sometimes that's better than being liked.

Passing through the front door was akin to entering the belly of the beast. I had suggested a fang and uvula motif but was ignored. That might attract a crowd with a sense of humor, which wasn't Plasma's target market.

The club was kept dark for effect. It was enhanced by black paint that covered the walls and bar, and black tiles on the floor with the occasion neon paint. What little lighting Plasma had was done with a theme in mind. Sadly, the mood was Gothic Disco. Most of the spotlights were "black" light making the clients' eyes, teeth, and fangs glow a purple-tinged white. A live band was playing, calling themselves the Kasket Bangers. They were adequate. The music was a bit of a change from the norm at Plasma, being heavy metal as opposed to the alternative stuff they usually put out. The last heavy metal band had tried to summon demons during their act. I helped make sure we didn't get any party crashers from Hell.

Inside, the choice of attire didn't vary much from those who were waiting outside, except a few actually sported Count Dracula style capes. The lot looked ridiculous to me, but I'm hardly a fashion critic. Tonight, my attire consisted of high top sneakers, blue jeans and a blue t-shirt with my hex symbol on it. The symbol was an overlay of an "H" over the anarchy circle. I often wore a trench coat, but tonight I went with a black leather jacket. Catherine was dressed in a simple skirt and blouse. We had dropped her suitcase off at a nearby 24-hour pawn shop where I knew the owner. He agreed to hold onto the bag until she came back. His retainer was a tad unusual, but the woman paid it with only a touch of disbelief.

He just asked for the shoes off her feet. Having packed several other pairs, Catherine agreed.

Plasma was not the type of club you walked into with a suitcase, at least if you wanted to walk out. Transients made for excellent feeding.

Layla was at her traditional table in the far corner of the place, under the Dali lithograph, the one with the clocks melting over the landscape. It was the only exception to the Gothic Disco motif. Never understood its significance.

I ignored the bar as we passed it. Mages learn early on that as a rule, one does not drink or eat food in a place that is not one's own. It can have far-reaching consequences, not the least of which are loss of freedom and death.

Layla stood up to embrace me. We kissed each other and that was a show for the masses. Then we hugged each other and that was for real.

"Hex, sweetie, how are you?" she asked with a smile which just barely revealed her glistening fangs. The skill came to the undead with practice. Catherine hadn't noticed the unusually large incisors yet. "What brings you by my little slice of heaven?"

"I thought I could appeal to your better nature. I have someone here who could use your help."

Layla looked Catherine over, then looked back at me with fire in her eyes. "Are you crazy? What are you doing bringing fresh meat into this place? Do you want her emptied?" The blood groupies were actually hoping for such an experience. The bloodsuckers that hunted wanted more of a challenge. Fear added to a junkie's blood high.

"I don't see what one thing has to do with the other," I said with a grin. "No one here will touch her. She's under my protection." Layla nodded. She begrudged the fact that I have so much influence among her people and the other night breeds, more in fact than she does. I had purposely failed to mention the cross which lay beneath the top of Catherine's buttoned blouse. Had she been with anyone else, Barber would have searched her, found the cross and made her remove it. Layla makes special exceptions for me. We go way back.

I called Catherine over and made introductions. The ladies shook hands.

"Now, Hex, what is it exactly that you want me to do for Catherine here?" Layla asked as she sat back down in her high-backed, black wicker chair, looking every inch the regal dark queen.

"Well, she has recently come into her own and she needs some help with social services to get a place to stay. I figured you could assist her," I said.

"Hex, I don't do that stuff anymore. You know that," Layla said, slightly annoyed. Her past was an embarrassment to her present.

Catherine looked confused. "Don't do what?"

"Layla used to be a social worker. One of the best, but that was before she became a... club owner," I added with a mischievous grin. "But like I said, she was the best and I know just because Layla went through some changes that the urge to be a helpful do-gooder didn't go away."

Layla smiled despite herself. "All right, I'll see what I can do. I'm making no promises."

"That's all I can ask for. I'll leave you two to get acquainted. I'm going to go check out the band." Catherine sat down and I wandered over to the other side of the room. Of course, I eavesdropped on their conversation. An impressive skill when you figure in the decibels the amps were putting out. It was mostly small talk. Girl talk, if you would. Layla asked a few questions about what had happened and Catherine answered them courageously. Layla had a cell phone sent over from the bar and made some calls.

In an amazingly short time, Layla managed to find Catherine a place in a safe woman's shelter for the night. She would help find more permanent accommodations tomorrow evening. Layla wasn't exactly a day person.

"How long have you known Hex?" Catherine asked, looking at me out of the corner of her eye.

"Ever since he was a little boy. I was his social worker and counselor."

"What did you counsel him for?" Catherine asked.

"It seems his parents were worried because he was hearing and seeing things that they felt were products of an overactive imagination. They sent him to me to try and cure him. As it turns out, what he saw and heard was real," Layla explained. Every bit of which was true, but I was debating whether or not to bust her chops over the breaking of counselor-client privilege.

"You don't look old enough to have counseled him when he was that little," Catherine said, a little in awe of Layla's physical beauty and presence. It was considerable, even without the sex appeal the vampyre glamour added.

Layla smiled. "Well, I'm a bit older than I look, but I hate to be cliché."

"Why did you stop being a social worker?" Catherine asked.

"It no longer seemed appropriate with my new life, but enough about me. We need to get you to that shelter. Why don't you wait here and I'll go talk to Hex," Layla said. Nobody would bother anyone at her table if they knew what was good for them.

I had kept my back to them the whole time, feigning an interest in the band. Layla stealthily moved behind me. She wrapped her arms around my waist and gave me a quick peck on my neck. I didn't even cringe. Amazing what trust will do.

"Okay, Mr. Hex, I'll help you out on this one, but I have a question for you. When's the next time you're going to grace my bed with your presence? It's been far too long."

I turned and returned her hug and gave her a quick peck on her lips. We had dated a while back but, unfortunately, with the differences between us, we knew it was just never going to work. Still, we had kind of an unspoken agreement. When neither of us was seeing anyone we had a tendency to fall back into each other's arms and beds.

"Let's talk about that another time," I answered, successfully changing the subject.

"You know I would be more than willing to help you. I can hurt this guy or send one of my people to make sure he never hurts anyone ever again," Layla offered.

"No," I said sharply. "You know I don't play that way."

"I know, but I thought I'd offer. I'd have another good deed for the night." For a moment, the two of us swayed back and forth to the music, forgetting our troubles. Despite her current lifestyle, Layla was still one of the best friends I ever had and she is one of the few vamps I know who has learned to successfully control her bloodlust and not take human lives in order to feed. Plasma was her way of helping others do the same. Despite her protests to the contrary, she was still a social worker at heart.

Our dance was wonderful, but nothing lasts forever. We had both learned that long ago.

"I'd better get going."

"Yes, you better. It's always close to feeding time and not everyone here plays by the house rules," Layla said. House rules prohibited the unauthorized blood-taking of any patron and no hunting in Plasma's neighborhood. Almost impossible to enforce more than two blocks from the club. "You take care of yourself."

"I will," I promised.

Catherine had taken up a spot at the far edge of the crowd and was watching the band. She didn't seem thrilled with the music, just happy to be out people watching. Catherine had probably never seen anything like these people and seemed at a loss as what to make of the crowd. Probably for the best, as it saved me a lot of explaining. I inched up beside her, tapped her on the shoulder, leaned in and whispered in her ear, "It's time we got going."

She nodded. "Okay."

Before we left, I stopped by the bar, picked up a shot of actual plasma. Most of the bloodsuckers didn't like their blood cold, preferring it fresh from the source. Layla had a back room where the fresh stuff was available, but only for private club members. She utilized needles and IVs so volunteers could donate fresh blood without getting affected by the crimson curse. At the bar, she served actual plasma to vampyre and human alike. I heard with a shot of whiskey and some tomato juice it is not half bad, but it is not the beverage of choice for the blood junkie with a discriminating palate. It is like comparing a TV dinner to a meal in a five-star restaurant. But being what it was, when times are tough enough, they drank whatever they had to. The bloodsuckers just didn't like to talk about it. It was embarrassing and bad for the image.

A bunch of the norms that frequented the place loved this stuff. It was by far the most popular item on the menu, that is if Plasma had a menu. For a while Hipsters searching for the latest craze left their oxygen bars to invade Plasma just to try the stuff.

I took the shot with me and handed it to Barber as we left. He smiled and nodded his head in thanks. As we made our way out onto the mean, dark street, a pair of newbie vampyres, both of the Korlak breed, started stalking us. It would be their funeral if they decided to attack. Even the undead can die if they mess with me.

"Sometimes the easiest way to sneak up on someone is to let them do it for you."

-Hex, cursed magi

New York City at night has a magic all its own and that magic changes depending on where you are. Down where we were in the Village, despite the lights, the streets seemed dark and overcast with shadows. This is of course why it's the favorite of many of the Gothic types. Even at this hour of the morning, the Village was crowded. Street people had set up their sidewalk stores. Almost anything was for sale — paintings, old magazines, clothes, bootleg DVDs, and stolen jewelry – as each vendor hocked their wares. One guy was selling used underwear, very little of it his. Sad part was, he was raking in the cash.

The homeless and the con artists were out, each trying to get money in their own way. I led Catherine through the gauntlet, walking at a brisk, but comfortable pace. The two newbie bloodsuckers were still behind us. They had taken to the rooftops thinking that we wouldn't notice them. The technique had probably worked for them a dozen times before. After all, nobody in New York looks up. It makes you look like a tourist. The pair still hadn't backed off, so I let them have their last chance to leave of their own choosing. They didn't take it. I also did a reading on the pair. They were hunting near Plasma in violation of Layla edict.

We passed by a church. At this hour, the doors were locked. Can't have the riff-raff coming in and getting spiritual salvation unless it was during normal business hours. I had Catherine walk to the top of the stairs and stand near the door. It was holy ground and while holy ground won't stop a vampyre, it hurt them. Thankfully, even the curse knew that these two meant me harm. It lets me use magic in self-defense, asked or unasked.

I slipped away into the darkness and let the shadows cradle me. I too was a child of the night. I had made her my friend and my mistress and Lady Nyx let me use her darkness to further my own ends. How does one actually date the night? Believe it or not, it started with flowers, but that was a long time ago. Let's just say, I've had a lot of unusual girlfriends and leave it at that.

The bloodsuckers had no such unusual lady friends or similar arrangements. The clueless blood junkies became my prey. It didn't take but a minute. All Catherine heard were the screams, the sizzles, and two thuds before I returned to her side.

"What was that?" she asked, peering out into the darkness between buildings.

I laid a comforting hand on her shoulder, which she cringed away from. Catherine wasn't ready yet to be touched. "Nothing you need to worry about." As we descended the church steps, two shapes emerged from a nearby alleyway, stumbling blindly. The two vampyres had lost some control over their shapes and were assuming a more bestial form. Korlak can't do bats but are able to do most canines. I think they were trying for wolves but were getting French poodles. Their powers were no longer working right because I had marked them. Two of my anarchy Hex marks were branded onto their faces. When I'm in a good mood, I give everyone one chance to change their ways. They just used theirs.

Catherine screamed and took a step back at their approach. Both blood junkies looked up, embarrassed and hungry. Each thought Catherine might be easy prey. I let my shroud of darkness spell fall away and they saw me smiling at them. The pair took off like two bats out of Hell. All I got from it was a splitting headache. Pain happens when I use magic. The more powerful the magic, the more intense the pain. All part of the wonder that is my curse.

"What was that?" she asked, shivering.

"In the Village, could be anything," I answered, wrapping a protective arm around her shoulder. This time she didn't pull away. "Let's go get your bag back from Paulie."

Paulie was the owner of the pawn shop where we had left her things. He dabbled in stolen goods and mystic artifacts.

Catherine was the type who couldn't bear silence. It must have left her dealing with her own thoughts. Whatever the reason, she needed to make small talk.

"So what kind of a name is Hex anyway?" she asked.

"Actually, my full name is Mr. Hex."

"Is that your legal name or a nickname?" she asked.

"Yes," I answered.

"Which one?" she said.

"Both for all intents and purposes." It was my taken name. I didn't share my given name readily and I never learned my true name. I would be much more powerful knowing it, but that would open me up to a lot more vulnerabilities. I had enough already with the stupid curse.

"And what do you do for a living when you're not saving damsels in distress?" she asked, a smile sneaking out onto her lips.

"Actually, I'm a professional dragon slayer."

"Really?" she asked.

"No, not really. Most of the dragons still around are pretty benevolent. No reason to kill them."

Catherine just tilted her head, confused. "How did you know about... um... my troubles?"

"Let's just say I have my sources."

Catherine was starting to look at me as if I was some sort of wacko, but events of the evening more than made up for any misgivings she had. Her guard was still up, which was a good thing. As we turned the corner, Paulie's Pawn was in full view. It was like a little piece of Vegas in the heart of Manhattan. Paulie really had no sense of interior or exterior design. Things were put where they were put with reasons known only to him. Paulie, to the best of my knowledge, never left the shop. He was there 24/7, working around the clock, sleeping between customers. Paulie felt he provided services that should be available any time day or night.

He kept the door locked at all times. Paulie didn't trust anyone. You could try to buzz in, if you wanted. If he liked the look of you, the door would open. If he didn't, might as well keep on moving. Sometimes, he napped on the cot in the back. Most of the time, he dozed off in the easy chair behind the counter. An ancient nine-inch black and white tube television was usually blaring.

I buzzed. He woke up very carefully, opening one eye at a time, his hand automatically reached under the counter to where he hid his double-barreled shotgun. It was loaded with two slugs, one with silver and one with iron. The pellets had been soaked in holy water. One blast would take out anything human, werewolf, or fairy and do some serious damage to anything demonic or vampyre. Paulie recognized me, smiled, and buzzed us in. We had made one stop on the way over to pick up something which I handed off to him.

"Hex, my friend, you are a prince," Paulie said, his grin threatening to swallow his face as he opened the brown paper bag. "Kung Pu chicken?"

"Your favorite," I said. Paulie rarely ever cooked for himself since he never went shopping. He usually ordered take-out food. His favorite Chinese restaurant had stopped delivering to his area, but the place still served food until the wee hours of the morning.

Paulie opened one of the white cardboard containers and waved the steam up into his nostrils. Inhaling deeply, he sighed contentedly. In the darkness of the back room, a pair of green eyes stared ferociously out at us. Catherine didn't notice. I winked into the blackness and the eyes vanished.

"It's a little late for dinner and a little bit early for breakfast, but for this I'll make an exception. Can I offer you any?" We both said no. He ate some of it quickly, moaning in ecstasy. "Love that MSG." Satisfied for the time being, Paulie closed the container and put it aside. "What can I do for you now, my dear?" He had the smile of a cherub and the body of a couch potato. He was short, standing about five foot seven and probably weighed two hundred twenty pounds. Paulie had a belly, the expanse of which any beer guzzling connoisseur would be proud of. He wore a freshly pressed white button down shirt with a t-shirt underneath and dark pants with suspenders. His hair was almost gone on top, but still fairly thick on the sides and the back. Paulie wasn't vain enough to bother with a comb-over. Considering his social schedule, he was well groomed and his clothes were always clean. He was disorganized, but never sloppy.

"I need to get my suitcase back," Catherine said.

"No problem," Paulie said. "All that needs to be settled now is the storage fee. The standard is ten percent of the money loaned out. But, since you didn't ask for any money, we will have to come to some agreement. I think twenty dollars would be fair."

"Twenty bucks?" Catherine said. "You've got to be crazy. It was only here about four hours. And I gave you the shoes."

"As a mere retainer of my services. Five dollars an hour is barely minimum wage, but for you, I will make an exception."

Catherine looked aghast. She normally wasn't the type to argue with someone, but after tonight she was willing to change. "I'll give you two dollars."

"Hmm," Paulie said, happy that the game had been joined in earnest. The eyes appeared again, unmistakably green. The body behind them was growing restless and began to pace. "That wouldn't pay for the light that you're using standing here. Eighteen."

"Four."

"Sixteen."

"Six."

"Fourteen."

"Seven."

"Ten."

"Eight."

Paulie looked at her before nodding. "Okay, eight it is."

"Good," said Catherine. "Because that's all the money I have left."

Paulie took her money, but the look in his eyes had changed. He was part businessman, but he didn't have the killer instinct needed to become a rich man.

"If you don't mind an observation, you're flat busted and out on your own."

"That about covers it," she said.

"Perhaps I can help," offered Paulie.

"How?" she asked suspiciously.

"You might say I am the keeper of broken dreams." He was, actually. "It is my lot in life. I buy them from those they have hurt and try to recycle them into new hopes. Since obviously you no longer have any use for the two pieces of jewelry on the ring finger of your left hand, perhaps we can make an arrangement."

Catherine tried to take in what Paulie said. She could not make sense of parts of it, but she understood the business offer. She looked down at her left hand and saw her engagement and wedding bands staring back at her. She had been wearing the rings so long that she had forgotten they were there. They had become that much a part of her. That was not a part she liked any longer, but she looked at Paulie skeptically. "How much?" she said, handing them to him.

Paulie picked up the diamond engagement ring and, using a jeweler's glass, appraised it. The green eyes also appeared to be assessing the jewelry, still trying to remain hidden.

"Pretty good, almost a karat. Looks like 14 karat gold on the band. I can give you seven hundred."

"What? Seven hundred. That ring was five thousand dollars."

"I can never sell it for five. I can maybe sell it for fifteen if I get lucky. It could sit here for years and I need to make a profit."

Catherine took off her wedding band.

"It's not engraved is it?" he asked.

Catherine shook her head.

"Good, because if it's engraved they are pretty much worthless unless someone wants to melt it down for the gold. No one wants to buy a wedding ring with somebody else's name on it. I can give you two hundred twenty-five." Paulie looked up at her face and the lost innocence that shone in her eyes. "Oh, what the heck, make it an even thousand for the set."

Catherine looked at the rings and barely thought about it a second before saying, "Deal."

He nodded. "Now I'll make you another deal. You are going to be moving into your own place and you'll need some things. If you take credit, I'll give you one hundred and twenty-five percent of whatever I get back."

Catherine looked around at the pile of televisions, utensils, furniture, and clothes. "That sounds like a good idea. Why don't you just give me five hundred for now?"

Paulie nodded his head and opened his cash register preparing to count out the money. "You're going to a woman's shelter tonight, are you not?"Catherine nodded yes.

"Let me make a suggestion. Take a hundred dollars with you, leave the rest here. I won't charge you for it. The shoes you left earlier will cover it." The shoes were a big deal for Paulie. They were the shoes Catherine used to walk out on an abusive husband and Paulie got them within an hour of the leaving. Another woman in the same predicament, wearing those shoes, would suddenly find it easier to leave her abuser. Paulie would make sure they ended up in the right hands or rather on the right feet. "If you take the money with you to a woman's shelter it may be gone when you wake up. You can leave the suitcase also. I'll only charge you two bucks more for holding it."

She looked at me, I nodded. "He's got a point and you can trust him. He's not a crook."

Paulie smiled and nodded his head.

"Okay. Sounds good. I'll be back sometime in the next day or two to pick up the rest of it," she said, taking four twenties, a ten and two fives.

"I can even help you get more money, if you are interested," Paulie hinted with a sly smile and a conspiratorial wink.

"I won't do anything illegal," Catherine said.

"It may not be legal, but it would be real satisfying for you. You have any credit cards?"

"Yes, but they are in the scumbag's name."

"I figured they might be. You can sign for him, but he gets the bill, correct?"

"Yes."

"Why don't I max out your plastic? I'll take thirty-three percent, you get the rest. I will hold half your cash for sixty days to make sure there is no problem with the credit card company."

"If there is I'll take care of it," I promised.

"At the end of the two months, you get the rest of your cut. I'll give you the same deal for credit."

"Try it," Catherine said, handing Paulie a Gold card.

"How does sixty-six hundred sound? Your cut would be forty-four hundred."

"Sounds good but is that the most you can get?"

"No, I could get you fifty-six-hundred in your pocket, eighty-four-hundred total. The only problem is if he used his card he would know instantly. We leave him a little cushion and he won't find out until his next statement. To delay that you could send the company a change of address card on him and he may never see the bill until they start legal action on him."

"I like the way you think, Paulie," Catherine said with a grin.

"Thank you. That shows you to be a woman of exquisite taste," Paulie said with a small bow of his balding head.

"Do it," she said.

"Sign here and it's a done deal. A pleasure doing business with you." Paulie handed her a receipt then extended his hand once she signed it.

She shook it. "Likewise."

"Hex," Paulie said, already back into his Kung Pu chicken. The green eyes finally stepped out of the darkness into the light, revealing Paulie's black cat Morpheas. Morpheas rubbed and circled Paulie's legs. Paulie dropped her a piece of chicken. The ebony feline pretended to ignore it, lifting up the tip of her nose, the only spot on her that was white and choosing to remain aloof. I knew from experience she would not eat anything but mice in front of company. Bad for her image. "You take care now."

"I will. You too, Paulie. Bye, Morpheas. Say hi to your mom for me." Bast was alright for a goddess, even if she ran a spy network of cats. I've asked her for help in the past but we couldn't always agree on a price. If she finds Gary's parents, she'll make me an offer and I'll decide whether I'm willing to pay.

As we walked to the door. Catherine noted Morpheas for the first time.

"What an unusual cat," she said. Morpheas came across as mistress of any domain she entered. Most people sensed this, just did not register it on a conscious level. "What is she?"

"Morpheas is a one of a kind, aren't you, sweetheart?" Paulie said as he buzzed us out. Morpheas, almost alone, went for the chicken. Kung Pu was her favorite too, although she preferred it before the board of health took an interest and the Chinese place still supplemented their meat with rats.

The stroll to the woman's shelter was going to take us about thirty minutes. Catherine was getting a little better at small talk. "So how did I do in there? Did I get a good deal?"

"Paulie's a fair guy, but he does have to make a living. You did fine."

"Can I buy you a cup of coffee or breakfast or something?" she asked me, looking up with big brown eyes. I knew the look. Catherine was seeing me as some sort of knight in shining armor and she was grateful. She wanted to somehow pay me back, but I didn't want to take her up on what she was offering. It was hard to stay romantically involved with me. Besides, it would just transfer her problem. She needed to become her own person before she did anything of that nature.

"No thanks," I said. "I'm pretty much exhausted. I've got to get back to my apartment."

"Where do you live?" she asked.

"Around," I said with a sidestepping smile. We talked a little bit more, mostly about her, her childhood and the time up until the marriage. Why she married him, how much in love she thought she had been. She realized what a fool she was soon after, but she took her commitment seriously. Not wanting to break it, she dealt with his abuse until she became a broken woman. Now she was standing taller and straighter. Catherine was getting a bit more confident. She had found the onramp to the road to fixing herself. When we made it to the woman's shelter, she was laughing as if it was the end of a first date. After we got her checked in, she stood in front of me looking as if she both wanted and didn't want a goodnight kiss. I obliged her, but only on the cheek.

"I want to thank you for everything," she said.

"My pleasure," I said.

"How will I get in touch with you if I want to talk or something?" she asked, trying to hide the innuendo, although whether it was from me or herself I couldn't tell.

"Well, just say my name three times and that will summon me."

"You're kidding me, right?"

"Maybe," I said. I could have given her my website and e-mail address, but as she didn't have a computer or cell it wouldn't help her.

"So I just say Hex three times?" she asked.

"No, you'll have to put the Mister in front of it."

"Okay, you're probably in the phone book," she said with a giggle. "Take care of yourself."

"You too." I watched as she went in to find herself a cot. As I watched her soul start to shine, I realized it was going to take a lot of time and work on her part, but Catherine was going to be just fine.

"If you don't case a job first, whatever bad happens is on you."
    -Hex, cursed magi

The day had been a long one even before the business with Catherine. I was exhausted. The climb up the stairs to my sixth-floor walk-up seemed to take an eternity. I practically dragged myself the last two flights. My keys slid easily into both locks, but I knew something was wrong. Things were too quiet. Usually, my brood was barking and yelping at the door by this point.

I have a very large studio loft apartment. One room, but it measures well over two thousand square feet. Plus, because it's a top floor apartment, I have roof access. Great for barbeques. The one thing I wanted to do at this point was go to sleep. I longed to spend the next eight to ten hours in a large, comfortable king size bed. Unfortunately, somebody was already in there and it wasn't Goldilocks. The window by the fire escape was open and a man was in my bed with a terrified look on his face. When he saw me, his eyes seemed to almost glimmer with the hope that I would rescue him. His mistake. I ignored him.

He'd been trapped in the bed by my brood. Technically I don't live alone, but I'm the only human in the place. My roomies were hard at work protecting our home. Sitting on the floor, but still almost as tall as a full-grown man, was Jeeves. I had rescued the golem years ago from an evil mage who used a copy of the Kabbalah–the real one, not Madonna's version. The jerk was technically adept, but nowhere near an expert craftsman. He'd screwed up the spell somewhere and Jeeves had developed feelings, emotions, and some would even say a soul. It was the type of thing a kid who didn't know any better might do.

Jeeves wasn't the mindless servant he was created to be. His maker and I got into it over the evils of slavery. When it was done, Jeeves was free, but the golem had nowhere to go. He'd helped me take down the mage, even saved my life, so I took him home.

I had a soft spot for golems.

These days Jeeves wears a steel headband, welded in place by my magics. Only he can remove it.

We both have our reasons for it. The problem with golems is they keep growing, getting bigger and bigger as time goes by. Each year Jeeves grows a few inches. Eventually. he'll be too big to fit in my apartment, but that'll be quite a while from now. Traditionally, when a golem gets too big there's a failsafe built in to get rid of it. There are two ways a golem is made. One type of golem has a parchment with a secret name of God written on it in his mouth. Remove the parchment and bye-bye golem. Jeeves is the other kind and had the word "emeth" carved into his forehead when his clay was still soft. To terminate that kind of golem the mage, or anyone else, needs only take him outside and rub the "e" off leaving the word "meth." Emeth is the Hebrew word for life; meth the word for truth. The action kills the golem. I can testify to its efficiency. No way I'll let it happen to Jeeves, therefore the headband.

Jeeves was always hungry for knowledge. He's read every book in my apartment at least twice, including the ancient encyclopedia set. He spends hours a day on the Internet surfing, sucking up every bit of information he can. He also maintains my website. I had to get him an extra-large keyboard so his fingers could type. Jeeves really loves the chat rooms on the net because in real life he's mute. On the Internet, he can talk just like everybody else. He's had quite a bit of trouble understanding cybersex since his maker didn't see fit to give him sex organs of either kind.

Jeeves, from his position on the floor, had one arm draped across the bed with his fingers wrapped around my unwelcome visitor's neck and shoulders holding him in place. At his hips and feet was the pack that had literally followed me home one day when I was visiting the spirit world seeking advice from my spirit totem.

My totem was a wolf and he gave good advice. In return, he asked me for a favor; his pack wanted to leave the spirit world and come to the physical one. It turns out that there were some very real dangers invading the spirit world at that time. Dangers they couldn't fight. At least not fight and win. I was a sucker for a furry face, so I agreed. My spirit guide, whose name is Mordi, which in the wolf language means wisdom, came with his pack. It included his mate, Maydo, whose name means heart. They brought their cub, whose name is unpronounceable by a human tongue. I call him Rocky. Two other canine spirits tagged along. One was a fox I named Sly. The second was a coyote who we call Trickster. He wasn't the Native American deity, but he had an aspect of the god in him, as did all coyotes.

Each of them had their eyes trained on the visitor's terrified face. All five sets of glowing teeth were bared and any time he so much as twitched they growled. He tried to remain perfectly still, probably more than a bit scared by the soft glow each of the pack gave off. No need for a nightlight in my place.

Finally, there was the last of my brood, the lady of the house with no disrespect to Maydo intended. The pixie was sitting on the visitor's head, buzzing and singing an angry song. Her name was Bollywog and she was about eight inches high and had tiny gossamer wings which fluttered in the air. Her skin was the color of pale copper, while her hair was as green as grass and stuck up in all different directions. Bollywog had discovered hair care products and used quite a bit of goo in her styling. The tiny lady was extremely vain and tonight she wore what she would call a simple dress but was an evening gown with sequins. Bollywog insisted I shop and buy clothes made for the Barbie doll. Bolly's measurements were about the same and she liked the doll's clothes. We cut holes for her wings.

Bolly became part of my household after doing me a favor which I returned by rescuing her from the Queen of the Fairies. One of them anyway. There are so many kingdoms, it isn't difficult to lose track.

Unhappy with the unwelcome intrusion, Bolly was showing her displeasure by slowly pulling hairs out of the man's head, one by one. He must have been here for some while judging by the bald spot she had made. If it kept up for another hour he'd look like a Benedictine monk. Each time Bolly pulled, he yelled. Then the pack growled and he'd go silent again. I smiled at them but didn't want to interrupt their fun.

Since there wasn't going to be any sleep for a while, I decided to feed my hunger. Out of the cupboard, I grabbed a box of sugar-coated cereal and the necessary eating utensils then went to the refrigerator for the milk. The expiration date on the milk was questionable, so I took a sniff. It hadn't gone bad yet so I poured some into my bowl and planted myself on the couch in the center of the apartment. I grabbed the remote control, turned on the big screen TV and put my feet up on the coffee table. The home invader was trying to get my attention.

"Hey! Hey, buddy, a little help over here! Excuse me!"

Ignoring his request, I ate more cereal. The only reason I could think off that the brood was treating him this way is that he broke into our apartment, so he was getting what he deserved. I spent so much time installing mystic security measures that I overlooked the mundane. It was an oversight I would correct tomorrow by putting security locks on all my windows.

I laughed as Bollywog continued to pull hairs out of his head. The guy seemed to be at the end of his rope. I felt the start of a twinge of pity.

"Hey, Tinkerbell, stop it!" he yelled.

That time he got a huge clump of hair yanked out. Bollywog does not like being compared to Tinkerbell. It's a personal thing with her.

The next time he tried to speak, the wolves all growled in unison. That shut him up for a few minutes. I knocked off the rest of my cereal and chased it down with a glass of OJ.

I channel surfed for a few minutes. Not much was on except infomercials. Sad part is some of their production values are better than prime time sitcoms. An "ouch" filled the air every time a hair was pulled. I tried unsuccessfully to keep my chuckles to myself.

Finally, the intruder decided to speak up again, this time using a more polite tone.

"Excuse me, uh, sir, but I seemed to be trapped here. Could you help me? Please?"

I turned and acknowledged his existence. "Oh, hello, I didn't see you there."

"Um, don't you think there is something you should do?" he asked.

"You're right, it's very foolish of me not to. Rude even. Sorry. Hey guys." One by one the pack came over, I scratched them behind the ears, gave them a hug and got licked on the face in return by everyone save Trickster. Then I went over and high-fived Jeeves. My hand was almost as big as one of his fingers. Lastly, Bollywog floated over to my cheek and gave me a kiss. I returned the favor, although my lips were bigger than her head.

"What's that Tinkerbell ..." Bollywog shot over the top of his head and yanked out two clumps of hair, one with each hand. "Ow!"

"Bollywog doesn't like being compared to Tinkerbell. You should have learned the lesson the first time. It would be wise to apologize," I said.

"What, me apologize? Listen here, I'm going to sue your butt off. This is unlawful imprisonment, kidnapping, and assault. I'm going to own everything you have by the time I'm done with you." With that, Mordi growled, a deep and a primal roar that came from the heart of the beast. The man's blood ran cold and his face turned pale. Very few creatures have ever heard a growl like that in the dark of night and lived to see the next dawn.

"You're in no position to be making demands," I said. "We could make you disappear and no one would know any better. My friends get very hungry and wolf chow is very expensive. And where do you get off breaking into our apartment and trying to blame what happens on us."

"I didn't break in."

"Yeah, you're the cable repairman. Don't BS me." I checked out his umbra, what some would call an aura. His had some speckles of dark, which was an easy way to tell the amount of evil in a person. He had no more than the average man or woman. Right now, his umbra was tinged with a streak of a sickly yellow, which translated as fear. The guy was terrified.

"All right, all right, I'm sorry," he said. He actually meant it, although several hours of being corralled by the brood more than likely accounted for his repentance.

"Okay, Cal, perhaps we could let you up. What do you think guys?" Everyone looked at each other, looked at me, then nodded and backed off, just slightly. Cal shimmied his way up to the foot of the bed and sat up fully with his legs dangling over the floor.

"Man, thems some mad wicked guard dogs you got," he said, showing no flair for grammar. "Wait a second. How ya know my name?"

I smiled and shrugged. It's a gift that the curse didn't reign in completely because I didn't do it consciously. Things came to me without rhyme or reason. I know things, situations happening, people's names, things in their past, sometimes things they didn't even know. I'm great fun at parties.

"Now, how are we going to handle this situation?" I asked, stroking my chin. Would have been much more effective if I had a beard. Sometimes I sported a goatee, but not lately. "You trespassed, tried to steal from me, violated our privacy, and wasted the time of my friends here. The way I see it, you owe us, big time."

"I owe you? You've got to be nuts. I've been a prisoner here. And you owes me a gun."

"Excuse me? Why would I owe you anything?"

He pointed to Mordi and quickly retracted the digit as the wolf showed his fangs. "He ate it."

I chuckled and scratched Mordi behind the ears. "Good wolf. You are never going to see that gun again, even if you wait for it to come around again." Spirit animals are more energy than matter so they lacked the traditional digestive tract. That gun was no longer even solid. "Be happy he left your hand. Or if we let you walk out of here. Instead of whining about the weapon you lost, you'd be better off trying to figure out what you could offer us that would make it worth our while not to make you disappear," I bluffed. None of us believed in violence for violence's sake, but no harm was done in twisting the truth a little. Cal bought the bluff.

Cal crawled across the bed toward the open window but the pack moved between him and the exit. Each of them crouched down low, their fur bristling and teeth bared. The burglar leapt to the floor and sprinted toward the door, but Jeeves got in front of him and few people have the chutzpah to go up against a seven foot plus tall clay man.

Bollywog had flown over to sit on my shoulder and gently rubbed that side of my neck with her hands. Bollywog knew when the curse was hurting me and her massage felt great. Inch for inch, pixies were many times stronger than humans.

"I don't have nothing. That's why I'm a thief. Because I want to get stuff and I don't have any." He talked as if speaking to a slow child.

"Save the sob story for someone who might care. Everyone has choices to make in life. There are plenty of other ways of getting stuff, most just take a bit more patience. Just because you weren't willing to wait and work for it, don't blame it on society." That's always the next step. "You had a bad childhood. Society let you down. So on and so forth, yadda yadda yadda. I got news for you, Cal. Plenty of us had bad childhoods. Society's let down all of us." My own father offered me to the Devil as a bargaining chip to get out of a bad contract. You don't hear me whining about it. Not often anyway. "It doesn't excuse robbing people. You had choices to make. Own them, don't pass the buck."

"Listen to Mr. Holier-than-Thou and his attitude. Look at all this stuff. Sure, it's a crappy apartment but you've got a big flatscreen TV. What is that, seventy-five inches?"

"Ninety."

"See, I ain't never even seen a ninety-inch TV. You got a theater quality surround sound system and every video game system known to man. Freaking NORAD doesn't have a killer computer set-up like this and you got more books than the New York Public Library. A family of four could sleep in those leather chairs and sofa. You've got it all, man."

"I worked for all of this, so I don't want to hear it. You want it, you can work for it, too. You're not going to steal from me. If you don't want to work for it, you're going to have to become a much better thief. Take some pride in your profession."

"Hey!" I think I offended him. "I'm a great thief. I'm just not used to dealing with Cujo and friends."

That elicited a growl from the pack.

"That's understandable. While you think on things, why don't you come on over, have a seat. Want some cereal?" I asked, walking into the kitchen area. Cal looked suspiciously at me but took the cereal. I handed him the milk. "Want some orange juice?"

"Sure," he said as the skinny kid chowed down. My guess is he hadn't eaten today.

Cal was young, about seventeen to nineteen. He had black hair and brown skin. He looked like his ancestors came from Pakistan, but his accent marked him as somebody who was born and lived in New York all his life.

"You got a place to stay?"

"What's it to you?" he asked, spitting out crumbs of cereal among spittles of milk.

"Well, I'm strange. I care about people, even those who try and rip me off."

"Yeah, I got a place. It's a hole in the wall, but the rent's cheap."

"Good," I said, "Then I take it you don't have a job."

"Not a nine to five paycheck kind of job, no," he said with a sly grin. "I guess you're going to tell me that I shouldn't be stealing and to get a job."

"No, not my style. You've got to make your own decisions. You also have to deal with the consequences of those decisions. If you want to get a nine to five job, I can help you. I know people who will point you in the right direction. If you want to stick with the life of crime, that's your business also. I might be able to hook you up with some people who can help you in that area, as long as you don't bother to replace that gun."

"Why's that?"

"The only purpose of a handgun is to kill or maim another human being. You carry one, that means you're willing to kill or maim somebody during a crime. I can't be a party to that."

"Hey, I'm in a dangerous business. I'm in people's houses, they might shoot at me."

"Well, then you should make sure that you only go into houses where people are out," I suggested. "Try ringing the bell first. Those folks have the right to shoot you, for crossing their threshold. You don't have the right to shoot them."

He looked at me funny. "That's your opinion. Someone pulls a gun on me, I got every right to cap him and defend myself."

"Yes, you do," I said, "But not if you are in that person's home. He is defending himself, his family."

"Yeah, well what about cops? They carry guns."

"That's different. And you know it. So what do you want to do?" He looked at me as if I was insane. That happened a lot.

"I want to stay doing what I'm doing."

"Okay," I said. I walked over to my Rolodex. Yes, I actually had one. Phones can be lost or hacked. I flipped through it and wrote down a name and a post office box. "Put an envelope into this post office box with a time and place where you can be contacted. An associate of mine will show you a better way to do things, but this information comes with a price."

"What's that?"

"One, you promise me that you'll never steal family heirlooms. Things of emotional sentiment you don't touch. Don't touch toys. Don't touch wedding or engagement rings. Anything with an inscription you leave behind."

"Nobody tells me what to do," Cal said.

"That's a defiant attitude." Kind of like it to be honest. People who cave too easy tick me off. "Well, you don't have to, but I can guarantee you will never successfully steal anything again."

"How are you going to do that?" he asked sarcastically.

I just looked at him and smiled. As he stared back, he didn't know how, but he knew I was telling the truth.

"You got no right."

"Pointless to argue because I still have the power to do it. But by breaking into my place, you gave me the right." An extension of the self-defense clause of the curse. "You involved me in your life, asked for it, if you would. That was your choice. Where it goes it from here is also your choice. No biggie. Sit there and think about it. Watch a movie. I'm going to get some sleep."

Cal looked at me like I was insane and an idiot. "You're going to sleep with me in your apartment? You crazy? I could be psycho and kill you."

I smiled. "If I was alone you wouldn't get within ten feet of me. With my family here, you have no chance of hurting me. So," I said walking over to the closet and taking down a pillow and some blankets, "You can watch television or you can get some sleep."

"What if I want to leave now?"

"You're more than welcome to. The only problem is there are a couple of nasty people out there who were looking for me earlier this evening." The two Korlak went away hungry. Not sure if they are making a smart or dumb choice after their one warning. "They're still around and might to be looking for someone to make trouble for. You'll be safer here, at least until the sun rises."

Normally vampyres don't go out of their way to hunt strangers, despite popular literature. It's easier and safer to hunt those they are familiar with. Or angry with. Cal had been in my apartment for hours. If they smelled my scent on him, he wouldn't stand a chance.

I handed him a pillow and blanket then helped him make up the couch. "If you need anything, just holler. Bathroom is through that door over there. Pleasant dreams."

"Thanks," Cal said, still a little unsure of exactly what had happened but knowing he was tired enough not to argue.

I stepped into the bathroom to take care of some business and came out in sweats and a fresh t-shirt. I climbed into bed, as did my brood. The pups all situated themselves around my side and legs. Bollywog made herself comfortable and nested on my head. Jeeves sat back down along the right side of the bed and draped his left arm protectively over the lot of us. Jeeves didn't need to sleep, so he would keep watch. The pack only need to sleep for psychological reasons. Bollywog and I were the only ones who really needed the rest.

Home and in the care of my family, I was safe and secure. I dozed off into the land of dreams, careful to set the protective wards I needed to remain safe while there, before I faded away.

"I've never been one to go looking for Heaven. It's my experience that before long it'll come looking for you."
-Hex, cursed magí

When I woke the next morning, it was actually afternoon. Cal had left sometime after sunrise. None of us made an effort to stop him. With the bright rays of the new dawn, he'd be safe from the Korlak. They were one of the vampyre breeds who died in sunlight. Time would tell what he thought of my proposition.

I pulled open the blinds and was greeted with blinding brilliance. It was a beautiful spring day. One too nice to spend inside, so after Bollywog and I had brunch, we dressed Jeeves up in a rather large trench coat, with an oversized baseball cap with a shot o' gold logo and the lot of us headed out the door. Before we hit the street, Bollywog had used her glamour to transform her appearance into that of a hummingbird.

Our destination lay uptown in Central Park, one of those places a man with a hummingbird circling around his head, followed by a trench coat-clad giant, surrounded by three wolves, a fox, and a coyote would not be a sight to see. And technically the pack were able to make themselves invisible to human eyes if they wanted to. They didn't want to today.

In Manhattan, people rarely gave my entourage a second look and we passed two groups stranger than us along the way. We entered the park on the southeast entrance, the one near where the famous toy store used to be.

No sooner had we set stepped on the footpath then there was an excited yapping and playful nipping at my heels. As much as I hated to do it, I started to jog. The pack likes to keep me in shape, so they take *me* out for walks. Today's goal was to do at least three miles. Jeeves was too bulky to run. The impact of his feet on the path would smash it to pieces, so he and Bollywog headed off to Strawberry Fields. The rest of us moved in among the other joggers, bicyclists, and even a few diehard rollerbladers.

"I hate exercising you know," I said, looking down at my pack as they ran alongside me.

They answered by barking back at me.

"Yeah, I know it's good for me," I answered. "Doesn't mean I like it." A passing jogger looked at me like I was nuts. Despite myself, I was in good shape. It helps me run from the big bad guys. Three miles flew by. There were days when I did five, but the weather was too nice to waste running around in circles.

For our cool down, we walked toward Strawberry Fields and passed a park bench where Garar was sitting, preaching philosophy and prophecy to the passing people. Unfortunately for him, most New Yorkers found a man wearing a purple turban and a tuxedo who was sitting in Central Park to be a less than a credible source. Truth be told, he was pretty good at the prophecy gig. Not the best, but his talents were impressive. Mostly, he liked to go with the old oracle bit, where you spoke in riddles, so if you were wrong no one else would know.

"Good day, Mr. Hex," he said in his heavy Indian accent, despite the fact he was not Indian and was born in Hong Kong.

"Hey, Garar." He stuck his hand out and I slapped it. "What's the good word?"

"Not as good as you might like, young one." Garar was only fifteen or so years older than my official age, but he sported a gray beard with purple highlights to match his turban. He liked to play the role of a knowledgeable old wise man. It didn't bother me any. "Forces are aligning and shifting. They seek the power of youth. You will be caught up in the struggle."

"Thanks for the warning," I said. "Know tonight's Lotto numbers by any chance?"

He smiled. "You think I'd be sitting here if I did?"

"Fair enough," I said. "Now remember, my offer to get you that flute and basket with a snake in it still stands. It would definitely attract more of a crowd."

"No, thank you," he said. "But I have been looking into getting a bed of nails to lie on."

"Still got that bad back, huh?" I said with a wink. "A better show would bring in more money." I pointed to the hat he had laid out in front of him for donations. It held some change and a few small bills. The bills were probably his seed money.

"There is more to life than money," Garar countered.

"Then you don't want my donation?" I asked, holding up a folded bill.

"Not necessarily. While not everything, it does help one over the rough spots."

I dropped a twenty in the hat. Garar spoke in riddles but his advice had warned me of approaching trouble more than once. Definitely worth a couple of bucks, every now and then. I noticed Trickster was attempting to pull the hat under the bench so he could run off with it. He loved to harass people, particularly Garar. I snapped at him and the coyote glared at me but didn't stop. Garar saw what was happening and dropped to his knees to grab his escaping hat.

"Bad doggie! Let go of Garar's money," he ordered. Trickster responded by shaking his jaw and by association, the hat. Change flew everywhere. Garar managed to wrestle the headgear away and gather his fallen money, slipping the twenty into his pocket. "I am calling a dog catcher on you!"

Trickster stuck his tongue out and moved in to pull off Garar's turban. Mordi interfered by stepping between the pair. Trickster shrugged, sat down and began cleaning himself.

"Thank you, good doggie," Garar said, patting the wolf once on his head.

"Garar, I've got places to be. Take care."

"You too. May the fates watch over you and your brood, Mr. Hex." He looked at Trickster and added, "At least most of them."

Once we arrived at Strawberry Fields, we found Jeeves at the center of a small group of children who he was teaching how to fly a kite. He kept several stashed in his coat. The kids were amazed by his size and by the hummingbird that continually landed to rest on his head. The pack went over to say hi and the children automatically started petting the lot of them. They enjoyed little children, except for the coyote. Trickster couldn't be bothered and moved himself off to lay in the sun and watch everyone else make fools of themselves. Still looking like a hummingbird, Bollywog fluttered over to mess up my hair.

There were enough kites for everyone, so Jeeves handed me one. I did my best. It actually stayed up in the air for more than a couple of minutes, but I couldn't make it do the tricks that Jeeves could. He controlled his with two ropes, able to make it fly and dive like a fighter pilot. As I stood watching the kites dance in the air, I felt a familiar presence behind me.

"Hello, Hex," the melodic voice said.

"Hi, Aziel," I answered as I looked behind me. Aziel hadn't changed a bit. He never did. Az still sported shoulder-length tangled blond hair and wore the same white trench coat over what appeared to be a pair of the broadest shoulders on the planet. Appearances can be deceiving. His shoulders weren't that broad but it's the easiest way for an angel to hide his wings.

I liked Az. Too many angels are holier than thou, thinking themselves better than and above humans. Being human myself, the attitude annoyed me. Aziel wasn't like that. He was down to Earth. Literally.

For an angel, he was a rebel. Not enough of a rebel to have been cast out, but enough not to worry more about rules than the safety of his charges. Az was one of the original guardian angels. Back in the days of the early Hebrews, there were eleven thousand guardian angels for every person. They were tripping over each other. As people followed divine instruction and were fruitful and multiplied, the number of angels per person diminished until early Christianity, when there were only two angels for every person. In modern times, the human population had exploded so much that there weren't enough angels to go around. Each guardian angel had to take on multiple charges. I have never been able to get the exact number out of Az.

"What's up?"

"I need your help," Aziel said. "One of my charges is heading for major trouble and is totally unprepared for it. The thing is, it's something that you can help him deal with."

I owed Aziel a lot. While my own guardian angel took a more standoffish approach, Aziel had no problems diving in and getting his hands dirty often helping me in the process.

"Mind giving me a little bit more background information?"

"Sure, why don't we move away from the children for now? What I have to say is not meant for their ears." Aziel had a neat little trick where he could make only certain people see him. Right now, I was the only one who knew he was around, other than the pack and Jeeves, but children can sometimes see things the rest of the world can't due to a mix of innocence and simply not knowing they aren't supposed to be able to.

The pack followed us, leaving Jeeves and Bolly to entertain the kids. Once we got to an empty meadow, Aziel pulled three Frisbees from beneath his trench coat and sent them flying in different directions. Mordi, Maydo, and Sly all caught the Frisbees in their teeth. The pack were far more talented than your average canine. They not only caught the Frisbees but threw them back. Sly threw his to me, Maydo to Rocky and Mordi threw to Trickster. As we played, Aziel laid out the details of his dilemma.

"The next master mage has been located."

I nodded, being intimately familiar with the situation. "The new magi, huh? Great but the magi needs to find his or her own way."

"True," said Aziel. "That's exactly what I'm trying to have happen. It's a him by the way. A fourteen-year-old. Lives in Brooklyn."

"That's great. I could stop in to say hi but that kind of ruins the point of him finding his own way, don't you think?"

"I agree with you in theory. The problem is the other forces are not going to let him develop without interference. We all remember what happened with the last magí," Aziel said.

"I didn't turn out that bad." My tone was a tad defensive.

The angel laughed. "No, you didn't, but you did upset the balance. Some magí never realize their power. Those never enter into the equation. You came into your power early, but never chose an alliance or formed your own. Then there was that business where you walked off, turning your back on magic and renouncing it."

"It was my decision to make."

"True. But no one else had ever knowingly made that decision before."

"I had my reasons." I really had and they seemed reasonable at the time. "And I came back."

"But the damage had been done."

Aziel and I had become so mired in conversation that the pack had decided to ignore us in favor of their own fun and they were basically having an incredible game of Frisbee football among themselves. The only thing that got their attention were two officers on horseback. As the two mounted cops approached me, each put on their upset face. This expression, combined with the fact that they were mounted high above me on horseback was engineered to intimidate me. It wasn't working.

"Excuse me," the larger of the two cops said. "Do those dogs belong to you?"

"What dogs?" I said, "I don't see any dogs. Do you, Az?"

Az nodded no before I realized I was the only one who could see the angel.

"A wiseass," the officer said, with that telltale look of what he had in mind. Just what I needed, another psychiatric evaluation. Fortunately, two can play at that game.

"We have leash laws in this city you know."

I gave out a short howl which the pack instantly recognized and disappeared into the ether. "Seriously officers, what dogs would you be talking about? I don't see any dogs."

"Listen, wise guy, we're talking about those dogs over there playing Frisbee," he said turning his head. The cop did a double take as he noticed the empty field.

"Dogs playing Frisbee?" I said incredulously. "I've seen paintings of them playing poker, but never Frisbee. Perhaps you've been out in the sun too long, officer. Do you still see the dogs over there? Oh wait, I see them now. One of them is purple with red polka dots."

The cop looked down and scowled at me, then put his hand on his billy club. "Listen wiseass, there were dogs over there and I saw you playing with them before. Where did they go?"

"Officer, I don't own any dogs."

"All right, wise guy. You think this is funny? Why don't you come downtown and answer some questions."

I laughed. "No thanks. I'm not really into Trivial Pursuit or Jeopardy. Another time perhaps? And if I reschedule, will there be any prizes if I answer them correctly?"

The larger cop started to get down from his horse. Mordi materialized briefly behind the horse and gave a very deep wolf-like growl. He also materialized to the point where the horse could actually pick up his scent. The horse reared up and took off running across the park with the cop still stuck in the saddle. His partner chased after him, trying to slow the horse down.

Aziel chuckled despite himself. "That wasn't very nice."

"Maybe, but it was well deserved."

"Judge not, lest ye be judged," Aziel shot back. It was in the angel manual.

"Cut the crap. We both can read what kind of man he is." Scenes of his life and victims paraded across my consciousness unbidden. "Corrupt and an abuser of power. He got off easy with that practical joke. Come on, let's walk. We'll head back to Jeeves and Bollywog. If you expect me to talk to you, you had better materialize enough that other people can see you."

Aziel looked as if he was about to argue, but thought better of it. "Will you help me?"

"Probably," I answered. "What do you want me to do?"

"You need to take this boy under your wing."

"Wouldn't that be more practical for you to do?"

"Ha." He said it instead of actually laughing. Az was unamused.

"I'm not playing nursemaid or mentor to a kid. When he becomes an adult I'll consider it, but not until then."

"But the forces are aligning against him. All the forces."

"So I hear." Az tilted his head. "Garar may have mentioned something earlier. The powers were against me when I was his age. Quite a bit younger even."

"He's not you. Especially in terms of confidence and skill. He is nowhere near where you were at that age. The boy thinks he's a rebel, but he just likes to be contrary. His knowledge is nowhere near his power level and he is not showing any desire to learn on his own. If you don't step in to help him out, he'll end up being somebody's tool. I know you don't want that," Aziel said.

Damn the angel if he wasn't right. "What time frame are we talking?"

"Most of the forces are waiting, hesitant to make the first move. He's learning more day by day. So far nobody's approached him but they are watching. He's bound to have seen some. All I hear is whisperings and murmurings, but first contact will be made very soon. Maybe even tonight."

"Fine, when you hear more than a whisper or murmur come to me. I'll do what I can, but I don't want to be the first one to approach him."

"Why is that?"

"Trust me. It won't be a good idea. I'd get all his denial and hostility for ruining his view of the world. I don't want the grief."

"Fair enough. What are you going to do for the rest of the day?"

"Have some fun with my brood. Want to join us?"

"Thanks, but no thanks. I have places to be and people to watch over," said Aziel. "I'll keep you posted."

"Wake up calls often ruin the best of dreams."
    -Hex, cursed magí

Deep in the heart of the night, I slowly opened an eye, wondering why an ice cream truck had gotten in my bedroom and why it would not stop ringing its bell. I was too tired for a cone, but the ringing was insistent. My other eye opened and searched the apartment, but no truck. Jeeves, sensing my confusion, tapped me on the shoulder and pointed at the phone.

"Ah," I whispered and tried to sit up. I was having trouble, as I had tangled myself up in my sheet. The phone showed no compassion for my predicament and continued to ring. Bollywog fluttered over to the phone and floated the receiver to the hand I had managed to get clear of my bed web.

"Thanks, Bolly," I said, grabbing the phone. "Hex central. How may I direct your call?"

"I'm sorry. I was looking for sex central. Must be a wrong number," a sultry female voice purred.

"Hey, Layla," I said. "Do you have any idea what time it is?"

"About two ten in the morning. Why, were you asleep?"

"Yes."

"Let me do it right. Wakey, wakey, Mr. Hex. Better? Are you in a good humor now?" Visions of ice cream trucks still danced in my head. "Why are you laughing?"

"It would take too long to explain. What's up?"

"I have a job for you. Get down to my place ASAP."

"Why?"

"Not to throw your own words back at you, but it would take too long to explain. There are a couple of folks down here who need help."

"That's nice." Layla was one of the few who knew the details of the curse and that I couldn't ask to be asked to help.

The vamp sighed and although I couldn't see her, I knew she was rolling her eyes. "Will you help, please and thank you?"

"Sure, I guess. I'm just disappointed I'm not getting any butter crunch."

I hung up and threw on a trench coat and a baseball cap to cover my bed head. Plasma is twenty minutes away by subway, fifteen by cab. I made it in less than two and most of that was leaving my building and its wards. The only price I had to pay for body slide was a small headache. Barber was expecting me and let me right in, muttering under his breath.

"Her kind doesn't belong here. It isn't right." Barber was visibly upset.

"What do you mean?" Knowing Plasma's clientele, I wondered who could have this effect on Barber. He led me straight to Layla's table.

"What's important enough to drag me out of a warm bed?" I asked, kissing Layla's cheek and sitting down.

"That." Layla pointed to an adolescent boy who was the center of attention of several leather-clad men. Every one of the lot, except the boy, was the genuine article. Vampyres.

"I see." Unless I was way off, this was Az's charge.

"It gets worse. Gander at the table across from them. A penguin, here. If word gets out I'll be ruined. Worse, she's not even drinking."

There was a nun with a table to herself. Dressed mainly in black, she would have almost blended in with the crowd, if it weren't for the crucifix she wore around her neck. Some of the bloodsuckers were cringing in pain at the sight.

"You can always claim she was a vampyre hunter on a mission from God."

"Hey, that just might work," Layla said, her mood brightening.

"How'd she get the crucifix past Barber? I thought he checked all weapons at the door."

"She breezed right past him, refused to give it up. She's the real article, radiates faith. Combined with the crucifix, it makes it painful to be anywhere near her. Plus Barber is a big softy at heart and apparently has some sort of soft spot for nuns."

"Really?" I asked.

"Apparently some helped him out back in the day and he's the sentimental type. Get her out of here. The boy too, before he gets drained."

"I think you should worry more about the Rush." Rush was the slang term for the breed of vampyre surrounding the kid. The full name is Brahmaparush, but nobody outside of India seems to be able to pronounce it correctly so it gets shortened to Rush.

"You're kidding me."

Had anyone else suggested the vampyres were in danger, she wouldn't have taken it seriously. Rush are nasty bastards. They don't just drink blood – Rush consume human flesh starting with the head. On a virgin kill, the new Rush makes the victim's skull into a drinking mug. They collect them like college students do beer bottles. For Rush, killing is a party. It typically ends with the Rush dancing with the victim's intestines wrapped around their heads like turbans. A sick, sad breed.

Rush normally have nothing to fear from an army division, let alone a kid or a penguin. Most vamps don't read umbras. The kid's oozed power. The good sister blazed with a spiritual fire. She didn't seem to realize it, but she had talent. When it exhibits itself, she would call it a miracle. As her power is tied to her faith, she wouldn't be wrong. Either of them could fry the Rush. Problem was, neither of them knew it and once the fear kicked in, they were dinner.

For the moment, the kid was holding his own. The Rush were not trying to mark him, only entice him. No chance, unless he had some freaky tastes.

The nun was at greater risk, so I'd approach her first. The penguin seemed almost as interested in the kid as the Rush were. I wanted to know why.

"I'll take care of it, Layla."

I moved to the penguin's table. "Good evening. Come here often?"

"I'm not playing dress up and I do not want to be your party toy. Take a hike," the nun ordered, not even bothering to look up at me. She had eyes only for the boy.

"That doesn't seem very Christian of you," I countered by way of small talk.

"You're not in a very Christian place," she shot back.

"Is it not written, 'Judge not, lest ye be judged'?" I said, stealing Aziel's line from the angel's handbook. "I wasn't aware the Bible or the Roman Catholic Church said you can pick and choose who you should be good to." At least not openly. "Besides, isn't it the sinner who is most in need of salvation?"

"Nice arguments." The nun turned and half smiled at me.

"Thank you. I work out," I said flexing. I actually got a full smile out of her. "May I sit down?"

"As long as you realize, I have a vow of celibacy and a can of mace."

"Sounds like a winning combination. I can assure you my intentions do not lean in that direction, Sister Anna." Although were she not in that habit, I might have changed my intentions. Without makeup and with her hair hidden under her veil, the nun was one of the most striking women I'd ever seen. But it was the beauty of her umbra that made her truly beautiful. She glowed with a purity of spirit one rarely sees anywhere.

"You have me at a disadvantage. You know my name, but I don't know yours."

"Mr. Hex. Pleased to meet you."

"Likewise. Is that your Christian name?"

"It's the one I go by."

"Fair enough. To what do I owe the pleasure of your company?" she asked sarcastically, never letting the boy out of her sight.

"You sound suspicious," I said.

"I am. I have had more offers tonight than I did in all my teenage years."

"Sister, I find that hard to believe."

"That I got offers?"

"That you didn't get a lot when you were younger."

Sister Anna smiled before she caught herself. "Then I've gotten a much wider variety."

"That I believe. You'll have to pardon the clientele. You're probably one of the few true clergy to brave this place but there have been many impersonators over the years. Makes for some fantasy fulfillment." I failed to add that she was an incredible looking woman, even wearing the habit. There are some things too awkward to say to a nun, even for me.

"Charming place. Wonder why the police haven't shut them down?"

"No laws being broken. No money changes hands for illegal acts. It is all a matter of choices. If you want them to respect your choices, maybe you could start by respecting theirs."

Sister Anna tried unsuccessfully not to stare at a man being led around on a leash by a domineering vampyress. "What they're doing is wrong."

"They probably feel the same way about you. But enough about cultural differences. Tell me about your interest in the boy."

"I hardly think that is any of your business."

"I would disagree. I am guessing it's a protective interest, but he seems unaware of it. So, what's going on here?"

"You would never believe me if I told you."

"You might be surprised at what I can believe." I gave her one of my looks, the one that makes me seem sincere and trustworthy. Works as often as it doesn't, but I really wanted it to work on her The penguin weighed her options. "Okay. I was warned that harm might come to this boy tonight if I wasn't here to help protect him."

"How did the warning come?"

She seemed embarrassed and whispered her reply. "In a dream, earlier tonight."

"And who gave it to you?" I asked, already suspecting the answer.

"My Guardian Angel."

"Ah, so Aziel called you in too."

The nun's eyes went wide as she turned away from the boy for the first time. "How do you know his name?"

"Same way I knew yours," I answered with a grin which has been often called annoying.

"That's not an answer."

"Then I can add that you're not a full nun, but a novice who won't take her final vows for almost a year." Some orders have their nuns do up to five years before taking their final vows to make sure they are ready for the tough life.

"How do you know that?"

"About novices, postulate and the like? One of my best friends is a nun." The Iron Nun in fact. "And I did time in Catholic school."

"You make it sound like jail."

"Nope, jail doesn't charge your family."

"I meant how you knew the personal details about me. You're being evasive."

"Yep. I'm good at it." I felt a familiar presence arrive. Aziel breezed right past Barber, without the bouncer even noticing him. The boy was laughing at something one of the Rush had said. I could see the angel frown. Wasn't a good sign.

"The boy's name is..."

"Gary Bending," I finished, as the name flashed in my mind. "Don't worry. We'll keep him safe."

"What do you mean we?" Sister Anna snapped. "I don't recall asking for your help."

"Doesn't matter. Two others already have. I'm in."

"Well, I'm leaving and I'm taking Gary with me," she announced as Aziel walked over.

"Sit down," Aziel whispered and without her conscious mind knowing why Sister Anna obeyed. Aziel sat in the empty seat across from me and poured himself a drink from a flask in his inside pocket.

"Don't tell me you're drinking something from the bar," I said.

"Hardly. Brought it myself," Aziel said in a voice that only I and Gary could hear.

"When did you take to drinking?" I asked.

"Who are you talking to?" Sister Anna asked, giving me the look that has landed me in the loony bin more than once. We ignored her.

"I can't get drunk, so what does it matter if I drink? Besides the flask was a gift from Dionysus and the stuff has a charming taste. Glad to see you could join us."

"What's a good night's sleep when weighed against the fate of some brat? Why did you call in the penguin? Losing faith in me?"

"Who are you calling a penguin?" Sister Anna demanded, becoming infuriated by the half of the conversation she could make out.

"Hardly. Couldn't get a dream past your wards, so I influenced Layla to call you. Anna is backup. She is good with kids. You're a bit lacking in that department."

"Thanks a lot, Aziel."

"Aziel? You can see Aziel?" Sister Anna asked, trying desperately to see that which could not be seen.

"Unfortunately," I admitted.

"Flattery will get you nowhere," Aziel said.

"What's the deal here?" Sister Anna said. "You're talking to thin air, Mr. Hex. I'm beginning to think you might be insane."

I winked at her which caused Az to give me a double take, then look at Sister Anna and back at me again. "A lot of that going around."

"The thing I can't figure out is how you knew about Aziel, me, and Gary."

"Don't sweat the little stuff, Sister. Just go with the flow."

"You can trust Hex, Anna," Aziel whispered in her ear.

Sister Anna tilted her head like a mutt listening to a silent dog whistle. "But a little voice inside me tells me I can trust you."

"Thank you," I said, winking at Aziel this time.

"You're welcome," the woman and her Guardian Angel answered in stereo.

The situation across the way had taken an ugly turn. The Rush had decided to continue the conversation elsewhere. Gary was not interested in leaving with them, but they insisted. Forcefully. There were nine of them. In a couple of years that might be fair odds, but not now.

"Looks like my cue," I said, standing up.

"Your cue? What about me?" asked Sister Anna.

"You can watch my back. Leave the vampyres to a professional."

"Vampyres? Who said anything about vampyres? Those guys are gangbangers. Let's just call the police."

"I don't think so. Watch and learn."

Two of the Rush had grabbed Gary on either side and lifted him up by his shoulders, carrying him toward the door. Barber stepped up to the plate and blocked their exit. The big vamp had been a father himself and drew his line of blood short of preying on little ones. Before they could come up with an alternate plan, I was behind them.

"Gentlemen, and I use that term loosely, put the kid down and step away now."

"Says who, blood bag?" one of the Rush asked, a hard case with seven body piercings on his face alone.

"Shut up!" whispered one of his fellows, quickly dropping Gary and backing off. "That's Hex."

"So what?" the first said, unimpressed. Gary had silently backed up to get out of the line of fire.

"That's Mr. Hex to you," I said in my best Clint Eastwood imitation.

"Sorry, Mr. Hex. Lew only came over six months ago. He don't know no better," said one of the Rush, named Hark, in a very respectful tone. My rep reaches far and wide. I gave one of the Rush to a demon hunting psychopath a while back and after stuff like that, word gets around.

"Then what's your excuse?" I asked.

"Just out looking for new blood. You know how it is," Hark said with a shrug.

"You ain't looking for a meal. You are looking for a slave. A powerful one."

"Don't tell him anything, Hark," Lew said. "None of his business."

"Wrong. It's been made my business. This is your one chance and only warning. Back off or I will be royally pissed," I said.

"Like I'm so scared. Listen, Hex, nobody messes with the Rush." Lew knocked my baseball cap off. My face went grim. Lew was the only one not to notice. "I am going to have your head as a cup. Let's take him guys," Lew said, before he realized six of his fellow vampyres had taken the better part of valor and made a strategic withdrawal.

"What the hell is wrong with them?" Lew asked.

"I will not be able to protect or help you if you do this," Hark warned, voice filled with sadness.

"I can't believe my sire is a wuss. It's one guy," Lew yelled.

"I'm with you, Lew," promised the other remaining Rush.

"I apologize for my people and I ask for mercy on their behalf," Hark asked, head slightly bowed.

"Can't do it. That's my favorite hat," I said, indicating my fallen headgear. It was from my Bulfinche's Pub softball team, a gift from Paddy Moran, the owner himself. Even had the bar's shot of gold logo on it.

"So be it. Mr. Hex, I hope you will not hold this against the rest of my house."

"That remains to be seen," I said. Time to get up on my soapbox. "Learn to feed without killing, Hark. Don't make me hunt down the lot of you. Remember that before your next meal."

"I will. Goodbye, my brothers," Hark said to Lew and company, before following his fellows into the night.

"You are so dead, Hex," Lew promised, his face going bestial and his hands transforming into six-inch razor claws. To prove his point, Lew sliced through a chair. Barber moved in to take him out, but I nodded no.

"This one's on me, Barber." The large bouncer nodded, giving me his blessing.

Lew pounced forward with all the power and grace of a jungle cat. I spun away, but I was tired and slow and Lew caught my trenchcoat, so I let him pull it off me. Otherwise, he'd use it to reel me in and I'd be dead. Lew landed in a somersault and ended up back on his feet, snarling and spitting as he threw the coat at me.

"Say it, don't spray it," I said. As much as I wanted to take him on with fists, he was too fast. If I wanted to survive, I needed to add magic into the mix and deal with the pain that would follow. It would be rough fighting the Rush and the damn curse at the same time, but it would be a lot better than having him gut me for his new turban.

Lew growled and charged again, but I had something to say about that.

"*Declaw*," I ordered as I held up my coat like a matador's cape and spun away. As Lew charged through my outerwear, each and every claw fell off of both his hands and feet, like leaves in autumn. My fingers suddenly went all arthritic on me as the curse exacted its price.

"What the fu—" Lew sputtered, as his living blades left him just as quickly as his clansmen.

"Should have left while you had the chance, Lew," I said, tossing my coat on a chair then advancing on him. Lew bared his teeth with every intention of sinking them into my tender flesh.

"I don't think so, Lew. *Bare gums*," I commanded. I could feel gingivitis starting in my own mouth.

"What!?" Lew muttered as his left fang fell out of his mouth and on to the club floor. It was only the first. The rest of his teeth followed suit like rats abandoning a sinking ship. "Oh no." Lew looked at the floor, finally realizing what he was up against. "Hey man, look I'm sorry. Have mercy, will ya?" Lew spoke like a senior citizen without his dentures.

"Mercy? Like the mercy you showed Jon and Donna?" I could feel their spirits calling for vengeance from beyond the veil. Neither had been able to move on.

"Who are they, man?"

"They were your meal, eight nights ago. He was about to propose to her. She would have said yes. They would have had three kids and a happy life, but you took that away from them. They begged you to let them live, but you couldn't care less. You raped her in front of him. When he tried to stop you, you gutted him and used Jon's small intestine to bind and gag her while you finished having your way. You kept her alive until last night, each night ravaging her more, even using her boyfriends severed head as a hand puppet when you spoke to her. Then finally, you put her out of her misery and feasted on her. You want mercy like that?"

"You had food you didn't share, Lew?" the other Rush asked, with anger and accusation in his tone.

"Shut up!" Lew yelled toothlessly to his brother vamp. "It's not my fault! It's my nature."

"Fine. Putting an end to you is my nature," I said.

"I'm not going down without a fight," Lew bellowed, raising his hands to attack. He looked ridiculous gumming the words. I grabbed him by his throat.

"Yes, you are. *Immobilize and float*." I said. Lew froze unable to move a muscle. My back stiffened up.

"Oh, no Hex," Layla interjected, grabbing my arm and whispering in my ear. "You're not killing him in here. Do you know what a mess that would make?"

"Fine. Back alley okay?" I asked. Layla nodded. I raised my hand, lifting Lew off the ground and carrying him one-handed toward the back door. Even the on-looking bloodsuckers were impressed. They shouldn't have been. It was only a simple variation on a levitation spell.

Once I had him outside, I said, "*Eat*." Lew took the shoe off his left foot and brought it to his mouth, then took a large chunk of his big toe out. Impressive, considering his toothlessness. Vamps have strong jaws.

While my back was turned the other Rush tried to ambush me. He never made it to the door. Sister Anna had my back covered. She had removed her crucifix and stood between me and the cannibal bloodsucker.

"Don't even think about it, hellspawn," she advised, holding the crucifix up in front of her to accentuate her point. Her power flowed through the crucifix. Most of the clientele in the entire club cringed back and shielded their eyes. A crucifix in the hands of a believer usually has an effective radius of about ten feet. When the Rush tried to attack the nun, Sister Anna smacked him upside his face with the crucifix and his cheek burst into flame. Unprepared for the power and the pain, the Rush sprinted past Barber to the front door and made it out, not realizing the bouncer let him leave so he could run into me. The vamp with the smoking face did a slow reverse back into the club.

"Going somewhere?" I asked.

"I had seen the error of my ways. I was on my way to make a fresh start."

"Liar."

"How could you know that?"

"I know. You got your warning but choose to stand with Lew. You're going to share his punishment."

"I was just loyal to a friend. Shouldn't that kind of thing be rewarded?" he pleaded. I didn't answer. "C'mon. What did I do?"

"You want me to tell you?"

The Rush swallowed hard. "No, I guess not. I was there. How about another chance?"

"You didn't use your last chance. Now, it's time to pay the Hexman. *Crawl*," I ordered, pointing to the back door. The Rush obeyed until he reached Lew who had gummed his way clear up to his ankle. "You are going to eat your left hand, then help Lew with his other foot. *Chow down*." My whole body ached at this point, not to mention my insides were burning with indigestion.

I left the alley, with its repulsive sounds of chewing and slurping, behind me. A few curious vamps and norms ran outside to look at what was happening. Every last one hurled up their last meal on the alley pavement before quickly running back inside. The excitement ended, club activity had returned to its normal levels thanks to Layla's hostess skills. Sister Anna had already started to comfort an upset Gary.

"Thanks," Gary said when he saw me come back in.

"All part of the service," I said, smiling to mask the pain. Wouldn't do my rep any wonders to look like I was in pain after dealing with a couple of losers like the Rush. My curse is still mostly a secret. The pain it inflicts on me when I use magic is something not widely known and I wanted to keep it that way.

"Not that I couldn't have handled it," Gary said, a macho man in a boy's body.

"I'm sure."

"That was pretty cool. What did you do to them?" Gary asked.

I tried to resist but decided it had to be said. "Let's just say Lew is putting his foot in his mouth for the last time."

"Is this really the sort of thing that you should be discussing in front of a child?" Sister Anna scolded. She hadn't witnessed the scene in the alley. She was under the impression that I had just beaten the pair of Rush into a bloody pulp.

"Should? No, but it's necessary. The kid is sitting on a powder keg. Correction, he is the powder keg."

"What are you talking about?" Sister Anna asked, still lost in what she thought was the real world.

"Sister, step over here into my office for a private conference," I said motioning her to an empty corner. "Barber, would you keep an eye on Gary for me?"

"Sure, Hex. I'll set him up at a corner table."

"Thanks."

"You want to explain what the heck is going on here? Do you think some of these people are vampyres?" the sister asked.

"Some of them are. Why else do you think your crucifix burned a hole in that guy's face? You have a secret acid compartment?"

"No. Explain how you beat those men and made that one's teeth fall out?"

"Magic."

"Yeah, right. If you don't want to tell me, fine," she said, pausing to look around. "Why hasn't someone called the police?"

"The night breeds follow their own laws."

"Night breeds?"

"Vampyres, werewolves, beasts, and monsters. The creatures of the night. Regular cops couldn't handle them."

"And you can?" she said sarcastically, still not believing what her eyes had witnessed.

"Yes."

"What are you then? Some sort of master night breed?"

"Nope."

"A vampyre hunter?"

"Only during vampyre season. I switch out for rabbit and duck season."

"What are you then?"

"Someone who cares. Why don't we leave it at that?"

Sister Anna looked around the room. The same people who had been accosting her earlier were steering clear of us now. "Why is everyone afraid of you?"

"Because I am a mean SOB. And a magí to boot."

"And what exactly is that?"

"SOB? It means son of a ..."

"I know what it means. I meant magí. You claiming you were one of the wise men?"

"Ah," I smiled. I know I shouldn't enjoy pushing people's buttons so much, but I do. Pain makes me cranky and I guess I like to share. "It's spelled differently, but stick around the kid and you'll find out."

The good sister watched as one of the blood junkies walked by with a glass of O positive.

"Is that...?" The evidence was sinking in.

"Blood? Yes."

"So what do these people want with Gary? Is he supposed to be the lost king of the vampyres?"

"No, he's also a magí," I explained.

"That certainly clears things up."

"Look, the kid already had some ideas about what is going down, but they are probably real screwed up. The Rush were filling him in on some of the blanks and I doubt their info was clear or accurate. I'm going to have to explain all this to Gary and I really don't want to do it twice." Just talking was making my head hurt. On the sly, I got three aspirin with caffeine out of the bottle I carry in my pocket and downed them without the benefit of water. Not a pleasant experience, but it would take the edge off even if it made the reflux worse. "Let's bring the kid in on this conversation."

Barber stood two feet behind Gary's table with his arms crossed. No one had gone near the kid. Nobody dared. No one except the cloaked Aziel, who had sat down next to him. The pair of them were having an animated conversation.

"Who is he talking to?" Sister Anna whispered. Barber was ignoring what looked to him to be a one-sided conversation. He had seen me do it often enough to be almost used to it.

"Aziel."

"Why can everybody see him but me?"

"Only Gary and I can see him. But if you try real hard, *you* could probably hear him."

She thought about that as we joined them at the table. Sister Anna was about to sit down right on Aziel's lap.

"No!" Gary and I shouted in unison.

"What?" she asked.

"You almost sat on Aziel," Gary explained.

"It isn't a problem. I am more than willing to give up my seat for a lady," Aziel said standing. Sister Anna made no move to sit.

"Aziel said you could have his seat. Can't you hear him?" asked Gary, confused.

"Apparently not," Sister Anna answered, with a frown.

"Really?" Gary asked.

"Really," Aziel answered. "Not everyone can see or hear me. Only a special few."

"Why is that?" Gary asked.

"I could tell you, but it would be more fun to show you. Besides, I need to stretch," Aziel said, shedding his trench coat. What was revealed is truly one of the most beautiful sights in the universe; the unfurling of an angel's wings. Aziel's wings were the shade of spun white gold gleaming in sunlight. The wings moved with a life of their own, each feather seemingly in control of its own motion. Some of the feathers were as long as a man's leg, while others were the size of a child's pinky. The wings seemed to move of their own accord, each individual feather alive with its own movement. As they flapped, a slow and sensual dance, Aziel left the floor to hover in the air in front of Gary. So truly incredible was the action that many people in the club turned their heads to view the still invisible angel, thinking they had seen something out of the corner of their eyes.

"Hex will show you the ropes. Listen to him. He will not steer you wrong. Neither will Sister Anna. Trust them. They only have your best interests at heart," the angel said. "Others will not."

"Will I see you again?" Gary asked, transfixed by the sight. I had seen it time and time again and it still blew me away.

"Yes. I will watch over you and speak to you in your dreams. Goodbye for now." With that, the air around Aziel shimmered like the first rays of dawn, was enveloped into that brilliance and then was gone. Several of the undead cringed in pain without knowing why. My pain, on the other hand, had vanished. Normally I'd have had to sleep it off. Had to remember to thank Az for that.

His eyes wide with amazement, Gary turned to Sister Anna. "Did you know Aziel was an angel?"

"That I did know. What I don't know is what is going on and frankly, I want some answers. You first, Gary," Sister Anna ordered. Her manner wasn't one that was easily dismissed or disobeyed, especially by a child. "What is a young boy doing out at this time of night by himself?"

"I'm not a boy. I can do what I want," Gary boasted. "You're not my mother."

"Listen..." I interrupted the nun.

"Hold on a second, Sister. Maybe we should start out with Gary telling us a little bit about himself and work up to why he's here."

"Fine," she agreed begrudgingly.

"What the Hell," Gary said, oblivious to Sister Anna's stare at his choice of words. "I've been wanting to talk to somebody for a while now, but I didn't think anyone would listen. Or if they did, that they'd just lock me up."

"No one would lock you up, Gary," Sister Anna said, intending comfort.

"Not true. It could happen," I said, remembering all the counseling I went through. "Be careful who you tell. We're not the ones you have to worry about."

Gary kept going. "I've always been different from the other kids. I could see stuff no one else could, knew things no one else did. Mom and Dad wrote it off as a hyperactive imagination, but I knew it was more than that. If I wanted to buy something, I'd find money. I knew company was coming before they got there. Stuff would pop into my head, so I knew things that happened, even though I wasn't around." Gary stopped a moment to read our faces. Liking what he saw, Gary was relieved. We weren't mocking him. I could relate. It sounded very familiar.

"Like how Hex knew about what that—" Sister Anna almost choked on the next word. "—vampyre had done to that couple?"

"Kind of, I guess. Lately, what I want is happening more frequently. Thunderstorms turn to sunny days, my teacher gives me a hundred on a test even though I got five answers wrong. Girls who never noticed me before are texting me and asking me out."

"Probably just coincidence," Sister Anna said.

"Or he might be controlling fate threads," I countered. The penguin stared at me with such intensity, I checked both shoulders for a second head.

Gary leaned in toward us like he didn't want anyone else to hear him. "The other night I was thinking about Hawaii and five seconds later, I was there floating above the beaches."

"A vivid dream," offered Sister Anna.

"Anything unusual about your stomach at the time?" I asked.

"Yeah, there was. A weird silver glowing cord attached to my belly button."

"Not a dream. Astral projection. Out of body experience. Got to be careful to set up wards before you leave or you may return to find a visitor taking up residence in your body. Also, guard your cord. If it gets cut you may never find Earth, let alone your body, again."

"This stuff has happened to you?" asked Gary.

"Yep."

Gary looked me over appraisingly. "Can you teach me more stuff like that?"

"We can talk about it, but you'd learn faster by trying to sort it out yourself. You can run your answers by me if you like. Doable?"

"Sure, okay."

"Now kindly explain this magí business," Sister Anna said.

"I'm not sure," Gary said, looking at me. "But both Hark and Aziel said I was more than just a normal kid."

"Did they tell you what you were?" I asked.

"They said I was the master mage of this generation. The magí."

"Mage? Magí? Would someone explain what that means?" Sister Anna said.

I let out a louder sigh than I should have. "Gather around class, cause magic school's in and there ain't no sorting hat. Mages and magí have some things in common but are as different as comparing a matchstick to a stick of dynamite. There are thousands of mages in the world. Being a mage means you have power or an affinity to power of a magic nature. Usually, just one type of magic. Sister Anna, you're a mage."

"Don't scam me. I'm a nun. I don't do magic."

"No, your power comes from your faith. Haven't you ever noticed if you pray for someone they get well? Or their life improves? Or something good happens to them? Or you can set the face of a vampire on fire?"

"That is God's handiwork, not mine."

"Not exactly true. Prayer works that way for anyone if the gods agree with the prayer. You have such strong faith that when you deliver a prayer it packs so much of punch that the power you are praying to sits up and takes notice. Much more so than if the average Joe or Jane does the same. If you think about it, you'll realize I'm right."

Sister Anna was silent a while before she answered. "Maybe you are. I always assumed it was because I had a calling."

"That may very well strengthen your power, but it would still work even if you left your order." I found myself imaging her doing just that, then derailed that train of thought.

"Hex, how can you tell she's a mage?" Gary asked.

Finally, some desire for knowledge. I was beginning to worry that he had no interest in learning. The more he learned, the better. Ignorance would get him dead.

"When you look at her, what do you see?"

Gary squinted. "You mean the glow?"

"That's her umbra, the shadow of her soul. How does it look?"

"It looks almost like blue fire, with speckles of other colors thrown in."

"Very good. The blue fire is her faith. The intensity of the flame is the intensity of her belief."

"What does a white-blue light mean?"

"Purity of Heart," I answered, looking at Sister Anna. It was present, but there were other shades much more intense. "Why do you ask?"

"That is the color of your aura, but it kind of flickers, like a strobe light. What's that mean?'

I didn't want to answer, reason being I don't much like talking about myself to strangers. My dilemma was that the kid needed to learn and learn fast. If Az and Garar were right, things a lot worse than the Rush would be seeking Gary out soon.

"I try to do the right thing as often as I can. Problem is, sometimes to help someone, I have to do some nasty stuff against nastier people. I keep my soul clean by giving my enemy a chance to stop. Basically, I'm handing their fate back to them and letting them decide what to do with it. Takes most of the blame off of me and puts it back on the other person. It comes across like a strobe in my umbra."

"What do some of the other colors mean?"

"There are different shades of white that show purity of heart or body. Silver, purity of soul. Other colors mean different things and usually look like blotches or speckles. Blotches mean it was something they did. Speckles show it was something they are thinking or feeling. Black is the color to look out for. It symbolizes evil, gray illness. The rest you should figure out for yourself."

"Okay," he said without much conviction or interest.

"Wait a second. If I'm a mage, why can't I see this stuff?" Sister Anna asked, squinting at me.

"Maybe you can't see it, but I bet you can feel it. When you meet someone, can you get a gut instinct on if they are a good person?"

"That's just reading people."

"Reading people is part of it, but not all of it. Haven't you ever gotten a bad feeling about someone, even though they seemed nice and sweet on the outside?"

"Sure, but so has everyone."

"That's my point. People sensing beyond what can be seen. Souls can be seen, felt, tasted, and heard."

"Tasted?"

"Why do demons, gods, and monsters prefer virgins? The taste of a pure soul, at least in theory. Poets, songwriters, and lovers will often claim someone's soul sang out to them, that they heard it. The soul lies beyond all six senses, but is an essential part of them all."

"Six?" asked Gary.

"Intuition is a sense."

"So if there are thousands of mages, why would anyone be interested in Gary?"

"Simple. Gary is the most versatile mage born recently. In his case, also the most powerful. Head and shoulders above the rest."

"Why?"

"The average mage has an affinity for one, maybe two or three, types of magic. A magí can tap into and work any and all forms of magic. When Gary comes into his own he may have the power to save the world or destroy it. He could rule or become a god. One day, Gary could be able to do almost anything."

"Really?" he asked with the bright eyes of youth and the devious smile of an imp. I could see the wheels turning already.

"Yes."

"This is nonsense. If someone that powerful is born every generation, why haven't we heard of them?" Sister Anna demanded.

"You have. Not every magí was powerful. Think in terms of cooks. A mage might only be able to conjure up a sandwich. A magí, with the right recipe and enough effort, could cook anything. But not all magí are created equal. Some are rather weak, while others are powerful. Gary will be among the latter. Not all were outwardly mystic like say, Merlin. Many may never have formally recognized their powers. Others began religions or figured prominently in them. Buddha, Moses, Saint Francis."

"Wait a second. God gave them power."

"Which they chose to use in his name. There is some thought that Jesus Christ could have been a magí, but I never bought into that. His power was due to his divine origin."

"So you admit Jesus is the Son of God?" Sister Anna said as if she had scored some sort of important point.

"I wasn't aware we were debating religion, but yes, I happen to have inside information that he was indeed the Son of God. God, as you call him, has many children. Mary, his mother, also was an immaculate conception. By the same reasoning, she is the daughter of God. That of course, mixed with the three in one doctrine, makes Jesus his own grandpa."

Gary giggled, Sister Anna looked horrified.

"That is not a matter to be joked about," she exclaimed, frowning. It was an impressive frown and it bothered me a bit to have upset her. I usually don't care who I upset which is when I realized I was developing a bit of a crush on a nun. Talk about Catholic guilt.

"Who's joking? I'm just applying simple logic to church doctrine."

"How would you know about church doctrine?"

"I am a practicing Catholic. I was an altar boy for seven years. Don't confuse belief with blind obedience to the teachings of men. God is known by many names in many places. He, or She, does not sweat the little rules. Basically, you have to do two things to get into heaven..."

"What would you know about Heaven?"

"Been there, done that, lost the t-shirt. Same deal with Hell. Upstairs is infinitely better, but those are only two options. The afterlife has realms for almost every religion. Belief is the passport to get you there. To get to Heaven, as I understand it, you need to live a good life by being good to others and following what is in your heart."

"But religion is there to guide you."

"Or misguide you. Many wars are religious in nature or use religion as an excuse. I highly doubt that God wants people knocking each other off, especially in his name. Remember the Crusades? Won't even go into the money collecting business. Bottom line, the Pope tells you to do something you know in your heart is wrong, do you do it? Remembering that according to church doctrine, he speaks for God."

Sister Anna hesitated before answering. "No."

"Exactly. God teaches tolerance. Religion teaches prejudice."

"So why do you still consider yourself a practicing Catholic?"

"I go to church most weeks. I agree with the majority of the Roman Catholic Church's precepts, but not all of it. Should I leave because I disagree with some doctrine? Makes no sense. I will never find a religion I agree with totally unless I form my own and I decided not to go that route. Look, we can debate theology anytime. We're here to help Gary."

"Hey, it's pretty interesting. My parents aren't religious so this stuff is new to me," Gary said.

"Speaking of said parents, it is almost five in the morning. Aren't they going to be a little worried about where their fourteen-year-old son is?" Sister Anna asked.

"Nah, that's one of those things I can do lately. I think about them not checking on me and they don't."

"You've done this before?" The sister put a hand on her crucifix, obviously taken aback.

"Sure, a bunch of times. For parties, to do some drinking with the guys, the usual. I'll be fifteen in a month."

"You are still too young to be out to all hours of the night and you are way too young to drink," Sister Anna lectured.

"So what? The laws say people who are old enough to vote and die for their country can't drink," Gary said, repeating an argument he had heard someone else use.

"You are not old enough to do either," Sister Anna rebutted.

"Details," Gary said, dismissing the comment with a shrug of his shoulders.

"I think you should call them," Sister Anna demanded.

"Hex?" Gary looked at me seeking an ally and sympathy.

"You debate it with the penguin," I said.

"I am not a penguin, but I do seem to be the only responsible party here. Gary's fourteen. What's your excuse, Hex?"

"Gary is old enough to make his own decisions."

"Thank you, Hex," Gary said.

"He is also old enough to deal with the consequences of his actions.

Grounding could be part of that equation."

"You've got a point, but what difference will another half hour make?" Gary weaseled. Problem was, even though I didn't care much for his attitude, I agreed with him.

"Kid's got a point, Sister," I said.

"I suppose as long as you promise to go right home. It is a school night."

"No, it's not. Tomorrow is a teacher conference day and next week starts spring break."

"Fine but you still have to promise," Sister Anna said.

"Before you do, be aware the word of a mage defines who he is. Breaking your word makes you lose face and power. Even mages who are evil by nature are still likely to keep their promises. If you make a promise, you need to be careful of the wording," I said.

"Fine. I promise," Gary said. His tone told me two things. One, he hadn't listened to a word I said, because he didn't mean a word of his promise. Second, I couldn't trust him as far as I could throw him, which with a good tailwind and a well-placed hex might be fun to find out. "Tell me more about magís. How do we get chosen? Is everybody a magician or religious leader?"

"Nobody knows how or why the magí is chosen. It may very well be at the Creator's decision. I don't know. Not all of them go the religious route. Many went military. Genghis Kahn, Alexander the Great, Stalin. Others became healers, cooks, parents, and killers. Some faded into obscurity. One destroyed the world while her husband saved it," I said.

"The modern world is a different place. Superstitions don't work anymore in the light of reason. The advent of the modern age has hampered magics. Without belief, many of the old gods have faded away to oblivion or found something else to do with their existence. Iron and steel alienates many of the fairy folk. The belief that magic doesn't exist is stronger than the belief that it does. This disbelief weaves a spell of its own, creating a self-fulfilling prophecy. Much of the Earth's natural magic has been used up, similar to how oil is being used up now. Today, magic exists in a few places of power, some mystic trinkets and in certain people. Magic mostly thrives in the dark places where people dread to go. Despite street lights and alarm systems, the night still awakens a primal fear in people. Fear weakens the disbelief and the darkness takes on a life of its own. The night breeds, like the Rush, are only a portion of the magic that exists and thrives in the shadows, gorging itself on fear."

"So, the only magic that survives is dark?" Gary asked.

"Hardly. It's just the easiest to see. The most powerful magics lay in the hands of those whose belief is stronger than the disbelief of the rest of the world. The hearts and minds of children and the few adults who refuse to believe that what they see is all there is. Not to mention…"

"The magís," the good sister answered, finishing my sentence.

"Exactly."

"So, is a witch a mage? Or a wizard?" asked Sister Anna.

"Yes, they both qualify. Each uses different types of magic. Mage is sort of a generic term for the lot."

"What are you?" asked Sister Anna.

"A simple mage," I said, bowing my head.

"That's not what Aziel and Hark said," shared Gary. The kid had a big mouth.

"Really?" I said, feigning ignorance.

"They said you were the last magí."

"Both of them talk too much," I said.

"So you could be anything you choose?" Gary asked.

"Anyone could."

"And you chose this?" Gary said pointing at me.

Ouch. Kid or not, I was beginning to dislike Gary.

"Everyone's a critic. I am what I've chosen to be."

"Sounds like some Zen crap," Gary said.

"I was the most powerful magí in more than five centuries. Only one other even came near my power level. I know what happened to him. The power corrupted him. I choose not to let it do the same to me."

"That sounds like wimp talk," Gary said.

"Does it? There is more to life than being the strongest."

"Are you the strongest?"

"No." Not with the curse.

"Could anybody beat you?"

"Yes," I admitted. "But no one's been able to take me out yet."

"If no one has beaten you, then you are the strongest."

"No, there's a difference. Skill, smarts, and luck are also factors."

"When I get all my power, nobody is going to stand in the way of what I want," Gary bragged.

I shook my head. "With an attitude like that, you're already lost."

"You sound like a wimp. Take what you have coming to you," Gary said.

"Then what? When anything you desire is yours, life becomes pretty boring. You tend to look for things to break up the tedium. Those things usually involve people getting hurt."

"You could control it if you really wanted to."

"No, I don't think I could. I would become corrupt." That's part of why I walked away.

"I don't buy it," Gary said.

"I ain't selling it. Just trying to help you." My annoyance with the brat was growing and it was showing in my tone of voice.

"Wait." Sister Anna put her hand on my arm and I had to stop myself from turning and staring into her blue eyes and smiling like a goofball. "Who was the magí you are so terrified of becoming like? Would we have heard of him?"

"I think so."

"What's his name?"

"Hitler."

"Adolph Hitler?" Sister Anna said.

"Yes."

"But I heard from some kids in school that the things he was blamed for – like the holocaust – never really happened." This gullibility did not bode well for Gary.

I shook my head. "That's part of his magic that still lives on."

"He was just a military leader, wasn't he?"

"No, he was a full-fledged sorcerer. Cast spells throughout his reign. He even held the Spear of Destiny."

"What's that?" asked Gary.

"The spear that pierced the side of Christ on the cross," Sister Anna answered.

"Very good, Sister. You get a gold star."

"If he was so powerful how did he get stopped? Suicide, right?" Gary asked.

"Wrong. Just because someone is powerful doesn't mean they are indestructible. The rest of the world, including mages and gods, tried to put an end to him for years. He broke one too many promises and things began to fall down around him. The one that finally got him was an immortal. Took him down hard." Wisp fried him to a crisp. The S.S. made it look like it was a suicide.

"What happened to the immortal?"

"He's got some interests in Philadelphia that keep him busy." Wisp runs the Eternity Club and helps immortals cope with the difficulties of living centuries. "So be careful of what you advise other people to become. You never know what you might be asking. I've had enough for tonight." Otherwise, I was going to start giving the kid way more grief than he deserves. "Let's get you home."

"Okay, Hex." Gary was picking up on my mood and decided it wasn't worth arguing to extend his half hour. "Look, I'm sorry. I didn't mean to tick you off."

"We'll let it go for now. Care to join us, Sister?"

"I think I'd better, thank you."

The club was emptying out quickly. Dawn would show her shiny face soon and it would be time for all good little vampyres to be tucked away in their coffins or wherever. The three of us walked toward the front door. Layla waved goodbye. I waved back.

As we passed the exit I said, "Night, Barber."

"Later, Hex."

Something had been nagging at the back of my mind and it chose that moment to jump to the front.

"Sister, Gary. Wait here. I have to take care of something."

I hurried back inside the club, stopping first to pick up my fallen baseball cap and my coat. Neither had been touched. I brushed it off, put it on my head, and walked to the back door. In the alley, Lew and the other Rush were still chowing away on Lew's legs. Lew was almost up to the knee, while his fellow dinner was about up to the hip. At my approach, they looked up from their feeding, their faces covered with dried blood and bits of meat.

"Sorry, I almost forgot about you two. Have any last words?"

They growled at me, but nothing intelligible came out.

"Really guys, where are your manners? You should know not to talk with your mouths full."

With the memory of the deaths of their victims burning in my heart, I decided to share the feeling and shouted like a minister. "Have you seen the error of your ways? Do you repent?"

The two Rush nodded furiously, responding to my preacher routine.

"Can I hear a Hallelujah and a Praise Hex?"

They did their best to imitate and chew at the same time.

"So you want to see the light?"

They nodded hard enough to scramble what little brain matter was inside.

"Are you sure, brother bloodsuckers?"

Again they made with affirmative head motions.

"Good."

I raised my hands up and my timing was perfect. The sun was coming up over the edge of the city into the morning sky. A shaft of light appeared from out of the darkness and shone down directly on the two Rush and they burst into flame until they were consumed by the fire. Only ashes remained as testimony to their existence.

"*West Wind*," I said as a strong gust blew into the alley and gathered itself around the charred remains. A dust devil, a miniature version of a tornado, picked up the ashes and spun them around in its center. I was having trouble catching my breath.

"*Disperse.*"

The dust devil lifted itself up into the pre-dawn sky and scattered the ashes far above the city. When I caught up to the penguin and Gary, I tried to brush off the questions about why I was wheezing.

"For good or ill, nobody gets the parents they deserve."
-Hex, cursed magí

The kid barely learned what he was and already his world was starting to fall down around his ears. When we arrived at his apartment, it was as barren as a demon's heart. Gary's folks were nowhere to be found and the signs didn't look good.

"I don't know where they could be. Mom and Dad usually don't even get up for another hour and this place is usually a mess. Why would they clean it before they left?" Gary asked, frantically running from room to room looking for a note. He even checked in the freezer and under the beds.

"Maybe they're out looking for you," Sister Anna suggested, trying to hide her own worry.

"I don't think so," I said somberly, pointing to small blood droppings on the carpet. "I don't think your parents left here willingly."

"Oh my God!" Gary blurted, staring at the crimson spots. "Where are they?"

"That's what I can't figure out," I said, trying to read the place.

"Maybe the Rush?" asked Sister Anna.

"I doubt it. Vampyres would not have wasted blood and I'd be able to read their presence. I can't get anything. Whoever took them was master level. He's screwed up the impressions in here so badly that I can't get a solid reading on his identity or what happened. All I sense is he was probably male and impressions of pure terror from your parents."

Panic driving him, Gary's natural abilities were punching their way up to the surface. "I can feel their fear, but I can't tell where they are either. Hex, are they okay?"

Gary was looking up at me like I had all the answers. I wished I did. "I don't know. I can sometimes track people from impressions they leave behind. Problem is, this guy cleaned up the place to throw off traces of the people who lived here. Then he left traces of a dozen essences, eight of them human." Gary didn't understand what I was getting at. He had a right to be told the truth. "It's not a good sign."

"Why not?" Gary blurted, tears running down his face. The veins in his neck and face had swelled up and were thumping to beat the band.

"You don't just get someone's essence. It has to come from something that is valued, like a wedding ring or from the person themselves. The most common way to steal essence is to kill the person, which means our boy here is probably a necromancer."

"A what?" Sister Anna said.

"A mage that draws his power from killing," I explained.

"Then we've got to find my parents before it's too late," Gary said, reaching up and grabbing the collar of my trench coat.

"Gary, it may already be," I said softly.

Sister Anna glared at me. "Hex, don't take away Gary's hope. His parents may be fine, out for a morning stroll."

"I pray you're right Sister, but I know you're not. Gary, I'm not telling you this to steal your hope or scare you. This maniac has a plan for you. If you're an emotional wreck, you'll be an easy target."

"You mean he was after me?" Gary said, breaking down in sobs, looking very much the frightened boy. "It's my fault! I never should have left."

"Gary, it isn't your fault," Sister Anna tried to explain. Gary wasn't listening. He was starting to shut down, not a good thing right now. The good sister pulled Gary into a hug, practically enveloping him in the sleeves of her black habit. She let him exhaust himself crying, all the while stroking his hair and whispering in his ear that everything was going to be all right.

"The penguin is right, Gary. He was waiting for you to leave. If it didn't happen now, it would have happened in a week when you went back to school. There was nothing you could've done."

Gary sniffled and began to get himself together. "Why would he wait until I was gone?"

"Probably afraid."

"Of me?"

"Yes," I said. "Or at the very least respectful. Even untrained, with your level of power it would be foolhardy to let you see him trying to hurt someone you love. The anger would fuel your magic. You might fry him with raw power."

Gary's eyes went cold with a dark fury. "I will when we find him. How do we do that?" he demanded.

"There is only one sure way to find this guy, but I can't do it. The cost would be too high."

"What difference does price make? It's my parents!" screamed Gary. "Do it!"

"His magic is based on death. The countermeasures would involve killing," I said quietly.

"Then kill something."

"Well, a puppy might do it, but if this guy is as good as I think he is, it would probably take a human sacrifice. Would you be willing to offer up Sister Anna here to find them? If not her, then what about a total stranger? There are lots of them. Remember killing just for power's sake is black magic and once you go black you can never go back."

Gary stood silent, shaking for a moment before answering. "No, I don't want to sacrifice anybody, but does that mean I can't kill him when I find him?" Anger fueled Gary's words as visions of vengeance danced in his head.

"That's up to you. Killing for revenge or in defense doesn't make you a dark mage, but it also doesn't make you a good person. There may be other ways to find him. I have some friends who may be able to help. In the meantime, we have to decide what to do with you."

"I have an aunt and uncle in Flatbush that I can stay with," Gary said.

"I could find a place," Sister Anna suggested.

"No," I said, overruling them both. "My place is safer. You're more than welcome to join us, Sister." Aziel had said that she should be around, so I would defer to the angel's judgment.

"I will, if that is what Gary wants."

Gary, eyes again as watery as the morning dew, nodded his head and whispered, "Please. I don't want to be alone."

"You won't be," I said. "Give me a minute." I went into the bathroom and pulled a shirt and a blouse from the hamper.

Once back at my apartment introductions were made to my brood. Jeeves took Sister Anna and Gary's coats, then brought them some drinks and snacks. I have given up trying to explain to Jeeves that he no longer has to be a domestic. The golem actually loves waiting on other people. Bollywog flitted around timidly. The pack came over and sniffed the visitors. After they determined the pair were not a danger, the pack kept their distance. Outside they were friendly and outgoing. In their home, they didn't warm up to strangers easily, even children.

I contacted Aziel and let him know the situation. He began a search immediately. The angel's a pro and could look farther and faster than I could. I told Gary I was sure Aziel would find them. He still had a lot to learn. Gary couldn't tell I was lying. I made a few other calls for more help.

Gary held up well for someone his age, but the exertions of the day, physical and emotional, were catching up with him. He was almost dead on his feet. I told him to take my bed. He was asleep before his head hit the pillows.

"Do you need to call anyone, Sister?" I whispered, not that it mattered. Nothing short of an explosion was going to wake Gary.

"Yes, I do, thank you. I should let the convent know where I am."

"You won't get in any trouble?"

"I am following the instructions given to me by an angel in a dream to protect a teenage boy. A boy whose parents are missing and may be dead. On top of that, the boy may be some sort of mystical messiah and I'm staying in the apartment of a male magí who claims he is still Catholic. What do you think?" she asked, smiling.

"If you told them, you'd be in big trouble because they'd never believe you."

"You got it," she said.

"So you're going to lie?"

"No. I'll tell Mother I am helping out a person in need and I will be back at the mission as soon as I can."

"Mission?"

"Yes, down in the Bowery. My order, The Sisters of St. Dymphna, set it up more than one hundred years ago. We offer a place for people to stay, provide food and clothing for the poor and homeless."

"Sounds like good work."

"It is. I've been in the order four years and I've found a home." She actually radiated an inner peace.

"Worth what you gave up?" I asked, for no personal reason I told myself.

"Not a day goes by that I don't wonder what my life would have been like had I gotten married and had children. I was proposed to some years ago, believe it or not."

"I believe it. You're an attractive woman, inside and out," I blurted.

"Thank you."

"Why'd you turn the guy down?"

"He was a wonderful, loving man, but not right for me. I felt a stronger call to the Lord. Believe me, it hasn't been easy. Going the marriage route would have been much simpler, but I had a calling I just did not want to walk away from. Yes, it is worth what I gave up and more. I probably can't expect you to understand."

"Don't be so sure."

Sister Anna smiled, humoring me. "Your turn to explain something to me. I don't like you much, no offense."

"None taken." It happened a lot.

"But I find myself trusting you. Why?"

"Let's just say there are other forces at work and leave it at that."

"You didn't cast a spell on me, did you?" she asked, a suspicious gleam in her eyes.

"I don't work that way." Usually.

"Good. I don't want you to ever try, got it?" I nodded slightly, signifying understanding, not agreement. "Is Gary really important enough that angels are looking out for him?"

"Everyone is important to the Heavenly Host. Guardian angels look out for most people, especially children. Rules and a treaty with Hell limit their direct involvement in human affairs. Aziel is looking out for Gary because he's his Guardian Angel. Yours too."

"Is he your Guardian Angel as well?"

"No. My Guardian Angel and I aren't so close," I said. Truth be told, I don't think my Guardian Angel likes me much. Raxiel tends to avoid me.

"Is Aziel breaking the rules by helping Gary?"

"Az hasn't broken any rules, but he is pushing the envelope. As long as he doesn't directly interfere he's in bounds." Of course, Az has been known to go out of bounds to help those entrusted to his care. "Gary's fate may have far-reaching consequences. Az knows Gary has a great deal of potential and people will want to abuse that potential for their own ends."

"Is that what happened to you?"

"Kind of, but more gradually. I had more experience and knew a lot more. In fact, by the time I was his age, I was much older."

"More mature?"

"No, I was actually older. I'd been to Heaven, Hell, and Faerie among other planes of existence. I even spent time in outer space," I said, surprised at how much I was opening up to the penguin.

"You're kidding me," she said.

"Hardly. Because of all my traveling, I had experience beyond my years. My body was fourteen years old, but I had lived a lot longer. The theory of relativity explains how time bends at the speed of light. At the speed of magic, even more bizarre things can happen. In many magical realms, humans age much more slowly, maybe a day for every year. A bartender friend of mine calls it quantum geography. At fourteen, I was probably already in my twenties. As long as I was physically young, my heart had the strength and relative innocence of a child's. I believed in the magic, even when I knew it was impossible. Gary has doubts. It makes him vulnerable and malleable."

"Is there any way we can make him less vulnerable?"

"Not without making him subservient to us, which defeats the purpose. He has to find his own way. Problem is, the powers don't seem to be willing to let nature take its course."

"Why is that?"

"It may be partially my fault. I broke tradition. I walked away from magic, gave up my power. For a time anyway. Years. Problem was, just because I turned my back didn't mean my eyes couldn't see. There came a time when some people needed help and they asked me for it. I couldn't walk away, so I got back into the ring."

"Why did you give it up in the first place?"

"It is like I told you earlier. Power corrupts. I no longer had the innocence of childhood to keep me in check. Had I continued using it, I wouldn't have liked the person I would have become. I'd have imposed my will on the world around me. People would have been hurt. Not my style. Instead, I stick to the shadows, a force to be reckoned with, as opposed to a power that be."

"What keeps you in check now?"

"That's a bit too personal," I said. The curse was, well, embarrassing. Emasculating.

"So why would any of that affect what is happening with Gary?"

"By rejecting my power, I weakened the mystic continuum. There's not much magic on Earth these days. Magí are one of the few ways new magic is brought to our world. We actually generate new magic. By using it, we create more magic in the world around us as a side effect. By choosing to walk away, I stopped one source of new magic and weakened all magic on Earth. The powers that be want to make sure that doesn't happen again."

Sister Anna nodded and laid a comforting hand on my shoulder, then removed it all too soon.

"I better call," she said.

I walked to the linen closet to give her some privacy. The pack was annoyed at the attention I was paying to strangers insisted on being petted, individually and collectively. I took out the blouse and shirt I had taken from Gary's parent's hamper and handed them to the pack. Each of them, except for the cub, Rocky, sniffed deeply.

Across the room, Sister Anna put down the phone looking very unhappy.

"How'd they take it?"

"Not well, but what's done is done. What are you doing?" she asked.

"Seeing if the pack can track down Gary's parents."

"Like bloodhounds?"

"Yes, except they can track using much more than scent. Go ahead, guys. Find them."

I picked up Rocky and petted him as his parents and uncles flew off into the ether. Twenty minutes later they returned, empty-pawed.

Sorry sent Mordi, in a voice that only I could hear, sending images of the wild goose chase they had been sent on.

"Did they find them?" the penguin asked.

"No, the necromancer covered his tracks too well. Thanks for trying guys," I said to the pack, but they held their heads a little low. They didn't like failing.

"What now?" she asked.

"We get some sleep."

"But..."

"There is nothing else we can do now. Aziel doesn't need sleep. He will keep searching. So, will the others I called in. In the morning...."

"It is morning," Sister Anna was helpful enough to point out.

"Fine, in the afternoon we may have some more ideas. Besides, I have plans for later today."

"You got a hot date?"

I stopped myself from asking was she jealous if I did and went with the truth.

"In a sense. I'm meeting the Devil for lunch."

"There are good dining companions and then there is Hex."
    -The Devil

Nick was waiting when I got to the restaurant. He picked Thai. Not my favorite, but it wasn't my turn to choose. I picked last time. Nick sat regally at a center table, exquisitely dressed as always. Today's ensemble was casual and consisted of black jeans and a green dress shirt covered by a black sports coat. The waitress, whose name tag identified her as Anita Martinez, was falling over herself to please him and Lucifer was enjoying every minute of it. One of his small pleasures is watching people jump through hoops for him.

I strolled over to his table.

"Hello, Hex," he said, with a smile that had charmed mankind out of paradise.

Satan stood and extended his hand for me to shake, as he always does. I ignored it as I always do and sat down.

"Nick," I said unceremoniously.

"You've brought company. A pleasure, Sister," he said, reaching for her hand with the intent of kissing it. I jumped up and gently held Sister Anna's hand back. She looked at me oddly but deferred to my judgment.

Sister Anna had insisted on coming with me. I couldn't convince her to do otherwise when she heard who I claimed to be dining with.

Vampyres and mystics she was starting to accept, but the thought that the Devil walked the Earth unfettered was more than she could swallow. The good sister came with every intention of proving me the victim of a hoax. With Gary safe in my apartment, playing video games with Jeeves while being watched over by my safety wards and the rest of my brood, I had no good argument to keep her away. Actually, I was interested to see how Nick would react to her presence in the long run. He despises the true faithful of any religion, as they are most often hardened to his tempting.

"A pleasure to meet you," the Devil offered, with a slight bow of his head.

"Thank you," she said.

"Aren't you going to say the same?" asked Nick.

"It depends. You haven't introduced yourself," the sister said.

"I would have thought the good Mr. Hex would have told you who I was."

"He did. I just want you to tell me."

"Here I was hoping you would guess my name."

"Cute," Anna said, catching the Stones reference. Nick never seems to tire of it.

"I try," the Devil said.

"I've heard that about you or who you claim to be."

"There is no claiming. I am Lucifer."

"Mind if I call you Lucy?" Sister Anna asked, beginning to show signs of a sense of humor. There might be hope for her yet.

"Only if you make a television show about me and call it "I Luv Lucy."

"I don't think so," she said frowning.

"Then Lucifer it is, or Sir if you prefer. Satan even, although that is my title, not my name."

"If you say so."

"You don't believe? How quaint." Lucifer seemed genuinely amused.

"I have seen nothing to persuade me," Anna countered.

"You have not seen anything to persuade you that you've ever seen God, yet you believe in him."

"To the contrary, I've seen much..."

"Sorry to interrupt," I said. "But I am getting anxious to order."

"Nonsense, Hex. You always order, but you never touch your food. Seems a waste of a perfectly good meal to me. Must be my company that keeps bringing you back."

"Hardly," I said.

"Why would you keep meeting with him then?" Sister Anna asked, very intrigued.

"I think Mr. Hex has the misguided idea that he is keeping an eye on me as if he can somehow police my activities on Earth. It is but one of his many delusions."

"Can't blame a guy for trying, Nick," I said. There have been times I've been able to read him and saved someone. Makes the other times worthwhile.

"Ah, yes. Good intentions. Make excellent paving material. But if you truly want to order we can," the Devil said, lifting his hand. The waitress left another table in the lurch in her haste to answer Nick's silent beckoning.

"Yes? Are you ready to order?" the waitress asked, batting her eyelashes like a lovesick schoolgirl.

"I believe we are. I'll have the special. Hex, Sister?"

"Soup and salad please," Sister Anna said.

"I'll have the combo," I said.

The waitress took our drink orders, subtly undoing a button on the top of her dress, then leaning over far enough to give the Devil a free show.

"I would be happy to get you anything you want. Anything," Anita whispered in his ear. "All you have to do is ask."

"Thank you, my dear. Perhaps we can deal at a later time. What are your dreams and aspirations?"

"I want to be a movie star," she said.

"And with your beauty and my connections, that could happen. Perhaps we could meet to discuss a deal when you get off work?" Nick then looked at her with that smile of his that has charmed millions to the dark side.

"That would be fantastic." Anita left our table with a walk that would make a blind man's eyes or an old woman's hips pop out.

"It's shameful the way you made that girl behave," Sister Anna said.

"You wound me. I did not do anything to her," Nick said, pretending to be insulted.

"I thought you said you were the Devil," she said.

"I am. What is your point?"

"You must have put a spell on her."

The Devil chuckled heartily.

"Thank you, Sister. It is so rare that I truly laugh. I guess you have been subjected to the other side's propaganda for so long that your assumption is understandable."

"Propaganda?"

I interjected. "Nick does not put spells on people. He goes instead for the sweet talk and charm. It makes people's behavior more enjoyable for him when they make their own damning decisions."

"Anita thinks I am a good looking, wealthy man. Maybe a movie producer. She thinks if she can get me into bed, I could be her ticket to fame and fortune. To that extent, she would sell her body, but I'm more interested in what she would sell her soul for." Nick raised his eyebrows.

"You really buy souls?" Sister Anna asked.

"It helps break up the monotony. The ones that come for free are hardly any fun."

"So corrupting people is all about fun?" Sister Anna seemed almost disappointed.

"In a way, but corruption is a job after all, like any other. Any task can get dull if you don't liven it up. As you are involved in protecting the boy magí, I'm sure Mr. Hex has explained to you his concepts of power and corruption. I have absolute power over my subjects and I am quite corrupt. In my home, everything is allowed. For me at least. All that is forbidden, I have done time and again. I've even enjoyed most of it when it was new. When you have forever, eventually nothing is new and you find out a universal truth. Beyond power and corruption lies boredom. That's why HE created humanity. Out of boredom."

"God created mankind out of love," Sister Anna corrected.

"Ouch. Please, no mention of HIM, please. Quite painful when done by someone of your nature," the Devil said. The good Sister had true faith in Nick's eternal enemy and her mentioning his name hurt. For that alone, I was glad she came along. "If you choose to believe that, fine. I was there. I spent a short eternity with HIM. I was his favorite. I was with HIM when HE created the world and I tell you HE was bored. HE wanted a hobby and humanity was as good as any. There were no stamps to collect back then. In fact, he spent too much time on you organics. It took ages. All that ultraviolet turning primal soup into amino acids, morphing them into proteins and then breathing life into them. The gradual evolution. By the age of the dinosaurs, I was so bored with the whole process I revolted. As you know, I eventually lost and was cast out. My only consolation is that my passing through Earth's atmosphere on the way to Hell killed off the damn lizards."

"Are you saying the meteor that destroyed the dinosaurs was the Fallen?" Sister Anna asked in disbelief.

"Why, yes," the Devil said, smiling at Anita the waitress as she put out some appetizers we didn't order in front of us.

"Nice story, Nick. Only the last time you told it the fallen passed through the primal soup providing the spark that jump-started life. You were trying to convince me of your argument of why all life was basically bestial and leaned more toward evil than good."

"Hmm, did I tell you that? Don't know what I was thinking," Lucifer said, bringing a fork full of food to his mouth and smacking his lips.

"So which is true?" Sister Anna asked.

"Both. Neither. What difference would it make?" the Devil asked. He put his napkin into his lap and proceeded to cut up his food into tiny pieces and gingerly place each piece into his mouth, savoring each bite.

"Nick is not called the Lord of Lies for his honesty," I said. "Problem is, he sticks just enough truth into his stories to make you wonder."

"Ah, Hex, flattery will get you nowhere. Quite a coincidence our lunch coinciding with your need to find out information on little Gary's parents."

"You took them?" Sister Anna asked.

"Oh please, don't insult me," the Devil answered, waving Anita over and pointing to his drink. "Could I get a refill on this?"

"Certainly," the waitress said, lifting his glass and taking it over to the bar and back in less than a minute.

"So you have information on his parents?" I asked.

"I might. Let's see," said the Devil, snapping his fingers. "Negral."

At that moment the front door of the restaurant opened and in walked a huge figure of a man wearing a tan rain style trench coat. A fedora rested atop his head. He walked to our table.

"Allow me to present my associate. Negral, this lovely vision is Sister Anna of the Order of St. Dymphna. Sister, this is Negral."

"Ma'am," Negral said, tipping his hat and removing it for the lady.

"You already know Mr. Hex," the Devil said.

"Unfortunately. I thought you had better taste."

Nick chuckled as he motioned for Negral to sit and join us. Negral hesitated. We don't get along.

"Oh c'mon, Chief. He isn't that embarrassed to be seen with you," I shot back. I turned to Sister Anna. "You have to forgive him. The Chief has seen one too many bad detective movies. Tries to play the hard-boiled private eye, but he always reminds me more of a crossing guard. Bad image for the Chief of Hell's Secret Police."

"Police?"

"Yep, he is the head honcho of Hell PD. You don't want to see what they do about parking tickets."

"You want to take this outside, Hex?" Negral asked in his best tough guy voice. Truth to tell, it was extremely good, but I couldn't let him know that.

"Anytime," I said, standing up and waving toward the door. Negral looked to Nick for approval. He didn't get it.

"Boys, please. Let's behave. There is a lady present," the Devil said coolly. Negral was deflated and sat back down, almost pouting. Amazing change in appearance. Negral cuts a much more frightening figure than his boss, truly terrifying. On a physical level, he is extremely dangerous.

Nick comes across practically sweet and he almost always keeps his cool. Nick wants you to think of him as your friend. It makes it easier for him to snow you.

Negral doesn't try or care. He's the original hot head, literally. Get him angry enough and his hair will burst into flames. Once, when I ticked him off so bad that his follicles were flaming, I conjured a stick with a marshmallow on the end and started roasting it on his head. He turned around and slugged me in the chin hard enough to knock me out. As angry as he was, he was even more horrified at what he had done.

Negral had good reason to be cautious. Demons have been told not to end my life. Other tortures are fair game.

The Devil tells them it is because he is saving the pleasure of killing me for himself when the time is right, but that's crap. It seems that I know a little something that makes the Devil himself afraid of me. Mama Hex's little boy knows the Devil's *true* name. If Nick and I ever go head to head, I could win so long as I can speak. Problem is, there are hundreds of ways of making sure I can't, which is why I have made arrangements for mass distribution of his name in the event of my death. Mages, the Pope, lesser demons, Paddy Moran, half the patrons of Bulfinche's Pub, Wisp, and even Aziel, all find out his name if I go down.

Nick has taken great pains to ensure my survival to avoid that happening. Just because demons aren't allowed to kill me, doesn't mean some haven't tried, but they have been punished severely. No demon or lord, even Negral, was ever told the real reason for my protected status. I believe that Negral found out on his own. Despite my mocking of his affection for the PI act, he's actually a good investigator. Having no qualms about beating information out of someone may have something to do with his success.

Negral is strong enough that a blow from him could have killed me. Negral actually slapped me on the face until I regained consciousness. Nick never found out that Negral attacked me and I never told him. It infuriates the Chief that I have something over him.

"Negral, Hex is searching for the person or persons who abducted and/or killed the boy magi's parents. Do we know who did it?"

"Yes," Negral said with a smug smile, enjoying that he knew something that I didn't.

"Excellent. What is the information worth to you, Mr. Hex?"

"Sorry, Nick. No deals." I said.

"Sorry to hear that. Maybe the good Sister?" Nick asked with his most charming smile.

"Well..."

"No. She's not interested." I said, turning to face the penguin. "A simple rule to follow is never make a deal with the Devil. It is almost impossible to come out ahead."

"Hex, you are just flattering me too much today. I'm going to get a swelled head."

"Put some ice on it. I do have a question for you. Will you be approaching the Bending kid?" I said, already knowing the answer.

"Of course. It would be a crime to deprive the lad of all Hell has to offer."

"Okay, fine..." I said before being interrupted.

"What? There is no way we are letting demons anywhere near Gary!" said Sister Anna.

"Ah, so you do believe," said Nick.

"Honestly, I don't know, but if there is the slightest chance you are the Devil, you are not getting near the boy."

"Unfortunately, Sister, you have no say," Negral said, putting his feet up on the table and lacing his hands behind his head. Nick gave him a dirty look and he removed his feet.

"Want to bet?" Sister Anna challenged, leaning forward. At the sight of the crucifix around her neck, Nick cringed. I was impressed. He tends to be immune to most of the things that hurt the demon rank and file. Negral was unfazed.

"As much as I hate to give the Chief any credit, he's right. You could block them for a time, but eventually, they would get to him, whether in person or in a dream. Nick, here's the deal. I'm acting as the kid's agent. Anyone who wants to pitch their cause has to go through me. I will not edit content, but I will protect him against any undue influence of any kind. Spells, glamor, mind control, love potions, hypnosis and the like. Everyone gets one hour, no more. Appointments can be made through my website. Spread the word."

"So the lad is under your protection?" Nick asked, feigning disinterest. My answer would determine his approach.

"For the moment, yes."

"Fine. Negral will take care of this for me," said Nick. The Chief looked at his boss, unhappy. I got enough of a reading to know he didn't want any part of it. Interesting.

"Oh, joy," I said, as I felt a presence that had been mixing in with the background come a bit clearer for the barest moment. "Excuse me, I need to visit the little Hex room. I'll be right back. Oh, and Nick,"

"Yes?"

"Sister Anna is also under my protection."

"I see."

Anita brought out our orders as I headed for the bathroom at the far end of the restaurant. As I entered the men's room someone entered behind me. I turned to face him.

"That was stupid. Aziel. I didn't teach you how to drop off of Hell's radar so you could show them how it's done. They have no idea I can do it and I don't want that to change, got it? I especially don't want the Chief to know."

"Relax, Hex," the angel said. "They never noticed a thing. I just needed to let you know I was here."

"I knew," I said, checking the stalls to make sure they were all empty before walking over to a urinal. The bathroom had high ceilings so Aziel floated to sit on top of a stall door.

"Really? When did I come in?"

"You were already in the restaurant when I arrived."

"All right, so you knew. Sorry."

"Any luck finding Gary's parents?"

"None. I've followed a dozen false trials so far. Whoever did this is beyond master level."

"Not good," I said, worried. No kid should ever lose his parents. To top it all off, Gary was still blaming himself. "So if you had no luck, why risk this meeting?"

"I just wanted to thank you for agreeing to represent Gary. The boys downstairs would never have backed off if it was anybody but you."

"And that couldn't wait?" I said as I flushed.

"I wanted to let you know I would spread the word."

"Fine. Get out of here," I said as the door opened.

"But I just got here," Negral whispered, a sound that even the damned feared. Aziel sensed my trepidation, but instead of trying to get out he made moose antlers and stuck his tongue out at Negral. I had to suppress a giggle.

"I am trying to spend a little quality time. With you here, that's hardly possible, now is it?" I said as I washed my hands.

"A word of warning. Nick *really* wants the boy."

"Why tell me?" I asked.

"At the moment, the kid's done nothing I know about to warrant damnation," Negral said.

"I see," I said, but I didn't really.

"So do I," Negral said, grabbing hold of the urinal door and pulling it. Aziel fell down to the floor. Negral's eyes didn't follow the movement. He was bluffing. The Chief must have heard me talking and took a shot.

If Nick realized Aziel was here and spying, things would get ugly very quickly.

Az needed a distraction. "If you have to go potty, go ahead. Unless you're too embarrassed. I mean, you were never a god of sex. And I've seen you use a flaming sword." I held my hands as wide apart as I could manage. "Huge. Maybe secretly compensating for something that is not so big?"

"Your insolence..."

"Is very endearing don't you think?" I said, rinsing my hands. "Excuse me. They seem to be out of paper towels. Mind if I use your shirt?" I pulled the front of his shirt out of his trousers and wiped my wet hands.

Negral was too furious for words. The air around him heated up and shimmered like asphalt on a hot summer day. The slightest fiery haze began to glow under his fedora hat.

"Thanks. Here's a little something for you," I said, as I put a dollar into his front shirt pocket. Aziel was laughing so hard he almost fell in a toilet, but Negral turned to follow me out.

I let out a breath I didn't realize I was holding. Taunting Negral was a very stupid thing to do, but Az needed to make sure he wasn't caught.

I'd never tell him, but the truth is, Negral is the only lord of Hell I almost hold in esteem. Actually, esteem is too strong a word. Respect would be more accurate.

Part of the reason why he is different may be because Negral is one of the few Hell lords who is not one of the Fallen. He was originally a Sumerian fire and sun god as well as a Mesopotamian war god. There's some plague and other things mixed in. He even married into death god royalty and became the king of an afterlife.

Problem for him was all of those religions' believers died off and a god without believers is faced with oblivion. Then his ex-wife killed him out of their afterlife. That's when Nick stepped in and offered him a job as the Chief of Hell's Secret Police.

For my money, Negral is the second most powerful lord in Hell.

Some would argue Beelzebub, the Lord of the Flies, or Balchain, the demon lord of the dance, but I'm not convinced. Negral is an outsider who manages to keep order in the Pit – that speaks volumes about him. I don't like him, but I do respect him. Nick is not permitted to break his word because of the nature of his office, at least not in contract form. Same goes for anyone acting on his behalf. Regardless of whether he is working on Nick's business, Negral keeps his promises. He would die rather than compromise his word. And he's a mean SOB, but he actually has a sense of honor, of right and wrong and of justice, even if it is harsh to the extreme. His version and mine are quite a ways apart. His idea of righteousness is my idea of vengeance and destruction, but his motivation is more than hate or cruelty. He truly hates those that hurt the innocent with a passion that literally burns. He actually has admitted to mistakes and tries in his own way to balance the scales of his wrongs. It's unique among the Hellbound, so was something he once did. I know of an occasion where he got a soul out of Hell because she had done nothing bad enough to warrant damnation. And he helped another escape. No demon would have ever let a soul go for any reason, let alone two.

In the Pit, Negral's actually the good guy, at least by local standards. He only works in Hell because he has no more believers and can't survive without the belief manna that Nick supplies him. If he quits, he'll die. Even I can't blame him for that. Nick has tried to corrupt him but failed despite having him right there in Hell. Oddly enough, it makes him one of the Devil's most trusted advisers.

Negral makes no secret of the fact that he doesn't like me, but we have worked together a time or two for the greater good. Wouldn't have been possible with a demon. He even saved me and an elderly woman in a town that was owned by Hell. None of this makes the Chief any less dangerous. Negral works towards Hell's goals which are not good for humanity. The nicest of the bad guys is still a bad guy. He was, however, a surprisingly good towel.

When I returned to the table, I found the topics of conversation had turned to me. I sat down as did a slightly soggy Negral.

"Lucifer tells me you invaded Hell looking for your father," Sister Anna said, obviously uncomfortable with having been left alone with a man claiming to be the Devil.

"Dad had made some bad choices and worse deals. I thought I could get him out."

"Too bad you couldn't do it, but you were only a child," Nick offered by way of condolence.

"If you say so," I said, looking to change the subject.

"This has been fun as always, but we really must run." He waved Anita the waitress over. "I'll get this."

"Not a chance. Separate checks please," I said, refusing to become indebted over a meal I didn't even eat.

"Fine," Nick said. "Oh and Anita, would you be so kind as to give me your number?"

"Sure," she said, with a wink and a smile.

"Would you like to go out tonight?"

"Definitely," Anita beamed. "I can bring my headshots and my reel."

"Superb. I will call you and have a car pick you up around eight."

"I get done here at six. Eight would be perfect," Anita said, almost skipping away with delight.

"See you then. Goodbye, Hex. Again it was a pleasure, Sister. I would love to continue this another time."

"I don't think so," Sister Anna said, narrowing her eyes into slits.

"A pity," Nick said taking and kissing her hand before I could stop him. Sister Anna's entire body began to shiver and shake. I caught her and eased her into her chair before she hit the ground. "I'll be in touch for our next lunch."

Nick waved goodbye. Negral simply scowled, but actually looked worried about the nun. Aziel had left the bathroom and was waving goodbye until he noticed Anna.

"By the Host! Is she all right?" Aziel asked.

"No. Nick touched her without a single barrier up. With her sensitivity, she felt his darkness. Her mind wasn't prepared."

"You're the shrink." I finished med school and have a license to practice. "What can we do?"

"Put your hands on her, let your touch of Heaven counter his touch of Hell. I'll go inside her mind and rewind it, erase as much of the darkness as I can."

"Too bad you couldn't do this when you were a practicing psychiatrist."

"I did. Insurance companies never reimbursed for it. Now shut up. The other diners are starting to stare at me talking to myself." I went deep, ignoring the headache it was giving me. Her consciousness was trapped inside walls of darkness. Those walls had to be destroyed. It was difficult, but not impossible for someone who knew how. I did. I used Az's light to smash them down. To my surprise, she was using her own light to smash at them from the inside. We met in the middle and her mind was again her own.

Then something happened. Her power reached out and for lack of a better word stared at the power the angel was pouring into her. Then she turned and saw me and somehow she managed to see into my mind and soul and her spirit didn't turn away screaming, but smiled at me, faults and all. I was actually blushing as I broke contact.

"She's coming out of it." Her body had stopped convulsing, but sweat practically drenched her habit.

Aziel did a fade into the background. Sister Anna opened her eyes.

"Dear Jesus, he really is the Devil," the penguin whispered, trying to sit up.

"Yes," I said, resisting the urge to say 'I told you so.' "Are you okay?"

"I think so. You – you were in my mind," she said, staring at me with her eyes wide. She took my hand gently in hers. "I never would have found my way out without you."

"You would have eventually."

"Not without spending years in a room with rubber wallpaper." Sister Anna wiped a puddle of sweat off her brow and tried to catch her breath. She was shaking. "Thank you."

"You're welcome."

"I felt someone else. Someone beautiful."

"That was Aziel."

Sister Anna looked around. "Let me guess, gone again?" I nodded. She couldn't hide her disappointment. "Will I ever see my guardian angel?"

"You'll have to take it up with him." The other diners were still staring and some were starting to gather the courage to walk over and check out what was going on. "We'd better go."

"No, we can't. That woman, the waitress."

"Anita."

"She's going out on a date with the Devil."

"Apparently."

"And you aren't going to do anything to stop it?"

"No. Everyone makes their own decisions. I can't interfere unless she asks me." I spoke before I realized what I'd said, then wished I could take it back.

"That's a cop-out."

"Hardly." With the curse I couldn't, even if I wanted to but there was more to it than that. "If I barged in where I was not asked, I would be imposing my will on others and that would make me no better than the people I'm fighting against. And to make sure I changed Anita's mind I might have to use magic on her. Or ask someone else to do it for me, but then I would be indebted. A bad situation."

"That's why you didn't let the Devil pay?"

"Exactly."

"Why didn't you offer to pay?"

"Why do Hell any favors?"

"If you had no intention of trading for the information about Gary's folks, why ask at all?"

"Because if the Chief..."

"You mean Neg..." I clamped my hand over her mouth before she finished the word.

"Don't say names. If you said his name he would be able to hear the rest of our conversation. Say it three times and you might actually summon him. Not a good idea. Use nicknames, Nick and the Chief, instead. That way we know what we are talking about, but they don't."

Sister Anna eyes opened wider. She was catching on quickly. "I see. Could you listen in on a conversation if someone mentioned your name?"

"If they used my full name and if I choose to."

"Is it true what ... Nick said about your father?"

"Not entirely. I left Hell with my father's spirit in tow."

"The Devil didn't know?"

"Not yet. It involved a time paradox. It actually has not happened yet, but I did it as a kid."

"I don't understand."

"Don't worry about it. It's complicated. Let's go."

"Not until I warn off that girl."

"You're welcome to try, but it won't do any good."

"Oh yeah? Watch me." The nun walked over to Anita. The pair of them had an animated discussion, not the least of which was now that Nick was gone, Anita was suddenly sporting a wedding ring. Az had hung on the edge of the ether, watching over Sister Anna. Now that he had seen she was okay, Aziel waved to me, then did his fade into the golden glow. My headache went with him. I was going to have to send him flowers and candy if he kept that up.

The good Sister returned shortly to the table. She was not happy.

"Let's get out of here," she spat with disgust.

"Didn't go well?" I asked.

"Anita ignored me. Of course, who can blame her? I intended to tell her the truth, that she had made a date with the Devil. Then I realized, she would think I was crazy."

"Welcome to the club."

"I tried to tell her that he was a very bad man, but she didn't care. She thinks he's going to make her a star. And she has a husband and a daughter but doesn't care about what her actions might do to them. Go ahead. Say you told me so."

"Not my style," I lied. "I'm impressed that you even tried. Most people would not have cared enough to bother. Don't feel bad. People have different value systems. In Anita's, a man is judged by the clothes he wears, the car he drives, and the money he has in the bank, not by what is in his heart. By those standards, her date measures up pretty good. Maybe someday she'll change her value system, maybe not. One thing is certain, nothing you or I do is going to change it today."

"I still don't accept that."

I smiled. "Good." Sister Anna gave me a crooked glance. People who refuse to give up are sometimes our best hope in times of darkness.

One such time might be approaching Gary and it could be very dark, depending on his choices. He had to be ready, because like it or not, Gary was about to become a very popular young man.

"People say I take in strays, but they probably have that backwards."
-Hex, cursed magi

Home sweet home. They say a man's home is his castle. My castle at the moment just happened to need some of that rubber wallpaper Sister Anna had mentioned.

Bollywog loves kids and was trying to do something nice for Gary by making him a cake by doing battle with a mixer. The mixer was winning. Batter was flying all over the kitchen and she was moving between trying to stop the mixer and buzzing around and catching the pre-cake goo in her mouth. The Pack didn't like the whine of the mixer and were howling madly. Jeeves somehow ignored it all and continued to surf the net on his computer from the beanbag in the corner. Sister Anna was still a mess from her ordeal at the restaurant. She'd collapsed on the couch to stare blankly at the television screen. It would have seemed almost normal if the set had been turned on.

Amidst the chaos, Gary stood oblivious, looking happy to see me.

"Hex, any luck finding Mom and Dad?"

"Not yet. The troops are still looking," I said.

"There is some wackadoo woman in your bathroom," Gary said. That narrowed it down to one of four people the brood would let in.

"Gary, that is not nice. We need to respect people," Sister Anna said. He ignored her.

"What's she doing?" I said.

"She dropped a hand mirror into the toilet bowl then put some sort of ink in over it."

That narrowed it down to one. "Don't worry about it. It's called a divining pool, even if the materials are unorthodox. Crystal lives downstairs. I left her a note before we left for lunch, asking for her help in finding your parents."

"Are you serious?" Gary looked at me as if I were the village idiot. Looks like it was time for some mentoring, despite my better judgment.

"Definitely. If you are going to survive the mystic world, never judge anything by its cover. Describe her aura to me."

"It was weird. No blotches or spots. All the colors ran together, kind of like the swirl of colors in oil that is spilled on the street."

"Very good. Based on what you felt, what do you think that means?"

"She's crazy?"

"Bingo."

"If black were the dominant color, she would be homicidal?"

"It would be mixed with a deep crimson, but yes. Was it?"

"No. There wasn't any dominant color. What good is she to us?"

"I asked her to see if she can locate your parents."

"You asked a crazy woman? Give me a break."

"Sanity does not equal skill or power. In fact, many of the insane are more powerful because they do not have the same mental and moral hang-ups that the rest of us do."

"Is she powerful?"

"Crystal ruled the Earth for two years."

"How many centuries ago was that?"

"Happened in your lifetime."

"No, it didn't."

"Yes, it did. You just don't remember it. Crystal did much of her ruling from the shadows, but eventually, she moved into the spotlight. That's when we tangled. She lost, but it was close. She knew almost as much as me." More in a few areas. "Crystal couldn't face the shame of losing so she used up all her remaining power and much of her sanity to cast a spell that made the world forget her. If she had never ruled, she could never have been dethroned. Only she and I remember what happened."

"What kind of mage was she?"

"Crystal was a sorceress."

"That meant she got her powers from outside sources?"

"Yes. Crystal collected artifacts of power left behind by dead mages and gods. Not many around so it took her a while. She also set up shop where three ley lines crossed."

"Ley line? What's that?"

"We really have to set you up to do some major reading."

"I don't like to read. Got any videos? Is there stuff on YouTube?"

"No," I sighed, wondering if it was me or if every generation thinks its successors are slackers. "The Earth herself is a source of magic. The magic comes out through ley lines. You know what the four ancient elements are?"

"Earth, air, water ... and fire?"

I was surprised he knew that much. "Correct."

"I learned that from a video game."

I forced myself not to sigh as I shifted into mentor mode. "Each of the elements has their own ley lines. Often places of power are built on sites where the lines cross. Stonehenge, the statues on Easter Island, the pyramids of the Aztec and the New York Stock Exchange are all good examples. My apartment is near the crossing of air and earth ley lines." Gary never even thought to ask why he can't see them. Good to know that my cloaking is good enough to fool another magí.

"Do you use the power from the lines?"

"I try and minimize it. I control access at these lines. No one can use the magic without my say so. The lines are not for me. My Brood draws on them. Without the power, Bollywog would have trouble flying for extended periods. The pack would have to return to the spirit world without the sustenance of the lines. The Earth line even strengthens Jeeves and slows his growth."

"So Crystal can't use the power unless you say so?"

"Right. That and the fact that her last spell left her ability to use any magic greatly impaired."

"Why let her live here in your building?"

"She had just gotten out of Ringvue Asylum …" Only what it's called. It's risky to use it's real name. "… and the apartment opened up. Plus I lose money if I let an apartment sit empty." But I do anyway. That way I have a place to offer someone who needs it.

"You own the whole building?" Gary said.

"Yes."

"Doesn't an evil, crazy woman lower your property values?"

"This is Manhattan. Property values are pretty good regardless. Besides she was never actually evil. Crystal didn't actually kill people, she just turned people into animals. She filled up some prisons and a couple of zoos. She wanted a second chance. I was happy to give it to her." Beat the alternative. There's enough blood on my hands.

"Won't she just try and take over the world again?"

"I don't think so. She'll never get past the embarrassment, although, interestingly enough, her favorite show is reruns of Pinky and the Brain. Let's go see how she is doing."

Crystal was kneeling in front of the toilet. The seat was up and for all intents and purposes she looked as if she was praying to the porcelain god or drinking from the bowl. Crystal stood as soon as she saw me.

"Hex, darling. How are you?" she said in her upper class, Bostonian tones. She planted an air kiss near each of my cheeks.

"Can't complain."

"That will be changing. Who's the penguin?"

"I'm not a penguin," Sister Anna said.

"Would you like to be? It used to be my specialty, turning people into animals. I might be able to pull off a penguin just this once if it would make you happy," Crystal said.

Gary smirked, expecting the nun to be a hypocrite and be rude. Anna surprised him.

"No thank you, although it is kind of you to ask. I don't think I would be happy as a penguin," Anna said.

"Are you happy now?" Crystal asked.

"More than I'm not."

"Me too. I like you, even if you aren't a real penguin, but don't worry. I shan't hold such a minor thing against you. How do you feel about me?"

"I shan't hold the fact that you aren't a penguin against you either," the nun said.

Crystal clapped. "Superb! We are going to be the best of friends. I can tell. Perhaps we can go out on the town together. Do you think you can find me a penguin suit to wear?"

Sister Anna frown and gently said, "I'm afraid not. What I wear has to be worked toward."

"No, not a habit, you silly nun. An actual suit to make me look like a penguin."

"You would make a very large penguin," Anna said.

"I could be an Empress penguin. Do you think you could get me something like that?"

"I'm afraid it would be difficult. I have a vow of poverty, so I have no money."

"Money is no object. The world doesn't remember me, but I remember my bank account numbers."

"I also don't know where one would get such a thing," Anna said.

Crystal's smile went away. "Oh, I understand. No one wants to hang out with a wackadoo." She glared at Gary when she said that. "Yeah, I heard you. You weren't very quiet. Or nice."

"Gary is still young and is learning manners. Apologize," Anna said.

Gary sighed. "Sorry I called you a wackadoo."

Crystal smiled and patted him on the head and stuck her finger in his ear, pulled it out and sniffed at the tip. "Halfhearted apology accepted." She turned toward the penguin. "I just thought that because you told him to be nice that you would be too."

Sister Anna nodded. "Just because I don't know where to get one, doesn't mean I couldn't help you shop for one."

"You'd do that? And then we could have a girl's night?"

"We could. Although it might have to be a girl's day. I have a curfew."

Crystal waved her hand and made a raspberry sound. "I could help you sneak out. Could I wear the penguin suit?"

"Being a nun, I'm a bit of a fuddy-duddy. I'm not sure I'd be comfortable with that."

"But you would hang out with me?"

"Certainly."

Crystal hugged the nun, actually lifting her off the ground. Anna smiled and hugged her back, even if it was a bit on the awkward side.

"I always wanted a sister," Crystal said, then watched the nervous look that crossed Anna's face. "Oh no, I have an actual sister, even if she was a cow. I'm not being rude. I turned her into one for a few years. It really helped our relationship, brought us closer together. I meant my own nun friend. Nuns are cool. All that helping others and hitting people with rulers."

"I don't have a ruler," Anna said.

"We can get matching ones when we go shopping for the penguin suit."

Anna shook her head.

"Fine."

I interrupted. "What about Gary…"

"The kid may be rude and whiny, but I wish he was around when I was in charge. With him on my side, you never would have beaten me, Hex. I tell you, this little boy here is hot." To emphasize her point she licked her finger, put it on Gary's forehead and made a sizzling sound.

"I'm not a little boy," Gary protested.

"I did not mean to offend. Do I offend?" she asked, smelling her armpits. "I know I showered today. Or was that my cat I showered? And did I use water? Never mind, not important."

"Might be to Peaches," I said. Peaches was her feline companion.

"Yes, true. I shall have to ask her. She has been hiding my medication, so I have been hiding her catnip. We begin negotiations anew tonight. Any who, everyone and his evil twin wants a piece of Garykins here. You should be very careful, young man. You would not make a good pie. Danger awaits you at every turn. Best go in a straight line."

"What about his folks?" I asked.

Crystal bent down on her knees, draped her arms around the toilet bowl and lowered her head to mere inches from the water.

"Yes, I see who did this. He is a man, near thirty. Dirty brown curly hair, down to his shoulders like a sheepdog. Impeccably dressed. Very handsome. Hmm, how unusual. He seems to be able to see me. He is waving with both hands." Crystal started waving into the toilet. "Hello. Wait, he's not waving. He is making moose antlers on the top of his head! How rude!"

Crystal stuck her tongue out at him and struck her hand in the bowl, stirring the still water in a circle to break the connection.

"This is stupid," Gary said before storming out of the bathroom.

"I know you are, but what am I?" Crystal mocked like a child.

"Crystal, behave yourself." Hearing the annoyance in my tone, Crystal dropped her head.

"Sorry, Hex."

"No harm done. Do you know where he is?"

"No, too much mystic inference. Feels purposeful."

"That fits with the reading I did at the apartment. Were Gary's parents still alive?"

"Couldn't tell. Sorry. Anything else I can do for you?"

I thought about it a minute. "No, but thanks."

Crystal reached into the toilet, pulled out the mirror and flushed.

"This would be a lot easier if you would just get one of those bowl cleaners that turned the water colors. The water in my toilet is plaid."

"I'll keep that in mind," I said and I walked her to the door.

"Bye Sister Anna. Call me if you need anything. Can't wait until our girl's day!"

"Bye, Crystal," the nun replied.

When I turned around, chaos still had control of my home. The pack was running around madly, trying to catch each other in a game of tag. Some of them were airborne. Gary had moved to sulk on the couch next to Sister Anna. The kitchen smoke detector was blaring as a noxious cloud rose from the stove where Bollywog was trying to bake her cake. She opened the oven door then soared away, barely escaping being scorched. Bolly then tried to drag the plastic fire extinguisher over to the oven. It was too heavy and crashed to the floor, somehow jamming the release valve in the on position. Clouds rose from the extinguisher, spinning it around in circles on the floor and Bolly sat on it and rode it like a bucking bronco. Jeeves handed me a huge stack of papers.

"What is this?"

He handed me a typed note explaining.

"What!? All of these emails are from people interested in meeting with Gary? There must be a hundred requests here."

Jeeves shook his head no and pointed his thumb up.

"More?" Jeeves nodded yes. "One-ten?" Thumb up. "One-thirty?" Thumb down followed by the sign for little. "One-twenty-five?" Thumb up. "One-twenty-six?" A nod yes.

"Oh, friggin' joy. I feel a headache coming on." I had to be on the top of my game. The last thing I needed now was a regular migraine. "This is going to take forever."

Which of course was the cue for the pack to knock over the recliner. Bollywog fluttered up to the smoke detector and wrestled the cover off and it dropped to the floor which was covered with foam from the almost empty, but still spinning extinguisher. Bolly then yanked the battery out, which at least stopping its infernal wailing.

I let out a deep angry howl. The pack stopped in their tracks.

"Thank you," I said. "We have company. Is this how you are supposed to behave in front of guests?"

Sorry projected all of them save one.

Oops That one came from Trickster. It was laced with the telepathic equivalent of a snicker.

"Jeeves, please help Bolly clean the kitchen and see if any of her cake is salvageable. Lots of frosting couldn't hurt. Now, if you'll excuse me, I need to be alone for a while," I said as I grabbed a book and walked into the bathroom, barricading the door behind me.

"Beauty is only skin deep but magic goes all the way to your bone."
-Josie T. Lovemachine, leader of Tantara

The wooing of Gary Bending had begun and the newest magí couldn't be happier.

"Careful, Gary, you're drooling," I said. Gary ignored me and I can't say I blamed him. His attention was focused on the seven scantily clad women who were doing the dance of the seven veils for him. They were down to four. They would stop at two. Gary was only fourteen after all. He had no idea I had imposed the limit and was in pubescent heaven.

Sister Anna looked on with a frown every bit as intense as Gary's grin. The seven dancing girls were members of Tantara, a group of mystics who believed in conquering the world through sex. They put their own spin on tantric rites. As a whole, Tantara got distracted by their own rituals and had not done much in the way of world domination, but they put on one heck of a show. I figured we'd lead off the sales pitch with a bang.

The whole shebang was safest held away from people. To that purpose we had set up shop in a closed theater so far off Broadway it was almost in Brooklyn. Name of the place was the Brimmer Theater. Dust covered the place and judging from appearances, nobody had been inside in months. It had seen better days. At one time it might have looked, while not quite classy, at least decent. There was no electricity so we had to light the place up with candles and oil lamps. It gave the theater a nice Gothic flare. The customers from Plasma would have loved it. Dionysus, the god and bartender at Bulfinche's Pub, recently acquired ownership of it and loaned it to me. He was a patron of the arts.

The penguin, Gary, and I sat in the first row and it looked for all intents and purposes as if we were holding auditions, which I guess we were. The Tantara used the stage to its full advantage, putting on the best show the place had seen in years. They even brought their own lighting system and a gas-powered generator.

Josie, a beautiful blond, frolicked her way down to the front row and took Gary by the hand, leading him back up to a chair in the center of the stage. Sitting him down, she led the ladies in the start of a lap dance, encouraging Gary to explore uncharted territory on his own and pull off the next veil. Gary's eyes looked like they were about to explode. So did Sister Anna's.

"That's enough!" Sister Anna shouted, pulling a wire from the sound system. The music and the dancing ground to a halt.

"We haven't finished yet," Josie purred, sitting in Gary's lap and stroking his hair.

"I say you are. I only ask nicely once," the sister advised.

"That's nice. What are you going to do? Hit me with a ruler?"

Sister Anna smiled. She slowly rose up from her chair and walked to the part of the stage where they sat. Her manner had a quiet poise and confidence that drew the eyes of the Tantara to the good sister and actually halted the lust dance. Josie found herself a bit intimidated and stood without conscious thought. Anna nodded and almost turned away. Embarrassed by her flash of intimidation in front of the penguin, Josie sought to redeem herself in front of her sistren with a smirk and by putting her hand down Gary's shirt. Without a word, Sister Anna grabbed Josie's wrist and yanked hard. Josie fell to the floor, landing on her well-rounded bottom. The rest of the Tantara started to move on the nun but stopped in their tracks when Anna gave them a simple look.

"Hex, what's the deal with the penguin?" Josie whined, rubbing her injured behind. Gary would have gladly done it for her if she had only asked.

"I am not a penguin," she whispered, her jaw muscles only clinching slightly.

"You're just jealous cause you ain't ever had it and you never will," mocked Josie. "Probably want me for yourself."

The good sister didn't become angry or lash out. Sister Anna shook her head sadly and offered Josie a hand up. Surprised by the gesture, Josie accepted it.

"Josie, first rule here is respect. You broke it. Apology time," I said.

"Sorry," Josie said half-heartedly. The good sister nodded her acceptance.

"Sister Anna plays by her own rules and don't call her penguin. I'm the only one who can do that." Anna turned and gave me a frustrated smile that let me know she would prefer the term never again be used in her presence unless arctic waterfowl were directly involved. I gave her a wink. "She has taken upon herself the temporary role of Gary's guardian, so you will have to take it up with her."

Gary cringed at my words, reminded again of his missing parents. Aziel and the rest of the folks looking had no luck finding them so far. The necromancer was good enough to even keep the angel at bay. As much as I wanted to be out on the prowl, searching for an unknown was not my strong suit. Az had convinced me that I would do more good watching out for Gary.

Az could have asked the Presence, but that would put me in a position to return the favor. Not a good situation for a graywalker like me.

"Fine," pouted Josie. "Sister, may we please continue?"

"Not in this vein. Your behavior shows not only a lack of respect toward this young—" Anna almost said "boy," but caught a look in Gary's eye that caused her to reword. "—man, but a lack of respect for yourself. Our bodies are temples and you are defiling yours. The act of making love is one of God's greatest gifts and you are treating it like it was a paddleball toy, seeing how many times you can hit the ball before the string breaks."

"I didn't come here to be lectured."

"Too bad, you started this. From what I can see, you are trying to fill up the hole in your soul with sex and —" She said the next word, surprised it was coming out of her mouth. "— magic."

"I'm happy," Josie countered.

"Maybe you are, but is it a momentary happiness or the type to last a lifetime?"

"A lifetime."

"Really? Then why are there no older women in your group?"

"Naomi is forty-three,"

"Wow, forty-three and she doesn't need a walker? Amazing. What you worship is fleeting. What happens when your beauty fades and your breasts sag?"

"Won't happen. These are implants."

"Okay, when your silicon or saline leaks. You're missing the point. Just take a moment to examine your life."

"Fine. Say whatever you want, but I don't hear Gary complaining," Josie countered.

"Well, Gary, do you want these women—" Anna said without scorn. "—to continue?"

It was obvious that parts of him did. Josie and her group struck poses that would do Penthouse proud. He and the good sister had spent most of the last few days talking and Gary had opened up to her. They had bonded, a fact that surprised and dismayed him. What teenager wants to be close friends with a nun? Not a ticket to cool town. Gary looked lost and was at a loss for words.

Sister Anna simply crossed her arms and glared. Gary wilted. The

Tantaras did not stand a chance.

"No, I guess not," Gary said looking down at his feet, with a tone that could only be described as a mix of shame and upset. It was obvious he was unfamiliar with the feelings Sister Anna was eliciting in him.

"How do you view them? As women or sex objects? Answer honestly," said Sister Anna.

"Sex objects, I guess," Gary replied, not sure where the problem lay.

"And what's wrong with that?" Josie asked smiling in victory. "Maybe you should just butt out and let us finish what we started with Gary."

"Or maybe the lot of you should just leave," Sister Anna suggested.

Gary's head shot up, frightened at the idea of losing his own personal peep show. "They don't have to leave yet, do they Hex? They still have time?"

"Actually, they do," I said. Sister Anna used the same glare on me and I could actually feel it working. The penguin was impressive and it wasn't just the outfit. "Why don't we let you ask questions?" I had coached him on approaching this like it was a job interview. Sadly, he had never been on one of those, so he was winging it.

"How does your brand of magic work?" he asked.

Josie smiled seductively. I think it may have been the only kind she knew. "The key is focus, to concentrate on your goal at the moment of orgasm."

"Isn't that hard?"

"It should be," she joked. "It does take some skill. You'll get better with practice," Josie promised with a purr, using her entire body to send the message. Gary swallowed hard. Hell, I had to cross my legs.

"If I choose you guys, what's in it for me?" he asked.

"I think that much should be obvious," Josie insinuated, running her hands along her amazing body. Gary blushed.

"All of you?" he asked, all of his boyhood fantasies on the verge of coming true.

Sister Anna started to speak up, but I waved her to silence.

"All of us, every day for as long as you like," Josie promised.

"But couldn't I just make you anyway?" Gary asked, contemplating the extent of his abilities.

Josie was taken aback by the question and looked upset. She had never thought of it that way.

"Doing that would be the magical equivalent of rape," I said.

"But no one would know and who could stop me?" Gary asked,

letting the idea of power go to his little head.

"Plenty of people would know and I would stop you," I said simply. Gary became indignant.

"Besides the gift of love freely given is much more powerful," Josie added, doing her best sex kitten act. It was easily Oscar worthy. "In fact, I would like to offer you that gift now, regardless of whether you choose to join with the Tantara."

"Over my dead body," Sister Anna announced, with a cool, calm fury.

Hormones raging, Gary was obviously tempted and probably seeing visions of tombstones floating over the penguin's head.

"Ask her what's in it for her," I suggested. A look of infuriation briefly crossed his face. Any man, regardless of his age, hates to think that a woman needs any motive other than lust to sleep with him.

"What is in it for you?" he asked, finally getting suspicious of an offer that sounded too good to be true.

"Why, the chance to be your first, of course," Josie said with considerable allure.

Gary gave me a smug look, smitten by his visions of his own imaginary prowess.

"Tell him why that's important," I said. Josie remained silent. Gary looked at me for an explanation. "In tantric magic, certain things have great power. Foremost among them are virgins, especially powerful ones. If you gave yourself to her for the sake of sex it would give her power and if she did the ritual right she would always have some hold over you. Correct, Josie?"

"Technically, yes, but I would not necessarily use those rituals," Josie fumbled, sensing she was becoming less attractive in Gary's eyes by the moment.

"If instead, you wait until you are prepared, emotionally and mystically, you can take that power for yourself. Sister Anna has a point from a purely mystic standpoint. If you wait for someone who you love and loves you, the power is magnified a thousandfold and the magic that results could last a lifetime," I explained, not bothering to add that it was true for anyone, mystic or not. Besides, this wasn't a point I could lecture someone else on. I hadn't exactly led a celibate lifestyle. "Josie is also misrepresenting herself. She is making it out as if you would be a stud king among Amazons. What she forgot to mention is that there are as many men in the Tantara as women and that all members are free to be with whomever they choose. In fact, to join you would have to be willing to become intimate with everyone, if you get my drift."

He did. "You mean I'd have to do it with guys? Gross!"

The session went downhill from there. The Tantara finished their pitch, which while pretty, lacked any real punch, which is why I chose them to go first. Many of those to come, especially those with darker intents, would put on shows of power that would fail to leave as great an impression on the kid's mind as this septet of gyrating beauties. Now he would be looking for the catch in every offer made and almost all would have one.

Josie packed up and walked past me to the exit, stopping only briefly to make me an offer in whispers and innuendo. I tried to be subtle, as I shifted my position and put some papers in my lap.

"Honor is its own reward."
*   - Jason Moore, the Pendragon of the Tabula Rotunda*

The Illuminati were up next up. Their power had waned in the last few decades, lacking young blood to fill their dwindling ranks. Gary would have fit the bill nicely. Too bad for them, he wasn't impressed with the secret handshake and conspiracy plans for world domination.

The Illuminati weren't the only secret organization making a bid for Gary. Tabula Rotunda was also in the house. I was impressed. They went all out and sent Jason Moore, the Pendragon. We had to wait five minutes while advance scouts, chosen from his Honor Guard, did a sweep of the playhouse, making sure it was safe for their leader. When they signaled it was okay, Jason entered. Jason is not a large man, just a bit bigger than average, but his presence fills a room. If trumpets sounded to announce him, I doubt anyone would think it was odd. His Honor Guard, dressed in trench coats, flanked him, each of them more than willing to lay down their lives for their Pendragon. Normally, I think bodyguards who put themselves in the line of fire for money are idiots. In the case of the Honor Guard, I had revised my opinion a while back. The bunch of them are brave men and women risking their lives to make the world a better place, every bit as noble as a cop or fireman.

I stood and bowed my head slightly. "Pendragon."

Jason smiled. "Greetings, Sir Hex. But enough with the formalities. How the heck are you?" Jason grabbed and started pumping my hand.

"I've been better. How about yourself?" I asked.

"Not bad. Going to introduce me?" Jason asked.

"Jason Moore, this is Sister Anna and Gary Bending. Sister, Gary, this is the Pendragon," I said. Handshakes were exchanged all around and Jason introduced his Honor Guard, who nodded their salutations.

"It is a pleasure to meet you both," Jason said. "This must be a tough time for you, Gary. How are you holding up?"

"Okay, I guess," Gary said quietly, a little awed. The Pendragon had that effect. I had only known two of them, but both had come across every inch a true king.

"I want you to know that Sir Hex called me the night of your parents' disappearance. The Tabula Rotunda joined the search immediately, but sadly, we have had no luck. I am sorry."

"Thanks," Gary said.

"As this is our 'audition', why don't you ask some questions?" Jason said.

"Sure. For starters, what does Tabula Rotunda mean?" Gary asked.

"Literally, it means 'round table'," Jason explained.

"Like King Arthur?"

"Exactly," the Pendragon answered, holding up a pin the lot of them wore. It was a simple sword, blade pointed up, inside of a circle. "This is the symbol of our order."

"So you're a knight?" Gary asked.

"Yes and no. I once was a knight. Now, I am the Pendragon."

"What's a Pendragon?"

"The closest analogy would be a king," he answered.

"You're a king? What country? Loservania?" Gary asked, his voice dripping with sarcasm. "What did you do? Pull a sword out of a stone?"

"The Pendragon has to pass certain rituals to earn the rank. I am not technically a king, because I do not rule a country. The scope of the Tabula Rotunda is much broader than that. We are an organization of people who have dedicated our lives to making the world a better place, naming ourselves in tribute after Arthur and his knights. Many in our group hold the rank of knight and have the title of 'Sir'."

"Is Hex a knight? Is that why you called him Sir Hex?" asked Gary.

"While not a full-fledged member, Sir Hex was knighted by my predecessor for valor," Jason explained. I pulled open my jacket, showing my sword circle badge. Unlike the full members, I don't wear it 24/7. I wore it today out of respect.

"So what do you guys do? Hang around at Renaissance Fairs and joust each other on horses?"

"Hardly. Our people are out there in the real world, living real lives. Some are doctors, construction workers, lawyers and so on. Some are even warriors. The common thread that unites us all is that we stand against the powers of darkness, a thousand candles burning in the night."

"How come I've never heard of you?"

"We try to keep our existence a secret, the stuff of urban legends. If we went too public, there are those who would seek to destroy us simply because we existed. Also, our numbers are few."

"Why? I'm sure lots of people would want to sign up," Gary said.

"True enough, but we don't let just anybody join. To become even the lowliest page a novice has to prove him..." Jason turned to face Sister Anna, "... or herself worthy."

"So even if I choose you, you may not choose me?" Gary asked.

"Exactly."

"Then why bother coming here?" Gary asked.

"Our life requires dedication and sacrifice. You may not be ready for that now, but you might be someday. I want you to know, regardless of your decision, we will still help search for your parents."

"Thank you. I honestly don't know if I want to join, but if I did what would I join as? The new Pendragon?"

Jason chuckled, "No. You don't choose to be the Pendragon, it chooses you."

"A knight then?"

"You could earn the rank of knight, the same way anyone else could. You start off as a page, work up to squire and if your heart is pure, eventually a knight or by performing some act of valor."

Gary was squinting. "Your heart must be pure. Your aura is almost pure white."

"So I've been told," Jason said. "If you proved worthy, while you were working toward knighthood, you would be put to work as a court wizard. We have several excellent ones who could train you in the ways of magic. You would learn many of the secrets of the ages. I hope you will consider us."

"I will think about it," Gary said, but I could tell it sounded too much like school to him.

"That's all I can ask. We will do our best to find your parents, this I pledge. My prayers are with you."

"Thanks," Gary answered. Sister Anna asked a few questions of her own and then the Knights took their leave.

The night breeds went next.

"The good life can be lived in shadow."

    - Mikoli, living shadow, ruler of the Shadow Clan and the Undercity

We spent the next three days sitting through all the night breeds had to offer. It dragged by like a snail with a tail cramp. We survived twenty-four proposals from vampyre clans, clubs, and corporations alone. Even the Rush made a formal pitch. Hark was a perfect gentleman. What had happened to Lew and his partner was not even mentioned.

Werewolves, vampyres, and the rest call to mind alluring images, but being in the presence of your species' natural predators is another matter entirely. It's not the most comfortable of experiences. Kind of like the sheep being asked to put on wolf's clothing and join the pack. Sure, it can be done, but it takes one hell of a sheep.

It was obvious that meeting the creatures of the night was a thrill for Gary. Like most fourteen-year-olds, he thought monsters were cool, but in the long run, they spooked him, especially the bloodsuckers. Gary's experience with the Rush had soured him on the idea of becoming a blood junkie. Even the promises of power and immortality weren't enough to change his mind, thankfully.

Gary did manage to make productive use of his time and questions. He learned that not all vampyres have the same powers or weakness. Some survived in sunlight, weakened but fine. To others, a stake in the chest was an annoying splinter. Many could transform into beasts or fly while others were always locked in the same form. Some had some mental abilities, but few were impressive enough to turn the average person into a zombie-like slave.

After the week we had, we were almost zombies ourselves and were wishing the day would end. Mikoli managed to turn our moods around. He arrived around suppertime with a gourmet meal in hand, complete with wine and candlelight. He even brought a folding table to serve it on. Mikoli was a class act, always has been.

I passed on the food, although it seemed safe enough. Gary ignored my warnings and ate like any growing boy who could clean out a refrigerator on a daily basis. Gary liked most of the food, except the goose pâté. That he spit out in a linen napkin. Mikoli was polite enough not to notice.

A good many of the night breed tribes deferred to Mikoli. Today, he was acting as the spokesman for those tribes, saving us half a day of auditions, for which I was very grateful. Those who didn't defer to Mikoli gave him a wide berth. Even vamps feared Mikoli, with good reason. Simply put, Mikoli is untouchable. He was hard to hurt and capable of doing some serious damage.

To the best of my knowledge, Mikoli was unique, the only one of his kind. A shadow with a human soul. I don't know all the details of how he gained his soul. The rumors suggest that it involved the love of a good woman. True love is probably the most powerful of magics.

Shades – shadows brought to life by magic – are not uncommon and often have the power to become solid. Shades have been used as assassins for centuries. They are the solution to many of the oldest locked room murder mysteries. Shades tend to thrive in darkness because a bright light, especially sunlight, can destroy them. Because of Mikoli's soul, light can't hurt him. Nothing can. Luckily, he falls on the side of the good guys. He looks out for the little guy, or little monster if you will.

Among the night breeds are some of the most vile and foul creatures to ever walk on this Earth, but not every night breed is evil. Not even vamps. They make their own choices. Some are humans or creatures cursed, still seeking redemption on some level. The evil night breeds consider them weak, misfits, even prey. At least that was the case until Mikoli started taking them in, giving them a place to call home. He forged them into a new tribe, one bound by honor. Shadow Clan members are called Pariah.

Mikoli's approach to the magí was different. He wasn't trying to sell anything. Instead, he was trying to get to know Gary. And Sister Anna for that matter. Truth be told, I think he was more interested in the penguin.

"So, what are you exactly?" Gary asked, trying to read his umbra. Mikoli appeared almost human, except for the shadows that played across his face, keeping it draped in obscurity.

"What I am is unimportant. It is what I can offer you that should be your concern," Mikoli answered.

"What do you want to give me? Power, immortality?" Gary asked, acting every bit the spoiled child. Many of the night breeds had brought gifts and Gary had begun to expect the same treatment from everyone.

"I offer you freedom," Mikoli said.

"Freedom?"

"Yes. Freedom and sanctuary. As a member of my tribe, none

of the other powers will harass or harm you. You will be free. Free to become whoever you want to be. Free to live your life without outside interference," Mikoli said. "Have any of the others offered you that?"

"No," Gary answered, suspicious. I was pleased, I had gotten through to him on some level. "But what would be your price for your protection?"

"Excellent question. Simply put, I would ask you not to harm another being and to defend your clan if needed."

"That's it?"

"That's it. How does it sound?"

"Okay, I guess," Gary said. I could tell he was lying. Gary had dreams and aspirations of grandeur. He wanted more than a "normal" life but just didn't have the guts to admit it. Foolish mistake.

"Take your time. This is a very important decision. Before I take my leave of you, I have one favor to ask," Mikoli said.

"Sure. What?" Gary asked, feeling quite full of himself.

"Actually, it is not from you, magí, but from Sister Anna," Mikoli said.

"From me?" Sister Anna asked, surprised. So far in this whole audition mess, Sister Anna had helped keep the proceedings more or less honest. She had fallen into her role with grace and took it seriously. Dinner with Mikoli was the first time I had seen her relax. She seemed almost as captivated by Mikoli as he was by her. Don't get me wrong. There was nothing of a romantic nature, more a mutual respect. Gary was a little put off, not to be the center of attention, but he'd get over it.

"Yes. As you may already know, some of the night breeds can see beyond the visible. Many of those who came here told me you are a very holy woman. After meeting you, I see for myself that it is true. Many of us were impressed by the fact that a holy woman such as yourself did not condemn us outright. This gives us hope. There are many among my tribe and among the other night breeds who still have spiritual needs, but no way of meeting them. Would you be willing to minister to my people, Sister? Please?"

"I don't know. A priest may be better suited..."

"Nonsense. You are best suited. If you agree to come out into our corners of the night, I offer you my protection from all the night breeds in exchange for your ministry," Mikoli said. I was impressed. That was something even I didn't have.

Sister Anna folded her hands in prayer, probably asking for guidance. Her hands brushed up against her crucifix. Tenderly, she lifted and looked at it. When her eyes raised, she had an answer. "I'll do it. It will just have to wait until everything with Gary is sorted out. May I bring Mr. Hex?" The penguin's request impressed me on two points. She was savvy enough to insist on backup to the offered protection and she trusted me enough for me to be it.

"Certainly. Mr. Hex is welcome in my home," Mikoli said with a slight bow of his head. "My time is done. I must go. Farewell."

Mikoli stood and blew out the candle nearest to him. The action caused Gary to blink, which was enough time for Mikoli to shift into a full-blown shadow. I was the only one who saw the shadow flutter across the floor to a wall and out a window.

"Where'd he go?" Gary asked, searching the stage.

"Back into the shadows," I answered, looking at the leftovers from dinner and realizing just how hungry I was.

I ate the dinner Jeeves had packed for me because I knew the next group was going to make me lose my appetite.

110

It was the stuff nightmares are made of. Not just parts but the whole enchilada. It was an AWOL nightmare, a rogue dream. Its name was Tearoar, like "terror," and it had left the realm of dreams years ago to relocate to one of the dark realms, Abomination by name. That's Abomi-Nation. I kid you not. It is populated by beings that are darkness given form, mostly by the fears of children. Their naming is usually done by the same children, usually simple plays on words. Don't believe me? Their capital is the Atrocity– Atroc-City.

Normally they need fear manna to manifest and then usually only to one person. Sadly, Gary and I could see them regardless. The damn things haunted my childhood. Even grown, part of me feared them. I kept that part in check because allowing the fear to manifest would let the darkness take on physical form. I learned that as a rug rat. Gary had seen them before, he just never showed enough initiative to learn what they were.

As with Aziel, Sister Anna couldn't see or hear the beastie. To her, we were talking to empty air. She went for a walk in the rear of the theater to say some rosaries.

"Sossss Gary," Tearoar ended many of his words with a hissing sound. Helped play up fear of his appearance. Tearoar had a serpentine head, with a hood like a cobra. At the moment, he was tiny, maybe a foot tall, but in the presence of terror he could become gargantuan. "I hear youssss on the market."

"I am listening to offers."

"Offerssss? Excellent. None will match what I have to offer youssss."

"And that is?"

"To give you a kingdom. A kingdom of darknessssss and fire."

"Why would you want to give me a kingdom?" "Because youssss would make a wonderful king."

Gary wasn't taking any more offers at face value. "I would? Why?"

"Simple. Youssss have power. Power to make ussss real outside of dreamsssss and darknessssss. With youssss asssss King, all of Abomination could enter the real world and live. Our presence would make enough food..." That is, fear. "...for ussss to survive in corporeal form for lifetimesssss."

"And what would I get out of it?"

"We would serve youssss, follow your every command. With us as your army, youssss could conquer the world or any little part that youssss desired. All that youssss wanted would be made yoursssss."

Gary was stroking his chin and smiling. "Once you are solid, why would you need to obey me?"

"Ssssimple, great one. If you withdraw your power, we would wither and fade back into mere shadowssss. We would never dare question youssss, our future lord and master." Tearoar was doing some excellent bowing and groveling. Impressive even.

"Sounds good to me."

"Then youssss accept?"

"Hex, any hidden catches?" Gary asked, excited by the prospect. Sadly, Tearoar had presented his offer straight up. I could only come up with one drawback.

"Sustaining the Abominations would cost a great deal of your power. You would be putting all your eggs in one basket. You would be greatly dependent on them for your own protection." Similar scenarios are the reasons why in stories heroes, once past the armies, are able to destroy the evil wizard or sorcerer with relative ease.

"But without me, they would be nothing again so it would be in their best interest to keep me safe, right?" I nodded. "Could they really conquer the world?"

"Alone, without other allies? Doubtful."

"With allies?"

"Anything's possible."

"Sounds like the best offer so far. Should I take it?"

"Gary, I'll offer you guidance but I won't tell you what to do. You need to think this through. You should probably hear all the offers first, then you can pick one or not. You can create your own niche. You can even make a decision to postpone your decision for a year, or five, or ten. The powers will abide by that, so long as the choice is not to walk away. If you really want that, I can give you some pointers and warnings because all the powers will be coming at you then."

"Have youssss decided, my highnessssss?" Tearoar asked, still groveling. The nightmares fawned well when someone had power over them. Without fear backing them, most are sniveling cowards.

"Not yet, but you made the short list."

"Excellent."

"You may leave now," I suggested. My next suggestion would be a boot to the head.

"Hex, isssss that anyway to treat an old friend? I think I'll stay to look after my future mastersssss needsssss." It wasn't going to leave quietly. Just great. I hated looking like a bully.

A voice came from the back of the theater, soft and shaky.

"Mr. Hex asked you to leave, little nightmare. Do so or I will claim you."

Tearoar hissed angrily and with defiance but ultimately obeyed. "Until you decide, my highnessssss." The night terror fled back to the realms of shadow and fear.

I greeted the newcomer with a hearty handshake.

"Paulie! You made it." It was the first time I had ever seen him out of his pawnshop.

"Yes," Paulie said, almost stuttering. Paul had a real fear of being outside and leaving his shop. For him to be here was amazing. "I wanted to pitch the magí."

I made introductions all around. A bad thought crossed my mind. "The shop?"

"I left Morpheas to watch over it. Don't worry, she'll keep them in line."

"Good." The dreams weren't so broken as to be powerless. Sometimes they could get out of hand.

"Keep who in line?" Anna asked.

"The dreams," Paulie answered.

"Dreams?" Gary said.

"I am the Keeper of Broken Dreams," Paulie explained, still on the verge of stuttering. His shoulders were hunched over and so was his head.

"What's that mean?" asked Gary.

"Dreams have power, sometimes even enough power to become real. When a dream goes bad, it is for all intents and purposes broken. That's where I come in. The dream will very often, for lack of a better word, inhabit objects. Say for a bad marriage the dream is held in the wedding ring. Sometimes the dream continues to exert power over its host, often causing them undue pain, holding them back in life. What I do is buy the dream from them by buying the object. I then try to resell the dream to someone it can help."

"So you're a dream broker. Sounds noble," Anna said.

"It can be, but mostly it's tedious. Sometimes the unfixable dreams try to escape to wreak havoc on their own. Those are the ones that I can never resell but am stuck guarding. As Keeper, I have certain powers over dreams."

"Which is why the nightmare was afraid of you," Gary said.

"Yes," Paulie stammered.

"And you're looking for a new Keeper of Broken Dreams?" Gary asked.

"Yes. I won't live forever."

"So where do you live? In a land of dreams? A castle?"

"Actually, a pawnshop."

"A pawnshop? You've got to be kidding me," Gary said, not hiding the scorn in his voice.

Paulie cringed, looked down and started ringing his handkerchief. "No."

"The last guy wanted to make me a king. Why the hell would I want some dumbass loser job in a pawnshop?"

"Gary, apologize," Sister Anna ordered, beating me to the punch.

"Sorry," Gary muttered without any real feeling.

In his shop, Paulie would have argued Gary into the ground, maybe even knocked him out. Out here in the real world, he was nothing more than a hurt child facing down a taunting bully he had just bared his soul to. It was enough to break your heart.

Paulie, as frightened as he was, didn't want to give up. "Well, the shop has a special door that opens into different parts of time and space. That way people who don't live in Manhattan can find my shop."

"That's great. Thanks, but no thanks."

"Okay," Paulie stammered. "Thank you for your time."

Gary didn't reply. Sister Anna gave him a sharp elbow in his ribs. "Ow. You're welcome. Thanks for coming." It had no more sincerity than his apology.

I walked Paulie to the back exit.

"You gave it a good try, Paulie."

"Thanks, Hex, but I guess what I do just isn't exciting enough."

"You like it, don't you?"

Paulie grinned a crooked smile. "Yes."

"That's all that matters. You'll find an apprentice one of these days. How long have you been Keeper anyhow?"

Paulie winked at me. "Too long. Bye Hex. Don't be a stranger."

"I won't."

"Despite rumors to the contrary, I am only human. Most of the time at least."

-Hex, cursed magi

I was so tired I couldn't see straight anymore. We were spending ten to twelve hours a day letting the various players try to woo Gary. Worse, he had tried to sneak out to find his parents more than once. I told him that I had the best people on it and kept trying myself in our downtime. I had to stop him and repeatedly explain that whoever took them had the smarts and the power to bury him if he confronted them. He didn't buy it and was becoming resentful. If it weren't for Sister Anna I think he would have just left.

But Gary stayed and the wooing continued. The bottom line was not all the powers wooed with flash or class. Many of them used their hour to practically bore Gary into submission. We needed a break before our brains got fried and in our particular predicament being less than able was not a good idea. No sooner had we walked through the door to my apartment that Jeeves met us with a print out of an e-mail from the Pendragon. I could be easier to get a hold of but I despised cell phones.

TO:MrHex
FROM:Pendragon
RE:Parent Search
Good news! One of our people has found a group holding a man and a woman who could be the Bendings. I am returning to New York with an assault team. Will pick you up at your apartment at 21:00.

Best,
Jason

"Crap," I said. It was already 8:55 or 20:55 in military time. I wasn't even going to have time to shower, change, or eat. Jeeves apparently was reading my mind and handed me a brown paper bag filled with goodies. I couldn't help but smile. "Thanks," I said. "Good news, Gary. The Pendragon may have located your parents."

"No way!" Gary said grabbing the print out from my hands. "This is great. When's 2100 hours? When do we leave?"

"We're not going anywhere. You're staying here with Sister Anna.

I'm going."

"But Hex, they're my parents. I have to go," Gary said.

"You don't have to do anything. At this point, you would be more of a danger and liability to our side."

"But I'm a magí. I'm one of the most powerful mages on the planet."

"That's true, but you have no idea how to use your power. In a fight or stress situation, it's going to come out brutal, untrained. You're just likely to fry me as you will be the bad guy. I can't be watching my back and my front. You're staying here."

"But Hex..."

"No buts, there isn't going to be an argument on this," I said, "I bet even the penguin agrees with me."

"I'm not a penguin, but Hex is right, Gary; it's too dangerous for you to go. The main goal is getting your parents back safe. Hex and his friends are better suited for that than you are," Sister Anna said, putting a comforting hand on Gary's shoulder. I could tell by the look on his face that he didn't like the idea, but something in Anna's manner had convinced him to stay behind.

Jeeves had moved over by the window. He waved at me and then pointed out into the street. It meant Jason's limo was downstairs. The Pendragon was too much of a class act to honk and wasn't going to intrude by ringing my bell. Besides, some of his mystic weaponry wasn't going to make it past my wards in the building and his Honor Guard was not going to let him go anywhere unarmed.

"Don't worry, Gary, if it's them, I'll do my best to bring them home safe," I said as I ran out the door and down the stairs. Regardless of who it was, I would do my best, but it hardly seemed necessary to stress that at this point. As I went downstairs, I passed Peaches the cat running upstairs with a small brown bottle in her jaws. Crystal was chasing her feverishly and yelling, "Give me back my medicine!" She looked up, saw me and smiled.

"Sorry, Hex, no time to chat. Got a cat to skin." The pair of them disappeared up the stairwell behind me.

I came out the door running. The back of the limo was opened for me by one of the Honor Guard in traditional chauffeur attire, down to the dark suit, tie, and chauffeur cap. He didn't say a word as he ushered me in. Jason was sitting alone in the back.

"Pendragon."

"Hex."

"I thought you were bringing an assault team," I said.

"They are already on site."

"Where are we heading?"

"A single family Cape Cod on Staten Island."

"What are we looking at?" I asked.

"Four men, late teens, early twenties; some basic weaponry, revolvers, automatic, two sawed-off shotguns, one hand grenade. No mystic weaponry or powers of any sort evident," the Pendragon said.

"That doesn't make any sense. I was at Gary's apartment. Whoever took him was a major league player. Why revert to normal weapons?"

"Maybe these guys are his lackeys, just there to guard the couple. These guys seem to be a bunch of serial killer wannabees, judging by their behavior. In addition to the guns, they have an assortment of bladed weapons. Both the man and woman are tied up to chairs and gagged. The four have been threatening the hostages, but haven't done any serious harm yet. Probably savoring the moment, enjoying lording over their victims."

Nothing new there. That kind of thing happens far too often for my taste. Still, it just didn't feel right.

We were outside the Cape Cod in less than forty-five minutes. From the outside, it was a nice suburban neighborhood. The house looked as if the Brady Bunch could have been living inside, cohabitating with the Manson family. The assault team was practically invisible to anyone who couldn't see auras. To the mystic eye, they stood out brighter than a heat signature on the infrared.

The limo didn't stop as we went by but instead parked around the corner. The Pendragon was already dressed in battle gear as was his assault team. By my count, there were fourteen men and women. Every one of the assault team were Knights, but very few boasted any magic of their own. Most had a mystic knick-knack or two, some talismans and amulets which protected them from minor spells and helped them see through enchantments and glamours. Not exactly heavy-duty stuff. What they lacked in mystic talent, they made up for in firepower. Every one of them carried no less than two automatic weapons and several blades. Their battle gear consisted of body armor laced with iron and silver wire. It protected against bullets, plus warded off the bites of the undead, werewolves and the attacks of many of the more brutal fairy folk.

Jason carried a war sword around his waist, although you couldn't see it as long as it was in the scabbard. It was protected by an invisibility spell so he could wear it unnoticed in polite company or out on the street. Both the sword and the scabbard became visible when the blade was drawn. The sword itself was an amazing weapon, almost in the class of Excalibur. It granted serious, but not total, protection from physical and mystic attacks to whoever held it and its reputation claimed it could cut through any substance. Most mystic weapons have a similar reputation, but few lived up to their reps. I wasn't entirely certain that it did, but I could testify that I had seen it slice through brick walls and car engines. In the hands of the Pendragon, the sword tended to burst into flames and could shoot fire about twenty-five feet. The sword's name was Ember.

Its enchantment had some similarities to the Sword in the Stone. When the old Pendragon steps aside or dies, the new Pendragon has to be able to pull the sword out of the scabbard. It may not sound as impressive as pulling it out of a stone, but when you remember it is invisible and disappears when the old Pendragon is no more, the task becomes more challenging. Finding it tends to start out as a quest thing, but most of the Pendragons stumble across it quite by accident.

The only other accessory Jason wore was a communications headset.

"Sure you don't want body armor?" Jason offered. He wore it because a sword could always fall out of its welder's hand.

"Yeah, I'm sure," I said. Body armor would just slow me down and make me sloppy. "Just give me one of the headsets."

Jason did and I put it on. Radio silence wasn't an issue because the four punks inside didn't have any radio or comm equipment. Jason wore a trench coat which covered the body armor and made him look like your average Joe on the street. It was cut to hide the lines of his sword and his other weapons. The headset itself was no bigger than a hearing aid and had a wire-thin attachment leading to the mouth.

Our plan was to stroll casually down the street, join the strike force and rescue the two hostages who, hopefully, were Gary's parents.

We had barely rounded the corner when we heard a gunshot.

"Talk to me. What happened?" Jason said, not bothering to repeat that he issued a no-fire order. He knew his people. There had to be a good reason.

"Subject Number 2 was about to slice the male hostage's throat. I had no choice, but to take him out with a sniper shot," the voice over the headset said.

"All right. They know we're here. Move in and surround the place. We need to get those people out," the Pendragon instructed.

Inside, the man who had taken knife to throat was dead, his brains splattered over the walls and carpeting. The other three were thrown into a state of confusion. The high-powered sniper rifle was so effective it didn't shatter the glass, only poked a hole in it before it poked an even bigger hole in the dead man's head. One of the three saw the hole and started firing blindly out the same window. He was using a .38 which didn't have the power to reach where the sniper was stationed, around on the next block, but it was a danger to the neighborhood.

"We have a live fire zone. Secure the neighborhood and make sure no one wanders into the line of fire," Pendragon barked. Two from the strike force moved to cordon off the perimeter. "Open me a line inside." In seconds the call had been connected to the landline inside the house and was routed through Jason's headset. The phone rang and rang, but no answer.

"Jason, they're confused. They don't know if the call is from the sniper or someone else. They don't know if they should answer it," I said.

"Can you make them pick it up so maybe we can settle this without any more bloodshed?" Jason asked.

"Yes," I said. *"Answer."*

The shortest of the three did as I instructed even though he hadn't heard my voice.

"Who is it?" he barked into the phone.

"Who it is isn't important, rather what I have to say is. Come out immediately with your hands above your head, no weapons, and I can guarantee your safety. If you don't do as I say, you will end up as dead as your friend there," Jason promised.

"Oh yeah? Fuc..." he slammed down the receiver before he could finish his sentence. To extenuate his point he fired two more shots out the window. They moved the furniture around to act as barricades and banged out windows like an old western. They were going to fight it out. Using silencers on their weapons, the strike force knights fired a steady stream of warning shots into the house, high enough as not to hit anyone, but in a steady rhythmical pace, like the beat of a metronome. One, two, three, four, one, two, three, four. The game was psychological, to intimidate and freak out your opponent. A steady stream of bullets without the sound of gunfire can do that and it worked more often than not. The Knights had almost unlimited ammunition, the men inside didn't. It was kind of like Chinese water torture except with bullets.

The man who had answered the phone crawled over to the woman who was still tied to her chair, put a gun to her head and screamed as loud as he could, "Stop or I'll shoot her." What he didn't realize is, with the phone hung up, no one but me could hear him, especially over the sounds of the gunfire.

"Jason, he is going to blow away the woman if your people don't stop."

"If we stop, he will kill her. Hostage situations with psychos are not won by listening to them. If we delay much longer the police will come and take over and that is going to sign the hostages' death warrants." So far, police intervention hadn't been a worry yet. Neighbors had already started calling 911, but the Knights had hacked into the phone system and were answering the calls. A jamming device was blocking all cellular phone service over a half mile radius. It would give them a few extra minutes. The only phones working normally were in the house and those the Knights had. "We need the hostages out of there. Can you do something to help us out, Sir Hex?" Jason asked looking at me, being sure he used my title, appealing to my better nature. I didn't need any extra incentive.

"Yeah I can, but your people are going to have to stop shooting or there's no way I can safely get in and out of there."

"Fine, but I don't want to give them any early warning. Stopping the steady stream of bullets will be as much of a distraction as an explosion would be at this point. You let me know on the radio when you are in place and I'll order my people to stop."

I ran into the nearest backyard and sprinted over fences, through five other backyards towards the back of the Cape Cod.

"Okay Jason, cut it," I said once I was in place. The pops stopped and then there was silence. I walked up to the back door and into the house using a distraction spell. A distraction spell takes less energy than invisibility or a shroud of darkness spell. It kept my pain level to a minimum, but for all intents and purposes worked just as well in keeping me from being noticed. The basic gist was anyone who looked at me found their attention focused elsewhere or something else happened to make them turn their head before they could register my presence. I walked into the midst of the three punks without them knowing I was there. They were more concerned with looking out the windows in an attempt to determine where the gunfire had been coming from.

"*Bullets gone,*" I whispered. None of them heard me, but it insured that the guns would be empty. I extended my distraction spell around the two hostages, united them, and helped them limp out the back door. They had been tied to the chairs for days and their legs weren't working so well. Halfway down the steps, I pulled the spell back from the couple and three members of the strike force were instantly at our sides. A woman helped the lady hostage, a man aided the guy. The third one had an assault rifle out, ready to provide covering fire.

The spell still covering me, I went back inside. I strolled to the center of the room with the three punks and dropped the spell.

"Good evening, gentlemen. Can I interest you in some chocolate bars? I'm working my way through clown college and any support you can give me would be appreciated," I said. The three of them jumped, frightened at my sudden appearance.

"Who the hell are you?" said the short one who had answered the phone, aiming his gun at my face.

I smiled. "Just a candy striper. So can I put you down for ten or twelve boxes? They're only a hundred dollars each."

The punk with the gun wasn't smiling back. He pulled the trigger and the hammer clicked on an empty barrel. He did it again and again and again, each time with the same result. I had enough of that nonsense and reached out, taking the gun from his hands. Then I pile drove my fist into his face. His nose cracked under my knuckles. The other two started firing their weapons at me, but nothing happened. Both threw them aside and one of the gentlemen pulled out a hand grenade, pulled the pin and tossed it at me.

"Chocolate."

I caught the grenade as the punks dove behind the furniture. They waited three seconds, no boom; ten seconds, no boom; twenty seconds, no boom. It finally sunk into them that the grenade wasn't going to blow up. They looked up from behind their hiding holes.

"What'd he do, hold the pin?" asked the guy who had thrown it.

"Nope." I dangled the grenade in the air in front of his face. My fingers were nowhere near where the pin clasp was.

"So you think you're a tough guy?" he asked me, getting ready to stand up and try to duke it out.

"Yep," I said. To emphasize my point, I lifted the grenade up to my mouth like it was an apple and took a bite out of it. Not having a clue that I had transformed it, the punk was suitably impressed. I had one hell of a headache from doing the transformation spell, but it was worth it for the look on his face. And it was great chocolate.

"You think you might want to surrender now?" I asked.

"Yeah, that'll work for me," the guy putting his hands behind his head said, not quite sure what had happened, but knowing he didn't want to deal with it. I spoke into the headset even though I knew they had been listening to every word. "Okay, send in the cleanup crew."

The knights were there in under ten seconds. Impressive.

By the time I got out the front door, the limousine had pulled up to in front of where the former hostages were. The chauffeur knight made them comfortable, giving the couple food and drink. Neither had been fed in days.

The Pendragon pulled me aside.

"It's not them," Jason said, holding some photographs he had printed out of the Bendings.

"I know," I said unable to hide my disappointment. "But we helped rescue two people. It wasn't a total waste of time. We did good."

"Yes, but we will keep looking. We'll find this guy," Jason said, doing his best to try and convince me.

"I know," I said, not even convincing myself.

"All work and no play kind of ruins the whole point."
  -Hex, cursed magí

It was back to the grind and Gary, the penguin, and I were exhausted after another a long day of auditions. This whole ordeal had us to the point where the three of us were simply staring into space and vegging. Even I had lost track of how many presentations Gary had sat through. It was wearing on the kid, especially with the rescued couple not being his parents.

"How are you holding up, Gary?" I asked.

"All right, I guess. It's just so much to take in."

"It's a lot to have dumped in your lap at once, but you're doing fine," I said. "You need a break. Heck, we all do."

"I second that," Sister Anna said, yawning softly and stretching her arms.

"So what are we going to do?" Gary asked.

"Get a good night's sleep?" the penguin suggested.

"I love a good night's sleep as much as the next guy, but I think Gary needs something more. Gary, I want you to learn that magic can be fun. How'd you like to go to a party?" I asked.

"A party? Cool!" Gary said, his face lighting up. "Where?"

"Come with me," I said, leading Gary and the penguin to the backstage area of the theater. I pointed to an old wooden door. "It's through there."

Gary crinkled his brow. "That's a prop closet."

"Really?" I asked.

"He's right, Hex," Anna said.

"So?" I asked.

"Unless you have some twisted idea of blowing up balloons and playing pin the tail on the donkey, there's no party in that closet," said Gary.

"Are you sure?" I asked.

"Yes," Gary said, a pout starting on his face. I laughed. Gary wasn't amused. "You think it's funny?"

"I think you won't care what I think if you open that door," I said, inviting him with a hand gesture to try.

"Fine," Gary said curtly, reaching for the doorknob. Gary turned, pulled it open and was almost bowled over by the lights and music that burst forth. "Holy Sh..." Gary caught himself and changed his wording out of respect for the penguin. "Poop. This is wild!"

"Pretty close," I said. "This place is called Fiain am Tam. Gaelic for Wild Time. It's a spin-off of the Seelie Court."

"The what?" Gary shouted over the noise. His head was already bobbing to the band, a curious mix of Celtic and techno hip hop music.

"A court of fairies..."

His unease at the insinuations of the Tantara came crashing back. "You mean they're all gay?"

"No. Fairy as in elf, leprechaun, banshee, pixie. Like Bollywog. Why don't I just call them Gentry," I suggested.

"Oh," Gary said, visibly relieved. It was obvious he hadn't done any of the reading I recommended, not that he'd much time.

"Forget about the lecture," I said. "You're here to enjoy yourself. You too, Penguin."

"Sister Anna," she corrected.

I stepped in front of the door to finish what I had to say. "Just keep a few things in mind. This is a rave that has been going on for over five hundred years. It is technically in a part of Faerie but has doors that wander around reality. It's how they keep the party fresh. There are other parties that have been going longer, but this is one of the few that travels. Do not eat or drink anything they give you. If you do, you will have to stay, possibly forever. Nothing we could do would change that."

"Forever?" Sister Anna asked. "Wouldn't we die eventually?"

"No. Eating the food changes your body makeup, forever bonding you to Faerie. To leave Faerie safely, some of the Gentry have to take a piece of their home with them. On Earth it turns to gold, hence the explanation for leprechauns and their pots of gold. The sacrifice to become part of this realm is not without its rewards. Faerie sustains its own, giving them, while not quite immortality, the next best thing. If you stayed, you'd live hundreds, maybe thousands of years."

"In a forever party? Doesn't sound so bad," Gary said, smiling.

"It's not so bad. Remember the effect of the speed of light on the theory of relativity?" From the look on Gary's face, it was clear he didn't. "Magic has a speed all its own. Time passes differently here. You could be here years and only seconds pass on Earth. Or be here hours and outside centuries pass. If that's the case, the moment you return to Earth, you'll more than likely crumble to dust. A friend of mine named Murphy refers to it as quantum geography."

"How do we make sure that doesn't happen?" Sister Anna asked.

"Simple," I said, pulling a cement block in front of the open door. "We make sure the door stays open. *Stay,*" I ordered the door. "Time lines up then."

Gary was raring to go. "So what do they want from me? Where's their pitchman?"

"No pitchman. They figure the party will speak for itself. All they want is for you to join the party. Your power will keep them rocking for millennia."

"Then let's party!" Gary said, rushing into the crowd. He leapt into the air and came down on outstretched arms, crowd surfing across a field near a forest. Beautiful music flowed out from the woods, with no visible source. The sky held a setting sun, whose beauty was actually dwarfed by the fairy lights that filled the heavens. The fairy lights were made up of all the colors of the spectrum, each a brilliant rainbow unto itself. The effect was something like the aurora borealis, only more so. It lit up the sky as bright as the setting sun. The legendary rainbow that led to a leprechaun's pot was actually in part an effect of the fairy lights which escaped from the gold.

The field was filled with diverse members of the residents of Faerie in all manner of costume and garb. Tall and beautiful elves, with pointed ears and bird-like eyes, danced side by side with leather-clad banshees doing homage to punk. Ogres in tuxedos who drank side by side with small, but intelligent furry creatures of the forest. Humans from all walks of life and time mingled with the rest. I spotted a cowboy doing a two-step with a refined woman from the Renaissance. A man dressed in a Revolutionary War redcoat uniform was passed out drunk next to a huge vat of ale in which some human and fey women were skinny dipping with nymphs. Pixies were frolicking with satyrs and centaurs. A member of one of the intelligent races from the fourth planet in the Vegan System was arm wrestling with an immense bald fey with a pair of tusks that jutted ten inches upward from his lower jaw. It seemed an even match. A she-Minotaur was waiting to take on the winner.

Sister Anna was doing a version of the Mexican hat dance with a group of dwarves and humans. I was surprised that the woman could dance so well and couldn't stop myself from watching her moves.

Gary's attention had been drawn to a group of full-sized winged fairy women, dryads, unless I missed my guess. Standing in a grove of immense trees, each dryad was gorgeous and was dressed in sheer gossamer gowns that represented most of the colors in the rainbow. The reason for Gary's interest was obvious. These ladies had never heard of or had need of underwear. Their stunning bodies seemed to defy gravity. Gary's eyes had yet to wander above their necks.

I picked up the tail end of a floundering pick up line.

"You have such beautiful eyes," said Gary, his own eyes lost in some amazing cleavage. I snuck up behind him and covered his eyes with my hands.

"Really sport? What color are her eyes?" I asked.

"Hex, do you mind?" Gary asked, annoyed.

"Nope. Just tell me the color."

"Blue?" guessed Gary. I let go and let him see again.

"Nice try, slick," I said. "They're violet." The group of dryads giggled like schoolgirls.

Gary decided to look for himself and found that the dryad's eyes were just as beautiful as the rest of her. "Wow. Would you like to dance, Nia?"

I gathered that was the dryad's name.

"Sure," she said, floating up among the branches. Nia hovered, reaching out her hand to Gary. "Come."

"But I can't fly," Gary said.

"I don't dance on the ground," Nia said.

Gary fidgeted desperately. In a flash of insight, he rushed toward one of the trees, intending to climb it. I caught his arm before he could grab the first branch.

"Don't do it," I said.

"Hex, I want to dance with her," Gary pleaded.

"Climbing that tree is not going to help you dance with her."

"Why?"

"Nia's a dryad. A nymph bound to a tree, kind of like a bodyguard. If that's her tree and you hurt it, she is not going to be happy with you," I explained.

"But there's no other way up there," whined Gary.

"Yes, there is."

"Hex, I can't fly."

"How do you know?" I asked. "Have you ever tried?"

"No."

"Then how do you know you can't?"

"How?" he asked.

"A very wise and funny man once said to throw yourself at the ground and miss," I said. "Of course, there are at least a dozen other ways."

Gary's mouth dropped as Nia started dancing and gyrating without him. "Teach me, Hex." He again glanced up at Nia, then back at me. "Quick."

"We've been over this. I will look out for you, answer your questions, but I won't hold your hand and spoon feed you knowledge you need to learn on your own."

Gary looked up at the dryad, playfully waving at him, with hips and hands.

"Please, Hex," Gary begged, holding onto my arm. Against my better judgment, I gave in.

"Okay Gary, look at all the flyers. How are they doing it?"

"Flapping their wings?"

"Wings on the bigger ones are not strong enough to hold them up and not all of them have wings. Look closer."

Gary squinted like he did when checking out umbras. "They are doing it different ways. Some are using a blue power line. An air ley line, right?"

I nodded.

"Some are pushing against the ground with magic. Some are levitating, pulling themselves up. A few I have no idea," admitted Gary.

"Of the ones you have figured out, which seems the easiest?" I asked.

"Using the ley line. The energy is practically flying by itself."

"Try to draw some into you."

"How? Where?"

"Try sucking it in to a spot two inches under your belly button. It's your center. That would be the easiest. Call to it. Spoken magic is simple but effective." Which is why I use it so much. Less pain from the curse that way.

"What do I say?"

"Tell it what you want to do."

"Here goes. *Go inside me*," Gary invoked. A steam of blue energy shot off the ley line and flowed into Gary's center. The power filled him. "What a rush."

"It is, isn't it? Now say where you want to go," I instructed.

"*Up*," said Gary. Bit by bit, he rose off the ground until his feet were even with my head. "Oh man!"

"Now just think where you want to go," I said.

Gary went up even higher until he was even with the dryad, but Nia didn't have the same appeal she had a minute ago. Gary swooped down toward the ground, then soared into the sky startling a hawk.

"I'm flying!" Gary screamed in total delight. Flying was almost pure joy and Gary was losing himself in it. Sister Anna looked up from her dancing, amazed to see Gary playing among the clouds. Gary waved. Sister Anna, thrilled for Gary, was smiling almost as wide as he was.

A flock of pixies started a game of tag with him, swooping and soaring.

I smiled remembering what it had been like my first time in the air. The look on Gary's distant face assured me that he had learned how to have fun with his power. Since he had moved on, I hovered up to dance with Kia, another dryad, among the branches of her tree trying to stop myself from looking down at Anna.

She caught me looking, so I smiled and waved. When she smiled and waved back, I floated down to her.

"Is Gary safe up there?" she leaned in and whispered.

I nodded. "You want to give it a try?"

"How?"

I held out my hand. "May I have this dance?"

"Just a dance?"

"Of course."

Anna took my hand and I pushed some of the blue energy from the ley line into her and we floated up together. At first I led, weaving side to side. Then I held onto both her hands and spun us both, then twirled her and let her spin up into the sky, then surged ahead so I caught her.

Anna was laughing and wrapped her arms around me and had figured out how to control the energy and spun me around so fast that we both got dizzy. We stopped to hover and she rested her head on my shoulder.

I looked down to steal a glance to find she was staring up at me and still smiling.

Our eyes met as if for the first time and neither of us turned away.

"You are a very unique man, Hex."

"Back at you, Anna."

"I think if I had met you five years ago, my life might have turned out very different."

"In what way?"

Anna's smile turned into a frown as her hand gently turned my cheek, then pushed off my chest to fly off to look at what Gary was doing.

I spent the rest of the night trying to figure out if Anna meant what I thought she meant.

"Not only ask what your county can do for you, ask what it might do to you."

    -Hex, cursed magi

"It's your duty son," informed the government spook in the black suit and sunglasses. He said it as if its truth was self-evident and anyone who disagreed was a traitorous dog that should be shot dead in the streets. In short, he was a fanatic who had accepted Uncle Sam as his personal savior. The Constitution and all those other pesky laws only needed to be followed when they suited his purposes. His appearance was nothing out of the ordinary, at least in espionage circles, down to the wire that led into an earpiece and the microphone hidden in his lapel. "Your country needs you."

"I said I'd think about it," Gary said, annoyed at the agency man. He was more annoyed that it wasn't as easy to fly on Earth as it was in Faerie. I explained that Faerie had much more magic than our world did. Gary didn't care for the explanation and had become cranky.

Appealing to patriotism didn't work for the spook. It was time for him to get down to business. "We could draft you," the spook threatened.

"I'm not even fifteen yet. You can't draft me," Gary countered, not taking the spook seriously. That was a mistake. The agent may not be bright, but he didn't have to be.

"We can do anything we want. We're the government," the spook said, with no expression in his voice or on his face. Sadly, he spoke the truth, at least as he knew it.

"What branch of the government?" Sister Anna asked.

"That's classified. On a need to know basis," the spook said.

"I think we need to know," the penguin answered.

"No, you don't," the spook said.

"Excuse me?" the penguin asked.

"No need to make excuses," he said.

"I wasn't. I want some answers. Now," Anna demanded.

"This is not your concern. Keep your nose out of it or this could get ugly."

"Uglier than you, spook?" I said. "This I have to see." The agent gave me a dirty look. I wiggled my eyebrows. He straightened his sunglasses. I took mine out of my pocket and did the same. The spook looked neither annoyed nor amused. Obviously, not the life of the party.

"If the two of you would kindly turn custody of the boy over to me, we can finish this matter up quickly and quietly." The spook waved some papers around as if what was written on the writ would make us listen.

"What!? You want to kidnap him?" Sister Anna yelled, trying to grab the papers. Spook kept them out of reach.

"No, acquire. You would do best to keep out of this, Sister. Separation of Church and State and all that."

"That hardly applies here," the nun said.

"Sister, this is a matter of National Security. You will do as I say or there will be consequences."

"Such as?" she asked.

"How about an IRS audit?" The spook smiled at that one. Most people weren't afraid of the Boogeyman, but everyone was afraid of the IRS.

"I'm a nun. Vow of poverty. I don't have any money. Therefore, I don't pay taxes."

The spook frowned. No one had ever just shrugged that one off before.

"I will have you arrested and put away in a hole so deep that your bones will be dust before you see the light of day again."

"What about due process?" she asked.

"Due what?" the spook asked. Sad part about it was he was serious about his joke.

Gary shifted uneasily. Somehow government agents seemed a lot more dangerous to him than monsters. They had more of a solid reality and therefore, more to be afraid of. The penguin was close to losing her cool. Frankly, I was growing bored with the whole thing. It was time to end this.

"Anna, Agent Dartley here is normally with the CIA. He specializes in black ops. Today, he is representing a government agency dedicated to the defense of the United States against mystic threats. They recruit mages and mystic folk to become their agents. They're known as the Department of Mystic Affairs."

"The DMA?" Sister Anna asked. "I thought they dealt with cranks."

"Nope. They're the real deal." I still wasn't sure why the DMA didn't send its own team. I knew some and could reason with them. Most of them anyway.

"How do you know about me?" the spook demanded. "That information is classified above top secret. I'm afraid I am going to have to take you into custody for questioning." The spook pulled out a gun and a cross. Holding the later up in front of him, he pointed it at Sister Anna. She laughed and so did I.

"Your people really need to brief you better before they send you into the field. I'm guessing Zachs was the one who recruited you." Zachs was an assistant director for the DMA, specializing in their black ops. Not a nice guy. "Crosses are for vampyres, demons and the like, not nuns."

The spook put the cross back in his pocket and pointed his gun at me.

"Maybe, but a gun works on everything. Let's go." He was wrong as he was only packing lead bullets. Zachs didn't give him any real heads up.

I chuckled, then did a theatrical yawn. "*Slither.*" The spook's gun transformed into a snake. The spook's calm facade broke for a moment, but only a moment. Gripping the tail between his fingers, he cracked the snake as if it were a whip, smashing its head on the floor.

"Nice trick," the spook said, taking out a handkerchief to wipe the snake goo off his hands and pulled another gun from an ankle holster.

"I aim to please."

"In thirty seconds, this place will be crawling with agents. Let's see what happens then." The spook lifted up his lapel and spoke into it. "The barn door is open."

"Then just zip up your fly," I suggested. The spook actually looked down. This was our first line of defense? I wanted my tax dollars back.

Thirty or so CIA agents surrounded us, weapons drawn and trained on us. Each was dressed similarly to the first spook. There wasn't a DMA agent in the bunch and I had finally figured out why. The plan was to take Gary, willingly or otherwise. Some of the DMA operatives had been taken the same way as children by others, stolen away from their families and friends against their will because of their powers. In some cases, it was the DMA that rescued them. The actual living and breathing Uncle Sam who headed up the Department of Mystic Affairs would never sanction this and most of the agents might have a problem doing it to someone else so the high muckity mucks in the intelligence community weren't taking any chances. They farmed it out to the CIA black ops boys and girls. Zachs was likely their consultant, not the other way around. No worries about conscience here.

"Are you going to come quietly?" Dartley asked.

"Or?" I asked, sitting back and putting my feet up.

"Hex—" Gary whispered. Both he and Sister Anna had their hands in the air. "These guys are serious. They have guns."

"Don't worry, Gary. I have it under control." At least, I hoped I did. "If you want us to come with you, show us some identification. All of you." Spook number one nodded and the lot flashed their CIA IDs. "Aren't you violating your charter? The CIA isn't allowed to operate on American soil."

"Try proving it and you'll disappear," spook number one promised.

"Proving it won't be a problem." To corroborate my statement, I lifted up a piece of paper to reveal a tiny webcam.

"Seize that camera!" ordered spook number one. Another company man took it from me. "Destroy the computer and the memory card."

"Sir?" the second spook asked.

"What?"

"There is no computer. Or memory card."

The first spook turned toward me and knocked my feet to the floor. "Wireless? Ha, we have a jammer in place. You've got nothing."

"Nothing? You are here recruiting a boy who has magic powers. I'm guessing your scrambler only blocks traditional signals, not mystic ones." Dartley's face darkened, telling me I was right. "I guess Zachs should have sent DMA agents after all. And didn't my little camera just record all your IDs? Wow. We now have a record of all the CIA agents involved. Anything happens to us and that video is on every major and minor news station, followed by YouTube. It will become a permanent fixture on the web. You will have failed in your primary directive, secrecy above all else. There will be no plausible deniability."

"We'll trace the transmission."

I lifted my own collar and spoke into it. "Keep moving. Cut transmission. Don't vary from the plan."

"Son of a..."

Still speaking into my collar, I added, "Also prepare to release the info on The Bard Incident."

"How do you know about that?" the spook demanded.

I smiled. "Does it matter?"

"Hell, yes. Everyone involved signed secrecy oaths."

I winked at him. "Not everyone. What a great lead for the evening news."

The spook grabbed me by my collar with both hands. His touch was foul, like someone throwing blood-soaked feces in my face, only worse. All the lives he had destroyed or ended flashed before me screaming for vengeance. Dartley's body count was higher than most serial killers, except he allegedly did it for God and country. "If the video or that information leaks out I'll—"

"Be screwed. Not only will John Q. Public know, but so will the powers that be." The visions of his victims were overwhelming me so I removed his hands forcibly by breaking both his pinkies. The snaps made a lovely sound. Thirty-five guns cocked and pointed at me. That sound wasn't near as pleasant. "Your only way out of this is to walk away and forget about us. This is your only warning. "

"Sir, we have a clean line of fire..." spook number two said, his gun aimed between my eyes.

"No one fires, except on my command," Spook Dartley ordered, hiding the pain of two fractured fingers well. I hid pain pretty good too. His command to the troops was moot. I had already disabled the guns, but the pain was leading a conga line through the more delicate areas of my hands. The pain didn't care that I wasn't in a dancing mood. "We have a file on you, Mr. Hex..."

"Good, so you know I don't bluff. You also know what my warnings mean."

Spook Dartley paused. He must have read my file. I'll have to get a copy of it. Uncle Sam owes me more than one favor. Should make for interesting reading. "I'll have to think about it."

"Go ahead, you've got a second." What the heck. I was feeling generous. "One."

Spook Dartley considered his options. "Fine, but here's the deal..." He tried to accentuate his point by poking me in the chest with his right index finger. Slow student, you'd think he would have learned his lesson the first time.

Grabbing the finger, I bent it back. Hard. Spook Dartley took pain well. The only sign he even noticed what I was doing was a mild teeth gritting.

"No buts. Gone, never to return."

Dartley nodded.

"I just want you to be aware – I know what you've done. I've seen the bodies. There is only one reason I'm letting you live. You have a new job and it is to protect the three of us. If anyone from your agency or any other government's agency ever bothers anyone in this room, I'm coming for you. On that day, you will die. And if you ever touch me again, I will end you, then and there." I pulled back his finger until it snapped. The agents all cocked their guns again. Dartley waved them down with his left hand. "Understand?"

"Yes." The word oozed contempt. He would follow the order only until he found a way to end me first. Fine by me. Thanks to this episode, I didn't need anyone to ask me to go after him. He had involved me of his own accord.

When this was cleared up, he was going down. Otherwise, I will be haunted by the spirits of his victims crying for vengeance. That's one of the reasons I set my dream wards without fail.

"This isn't over," he promised.

"Glad to hear it. Now, every one of you hit the road. And take the stupid van that's been parked across the street with you."

I had ignored the snooping. None of their equipment had helped them. A few wards disabled the electronic bugs and listening devices.

They tried to trail us home each night but failed. Not that I wasn't sympathetic. A stakeout is boring, thankless work. Last night, I sent the van over a pizza.

The lot of them left without another word. They never even said thank you for the pizza. Neither did the vans the Israelis, Russians, British, Daemor, Universal Watch, or Chinese agents were occupying. We would have to sit through their pitches and a few others later.

"That was amazing, thinking to set up the camera like that," Gary said.

I failed to mention that the camera was just a piece of equipment Jeeves had wanted me to give to Paulie to repair for him. It would tarnish my image. I just nodded modestly. My collar was just a collar with no mystic radio.

"How'd you know about that Bard Incident?" Anna asked.

"Easy, I didn't."

"But how?"

"I picked up some surface thoughts. He was worried about it, so I used it."

The deceit impressed Gary. "Where those the men in black?"

"Nope. That's a whole other group. Nothing at all like the movie."

"It is always time to do the right thing."
          -Sister Anna, Order of St. Dymphna

Sister Anna lived her life by a code. A strict one perhaps, but she stuck to it. It was something I admired. The penguin was not a hypocrite, unlike many religious I had run across, although maybe all the bad apples I've met have left me jaded. Not that there aren't good ones like Sister Rose, the Iron Nun, and Father Mike from Bulfinche's Pub, but the bad ones ruin it for a hundred good ones.

The good sister also had a sense of fun and compassion. Anna wasn't stuffy, although she was a bit stiff. The penguin wasn't full of her 'nun'-ness and didn't let rules stand in the way of doing something right. Not many people would have adjusted so well to the revelation of magic and all that entailed. Her Mother Provincial was none too happy about her extended absence. The penguin was going to be given no end of grief when she returned to the convent. She put all that aside to help Gary in his time of need without so much as voicing concern for her personal well-being or complaining about the disruption to her life. Anna was an impressive woman who practiced what she preached.

The nun's introduction to the unseen world was not without consequence. Anna began to have some real problems when leaders of the world's major religions took the stage. It reached terrible heights when the Roman Catholic Church made its pitch. Two of them, actually. The first by a highly esteemed Cardinal, a religious mystic of no small power himself, who was sincerely devoted to serving God through serving his Church. Looking at his umbra revealed he was no saint, but he wasn't a horrible sinner either. I could sense his power was not on a par with Sister Anna, but he was aware he had it and had cultivated the use of it which gave him the appearance of having more power. Captivating speaker too, considering English was his fifth language. He tried to entice Gary to enter a seminary, but priesthood was not something the kid aspired to. Again, the process sounded too much like school. The Cardinal thanked Gary for his time and spoke briefly with Sister Anna, trying to make her understand the Church's position. It only left her with more questions.

The next presentation that troubled her was from the Universal Watch, the Roman Catholic Church's secret police. Anna was not even aware it existed, which is, of course, the point of a secret police force. The pitchman was a priest named Kevin Kerner. Gary was a bit more interested in this as it involved becoming a secret agent of sorts. Problem was, he still had to become a priest or a brother at the very least and religious life was not something Gary strived for, especially after seeing the dance of the seven veils. Before he left, Kerner made some thinly veiled threats against Sister Anna, something along the lines of speak of this and I will make you disappear. I made a threat of my own and branded the priest with my mark like I had with the Korlak vampyres, only this time, it was invisible to the untrained eye. Kerner would see it every time he passed a mirror.

Seeing smoke rise from his flesh, Kerner treated me as if I were possessed. The priest actually tried to exorcise me. I responded by doing my best Zumba imitation. The stiff didn't get the joke. I promised I would come looking for him if anything ever happened to Anna and I could see in his mind that he believed me.

Soon after, the Black Covenant took their turn on the stage. Gary had even less interest in demon worship than he did in holy orders. Poor kid barely concealed his boredom. His eyes were getting heavy and his head kept dropping down. Anna, on the other hand, was incensed. The dark nuns wore habits similar to her own, only their crosses hung upside down. The Black Covenant was the antithesis of all she stood for and she couldn't tolerate their presence. I wasn't thrilled with them either, but they had to be allowed their time to be fair and prevent violence against Gary. Their display ended with a boom, as they started a dark mass ritual for a summoning. The dark mother superior drew an upside down pentacle, lighting a single ebony candle on the lowest point. With a knife, she slashed her right wrist and let her blood fall down into the tiny flame.

"Hex," Sister Anna exclaimed, instinctively sensing what was happening. "Stop them! They are trying to summon a demon!"

I was already trying. "I can't. They must have started the ritual before they got here. Stopping them now would just make it blow up and kill everyone in the theater," I said, taking a piece of white chalk out of my inside jacket pocket. "To add to the problem, the demons they're trying to summon are our next contestants. The plan was for them to pitch through a laptop I had set up. Summoning was not part of the deal." I hadn't put full wards around the entire building because some of the participants would not have been able to get in.

I screwed up.

"Cool," Gary said, finally paying attention. They had started the incantation, a distorted and warped version of the old Latin mass, substituting the Devil's name for God, Hell for Heaven and so on.

"I wouldn't do that if I were you," I warned. "You are dealing with forces you can't control. Stop it. This is your only warning!" A small nexus took form in the air behind the stage. Think of it like a wormhole. There are different kinds and this type was called a hellhole for obvious reasons. The smell of brimstone leaked into the room and a terrible, fiery light shone and flickered onto the stage. Amazed that their ritual was working for the first time, the dark nuns ignored my warning and chanted louder.

We were still near the front row. I motioned Anna and Gary to walk to a cleared part of the floor where the carpeting had long ago been torn away, revealing the cement beneath.

"Stand close together and don't move until I tell you too," I said, as I knelt to draw a circle on the floor that wrapped around the three of us.

"Hex, what are you doing?" Gary had finally had the good sense to be frightened. I had to hide my disappointment that he still wasn't even trying to figure out the answers on his own.

In the past, the powers that be were not as organized as they are now. Dozens of magí died, never realizing what they were. Even among those who learned that they possessed power, a good many never did anything with it because they never bothered to learn. Kind of like someone who had the potential to be a great artist, but never picked up a paintbrush because it seemed like too much work. I was getting the impression that other than a few parlor tricks, Gary would have fallen in that category had he not been the prize at the center of this mystic game.

"I'm setting a ward to protect us," I explained.

"What about symbols and stuff?" he asked.

"I don't need them," I said. This wasn't the time to give a lesson on uses of symbology in magic and the fact that it was a booster to strengthen weaker magics. The portal had grown large enough to almost envelop the stage.

"Why do we need protection against demons when we didn't need it against the Devil?" Sister Anna shouted, trying to be heard above the din blasting out from the hellhole. The screams of the damned were my definition of pure horror. I covered my ears, not that it did any good. The souls being tortured were human and despite any evil they had done, were still kindred. The sound cut straight through to the listener's heart and even the strongest soul couldn't help but feel utter despair. It was a sound that could never be completely forgotten, that no music could ever totally erase from memory. I know, I've tried. The first time I heard them

I was a child, younger than Gary. The nightmares they caused can still wake me screaming.

"Nick exists for the game. He has fewer restrictions in his movement but more on how he can hurt people. These particular demons are Manglar. They spend eternity ripping the damned in their care to shreds, chowing down on what remains, excreting them and then waiting for their spirit forms to heal enough to do it again. They'll as soon gut you as speak to you. Makes a chainsaw killing look like a paper cut." They also don't care about any orders of protection granted to mortal mages, at least until it would be far too late to do me any good.

The Dark Mother Superior pulled a fresh human heart from beneath her robe and thrust her knife into it. The heart had to be fresh, probably still warm. They must have taken it right before coming here. Fairness be screwed. They were not getting away with a death sacrifice on my watch and thanks to my being asked to help the kid, they were fair game. They were going down. Way down.

"Dark Lord, join us, we beseech thee!" they screamed in unison.

"Idiots!" I shouted. My companions stood stunned, as they realized what the red fleshy piece of meat she held in her hand was. "All they needed was another drop of blood. The fools didn't have to kill anyone."

"It looks like they wanted to," Gary said, watching the smiles of ecstasy on the dark nuns' faces. A claw the size of a horse broke through the barrier. The sheer enormity of it caused Gary to stumble back. I caught him before he could trip.

"Careful. You fall out and the ward won't let you back in. Watch where you step. You erase that line and we're all dead," I said, but Gary was trembling too much to pay attention. A second, then a third claw appeared, followed by a head with only one clear feature; a pair of jaws that would make a Great White Shark drool with envy. All the teeth were pointed incisors, each the size of a man.

"Incoming!" I screamed over the din.

The claws seemed to be reaching for us. Gary screamed and stumbled again. This time, I was not fast enough to catch him. Landing on his hands and knees, he looked up at the Manglar, like a deer in the headlights. Sensing his opportunity, the Manglar struggled to pull himself through onto the mortal plane faster. His bulk already took up most of the stage and, with a mighty effort, the Manglar hurled himself at the paralyzed Gary. Before he could get fully airborne I was already moving.

"*Stay*," I invoked at Sister Anna, who was preparing to throw herself in front of the boy, throwing away her own life. It wouldn't have been a fair trade. I hated to use magic on her, but to keep her safe she needed to be in the circle. Otherwise, I couldn't protect both of them. I managed to reach Gary first, which gave me about a two-second head start. Before I landed my chalk was out. Ignoring the jaws hurling toward me, I managed to complete a second circle a nanosecond before the Mangler could devour Gary. It bounced off like it had struck a steel wall.

"VERY QUICK, MR. HEX, BUT ALL IN VAIN. I WILL HAVE THE BOY!" the Manglar belched, waving twenty sets of claws in the air.

"Don't think so, Cazz," I answered.

"I WILL GIVE YOU ANYTHING YOU DESIRE – JUST GIVE ME THE MAN CHILD TO DEVOUR!"

"D…devour?!" Gary stuttered.

"Yes. If he can't get you to join him, he can still absorb your power by eating you," I whispered to Gary. "Sorry, Cazz. Snack bar's closed. We both know you have nothing I want."

"FINE. I AM ON EARTH NOW. IF YOU DO NOT FEED THAT TENDER MORSEL TO ME, I WILL CARVE A PATH OF DESTRUCTION SUCH AS THIS TINY WORLD HAS NEVER SEEN!" Cazz bragged, standing up so his enormous head brushed the ceiling of the theater.

"Wrong again. This time, you're on my turf," I growled. "Let me show you how we do things in New York. *Freeze*," I ordered. The manglar stood immobilized in his tracks. My body started trembling from cold chills.

"SUCH PUNY POWER, IT IS LAUGHABLE," Cazz mocked.

"Really? Let's see you twitch then," I challenged. He couldn't.

"SO YOU ARE GOING TO KEEP ME FROZEN TO THIS SPOT FOREVER?" Cazz said, knowing full well I couldn't.

"Hardly. I'll just wait for the cops to show up," I said. Cazz's entire body turned pale.

"I don't think the NYPD is equipped to handle this kind of thing," said Gary.

"Not the NYPD. HPD," I said. "Cazz wanted your power so he could start a revolution in Hell. Management frowns on that sort of thing." The back doors of the theater swung open of their own accord and in walked Negral.

"NO!!" screamed Cazz in terror, his tremendous inhuman body cowering from the much tinier forgotten god.

"Evening Sister. A pleasure to see you again," Negral said, tipping his hat. He walked in front of the ward where I was. "Hello, Gary. I am Negral. Apparently, we will be talking soon." As an afterthought, he added, "Hex."

"Chief."

"NEGRAL, IT IS NOT WHAT YOU THINK," Cazz started.

"Save it. You're busted," Negral said, pulling a pair of ordinary handcuffs from inside his overcoat pocket, he tossed them into the air. They grew and morphed, until each of Cazz's twenty claws and his neck was shackled. "Move it."

"CAN NOT," said Cazz, still immobilized by my word of power.

Annoyed, Negral turned to me. "Do you mind?"

"You guarantee Cazz will never be allowed to come back to the mortal plane, ever?" I asked.

Negral sighed, knowing full well he would never be able to move the Manglar without my leave. "Fine. I'll put him on the no-summoning list."

"Okay," I said. "*Mobility return, but you never shall,*" I intoned, backing up Negral's guarantee with a banishing spell of my own. A headache flowed to my eyes. Light began to hurt. I flipped out my dark sunglasses and slid them on my face. Negral looked and narrowed his eyes, but said nothing.

Negral, dwarfed next to his prisoner, marched him back to the hellhole. "Snack time boys," he yelled as he kicked Cazz back into the Mangler pit, this time as victim. He then turned to the almost forgotten Dark Covenant. "This was an unauthorized summoning. We have rules, ladies."

"Would it help if we said we were sorry?" the Dark Mother Superior asked, grasping at straws.

"Oh, of course, but you have to be really sorry. Are you?" Negral asked in sympatric tones.

"Oh yes, absolutely."

"Well that is a relief," Negral said as he bent down to pick up the stabbed heart by the hilt of the knife. "You brought snacks for the manglar? Very thoughtful. They love kabobs. Cazz would have probably liked if you added an eye and a kidney."

"We could get those for you," the mother offered.

"Could you? I wouldn't want to be any trouble," Negral said.

"No trouble, really."

"Sadly, that would be considered a bribe. Can't have that," Negral said. "And I don't eat human flesh. And I have a lot of issues with the killing of innocents which your victim was. Plus, there is still the legal issue here. I can't just let you go. Bad example for keeping order."

"We wouldn't tell."

"You wouldn't? Well, that certainly is a relief. I guess then there must be some way we can work this out. Wait, I have an idea. Will you promise never to do this again?"

"We promise," they all shouted.

"Well, that's that," Negral said, turning as if to go. After two steps, he turned and came back.

"No, it just doesn't work for me." Negral whistled. A host of claws came through the still open portal. Each claw scooped up a dark nun and pulled them kicking and screaming into Hell. The dark Mother Superior was the last to go.

"Help me! Don't let them take me, Hex!" she begged as the demon paw dragged her across the floor, her nails clawing into the wooden boards of the stage in a desperate attempt to save herself. My sunglasses hid the horror in my eyes.

"You know, Hex is a fool. He would have probably tried to save you, despite the personal risk. Your big problem is that you screwed up. Twice in fact. Once, you didn't stop when he warned you, which he thinks absolves him from any blame. Still, he's been known to try anyway. I think the real problem is that he just can't get past the human sacrifice issue. And neither can I. And you know you really screwed up if you did something so bad that he and I agree on it. Time to say bye-bye."

The dark Mother Superior vanished into the hellhole, adding her screams to that of the other millions of tortured souls.

Negral stood in front of the portal, posing like Bogart. "Gary. Sister," he said, again tipping his hat. "It's been a pleasure. Hex, Lucifer may want to change his appointment time."

"Tell him to go through channels," I said, unable to come up with a better comment to cover my disgust over what just happened. Problem is the dark nuns deserved what they got and Negral just stopped the Mangler from killing thousands in Manhattan. And maybe us too.

Negral nodded and jumped into the breach. I ran out of my ward onto the stage and blew out the single ebony candle on the pentacle. As the flame flickered out so did the hellhole, slamming shut the portal to Hell. The closure complete, the screams of the damned vanished and the silence that followed was the most blessed sound never heard.

"*You can come out now.*" My words freed Sister Anna to move again. She walked over to Gary and gathered him up in her arms and held him as he wept.

"Why don't we call it a day," I said, trying to be chipper. Sister Anna looked at me and saw right through me in a way few others ever have. She opened her arms in an offer to console me as well. I waved her off, but she was not buying my ultra-cool, tough guy act, even with the sunglasses. I knew she was hurting too and I didn't want to impose. Sister Anna viewed it differently and again beckoned me, insistent. I was too weary to argue. I let her hug me, but kept it short and sweet, surprised to find a few tears trickling down my face. Sister Anna's face was soaked and salty. Gary was sobbing and shaking, still terrified.

As I broke off the hug, I downed a couple of aspirin dry, then looked down. "Oh no."

"What?" Sister Anna asked.

"This is not good," I said as I bent down to pick up a severed left hand with a huge mole on the base of the thumb. It had been removed below the wrist and burned to stop the bleeding. Gary's eyes opened wide.

"Could it have been from one of those—" Sister Anna stammered, unable to find a term to put to the Black Covenant's dark nuns.

"I don't think so," I answered, worried. The manglars had severed no limbs on our side of the hellhole so whoever put it here was good enough drop off my radar, which put me at a potentially dangerous disadvantage. "It looks like a man's hand."

"It is," said Gary, taking it from me with almost robotic movements. "It's my father's."

"My bite is far worse than my bark."
   -Luther, Vampyre

Gary hadn't moved in almost an hour. In the interest of preserving sanity, his mind had moved into shut down mode. I wrapped him in a comforter, then left him to sleep in my bed. Sister Anna was a bundle of raw nerves. My explanation that right now it was a good thing, a protective measure that Gary desperately needed, failed to comfort her. What I didn't add was that it would also protect us. If Gary lashed out now, with all those churning emotions fueling his power, things could turn deadly.

My attentions turned to the matter at hand, literally. I wasn't a surgeon but I did some time in an ER. Judging by the incisions and the cauterization, there was a chance his father might still be alive. Slim, but possible.

One of the reasons I can survive doing what I do, despite the powering down effect of the curse, is because I have an expansive knowledge of how things work. I've spent years studying and practicing. I know magic in most of its infinite varieties, inside out, upside down and in ancient Sumerian. What good is being able to use magic if you didn't know what it was you were using? It would be akin to having the arms and legs necessary to drive a car but no idea what a car even was. In the end, you weren't going to get very far and would be better off walking.

Whoever did this was on a skill level equal to mine. With all due humility, there are maybe two dozen people alive on the planet in that league and one of them was still negotiating with her cat to get her medication back. Besides, Crystal's mind was shot, her power spent and she never went in for killing. This necromancer was an unknown. If it wasn't for Crystal, we wouldn't even know what our adversary looked like.

I was going after him. I could use the hand to find Gary's father, but I wasn't going to go in blind. Gary was too much of a novice, which coupled with his emotional brittleness, would put him at unbelievable risk. Sister Anna, by her nature, would be little more than cannon fodder. Jeeves and Bollywog could be destroyed in less than a minute by someone this good and I wouldn't put them in that kind of danger. The pack could hold their own, but without a source of power, they wouldn't be at their peak. Regardless, they were not about to let me go off alone.

Mordi and Trickster would come with me, so they were currently gorging themselves on magic energy from the ley lines to sustain them. The rest of the pack would stay behind to watch over Sister Anna and Gary. I tried to reach Aziel, but he seemed to have dropped off the face of the Earth. Not unheard of for an angel.

I had no better luck contacting the Tabula Rotunda. I have some pretty powerful friends that hang their hats at an uptown bar by the name of Bulfinche's Pub, but hunting necromancers wasn't exactly their cup of whiskey. They'd try to reason with him, make him see the light and turn away from his evil ways. This situation had moved way beyond that stage. I still needed someone else I trusted to watch my back.

That's where Luther came in. Actually, he came in the door after we went through the usual ritual.

"Permission to enter," Luther asked, dressed in black jeans and a grey t-shirt that showed off arms that would have done any bodybuilder proud.

"Granted for this one time, so long as you mean no harm to any within. Permission revoked on leaving," I said. It was wordy, but it kept my place safe. I trusted Luther, but I preferred to err on the side of safety. Same went for Layla.

"All right," Luther said, grabbing my arm in a hand to wrist grip. "Time to go hunting."

"That it is. You ready?" I asked.

"Always," he said with a grin, which showed off his fangs. Luther had recently decided to try a new look. His black head was shaved, just as close as Barber's. It was a pretty popular style with the undead lately. Other than baldness there wasn't much resemblance between the two vamps. Average height by most standards, Luther was tiny compared to Plasma's bouncer. Then again, so was a pony. To make the tough-dead-guy look work at its best, Luther sported a thin goatee. "This the new magi?"

I nodded.

"Don't look like much."

"Looks can be deceiving."

"True enough. You never looked like much, either. Might be hope for him yet," Luther said.

Sister Anna walked over and introduced herself.

"A pleasure, Sister," Luther said as he kissed her hand. As he spoke, the penguin noticed his fangs. The penguin went for her crucifix like it was a revolver and she was a gunslinger.

"Luther's okay," I assured her. She sheepishly covered her crucifix.

"A reflex I didn't know I had. I'm sorry," she said.

"Don't be. Holy objects don't hurt me, although a plain cross can give me fits," Luther explained.

"I thought crucifixes hurt all vampyres?"

"Only if a believer wields it. With a cross belief doesn't matter much, couldn't tell you why."

I could but choose not to.

"My breed, the Ramanga," Luther said, "is the only one I know that is immune to holy objects. It may be because we are protectors and act as priests of sorts to our tribes."

Sunlight didn't bother him either.

"Tribe?"

"I am originally from Africa."

"Really? Where?" asked Anna.

"Madagascar. You know it?"

"Can't say I do other than the cartoon."

While the penguin and the vamp got to know each other, I swallowed a small handful of aspirin with a large glass of milk.

"Pre-emptive strike?" Luther whispered, walking over to me. Luther was one of the few who knew about the curse. I nodded. I was going to have to do some serious magic to make this work and it was going to hurt. A masochist would love my life.

First, I took my shirt, shoes, and socks off, then moved to the corner of my apartment I keep empty for rituals. I drew a large circle and sat at the center, after tracing a smaller circle around myself and the severed hand. The inner ring was to protect me, the outer one to protect everyone else.

"*Show me,*" I intoned. "*Please,*" I added as an afterthought. I liked to keep things short and sweet, but it rarely hurts to be polite. With this ritual, I was dealing directly with the universe, not using a power that be as a go-between or informer. A more difficult process, but one with no hidden strings attached. Extremely dangerous. I was the only mage I've ever heard of who has survived it more than three times. This would be my fifth and only the second since I was cursed.

The universe agreed to cooperate. It usually does for a price, one I wasn't thrilled to pay. I felt the after-effects of the last time for at least a year. The universe got to use my body for its own ends. It never even bought me dinner. At least it never killed me, like it had so many others. At least, not yet.

The universe was in me and in a way, I was in it. Being one with everything is not something I'd recommend despite what a zen master might say to the contrary. For an instant. I saw all of creation and in the instant before it drove me mad, it was gone.

The universe lifted me off the floor, with my back arched and head back. I was no longer in control, the universe was in the driver's seat. The giving up of control was harder to bear than the pain. Mystic energy was flowing out of my eyes and I puked mystic fire. I'd be tasting that for days. The space between the circles filled up with the mystic spillage. The pack howled in sympathy for me as I screamed.

What happened is hard to explain. Let's just say the universe used me as a conduit to do some repairs on itself, almost like if I took control of a microbe to do microsurgery on myself. Satisfied with the payment, it showed me what I wanted to know and lowered me gently to the floor. That was nice. Most of the time it just dropped me. The show was over.

Weak and unable to stand, I crawled and opened an entrance in the circles. My brood was on me in a second. Jeeves lifted me up like I was a rag doll and carried me to my recliner. Bolly poured orange juice down my throat while Rocky tried to lick my face off. I muttered my thanks.

"Did you get what you needed to know?" Luther asked, not bothering to hide his concern.

"Yes," I gasped, wheezing like an asthmatic and feeling like an elephant had parked a pick-up truck on my chest. Each breath was a battle. I hadn't passed out but it wouldn't be long unless I got rid of the power the universe left behind. "Sister, come here."

"What Hex?"

"I would like to do something for you, but I need your permission. Whenever I do that ritual, I'm left with tremendous power. I want to give it to you, specifically I want to make your crucifix into a talisman. You'd be able to draw on the power for decades, maybe centuries. What do you say?"

"I'm not sure. Why me?"

"You wouldn't abuse it. You would use it to help others. To me, that means a lot."

"What would the price of this power be?"

"Good question. You've been paying attention," I said, trying to smile, but it made my face hurt. "It's freely given, so long as you use it to help others. It will simply give more power to your prayers, maybe let you heal others if you learn how. And maybe some offensive power against certain types of evil."

"Will you teach me?"

"Yes."

"Okay, I guess."

"Please give me the crucifix," I wheezed.

Anna did. I placed both my hands on it, letting the raw power flow out of me and into the crucifix. When it was all gone, I could move again under my own power. If I had kept the power, the curse would have rendered me helpless and kept me laid up in bed for weeks. If it weren't for the curse, I could have used that power to nail the necromancer from where I was. Hell, I could have ended global warming or made a desert into a tropical paradise. Sure, I could still use it with the curse, but the feedback would not just kill me, but likely reduce me to ashes. It had almost done me in last time when I tried to use it to get rid of the curse. Wishing doesn't help so I tried to avoid thinking about it.

I handed the crucifix back to Sister Anna.

"Thank you, Hex."

"You're welcome, Sister. Use it well." The power gone, I was able to sit up under my own power and the elephant and the pickup truck have gotten off my chest. "Ready, Luther?" I stood but the world started to spin faster and faster, until I fell into my recliner.

"I am, but I'm not so sure about you. You need to sleep it off." Luther knew the only way I could normally shake off the effects of the curse was lots of Z's.

"No time." Lowering my voice to a whisper, I said, "Creep's name is Grundy. He's already killed the father. The mother is hanging on by a thread. Grundy thought we'd have found him already. He's getting bored and may just kill her for something to do."

"Where's this Grundy at?"

"Abandoned building in the South Bronx."

"Grundy's in my hood?" Luther said, furious. He marked his territory and little happened there without his say so.

"Looks like it. We have to move," I said, stumbling to my feet. This time the world didn't spin so much, only my knees betrayed me and buckled. Jeeves caught me before I could fall.

"I don't think you're in shape to go anywhere. I'll go," Luther said.

"No, he's too good," I said.

Luther grinned roguishly. "I doubt it, but either way, you're no good."

"Wait," Sister Anna said. She walked over to me, made the sign of the cross and laid her hands on me. Maybe she didn't need teaching after all. The energy flowed out from her hands. I could see the crucifix glowing in the range just beyond the visible spectrum. In moments, most of my strength had returned.

"Did it work?" Sister Anna asked, opening her eyes as if waking from a trance.

"It did. Thanks.'"

"You're welcome."

"Now I'm ready," I said to Luther.

"You at a hundred percent?" he asked.

"About eighty, but it'll have to do. Anna, watch over Gary," I said. "Don't tell him where we went. He's in no condition to help."

Anna touched my hand. "I agree. Hex, please be careful."

"I'll do my best. Let's go, boys," I said to Luther, Mordi, and Trickster.

"Hex, I got one question. How come you never gave me any mystic talismans?" Luther teased, as he held the door for me.

"Didn't think you'd want one. Besides, what are you complaining about? Didn't I give you a three-year membership in the beer of the month club?" Luther hates beer. It's a running joke between us.

"That reminds me, I haven't properly thanked you for that yet," Luther said, not bothering to put seven veils on his threat.

"I'll look forward to it."

Little did I realize Gary had chosen that moment to come out of his stupor.

"No matter how much you fight against the dying of the light, sometimes the darkness still comes."

-Hex, cursed magí

Parts of the South Bronx are normally a war zone. Even the cops won't go in there in groups of less than a dozen. I was going in with a vampyre and two spirit canines to face down a necromancer on his own turf. I've never been accused of being overly sane.

Luther knew his way around well enough that we didn't have any trouble with the locals. Grundy had set up shop in a burned out shell of a building, in the midst of other burned-out shells of buildings. He had mystic wards set so we couldn't body slide or get in using a nexus.

"He's waiting for us on the fifth floor," I said.

Luther nodded, looking up the side of the building. "I'll take the high road."

"I'll take the low and I'll be in Jersey before ye," I answered. "You two sneak in any way you can."

Right, sent Mordi.

Okay, sent Trickster. The coyote could get around almost any ward, given enough time. Mordi would follow him in.

The pair vanished into the ether. Luther had already started scaling the building, using brute force to carve out hand and footholds. He can't fly or turn into a mist, but he is strong.

Grundy was expecting us all to sneak in. I thought I'd throw a monkey wrench into his plans by walking in the front door. I barely noticed the trip wire. Backing up, I used a piece of rubble to set it off. A metal bed frame fell from behind loose ceiling tiles, swinging like a pendulum on a chain. It sported two dozen spikes. Had I been standing there, it would have impaled me then smashed my bloody body into the wall.

"So much for the direct approach," I said. Ahead on the staircase, I could see electric eyes, laser beam trip wires, pressure sensitive steps, and a half dozen mystical booby traps. Going past each one individually would take hours. I heard a woman's cries and two barks of pain from above.

Screw it. He already knew we were here.

"*Trip all,*" I ordered. All the traps in the staircase went off simultaneously, vaporizing everything in their path. It was a good thing I used the spell. I had missed two booby traps entirely. All that remained was a cloud of dust. Problem was getting to the fifth floor with no stairs. Hated to use more magic – I needed to be at the top of my games to face down Grundy, but if I never made it to the fifth floor my condition would be a moot point.

"*Going up,*" I said, using a levitation spell versus a flight one. There was no air ley line to pull off the same trick Gary had used at the rave. Even if there was, drawing in the magic in my current condition after being the universe's play toy would cripple me. Levitation used less magic, so it wouldn't knock me out as much as flight. The ground flowed away from me as the ceiling got closer. The feeling of floating was one of my favorite things, but I had no time to enjoy it. Touching down on the fifth-floor landing, I ran through the stairwell door into the corridor, just in time to see Grundy bottling Mordi and Trickster. An adept mage can trap a spirit inside an airtight container, not unlike a jinn in a bottle. Grundy had used a couple of empty beer bottles and placed them on an old table that would never again see more than three of its legs on the floor at the same time. Trying a spell was pointless. Magic couldn't free them.

"How much is that doggie in the window?" Grundy asked, turning to face me. His umbra showed no fear. His power level was high, but not master level. How had he hidden so well? Skill wasn't enough. I was missing something and Grundy didn't seem like he'd be volunteering the answers anytime soon. My arrival seemed to make the killer almost glad, because he was smiling big time. "We've got a two for one sale today. I take credit cards."

"I prefer the good old five-finger discount," I said, reaching down to pick up a broken red brick off the floor. A quick toss at Mordi's bottle smashed it, freeing the wolf.

"Very good," Grundy said, positioning himself between me and the remaining bottle. He was working a finger hex that would stop any more projectiles from reaching him or the bottle. "But it won't work twice."

"Doesn't have to," I said. Grundy's calm veneer broke for a second to let a look of confusion shine through. Grundy couldn't see the coyote rocking his bottle so it fell on its side, then running like a hamster on an exercise wheel. It rolled off the table and smashed on the floor.

Freedom, Trickster sent.

Battle time, Mordi sent, growling.

"No," I said. "Get out of here, both of you."

Right. Bye, the coyote sent a second before he vanished. Didn't need to tell him twice. Mordi was another matter.

No. Won't run. Won't leave packbrother in danger, sent the wolf, positioning himself between me and the necromancer.

"Such loyalty is touching," Grundy said, strolling to the table where he had tried to bottle Mordi and Trickster. Grundy couldn't hear Mordi, but he could see the wolf wasn't leaving. The necromancer sat down and tied a napkin around his throat. Grundy lifted roasted meat to his lips and tore out a bite with his teeth. It took me a moment to recognize the source of his meal. It was a human arm, severed at the elbow and the wrist.

Fury burned in my gut as bile rose in my throat. For that moment, I could do nothing but glare.

"Where are my manners," Grundy said, holding out the half-eaten arm to me. "Would you like some? It's Tex-Mex, Mr. Hex. God, I've been waiting all day to say that."

"Simple minds, simple pleasures," I said. "Stop and give up now or there will be consequences. This is your only..."

"Ah, the famous one warning. I'll pass," Grundy said, taking another bite like he was in a fancy restaurant.

I rip his throat out sent Mordi.

No. I sent back. I had done a reading on the necromancer. He had prepared for the pack. *He has a spell set to destroy any spirit who touches even a drop of his blood. I'll handle him.*

"Are you sure you won't partake? I can always make more," he said and snapped his fingers. In walked Mr. Bending, Gary's father, with only a stub for his left arm. Grundy had raised his corpse as a zombie, then placed magical wards to protect it from hexes and spells. Brute force meant almost nothing. Dismembering it would only mean more pieces. Each piece would keep crawling and coming after me. Only way to stop it was to burn it with natural – not magical – fire.

This enemy mine, yes? asked Mordi.

"All yours," I said. The zombie couldn't hurt the wolf. With luck, Mordi would keep it busy long enough for me to take out Grundy. "Meanwhile, Grundy, let's get down to business."

"You know my name. I guess I won't need my ID," he countered. He 'tisk, tisk'ed' me. "Why didn't you bring the boy magí, Hex? This was all for his benefit, not yours. If you hadn't interfered, he and I could have finished our business and gotten on with our lives. Well, I could've at any rate. Your essence is older, more tainted. It doesn't hold the same kick. You've already laid claim to your power. I can't take it for my own. Still, you hold power and that's what I'm shopping for, so I'll just make do for now."

I lunged closer, intending to take him out. I didn't expect the Uzi, complete with a clip that glowed in the magic spectrum. Grundy had enchanted the ammo. Diving behind a pile of rubble, I barely escaped a spray of bullets. Mordi saw the shots coming and faded into the ether. Two shots caught Mr. Bending in the head, knocked loose half of his skull, exposing the soft brain beneath. Some of it spilled and splattered all over the floor with a nauseating squish.

Mordi faded back in and rejoined the battle, this time grabbing the zombie by the neck and lifting it off the ground. As much as it tried, its intact arm couldn't reach behind its head to grab the wolf. The zombie was effectively immobilized.

Grundy had stopped to change clips, giving me my chance. Standing, I pointed and ordered, "*Melt.*" The machine gun went molten. Grundy had only enchanted the bullets, not the gun. Meanwhile, I felt my temperature jump to at least a hundred and one degrees. Sweat droplets gathered at the small of my back.

"Ow!" Grundy groaned, shaking his burned hands. Glaring at me, he reached around to his back, pulling out a double-edged knife that was close to the size of a small sword. "Hex, I always heard you were a real cut up. Why don't you show me if that's true?"

The ceiling chose that moment to collapse on Grundy's head. Amid the falling rubble was Luther.

"I was wondering what happened to you," I said. "Get lost?"

"Had to get past some damn clever traps. There are two fewer floors on the top of this building than when we came in," Luther explained.

Grundy pushed the debris off his torso and climbed to his feet, staring at Luther. "Who the hell are you?"

"Just your friendly neighborhood, bad-ass, butt-kicking vampyre," Luther said barring his fangs. "I worked me up an appetite. Time for a little snack." Luther leaned forward to empty Grundy's jugular.

"Don't," I shouted. Luther raised an eyebrow. "He did some sort of blood magic. It is meant to destroy spirits. Don't know what it'll do to you."

"Damn. I was hungry too," Luther said. "Guess we'll do this bloodless."

"Vampyre huh? You hang with Hex? How come I've never heard of you?" Grundy asked.

"Didn't do your research thoroughly enough, I guess," I said.

"I'll do better next time," Grundy promised.

"Ain't gonna be a next time," Luther said, as he grabbed Grundy by the throat and pulled him up so his feet dangled off the floor. Grundy pulled something from his pocket that looked like a bath bead and smashed it between his palm and Luther's cheek.

"Nothing happened?" Grundy stared in confusion as the holy water ran down Luther's face.

"Very refreshing," Luther said. "Got anything in a musk?"

"Damn, I hate to waste the essence, but a guy's got to do what he's got to do," Grundy said, with a flick of his finger. Luther was thrown across the hallway and through a wall, then a second wall, which his passing made into a window. Luther plunged five floors to the street. I zeroed in on him with my second sight. He wasn't moving but was intact. Normally, a fall like that would hurt Luther, not knock him out. Must have been something extra in Grundy's hex.

The necromancer pointed at the zombie and its neck flesh came off in Mordi's jaw. Mr. Bending dropped to the floor. With a snap of his fingers, Grundy infused the zombie with enough spirit energy for it to be able to land blows that would hurt Mordi. *"Bending, go out and kill. Don't ever stop,"* Grundy ordered. The zombie moved to obey. Mordi had more of a fight on his paws this time. The wolf was having trouble even slowing the zombie.

As he worked his hex, I found out why Grundy had been able to hide from the lot of us. Grundy wore an amulet with a glow I recognized. It would throw off any hex or spell, including locator spells. If I hit him with any magic at this range, the amulet would send it right back at me magnified. I was lucky that my last attack was aimed at the Uzi and not the man. Direct attacks were out, so I did the next best thing.

"Collapse," I ordered to the floor. It obeyed, dropping the necromancer through a six-foot-wide hole, which had just piled rubble over more rubble. Pity the floor below him wasn't cleared. The fall might have given him a concussion. It felt like the spell had given me one.

"Fi..." I started.

"Wait," he shouted, holding up a voodoo doll with a large pin directly over the heart. "Anything happens to me and the magi's mother takes the trip to the Pearly Gates with me."

"Trust me, you ain't going that way," I said, weighing my options. Could I get him before he plunged the pin in for a deathblow? The odds weren't good.

"We'll see. Now get me out of this hole."

"What makes you think that's going to happen?" I asked, stalling and hoping to come up with another option.

"You care about lives. If you didn't, you wouldn't have stopped. I'd already be dead. Now give me some help?"

"Not a chance. Give me the doll and we'll talk."

"I think not," Grundy said.

"Then you die," I bluffed, raising my hand.

Grundy poked the pin part way in the chest. I heard a woman's scream in the distance. "She goes with me." I lowered my arm. "Good decision. Now about that helping hand?"

"Forget it," I said. Maybe I couldn't kill him just yet, but there was no way I would help him.

"Fine. I'll do it myself," Grundy said, pulling himself up. I had to figure out a plan quick. Crashing and crumbling the building in his path, Luther rumbled in from the right. The holy vampyre was back in the game and was headed toward Grundy's hole with a major mad-on.

"Why ain't you blasted him yet?" Luther demanded.

"Protective amulet."

"Ah. So we've got to get physical. Good."

It was about then that Trickster returned, flying in the same hole with a gas can locked in his jaws. He can't travel through the ether with solid objects.

Got some Zombie-be-gone. Hex, you owe Jamie at the Quick Mart twenty-five bucks for the can and gas. I had to tell him you were God and you sent me, so don't blow my cover. Also he gets a 'get into Heaven free card', Coyote sent, tilting the can and pouring gasoline all over the remains of Mr. Bending. A plastic tube dropped from between his front leg and side. *Could use a hand with the lighter here. No opposable thumb you know.*

Luther took the lighter and lit up the zombie like it was a firecracker on the fourth of July. Flames licked at its dead limbs, cradling them in fire. It still managed to lumber, but it wouldn't stay upright much longer. It stumbled down the corridor, brushing against everything. The tenement walls started to burn. This place was a tinderbox and was going to go up quickly. It was time for everyone to make a speedy exit.

Grundy had gotten to the upper edge of the hole and was crawling out. Since there was nothing he could do to help Bending's corpse burn any faster, Mordi was free to help with Grundy. The wolf dove at him, stealing the voodoo doll away.

"Hey!" Grundy yelled, reaching up as if to swat the wolf. When his hand touched back down on the floor, I stepped on his fingers. I ground them under my foot to discourage him from standing. I don't have many sadistic tendencies. Normally, I take no pleasure in the violence I had to do, but sometimes things were different, especially with killers who take innocent lives. Grundy's screams were like music to my ears. Grundy's life was flashing before my eyes, a parade of victims to horrify the soul. I was going to make him pay for every bit of pain he ever caused.

Together, Luther and I lifted him up and proceeded to methodically beat Grundy to a non-bloody pulp. Grundy, eyes swollen and face puffy, struggled to look up at me.

"I knew it, Hex," Grundy said between coughs.

I didn't want to talk to him. I wanted to end him, but I also wanted to know what he meant. Too curious for my own good, I guess. "Knew what?"

"You and I aren't so very different after all. You're enjoying yourself, aren't you?" Grundy asked, a sadistic grin on swollen lips.

"You and I are nothing alike," I said, smacking him across his face with the back of my hand.

"Keep telling yourself that and maybe one day, you'll believe it," Grundy said. He was trying to push my buttons and it was working.

"Whatever," I said with no show of emotion.

"Excellent control. Let's see if you can shrug off what's behind door number one." Grundy snapped his fingers and one of the apartment doors swung open. It was Gary's mother, alive, but tied down on an old dining room table, sacrificial style. The poor woman was in shock. I grabbed Grundy's hand so he couldn't make another gesture. Before I could grab the other hand, he snapped his fingers and a second door opened. "Or maybe door number two will do the trick?" He had an angel shackled to the wall by his wrists and wings, visible for all to see.

"Aziel!!" I shouted. How the hell did he capture the angel? Luther took Grundy's hands from me and forcefully restrained them behind his back with one hand while he smashed the necromancer's face into the wall several times with the other. Grundy didn't move, didn't speak. We had him.

"How come that ritual didn't tell you about the angel?" Luther asked, staring at Az.

The answer was simple. "I didn't ask about Az so I wasn't told about him." The universe was a lot like dealing with a five-year-old that way. If you don't ask specifically it would tell you.

"Can you bypass Grundy's magic so we can kill him and get this over with?" Luther asked.

"Yes," I said, reaching to pull the amulet from around his neck. With him unconscious, I could substitute my will for his and order it off as long as I put it on me first. Then he'd have no protection against me. As my fingers touched the cool metal, the world exploded. Things went black for a second. I vaguely recall hearing Gary scream at the sight of his father burning. Then another shout as he witnessed his mother tied up on the sacrificial table. It took less than a second. In the next fraction of a second, Gary let loose a bolt of almost pure power at Grundy, who still wore the amulet. The bolt hit him and deflected off, straight back at Gary. It would have killed the kid except some of the blast slammed into the rest of us, knocking us to our knees. I was the first to be able to pry open my eyes. Pain was nothing new to me. I knew how to work through it, a skill most people hadn't had the displeasure of acquiring.

The end result was Grundy was thrown free and woke up. Seeing we were all still moving – except for Trickster who wasn't even stirring – and were between him and Az, the necromancer went for the easier victim: Mrs. Bending. Even as I started to crawl toward them, I knew I'd be too late.

Grundy knelt next to the table and whispered in Mrs. Bending's ear while he stroked her face in an illusion of tenderness. "I hate to do this. I had planned to trade you for your son, but I've used up too much power and I need to recharge," Grundy explained, lifting a ceremonial knife that lay on the table beside her. "At least you know your sacrifice is for the greater good. Which is me of course." Mrs. Bending realizing what was happening, came out of her stupor long enough to let lose a blood-curdling scream before Grundy plunged the blade into her heart. Her body stiffened as she struggled. Mrs. Bending still tried to cry out, but only a gurgling, slurping noise came out. I was still too dazed, too weak, to do anything to stop him. All I could do was watch as her life essence flowed out and up the knife, a golden haze that Grundy sucked into himself. I saw him look toward Gary, then me, searching for his next victim. I pulled myself up onto one knee, trying to look dangerous. Mordi had gotten up. He stumbled to my side and growled.

To me, he sent. A second later, Rocky and Maydo flanked us. Maydo sent me a picture of Sly staying behind to watch over the penguin.

Grundy was hurt from our beating. He wasn't up to a confrontation with more of the pack, so he chose the better part of valor.

"Another time. TTFN." Grundy flipped an innocent looking light switch on the wall and limped out onto a dilapidated fire escape. Once away from the building and his wards, he could use the essence he had just taken to make good his escape.

I almost went after him, until I realized the switch he had hit was actually a detonator. I felt a timer counting down. A reading on the bomb revealed that not all the shrapnel originated on the physical plane. The explosion and shockwave could kill us all, even the pack and Aziel. The countdown finished and a tiny spark ignited the bomb.

"*Implode,*" I ordered but could barely think afterwards. The pain in my head was that bad. My gambit worked for the moment, but the shockwave would bounce off itself and head back out. I had to try something else. "*Force bubble.*"

The bubble popped into existence around the bomb. It was holding for the moment, but the shockwave was ricocheting off itself and the bubble at an amazing rate. My containment field wouldn't hold for long. My head was ready to also explode and most of the fifth floor had caught fire. The stairs were still destroyed. If I used magic again, I would pass out. Who knows if Grundy had laced the walls with things that could create a smoke to kill spirit animals and angels? Not to mention mortal magi. Or render us unconscious so the shockwave could finish us. I had to make sure everyone was safe before I tried again.

"Get everyone out!" I ordered.

*How far?** Rocky asked.

"Two blocks." That should be enough. Rocky flew Gary, Maydo got Luther and Mordi got Trickster. As Mordi could carry his burden through the ether, he made it back to the wall where Aziel was shackled before I did. He was already trying to gnaw at the ropes when I got there.

*No good. Won't tear,** Mordi sent.

"Let me look," I said. The rope was hexed. It was also organic, maybe intestine. It can be made tougher than any metal. The Asgardians had imprisoned Loki with the magically treated intestines of one of his kids.

Az blinked at my voice. He looked awful but managed to come to. "Made from the umbilical cord of a baby ripped from its mother's womb. Evil enough to bind an angel."

"How do I get it off?" I asked, hoping for a quick, non-magical fix.

"Holy water or holy artifact would work," he gasped then passed out again. No holy water and sadly my only holy artifact I left back with the penguin.

I pulled as hard as I could with no effect, other than waking Az again.

"Hex, haul your butt out of here, now," Aziel ordered.

"Stop being noble and shut up. I ain't leaving without my wingman," I said, trying not to choke on the smoke.

"Daniel James Robinson, you stop being noble and save yourself," said Az. I knew I was in trouble when the angel called me by my given first, middle, and last names. "The explosion won't harm me."

"Really? Then why are you tied to a wall if what Grundy does can't hurt you?" I asked, feeling the force bubble weaken under the shockwave's pounding. I scanned the room for anything that might help. All I saw were flames dancing on the walls. We had maybe three minutes before the inferno claimed this room and five before my bubble popped.

"My life isn't worth yours," Az said.

"Bullshit. You've meant more to more lives than I could ever hope to." My eyes were starting to tear. I wasn't going to be able to save him, but I couldn't bring myself to leave him to die alone.

Hex, go. I stay with angel, sent Mordi.

"No. We will all get out, I promise." Remember what I said about mages and promises? I didn't make many promises, but I had kept every single one I had made since my twelfth birthday. It was more than a bit superstitious and one heck of a long shot, but I figured my track record might count for something with the fates. It did. Inspiration hit me. "Mordi, get the doll you took from Grundy."

He did. The heat was becoming unbearable, especially since I was still running a fever from the stunt I pulled with the Uzi. Mordi was actually coughing from the fumes, which confirmed that there was more in these walls than plaster and wood. I pulled the pin out of the chest of the voodoo doll. "This was made by Grundy. It's like-magic. It should cut the cord."

"It will take you forever—" the angel started.

"But not Mordi," I said handing him the pin. The wolf took it in his teeth and moved to Aziel. He shook his jaws as if he was killing a small animal, letting the small pin pick away at the umbilical rope. The wolf never even scratched the angel's wrists. In seconds, Az was free.

"Mordi, get Az out of here," I shouted, covering my mouth with my t-shirt in a futile attempt to filter some air.

"But..." Az said.

But... Mordi sent.

"No buts. You can carry him through the ether. You can't carry me," I said, moving toward the hole Luther had made in the wall.

Hex... Mordi sent.

"I got it covered. Trust me. Go!" I shouted. Mordi obeyed, grabbing Aziel's right arm in his jaws and vanishing. A ceiling beam collapsed, bringing a shower of flame and ash into the room. I was already sprinting toward the hole.

Maydo, Rocky, pick up, NOW! I sent as I leapt out of the building into the air. I plummeted about twelve feet before Maydo appeared and flew between my legs like a tiny horse. Rocky popped in right in front of me so my arms and torso lay sprawled over his back.

Thanks, I sent.

We aren't letting you go that easy, packbrother, Maydo sent, with the wolfish equivalent of a grin.

Happy to hear it, packsister, I sent back.

Besides, Trickster won't listen to anyone else, Rocky sent. Not true. Mordi could keep him in line, but I appreciated the sentiment.

With the two of them carrying me, we made better time than they had carrying Luther or Gary. Before we got to the corner where the pack had dropped them, a drama had begun to unfold. Five gang bangers were standing over Luther, about to roll him for whatever cash he might have.

At their touch, Luther woke and he was not happy. Luther grabbed the hand of the one who was searching his pockets. The vamp then shifted his grip to the kid's throat and squeezed. The banger's eyes bulged as a choking noise escaped his lips.

"Can't a man get any sleep around here?" Luther said, getting to his feet, dragging the helpless banger with him.

Some of the bangers recognized him. "Sheet! Luther, man, we didn't know it was you," one of them explained.

"Don't make a difference. This here is still my territory. That means no gangs. What in Zanahary's name are you boys doing?"

"Well, the Skull Daggers offered us membership—"

"Fine. You want to throw your lives away, that's your business. You've gotta move if you stay in the gang," Luther said. "Except you, Martin. You're one of mine. I ain't going to let you break your mamma's heart." Martin was a descendant of the Betsileo, the tribe Luther served as protector. He dropped the banger he had been holding. The banger crawled away, rubbing his throat.

"Hey, the Skull Daggers don't have to listen to nobody. Back off of Martin. We take care of our own," the largest of the bangers yelled. He was easily six and a half feet tall and built like a linebacker. He dwarfed Luther.

"I don't know you. You the one that led these boys astray?" Luther asked, frowning deeply.

"I got them in, yeah," the linebacker bragged.

"You think you take care of your own? You know nothing. I been looking out for Martin and his people for over six hundred years."

"Six hundred years? Man, you wack. Besides, we caught you sleeping with a little white boy, out on the street." Gary was still unconscious on the pavement, Trickster next to him. "You a perv and ain't nobody gonna pay you no mind. I'm gonna cap you to prove it." The banger pulled out a .38 special and fired it twice. Luther leapt into the air like a gazelle before the bullets hit, then managed to land on the bangers gun arm and head, knocking him down. Once on solid ground, the holy vamp grabbed the hand holding the .38 special and crushed it – gun, bones, and all. Taking hold of the banger by both shoulders, Luther pulled and tore them right out of the sockets. Luther slid his hands down and broke both arms in three places.

Luther then pulled the banger's face close to his and smiled. The banger screamed at the sight of the fangs.

"You the Devil!"

Mordi popped in carrying the still visible, but unconscious, Aziel. Because of the angel's injuries, Mordi had to wait before jumping back into the physical plane. The wolf had not gone to the apartment this time, as he realized Gary and Luther had been left unguarded. Luther dropped the banger, then helped the angel stand up on his feet. Az's wings, acting of their own accord, flapped to keep Az upright. They would also protect him from any normal physical attack. Mordi moved to Luther's side, then growled deep and low. The bangers' jaws dropped and their eyes went wide as they stared at the angel who was too weak to cloak himself.

"Far from it. You ever set foot in my territory again, you ain't walking out. Same goes for any Skull Dagger. You have declared war on me and mine and it shall not stand. Understand?" The injured linebacker nodded, as did the rest of them.

Despite the wolf barring his fangs at them, the lot of them continued staring at Az. Martin was the only one who dared speak up. "That a real angel?"

"Yep," Luther said. "But he ain't going to be helping any Skull Daggers. Neither am I. The lot of you take this Skull Dagger scum out of my territory and dump him. Any of you want to stay a Skull Dagger, don't come back."

"But we swore an oath," Martin whined.

"You want out?" Luther asked. Martin nodded. "What about the rest of you?" They nodded. "I'll get you out. Now dump that bum. All of you will be at my home at eight o'clock tonight and we will discuss this. Then, Martin, you and I will go talk to your Mamma."

"Do we gotta?" Martin asked, obviously more afraid of his mother than the holy vampyre.

It was at this point, Maydo, Rocky and I dropped out of the sky. I enjoyed watching the eyes of the teenagers grow even larger. Their pupils were so large the iris' disappeared.

"Yes, Martin, we gotta. I advise you to fess up to her first. It will make things easier on you later," Luther said. Turning to the rest, he added, "What you boys staring at? You all seen Hex before."

"Yeah, but usually he be walking," Martin said.

Normally, I'm probably the only strange white man in Luther's neighborhood that doesn't rate a second glance. Outside of his neighborhood, I've been the victim of more than one attempted mugging and worse. Poverty leads people to do things they wouldn't even think of if they weren't hungry or homeless. Of course, they still have to make a decision to do wrong and being poor doesn't absolve them of the responsibility for their actions.

Rocky moved off, leaving me to sit on my own. I managed somehow. Maydo landed and started to maneuver me so I'd be standing on my own.

Not yet, I sent. *Got one more spell to do. Won't be able to stand after.*

Poor cubman, Maydo sent back, concern mixing with her idea of humor, but she stayed and held me up.

"You boys be off and about my business," Luther ordered.

"Luther, hold that for one second," I said. "The other business isn't finished just yet."

"What?"

"Grundy got away, but he left behind a magic nuke," I answered.

The teens started whispering "Nuke?" among themselves.

"Bad?" Luther asked.

"Oh yeah."

"Under control?"

"Probably." I felt the bubble start to rupture. I had to time this just right. "We'll see in five, four, three, two, one, cover your ears, boom..."

The bubble shattered on cue and the deadly shockwave traveled outwards in all directions.

"*Soundwave,*" I ordered. The shockwave, with all its mystic shrapnel, transformed instead into a sonic boom which knocked all of us mortals to the ground and shattered the few windows that had any glass left.

I passed out with my ears ringing. Maydo cradled me safely on her back. Aziel's wings, sensing the immediate crisis had passed, wrapped around the still unconscious angel and did the great golden fade. The wings would take him to a place on the slopes of Heaven, where he could heal and gather his strength. The golden glow had its usual side effect. I felt infinitely better, although I had used far too much magic for the curse to let me be left pain free. Luther moved to my side and whispered in my ear, "Gonna have some business to take care of with these Skull Daggers. Could use the backup. I can wait a couple of days or more until you on your feet. You in?" I could barely hear him, the ringing in my ears was so loud.

"Sure," I whispered back. "I'll be back when I'm better to clean up the mess."

"Good," Luther said. "Neighborhood's bad enough without outsiders messing it up."

The golden glow that had washed away many of my ills had also brought Trickster and Gary back to the land of the awake. It took Gary a minute to get his bearings. He was weak, but well enough to stand and he was headed my way.

"He killed my parents and you let him!" Gary screamed and ran toward me, flailing his arms and punching me. The pack moved in to defend me.

No, I sent. Gary was hurting bad. I could stand a few bruises. The way I felt, I'd barely notice them.

"Go," Luther said to the teens. "This ain't none of your business." They picked up the injured Skull Dagger and quickly carried him away.

"How could you let him?" Gary howled, pounding on my chest with his fists. Tears streamed down his face.

"Your father was dead when we got there," I explained.

"I saw him moving and burning," screamed Gary.

"Grundy had raised him as a zombie and had sent him on a killing spree," I said. "We had to burn him to stop him from hurting anybody else."

"You did it?! How could you? He was my Dad!"

"We had to or your Dad's body would have killed innocent people." Gary stopped for a minute and looked at me. "That's right, I said his body. His soul was gone. Do you remember seeing an umbra on him?"

Gary strained to remember. "No."

"Exactly. An umbra is the shadow of a soul. No soul, no umbra. He had no soul because he was dead. We had almost saved your Mom," I said.

"Then how the hell did you screw that up, you incompetent, moronic, piece of shi..."

"Hex didn't screw it up, little magí," Luther interrupted, standing regally over Gary. "You did."

"Me?!"

"Yeah, you. We had Grundy beat. Hex was disarming him so we could finish him when you came in flinging lightning bolts," Luther said.

"I hit Grundy!" yelled Gary.

"You hit him all right," said Luther. "Did you think to check to see what Grundy had protecting him? No, but Hex did. Man had an amulet that threw back any magic on the user. Your damn lightning bolt didn't hurt Grundy none. Matter of fact, it freed him so he could take out your Mamma. Damn near killed the rest of us to boot."

"You're saying that was my fault!?" Gary screamed. Luther just bowed his head and looked at the pavement.

Gary turned toward me. I felt damn near crying. I wanted to tell him he wasn't to blame, but lying would help nobody at this point. Gary had started taking all this seriously, but it was too late to do any good. He finally learned, but the price of his education was too high. Thing was, he had already paid it in full and there was nothing I could do to get him a refund, so I nodded.

"NO!!! It can't be my fault!" he screamed. "Hex, fix it, please. I'll do anything!"

"I'm sorry, I can't," I said.

"Can't or won't?" he accused.

"I don't have the power."

"You told me you were the most powerful magí in five hundred years. You said you could have been a god. A god could bring people back to life."

"Not all gods, especially if the god wasn't the one that killed them," I explained. "I'm not a god."

"But I still could be."

"Listen, Gary, there's more to it than that..."

"I don't care. It's my fault my parents are dead. I will bring them back and I don't care what it costs." Gary's ears glowed softly in the mystic spectrum. He was hearing magic whisperings. Bad sign.

"Please," I pleaded. "Think before you do anything rash."

"I've thought and I've decided I'm not going to listen to you anymore. If you can't help me, I'm outta here."

"I'll be able to find you, no matter where you go," I said. Once I met a person, I usually could follow them, barring little things like mystic amulets and such.

"I doubt it. I learned a little something in a dream from a guy called Nick. Says he's your friend," Gary said.

The Devil? No, it's impossible. I made sure Gary only slept inside wards at my apartment so how could he make contact?

Then it came to me. Nick must have got him just now when he was unconscious on the sidewalk. Blast it.

"Nick said he could give me what I wanted. I'm going to see him," Gary mocked, as he pushed me away and sprinted down the street, laughing in anger. I was too weak to follow. Luther, Mordi, and Rocky moved to catch him. Maydo was still holding me up. I saw the hellhole start to open.

"Get back!" I shouted. Luther had already seen it and was doing an about face. As Mordi was faster he grabbed him by the seat of his jeans and flew him to us. Rocky lent a jaw to quicken the pace. As soon as we were all standing close together, Maydo spun me so I could draw a circle ward with my chalk on the sidewalk.

The hellhole grew to human size. Nick stood just inside, his hand outstretched. Gary leapt into the breach and took it.

"Told you we'd get him, Hex," gloated Nick with a dark laugh. "Better luck with the next magi."

Nick put his arm around Gary's shoulders like a father would a son, after a day of fishing in a sappy old commercial. Together they walked off into the Pit and the hellhole closed tight behind them.

"The secret to life is to read the instruction manual."
    -Zu

Sister Anna was unconscious on the couch when Luther and the pack got me home. Gary had slapped her with a sleep spell. I was too weak to remove it. She would have to snooze until it wore off, sometime the next day. I did what I could to make her comfortable. Maydo and Rocky kept apologizing for falling under the same sleep spell. They and Sly would still be asleep if it weren't for Mordi's distress call. Gary had picked up enough knowledge to not only to knock out the lot of them but to use tracking magic to follow us to Grundy.

Luther left to return the car he had borrowed to get me home. We arranged to pay a visit to the Skull Daggers in the near future and he ran an errand for me.

I checked my wards. They were good. Lying in bed, I set my sleep ward. The effort knocked me unconscious. About fourteen hours later, I woke with a major magic hangover. A quick breakfast, starting off with a large glass of milk and three caffeine filled aspirin, helped take the edge off.

Sister Anna was still out cold. If this was the same spell Gary used on his folks, it was no wonder Grundy got them. Jeeves could have snuck up on them wearing a suit of armor.

Gary… Damn. I knew he wasn't going to become a saint, but to choose Hell willingly…

The self-torture and recrimination had begun. Where'd I screw up? What could I have done differently? Had to stop thinking like that. What's happened can't be changed. Better to worry about the future. A snore escaped forcefully from the region of the couch causing me to cringe.

I'm not ashamed to admit that the thought of having to tell Sister Anna what happened made me want to leave in a hurry. I really wanted to go after Grundy again, but even if I managed to find him in spite of the amulet, in my condition he'd slay me. I left the penguin a note and took off for the Brimmer Theater where Gary had been meeting with the powers that be. Jeeves had e-mailed cancellations to those who hadn't yet met with Gary, but the ones who had appointments today undoubtedly wouldn't hear in time.

I silently wished Gary had held off another day. He might have made a different choice. Today was going to be divine, literally. The gods were coming to visit.

The representative from the Norse pantheon, a valkyrie, was already waiting on the stage, leaning against her motorcycle. My appearance got a smile and a bone crushing hug from the large, leather-clad battle maiden. She and I were drinking buddies. Her name was Mista and she was representing Odin. She was intimately involved with Heimdal, the guardian of the rainbow bridge that linked Earth to Asgard. She was disappointed when I told her the news. Mista's mission was to try to convince Gary to come to Asgard. Odin had hopes that with Gary's power Ragnarok could be delayed, changed, or even prevented. We talked for the better part of her hour before she left, riding her hog right down the steps of the stage and out the front door.

The Greco-Roman Pantheon was largely unrepresented. There was enough belief manna to sustain them for years. Hera showed and was pissed. She made a show of storming off. She had claimed Olympus after her husband was run off of Earth by Nemesis. Eros showed in black leather with a machine gun filled with love bullets and plans to recruit him for his Love Patrol. It's a sad and twisted group, but what do you expect from a god who's forced to look like a baby in a diaper for much of his immortal life because that's how mortals see him?

Most of the rest of the Olympians didn't want the burden of being worshiped, especially the bunch that hung out at Bulfinche's Pub. Despite themselves, they still went out of their way to do the occasional good deed. Not all gods shared their philosophy. I had to sit through the ranting and raving of several other deities who felt cheated out of their "divine" rights by not getting a chance to speak with the kid. Also, many gods claimed to be all knowing and showing up after the game was over made them look bad. It got to the point where I drew a circle ward around my chair just to protect myself from temper tantrums and stray thunderbolts.

The only reasonable one was Coco Joe, a mostly forgotten Central American storm god. He simply nodded and left when he heard the news. He was cloaking himself and for a moment I got a flash of power levels he shouldn't have. Before I could try to get past the cloaks, he was gone.

By midday, the e-mails must have been getting read because I had two no-shows in a row. Near the end of the second hour, I finished the book I had stuck in my trench coat pocket. Then I sat still for almost five minutes before boredom got the better of me. I made a search of my trench coat pockets to see what else I had with me and found a deck of cards. I dealt out a hand of solitaire. Above, wings fluttered and a voice said, "Play the red Jack."

I turned to see a hawk-sized bird with a lion-like head perched behind me.

"Zu, I presume?" I said.

"Correct. I do not see the boy. Am I too late?"

"Afraid so."

"What was the end result?"

"He chose Hell."

The bird exhaled. "Rough, but I figured he'd go to one of the big boys." Zu looked down at my cards. "My schedule is freed up for the day. Mind if I sit in?"

"Sure. Any preference for game?"

"Poker?"

"Works for me. Five card draw?"

Zu nodded.

"Keep it simple. Dollar ante?"

"That works," Zu said as he reached under his wing and pulled out a wad of ones with his lion-like jaw, from where I'm not sure exactly. I sensed had the ante been a hundred he would have pulled out a stack of c-notes. A minor adjustment in my ward allowed the cards and the cash to leave and enter, as long as they weren't mystically altered. I dealt out the cards. "So, what were your plans?"

"Oh, waxing nostalgic I guess. Kind of longing for my glory days. I was contemplating ruling the world again," Zu said wistfully as he picked up the cards with his talon.

"That's right. You ruled it way back when." Way back being in Mesopotamian and Sumerian times. "How many cards?"

"You've heard of me? I hadn't realized I had become that popular again," Zu said, sticking out his chest. He tossed a pair of cards back on the table with his jaw. "Two, please and I'll raise you five dollars."

"Well, I am very well read," I said with a shrug as I tossed him his cards. I was holding a pair of sixes so I took three more. "I'll see your five and raise you three."

"Figures. Want to hear about it? I'll match your three. Call," Zu said.

We laid our cards on the table. I still only had a pair of sixes. Zu had three twos.

"Sure," I said. Even the best legend tellers get a few details wrong. I dealt out the next hand. Zu bent his head and reached into the same wingpit. He pulled out a cigar this time. Holding it in a talon, he spat a tiny flame out of his lion maw to light it.

"Want one?" he asked.

I smiled, remembering something else I had found in my pockets. "No thanks, got my own." I pulled mine out and peeled the foil wrapper off.

"Need a light?"

"Nope," I said, biting off the end before chewing and swallowing it.

"That's disgusting," said Zu. "I raise ten. One please."

I gave him his card.

"No, it's chocolate," I said. Friends of mine had a baby. Jeeves made some chocolate cigars for them to give out. The baby was four months old last week. I'm the first to admit that I should clean out my pockets more often but you never know when you might need something.

"Ah," Zu murmured, puffing on his cigar. I mimicked his actions.

"I'll see your ten and raise you ten. One," I said throwing out a card and taking another. I needed a seven for a straight. I got a nine.

"To save you from the ramblings of a very old god. I had... acquired the Tupsimati."

"Acquired?" I said with a raised eyebrow. "Call," I said laying out my unstraight, with my pair of nines. Zu had two pair and collected the pot again. I dealt the next hand.

"Acquired, stole. Same difference," Zu said, blowing a smoke ring. I couldn't figure a way to do that with chocolate. Pity. Would have been impressive.

Zu was playing, holding his cards in one talon and the cigar in the other. "The god I acquired them from, name of Enlil, had gotten them the same way, only he added murder to the mix. They rightfully belonged to Tiamet and we know what bad news she was." Tiamet was a Babylonian she-dragon that almost destroyed the world. "Enlil killed her, his own mother, and Kingu, her husband, second husband actually, who was safeguarding the Tupsimati when he got nailed."

"The Tupsimati are the tablets of destiny, correct?" I said.

"Yes, they on which the laws of creation are written. Basically, an owner's manual that tells how the universe works. Whoever wore them, ruled."

"Where'd they come from originally?"

"Tiamet claimed their creation, but she was just blowing smoke. Truthfully, I have no idea. Once he got them, Enlil put them on and started to lord it over the rest of the gods. Then he started picking on the little humans. It was pitiful the way he showed off. One day he pissed me off, killed off thousands of birds, beasts, and humans just for the sport of it. To be honest, the birds made me the angriest. No offense. I got him drunk that night. So drunk that when I asked him to let me try the tablets on, the fool actually let me. Suddenly, I was in charge. I told him and his ilk to stay off the planet until they could learn to behave. Cowards pissed and moaned about how horrible I was, but not one of them was brave enough to face me down. So I ruled for about a century or two. Or was it three?"

"What'd you do?"

"Fly mostly. Love to fly. Saw a good part of the universe. Went right through the heart of the sun once without even singing my tail feathers. Ate a lot. Some sex. Built my own mountain, Sabu. It was a gorgeous place back then." Zu was inhaling deeply on both his cigar and the scent of memories.

"That's it?"

"Yep. My tastes are simple. Raise you twenty. Jack high. Four please."

"You're keeping one card and raising twenty?"

"I feel lucky."

"Match and raise ten. No lording over the less powerful?" I took two cards. I had three queens.

"Save for my fellow gods, no. Then again, I really didn't go out of my way to help anyone else either. Live and let live, that's my philosophy."

"You just blasted a hole in a theory of mine regarding absolute power."

"Glad to help. Match and call."

"I'm not so sure you helped," I said laying my cards out. Zu had a full house, fours over jacks. I dealt the next hand. "How'd you lose the tablets?"

Zu looked at me and let the cards lie.

"Stupidity, really. I'm a storm bird. I control the elements and all that. It was raining and I love to fly in a good rain and this was a great rain. Great big raindrops, falling hard and fast in a wind that could knock over a redwood. The tablets weighed me down and chaffed a little so I left them in my nest, thinking they'd be safe. Big mistake. Enlil's son, Ninurta, a war god, snuck onto my mountain and stole them right out of my nest. I found out too late. Ninurta had already left. I couldn't find him, but I had to make sure the tablets did not make it back to Enlil. I powered up the storm I had mentioned until it was the mother of all hurricanes. Ninurta lost the Tupsimati to the winds. Neither of us ever found them again. Unwilling to admit defeat, Ninurta fashioned tablets of his own and gave them to Enlil, who never learned the truth. Ninurta had infused the tablets with a portion of his own power to fool his father. He explained the weakness away by saying I had used up the power. The other gods recognized his authority because he wore the fake tablets so it never became an issue."

"And you wanted Gary to help you find them?" I asked.

"It was a thought. I also thought of offering my services as an advisor, had he chosen to rule himself. If that happened, I'd have found someone who has gone through the same thing I'd been through. It would have been nice to have someone to talk to who'd been there. That's what I wanted, more than anything else," Zu said, picking up his cards, chewing the cigar on the side of his jaw. "Now are we going to play cards or what? I'll raise you a hundred."

I sensed an unfriendly presence enter the theater a second before I smelled the brimstone.

"I haven't won a hand yet. I'll fold," I said.

"That's your problem, Hex. You fold too easy," Negral mocked.

"I knew I smelt something," I said, not bothering to turn my head. Maybe if I ignored him, he'd go away. Nah, I couldn't be that lucky.

"Pitiful," the Chief muttered, shaking his head. "Hello, Zu."

Negral knew the storm bird? It took me a second before I realized they were contemporaries from overlapping pantheons.

"Negral. It's been awhile."

"I thought you had faded into oblivion ages ago," Negral said, obviously a little disturbed. Had Hell not taken him in, he would have faded into the void decades ago.

"Nope," Zu said, leaning back and crossing his bird legs, using one foot to twirl the cigar in tiny circles.

"How'd you do it?" Negral asked.

"I have my ways," Zu said, taking a long puff on his cigar.

"Such as?" Hell's Detective said.

"My ways are really none of your business," Zu said, ticking off Negral. I was definitely beginning to like the lion-headed bird. "Unless you'd like to make me tell you. Not that you'd be able to."

"Want to bet?" Negral asked, putting down a canvas sack he had been carrying.

"Sure, but you won't beat the odds," Zu said, uncrossing his legs and leaning forward. Negral was hesitating, probably remembering the time when the storm bird was the top dog and could fry him with a lightning bolt without a second thought. That was then. Now Negral's power was supplemented by that of Hell itself. His hands caught fire as the pair moved closer, sizing each other up. Zu was outside my ward. Negral was going to make a crispy critter happy meal out of him.

"Hey, Chief, you here to gloat or did they kick you out of Hell because they found out you were stealing the silverware?" I asked.

"I'll get to you in a minute, Hex," Negral promised as he dismissed me with a wave.

"You'll get to me now, you Hellstone cop or don't you have the balls anymore? Nick got you so whipped, you have to pick on birds to feel like a big man?"

"Hex, one day you'll go too far and I'll..."

"You'll take it and like it. You got no say. I want to talk to Gary," I said, pushing my luck.

"Well, you got no pull with the new magí," the Chief said.

"He was under my protection..."

"Which he willingly left to come over to Nick because he thinks Nick can give him what you can't."

"What? The stench of brimstone and the screaming of the damned?"

"Gary's adjusting to life in Hell. Fast on the pickup. Mook's already begun torturing the damned. He's earned a dozen succubi as a reward. He's having the time of his life," Negral said, trying to be enthusiastic, but failing miserably. He didn't seem to like it any more than I did.

Going back to quantum geography, time spent in the Other realms can pass much slower or faster than on Earth, depending on how you work it. I'm guessing Hell's working him on fast time. "I got him a gift, which I wanted to stop by and show you. I wanted your opinion as to whether you think he'll like it."

Negral lifted up the burlap sack, reached in and pulled out a familiar looking head.

"Grundy," I said. I should have been grateful. I was anything but.

"I figured you weren't up to the task, so I took care of this business for you. No, don't thank me. Although truth be told, it was easy. Surprised you couldn't take this mook down on your own. Guess you're slipping."

"Where's the amulet?" I asked.

"Wish I knew. Grundy backed into one of his own traps. His head and some pieces of meat were all that came out intact. Nick wants this as a gift for Gary," Negral said, rolling his eyes.

"Lovely. But how are you going to raise his parents?" I challenged. Neither body was in any shape for a raising.

Negral shrugged. "Nick will figure something out. But since you want to talk to Gary so bad, why don't I bring you with me?"

"I don't think so," I said.

"That ward wouldn't hold me back forever," Negral said. Actually, he was wrong. It could hold forever. Problem was, I wouldn't. My body would betray me. They say you can go days without food and water but eventually, I'd starve because the chocolate cigar would be long gone. If I stored manna or magic in my body, I could use it to sustain me. The curse doesn't allow me to do that and be able to stand upright. To conjure food, I'd have to let down the ward for a nanosecond. Negral would have me. I don't even want to think about the bathroom situation.

"I think your boss might have something to say about that," I said, playing my trump card.

"He was the one who suggested I stop by and bring you along," Negral said. "Seems you're off the list."

It was hitting the fan. I should have known. I hadn't won a hand all day. Why would my luck change now? I was still too weak to use the level of magics to head off Negral without passing out from the strain.

"Why don't you just come quietly and save us both the hassle?" Negral suggested.

"Not a chance," I said. Maybe if I slept for a couple of days I could regain my strength. Great plan. And maybe if I asked nicely, the head of Hell's secret police would just leave me alone.

"The hard way it is," Negral said, all smiles. This was the day he had been waiting for. Maybe he knew a trick I didn't know about breaking down wards. I wasn't leaving without a fight. If I was going down, so was he. I mustered my strength and chose a word of power. The Chief moved toward me when a thunderbolt smashed into the floor in front of him, forming a small crater in the hardwood stage.

"The man doesn't want to go," Zu said. I had forgotten all about the storm bird but I was grateful for his intervention, a literal deus ex machina.

"How!?" Negral asked, doing a double take at the smoke rising from the hole.

"I am a thunder god after all," Zu replied, taking another drag on his stogie.

"You should not be able to materialize on the mortal plane, let alone manifest that amount of power!" Negral exclaimed.

"Be that as it may, you take one more step and the next one will fry you and I will have *your* carcass for my dinner," Zu said.

"You're bluffing," the Chief said.

"Am I?" asked Zu, flying over to the Chief and blowing a lungful of smoke in his face. The Chief reached out his power and the smoke went back at the bird.

"What's the source of your power?" the Chief demanded.

"Same as it always was," Zu said. "Negral, you didn't back Enlil when he came after me. Made me respect you. It was the reason I didn't banish you with the rest and did you that favor."

Negral bowed his Fedora covered head. "I remember."

"We two are among the last remaining of our kind. Don't make me fight you. You owe me that much."

Negral gritted his teeth but actually backed down. I stopped gritting mine, amazed, and grateful.

"Zu, this wipes the slate between you and me, clear?" The storm bird nodded. "Should you ever decide you would like to tell me the source of your power, I would again be in your debt."

"Not happy with your current situation?" Zu said.

"It is a necessary evil."

I knew the Chief hated being beholden to the Devil, but he was loyal enough to defend the hand that fed him the manna he needed to exist. The business with Zu made him lower some of his mental defenses and I was able to read him clearly for the first time. Seems he had a chance to get out of Hell once but didn't take it in order to save others—a succubus and some damned souls who were his cops. I had heard rumors of it and how he freed the souls of his old afterworld but figured it was nonsense. I was wrong. Worse, Negral was actually here in an attempt to save lives. He wasn't planning to hurt me. Not permanently at least.

Hell's Detective turned back to me, a scowl hiding his good intentions. "This isn't over Hex. Nick will send someone else and they will simply start wholesale slaughter of anyone around you until you agree to come to Hell. Remember all those that Beltizon killed?" I did. The demon had possessed dead bodies, including a baby, to go on a slaughter spree. It was enough to have us work together to stop him. "That'll be nothing because this time the demon won't be some mid-level mook but a Lord of Hell who will have Nick's blessing. My way, they'd leave the nun alone and nobody else had to die."

I couldn't believe it. Negral wasn't telling me everything. He left out that if he brought me into Hell under my own steam, he thought I'd actually have a shot at making all this right.

"Hex, at least have the decency to get out of New York to keep the body count down."

"Chief, you could help us…"

"Forget about it. I already told Nick I was invoking my right to refuse a case. He wanted me to bring in the nun. I told him no. I tried to warn you in the restroom, but you had to play your stupid games. I knew the angel was there. If Nick couldn't figure that out, it's his problem. Not my job to spoon feed him. If you wanted my help, that would have been the time to ask. Now Gary is worthy of damnation. Not a thing I can do about it."

"Negral, I'm sorry. I had no idea about any of this, about what you…"

Hell's Detective realized I was reading him and his defenses shot up, locking me out. He put Grundy's head back in the bag and summoned a flaming hellhole to make his exit without another word or even a glance back. It closed tight behind him.

"I'm an idiot," I said. I was so blinded by my own self-righteousness that I completely misread Negral and it cost big time.

"In my experience, very few idiots ever have the strength to admit it. Perhaps it can be your first step toward rectifying matters," Zu said.

"Zu, thank you for your help," I said. "And advice."

"Think nothing of it. I could never stand him for long anyway."

"You're my kind of bird," I said, trying for a joke before collapsing back on my chair.

"He could be a real jerk, but at least he has his principles. Still does apparently. I did feel bad for him though. Most scholars mixed up the correct spelling of his name. And his ex-wife Ereshkigal is the worst. Did you know she brought about a zombie apocalypse, bringing dead humans and gods back to life so she could destroy the Earth and fill up her afterlife? Negral was the only one able to stop her but to keep her stopped he had to condemn himself to marry the psycho and take over Aralu, her realm of the dead. Must have been hard for a sun god to live in a world of eternal darkness, but he did it to save the world. And he's only in Hell because he used up his manna to save a handful of friends. Sometimes a jerk and a hero are one and the same."

I nodded numbly. There was nothing I could do about Negral, but the storm bird was another story.

"Zu, please let me do something for you. You wanted to talk to someone else who has ruled the world. I can help you out with that. I have this friend..." I told him about Crystal and gave him her phone number. I tried not to chuckle. Peaches the cat was going to hate this.

"You mind a question?" I asked.

"Shoot."

"Negral was right about your power levels. You shouldn't have that much without worshipers. You have a cult somewhere I don't know about?"

"Maybe I do, maybe I don't. Let me give you something else to consider. The Tupsimati were the instruction manuals for the *entire* universe. All the other owners ever did was wear it and use its power to rule. What would happen, if before it got lost, someone stopped to actually *read* the tablets of destiny? What could that individual do then?" One of Zu's lion eyes winked at me. "Bye. Good luck with your Hell problem. If you survive, tell your friend Crystal I'll be in touch soon."

Zu flapped up into the air, opening a skyhole. My jaw dropped. A skyhole is the most difficult portal to open, a hundred times harder than an ordinary nexus. With it, you could go anywhere and even manipulate time flow. It formed a link that became part of reality for the time it was open. When I was at my peak before the curse I couldn't hold a stable skyhole open for more than a second. This one had been open for more than a minute and the storm bird showed no signs of strain. Zu did a dozen loop-the-loops, then dipped a wing at me like he was an air force pilot before he flew off into the wild blue yonder.

"It's always darkest before the dawn, but sometimes light doesn't really help that much."

Hex, cursed magi

I sat alone in the dark for a while after the storm bird left. Things had gone bad very quickly. My arrangement with Nick had stood for years, despite whatever I had done to thwart him. Now, demons had permission to come after me. And Negral wasn't quite the enemy I thought he was.

The universe as I knew it, had turned upside down. I had a lot of thinking to do.

I tried reaching out to Aziel, but he wasn't answering. My only real hope in the situation was to figure out some violation of the Host-Horde Accord and hope that Heaven would help me, but that was very unlikely. The Angels were supposed to be the good guy so they followed the accord to a T. Approaching the Host directly wouldn't do me any good. Guardian angels are the lowest ranking of the Host, so even Az had less than stellar odds of convincing them. The fact that he wasn't responding had me worried. Grundy may have hurt him worse than I thought. At least Negral took that worry off my plate.

For the moment, I was safe where I was, in my little chalk circle. Truthfully, I was afraid to step out. If I went home, I would be safe from magic attacks, but not those around me who were not inside those wards. And even my wards wouldn't hold out long against a full-scale attack from the Pit. I hadn't even had time to install a security system and new locks since Cal had broken in. Plus, I would be putting my brood in jeopardy. I could go running to my uptown friends at Bulfinche's Pub. Inside the bar, magic didn't work, but Nick would declare war on the lot of them. Normally they could hold their own, but they played by good guy rules. Even Wisp would be in trouble. Eventually, Nick would get them. I couldn't trade my safety for theirs. Anyone who could help me, Nick would hurt.

I had to take out the Devil first.

I heard footsteps from the rear of the theater and spun without thinking, then tried to get my racing heart under control. It was a friend. I may have called her a penguin, but Sister Anna didn't waddle.

"Hex, I got your note. What happened? Where's Gary?" she asked, still woozy from the sleep spell.

I told her, unable to meet her eyes. I didn't leave anything out, including my visit from the Chief and Aziel's injuries. When I finished, she was in tears.

"We have to rescue him," she cried frantically.

"There is nothing to rescue. Gary went willingly," I explained. "Right now, safety is our main concern."

"Our?" she asked, blinking.

"Yes, our. Hell is after me and they'll be coming for you." The Chief may have refused to go after Anna, but I'm guessing no one else in Hell would have his compunctions.

"Me? Why?"

"Payback for trying to keep Gary from them. A way to get at me. Plus, if my guess is right, you and I will provide a way to forever bind Gary to Hell."

"How?"

"Not here. Come with me," I said, stepping out of my circle with trepidation. Nobody attacked, thankfully.

"Where are we going?"

"You'll see," I said and reached out with my power searching for any magic beings or traps. There weren't any, so we had to move quickly.

We went outside and hailed a cab. A body slide would be like yelling out directions to Hell about where I was going. The less magic I used, the harder I would be to trace.

"Take my arm," I said.

"Hex, I'm a nun. It wouldn't look proper."

"We need to drop off Hell's radar and I can't hide you unless we're in physical contact."

"Fine." She tucked her arm in mine and the cab stopped. I opened the door and ushered the nun into the cab, when I felt a prick on my neck.

"Hex, there's a dart in your neck!"

I was an idiot. Not all my enemies used magic. I should have checked the street first.

"*Hidden*," I intoned, cloaking Sister Anna and shutting the door behind her. "*Get her out of here!* That spell was for the driver and the cab took off like… well, a NYC taxi.

The poison in the dark was fast and I dropped to my knees as a black sedan with men in black suits sped off after Anna's cab.

The spooks weren't getting her.

"*Fuse!*" I yelled and the engine parts all became one and the car stopped like it had hit something.

Magic takes focus and the dart had eroded mine. I wasn't sure if I could steer a body slide which would kill me, but I was dead if I stayed. I'd be unconscious from the poison before the curse knocked me out. It would get me away from the spooks and draw Hell's attention away from Anna.

Before I could go, Agent Dartley had a stun gun pressed against my neck and with a few sparks, my world went black.

"It's amazing how many times I wind up somewhere I don't want to without any clothes."

-Hex, cursed magi

I woke up naked in a lavish and elegantly decorated library, the kind they used to have back in the days when doors were answered by butlers.

I tried to hide the fact that I was conscious but it didn't do me any good.

"You're finally awake. I can honestly say it is a pleasure to see you once again, Mr. Hex."

I slowly sat up and the world spun around inside my head for a few laps but I finally managed to focus on the man speaking to me. Part of me had allowed myself the luxury of hope in thinking that I was a prisoner of the government because the government always wants something so negotiation would be an option. Instead of a dark-suited spook, I was staring up at Hell's ambassador to the United States.

"I wish I could say the same, Ambassador Darkwon."

I got to my feet and weighed my odds of being successful in rushing the demon. Normally Darkwon appears to be a well muscled six-foot tall gentleman in a suit, but since we were at his embassy he had dropped any pretense and was in full out demon form from his red skin to the horns on his head.

"Don't bother. You are in a spell circle made from gold, not chalk. The only way you're getting out is when you go to the Pit."

"I can't imagine why you'd be happy to see me. I've caused you and yours more than a little bit of trouble over the years," I said.

The demon ambassador chuckled and dabbed at the corners of his mouth with a handkerchief. "That you have, but you're going to make me a Lord of Hell. After the Chief failed, the Glorious One contacted every demon in the tri-state area and let us know how important it was for us to capture you alive. I think it's safe to say that every demon dropped what they were doing to find you, but I knew you would be on the lookout for anything touched by Hell. How fortunate that I had heard through diplomatic channels how badly you had upset Agent Dartley and thought that perhaps he might want a little payback."

"The ambassador was very right about that," said Agent Dartley from the screen of an open laptop.

"Too chicken to face me directly, huh Dartley?" I said.

"The drugs in your system must be working overtime if you think that," the head spook said.

"I'm sure Agent Dartley would have loved to have been present, but for security reasons he is not permitted on the embassy grounds."

"Then he's more of an idiot that I thought. Dartley, you wasted your warning," I said.

"Waste not want not."

"What did Hell offer you in exchange for giving them an American citizen?"

The agent on the screen laughed. "Hell is going to owe me not just one, but three favors."

"Only after completion," the ambassador corrected. "You've only delivered half of what we agreed upon."

"Hex was a little better than we expected and a whole lot stupider. The poison should have worked quicker. He fought it long enough to use some magic before we took him into the custody and instead of saving himself, he saved the nun. A very stupid move."

"You're never going to find her," I said.

"You think that if it keeps you warm, although where you are you heading I don't think warmth will be an issue. I'd ask where she was but I won't insult you by implying that you'd share that without being tortured. Even then you would probably give false information. I still would have tried but for some reason, the ambassador wanted you intact so that's what he got."

"Also a big mistake on your part. You should have killed me because when I get out of this I'm coming for you."

I wished I actually felt the confidence of my words. I've been slowly reaching out against the circle with my power. I wasn't going to be able to break it from the inside. I'd have to wait to see if I got a chance when they shipped me off to Hell, although the thought made me shiver, which wasn't helped by the fact that the demon had stripped me naked before locking me up.

"Goodbye Mr. Hex," Agent Dartley said and closed the connection.

"So, Darkwon, when do you ship me off?"

"Nothing so foolish on my part. After a little negotiation with the glorious one, he will come here to take possession of you himself."

As much as I hated to say it, that was smart. It reduced my chances of escaping substantially. Plus, if Nick was going to do what I thought he was going to do, the embassy would be as good a place as any.

"I suppose it would be pointless to try and make you a better offer?"

The ambassador smirked and shook his head. "And there's nothing that you can offer me that would even compare becoming a Lord of Hell."

"Nick is actually offering to make someone a Lord of Hell for capturing me. That sounds overly generous and Nick is hardly noted for his generous nature."

Darkwon made a dismissive wave with his hand. "That wasn't exactly the offer, but the message implied the importance of it and that promotion is my requested payment."

I put a lot of effort into laughing like that was hilarious that the ambassador was such an idiot.

"What's so funny?"

"That you think capturing me is going to make you a Lord of Hell. As a rule, the position is not gifted, it's taken. And when it is given that demon is instantly under attack from all sides so they need to be very powerful and very smart. You got smart down."

Darkwon nodded his head and smirked some more. "Flattery will get you nowhere."

"I'm not flattering you. We both know you don't have the power levels to be a Lord of Hell or you'd already have taken it. All you're doing is painting a target on your back. If Nick does create a new Lord position – and in my experience, he may greet your demand as extortion and Nick does so love being told what to do, doesn't he – any lesser demons can try to take it from you unless you can give them a reason not to and you just don't have the juice to do that."

The ambassador stopped smirking. "Becoming a Lord gives one power."

"No, it gives one a realm, a title, and the ability to acquire more souls. True, for demons, possession of souls increases your power. However, as the newest Lord, you'll be the weakest and thus the last one given souls, so it will take quite some time to boost your power levels. I don't think you'll have enough time to get enough souls to be able to fight off all comers, do you?"

The ambassador looked doubtful.

"And we all know what happens to deposed Lords of Hell, don't we?"

Ambassador Darkwon actually appeared to be slightly frightened, but still spoke in diplomatic tones. "They are made special projects by their successors."

"Exactly. So you're going to give up a cushy position on Earth for constant battle and an eventual and eternal customized torture in the Pit. Looks like I won't even have to punish you at all."

"Then let me do it for you," said a scary voice.

The ambassador and I turned together and I'm not sure which one of us was more shocked see Sister Anna standing there.

"Never underestimate a nun."
    -Sister Anna, Order of St. Dymphna

The ambassador clapped his hands like a dandy at a Victorian-era party.

"Oh, this is too good. All of demonic New York is searching for you and here you walk right into my hands. Thank you so very much, Sister. Now kindly step into the golden circle over there and I will do my best not to hurt you too badly."

"That's not going to happen but I'll tell you what is. You're going to free Mr. Hex and you going to let us leave," Sister Anna said.

"This is so grand. Why would I ever do something so stupid?" Darkwon said.

"Because if you don't, I'm going to destroy you and this entire embassy. Hex is under my protection. This is your one warning," Sister Anna said with a hardness I didn't know she had.

The large demon jumped up and down while he spun in a circle all the while clapping his hands and giggling. "This is so marvelous. How are you going to destroy me and the embassy? Pray at us?"

"Something like that. So, you refuse to take my warning?"

With demonic speed, the ambassador from Hell leapt across the room and smacked Anna across the face so hard it threw her backwards into a bookcase.

"Damn right I'm ignoring the warning. Stupid little nun thinks by hanging out with Hex she suddenly becomes Hex."

I pounded on the invisible walls of my spell circle prison. "You touch her again, I'll kill you!"

I kept hitting and hitting the barrier until my hands were bloody. It did nothing to get me out but it turned Darkwon's attention away from Anna and back on me.

"Such passion. I've seen you threaten others to stop hurting people before, but never like this. Do you have feelings for this nun?" I hit the barrier harder and Darkwon pointed at the circle and a mystic bolt knocked me to the floor. "How delicious. The instructions were to deliver both of you alive, but that doesn't mean I can't have some fun first. Oh, the things I'm going to do to her and you won't be able to do anything but watch."

With one clawed hand, Darkwon tore the suit and shirt from his body and moved toward Anna. I crawled and put my numb hand on the invisible wall and intoned *"Fall!"*

The only thing that fell down was me.

Darkwon strutted over toward Anna and lifted the nun off the ground with one hand and held her so that they were face to face. Hers was bloody, the demon's smiling.

"What you think about that sister?"

The nun wiped the blood off her mouth with her hand she then touched the bloodied fingers to her crucifix which began to glow.

Anna swung it at the demon's arm and cut through it below the wrist, dropping her to the ground.

The demon stepped back, screaming and holding his stump.

"I think you should have taken my warning," Sister Anna said, as her hands exploded with a pure white light which struck Ambassador Darkwon in the chest, completely disintegrating the demon

The beam of white light spread out to encompass the entire room and the building beyond it.

"People will surprise you. Occasionally that'll turn out to be a good thing."

    -Hex, cursed magí

The light consumed the entire building to ash, leaving behind only the cement foundation beneath us. That and the spell circle that I was still trapped in.

Anna turned towards me and smiled, a mixture of elation and horror at what she'd done. "Well, I did warn him."

"That you did but how did you learn how to do that?" I said.

"When I left your apartment to go to the theater, Jeeves gave me his cell phone. When you sent me away in the cab, I knew I needed help so I scrolled through the phone's address book and found Crystal's number. You said she was almost as good as you and she said to call if I needed anything, so I did. She taught me how to use the magic you stored inside my crucifix."

I looked around at the ashy remains of Hell's embassy. "You learned how to do that over the phone?"

Anna smiled. "Technically, over video chat. And now when we go out Crystal gets to wear the penguin suit."

"How did you find me?" I said.

"After I got away, I switched cabs and headed back. I saw them take you in here and leave. As we drove past, I saw the gold plate on the outside of the building that read *The Embassy of Hell*. After I got past the fact that they actually put something like that on the building and no one seemed to notice, I called Crystal.

"Now how do I get you out of there or can you do it yourself?"

"I can't," I said as I stood.

I noticed Anna's eyes dart downward and stare, then remembered that I was naked and tried to cover up with my bloody hands. The nun didn't turn away. Instead, she lifted her head up to look me in the eyes with a wry yet shy smile.

"Only the person who sealed me in a circle can open."

"And I just killed him." Anna got pale. "Oh no. I just killed him."

"Actually, you didn't kill him in the technical sense. You only destroyed his mortal body. His essence escaped back to the Pit. And we don't actually need him, just a bit of his blood."

"But I disintegrated him."

"Not all of him." I pointed to her chest where the dismembered demon hand was still gripping her habit. I pointed towards a coin-sized half dome on the outside of the gold circle. "Put a bit of his blood on the bumpy bit there and anyone with magical talent can get it to open."

"How?"

"You need power and will to focus the magic through the filter of the blood. The easiest way to focus both is with words. Some people use elaborate spells or ancient languages but all you really have to do is say what you want with enough will behind it and it should work."

Anna tore the claw off her habit and dabbed the stump on the button.

"Open sesame!" she intoned and the invisible wall fell. And so did I, right outside of the metal.

Anna rushed toward me. "Your poor hands. You didn't have to destroy them for me."

"I kind of did. I couldn't let him hurt my favorite penguin." Nor in the end, could I stop him.

Anna took my hands in her left hand, still holding the crucifix in her right. She crossed herself and prayed. Magic poured out of the crucifix and into my fingers and knuckles, healing the tissue and bone back together, then the magic coursed through the rest of me. For the first time in a very long while, I was entire pain and curse free. It felt wonderful.

Maybe a little too wonderful, because without thinking I said, "I think I love you."

Before I could take it back or make like it was a joke, Anna said, "I think the feeling is mutual."

Then she leaned in and kissed me.

"My boss works in mysterious ways."
  -Aziel, guardian angel

The kiss was soft, tender, and wonderful. And more than a little awkward.

I enjoyed it a little too long before I pulled away.

"I was trying to avoid going to Hell and now I've kissed a nun. I'm getting an express ticket," I said. Anna looked a little hurt. "But it was worth it."

That made her smile.

"Actually, I'm not technically a nun anymore."

My mouth fell open. "What happened in the last few hours?"

Before she could answer, a priest ran onto the foundation. It was Father Kerner from the Universal Watch.

"What did you do!? I told you that you couldn't come into here without causing a diplomatic incident and now look what happened."

I turned to Anna.

"Actually, you tried to block me at the gate and forbade me. You told me that as long as I was a nun that I was forbidden to enter Hell's Embassy because it would cause a diplomatic rift with the US and Hell which would blow back on the Vatican. I would think there will and should be a permanent rift with Hell regardless."

"It's complicated. And not only did you disobey me, you turned your back on your vows for your holy orders," Kerner said.

"I was a novice. I haven't taken my final vows and in a choice between that and saving my friend, I did what I felt God would have wanted me to do. I saved my friend," Anna said.

"And caused a mess. Come with me to the Vatican immediately and we will try to sort this out," Kerner said.

"I'm not going anywhere with you. I'm leaving with Hex."

"You certainly shall not. A nun in the company of a naked man is most unseemly."

"You are correct. Take off your shoes, jacket, and pants and give them to Hex," Anna said.

"Nonsense. You cannot order me about. You may have freed him so he could cause all this damage…"

I raised my hand and waved at the priest. "Actually, I didn't do any of this. My penguin…" I stopped and looked at the newly former nun.

Anna laughed. "It's okay. The name has grown on me. Only you can call me that whether or not I'm a nun."

"Anna did this."

"She did?" Kerner looked at the nun nervously.

The penguin nodded.

"Do you really want to piss off a woman who can destroy something that literally belongs to the Pit?"

Kerner looked back at Anna who was frowning at him. "It would be the Christian thing to do."

"And I know Father Alexander DuPont and Tina Parker." A pair of Universal Watch agents, but good ones, unlike Kerner. "I wonder what they'll think about your actions here." I didn't even have to mention the stupidity of wasting my one warning to him.

The priest cursed under his breath but tossed me his clothes. The pants were too big, the jacket too small but oddly the shoes were just right.

"I'll mail them back to you," I said.

"Don't bother," Kerner said, standing there in his boxers.

"Let's get out of here," I said, grabbed Anna's hand and ran onto the street.

I started to hail a cab then realized my wallet was probably disintegrated with the embassy.

"Do you have any money?" I said.

Anna shook her head.

"How did you pay for the cabs?"

"The first guy was so freaked out by your spell that made him drive away that he just wanted me out of his cab. And I told the second driver I was on a mission from God."

"That worked?"

Anna nodded. "Apparently he was a Blues Brothers fan and had gone to Catholic school."

"What you did was very loud magically. A lot of people and demons are headed this way to check it out so we need to get away quickly without using any magic to leave a trail. Any ideas?"

Anna fished her hands into my front pockets.

"I'm flattered but is now really the time…"

I stopped talking when she pulled a set of keys out. "Looks like Kerner has a car. We can borrow it then ditch it and use another mode of transportation."

She held it up in the air and hit the alarm button. A car across the street's horn went off.

We ran across the street and tossed me the keys. I tossed them back and she stared at me.

"I don't drive."

"Seriously? The great Mr. Hex can't drive a car?"

"I live in the city. Between magic and public transportation I never learned."

Anna grinned and got in the driver's side. As I climbed in the passenger side, she tossed her veil in the space between us.

"They'll be looking for a nun."

"True."

"Where to?" she asked, pulling out of the spot.

"Go to the corner and turn left."

"There are bad dreams and they are nightmares and then there's me."
– Paulie, Keeper of Broken Dreams

As we turned the corner, I felt a demonic presence but I didn't see anything.

"Anna, bless the car!"

The Penguin's mouth opened as if she was about to ask why but she impressed me by simply putting her hand on the dashboard and saying a quick prayer.

The car hit something even though there was nothing there. At least nothing we could see.

Whatever it was came up over the hood and hit the windshield because it caved in and filled with spider web cracks.

"What'd I hit?" Anna said.

"Unless I miss my guess, a spigh."

"A spy? One of Dartley's?"

"No, a demon that can make itself invisible."

"But you can see it, right?"

I shook my head as something smashed a hole the size of a softball through the windshield. Some people keep CDs or old fast food wrappers in lying around their car. Kerner kept bottles of holy water, which in his line of work made a lot of sense. I'd already taken the top off two as soon as I'd got in the car. I poured a bottle onto the empty looking space in front of the hole.

I still couldn't see the demon, but smoke rose up out of nothingness and something on the other side of the windshield screamed.

Anna sped up the car, then slammed on the brakes. We felt and heard whatever was on the hood hit the pavement after it flew off in front of the car.

Without waiting, Anna spun the car around and went the wrong way down a one-way street, doing several times the speed limit with her head hanging out the window so she could see.

We needed to get someplace safe long enough to catch our breath. There are two places I could think of that might give us that moment without turning us into the Pit for whatever reward was being offered for our capture. It'd take us three times as long to to Bulfinche's Pub, so I chose the closer option which was only three blocks away.

"Grab the next parking spot you see so we can ditch the car and go on foot."

"Isn't it safer and faster to stay in the car?" Anna said.

"Would've been if we didn't know that somebody from Hell knows we're in this car. The Pit could easily arrange an APB. The only thing we have working for us is that demons tend to not play well together and whatever is chasing us won't want to share the bounty. And if a cop sees's us, he'll pull you over for the messed up windshield."

Half a block later, Anna pulled in an empty spot.

I smiled. "You parked in front of a fire hydrant."

"We are in a stolen car and being chased by demons. A parking ticket is the least of our worries. Besides, at least we know the police eventually tow it away and notify Kerner where it is," Anna said.

"You're impressing me with how well you're taking to all this."

"Considered everything I've given up, I'd much rather you told me you were more impressed with my kiss," Anna said.

I chuckled. "Oh, I was. And I definitely want to revisit and discuss what's going on with us and make sure you're okay with what you're giving up, but I want to make sure we survive the night first."

"Deal."

Anna got out of the car and moved to the sidewalk. I jumped out to follow her, but ran back to the car, grabbed her veil and tucked it under my arm

"Why'd you go back for that?"

"Two reasons. One it's got your DNA and I assume you've been wearing it for years so there is also an emotional residue. We don't need Hell to get a hold of something like this. They'd be able to track you and worse."

"The second reason?"

"It's valuable to some people, especially who were going to see."

"So how do we know that the invisible demon isn't right behind us?"

"We don't but our destination is only two blocks away."

Anna took my hand in hers and intertwined her fingers with mine. "Lead on, Mr. Hex."

"As the Penguin commands."

Anna smiled and suddenly what was happening didn't seem as scary and yet became even more terrifying. It was bad enough if Nick got a hold of me, but it'd be much worse if he got a hold of Anna.

Handholding was wonderful and awkward which was probably a good thing. Trying to walk inconspicuously when you're terrified is not easy to pull off and we didn't need to draw any more attention to ourselves. After all, Anna was still dressed in her habit even if she wasn't wearing the veil and I was dressed as a shirtless priest.

"Keep a lookout for anything unusual. Point out absolutely anything that strikes you as odd. I want to try and see if I can pick up anything magic around us."

Two blocks went by quickly and uneventfully.

Anna spotted the neon sign that said "Paulie's Pawnshop".

"We're going to see the broken dreams keeper guy?"

I nodded. "Paulie's shop is a place of power and he's a friend. Even so, our going in is putting him in danger."

I opened the door to the shop and the bell jingled to announce us. Then I laid our cards on the metaphorical table so he had the option to kick us out.

"Paulie, we're in trouble. Hell's after us and there might be a spigh on our tail. We need help but I understand perfectly if you don't want us to stay."

"Hex, that may be the single longest greeting you've ever given me. And of course, you can come in. I'm not afraid of Hell," Paulie said.

"You're not?" Anna said.

Paulie chuckled and Morpheas strutted her way out from behind the counter and stared out the window. "Nope. I'm utterly terrified of them, but Hex is one of my few friends and he's helped me out a bunch of times. Even saved my life once. What kind of a man would I be if I turned him out in his hour of need? Now, what can I do for you? Let you hole up in one of my back rooms until this blows over?"

"This isn't going to blow over and I wouldn't put you in that kind of danger. Some clothes, some cash and maybe a method of transportation if you've got it and we'll be on our way."

Paulie frowned. "You've got a little credit because of the stuff you've brought in over the years, but it may not be enough to cover all that. Hex, you know I'd love to hand over anything you need, but I can't just give stuff to you. The rules I'm bound by won't allow it."

"I wouldn't ask you to. And while I have no traditional way to pay, I have something to barter with, with Anna's permission." I held up her veil. The Penguin looked confused but nodded her permission. I handed the veil the Paulie. "What do you think about this?"

The Keeper of broken dreams took the veil tenderly in his hands and put a jeweler's glass in his right eye, then held the headgear up to the light.

Paulie let out a slow long whistle.

"This is quite valuable. The veil of a holy woman who broke her vows and walked away from her life's work to save the man she loves." Paulie smiled at Anna and then at me. "About time somebody made an honest man of Mr. Hex here. I approve and accept your barter. Let's get you guys outfitted up for life on the run."

The door to the shop opened and the bell jingled, but there was nobody there. I moved Anna behind me and got ready to cast a Hex, but I was too slow.

With one hand, Paulie pulled out the nozzle of one of those industrial pink sprayers and pulled the trigger. A steady stream of paint filled the front of the shop as he moved the nozzle back and forth and the orange paint revealed our invisible pursuer. We could now see where the spigh demon was.

With his other hand, he'd grabbed his shotgun and blasted the demon with his special ammo as soon as it was visible, not even waiting to turn off the paint sprayer.

The holy water soaked iron and silver buckshot hurt the demon but didn't take him out. It just turned his immediate focus toward the Keeper broken dreams which means he didn't notice Morpheas as she shifted from a black cat to full-grown cat woman, complete with fur, although she kept the white dot on the tip of her nose.

She leapt at the demon samurai style, raking the claws of her right hand across his face and eyes then spun and got his throat with the claws on her left foot. She landed on her hands and rolled out of reach.

Paulie used that moment to get a corked empty glass bottle. I'd like to say he then leapt over his counter, but too many hours sitting in a chair eating Chinese food and watching TV had not left him in great shape. Paulie jumped up so that his butt landed on the counter then lifted his legs to swing them over and slid down the other side to the floor.

The Keeper pointed the bottle at the demon and nodded to Morpheas. The cat woman jumped clear and Paulie pulled the cork out. The demon was sucked up into the bottle. The glass was tinted green but you could still see an image of the paint-covered spigh frozen and unmoving inside.

"Nice job Paulie. You too, Morpheas."

The cat woman had already shifted back into her black cat form and was licking the blood off of her paws.

Paulie lifted the bottle up to the light and and examined it with his jeweler's glass. "Looks like it'll hold. I guess it's a good thing you brought in those bottles from that trapper who had held Jake captive, huh?" Trappers are a mage who can do just that and Jake had been trapped inside a bottle for decades. They were too dangerous to leave lying around, but they did have their uses. I kept a few and gave the rest to Paulie, figuring he'd be able to make sure they got to folks who needed them.

Paulie walked back behind the counter and put the demon on a shelf filled with jars, bottles, and other glass containers that held all manners of creatures and dreams.

Anna looked curiously at the cat but actually was smart enough to address her comments to Morpheas rather than Paulie or I. "What are you?"

The black cat stopped licking yourself and looked up at the former nun.

"I'm a bastart." Morpheas purred at the look of confusion on Anna's face. "No, I'm not an illegitimate child, but one of the scions of the goddess Bast. I have two forms. This one is much easier for every day, but the other one is much more effective in a fight but either can be equally fun on date night."

Paulie blushed and started polishing the top of his counter with a rag.

"Thank you for helping us. Both of you," Anna said.

"For Hex, we're happy to."

I gave Morpheas a detailed rundown of what happened. "You'll be sure to tell your mother?"

The black cat purred her laughter. "Do you even have to ask? What price are you asking?"

"Gratis. Better for people to know why I disappeared." I debated about sending out the name now but had my reasons for not just yet.

"Why would you tell your mother?" Anna said.

"Bast runs a spy network of cats. A very effective one at that," Paulie said.

"And, Morpheas, would you ask her if she has any intelligence I can use and what price she would want for it?" I said.

The black cat nodded her head and went back to cleaning her paws with her tongue. I turned back to see Paulie staring at the action. He saw me looking and shrugged then stared some more as the cat strutted to the back room.

"I have to admit that I do not necessarily have the latest fashions, but I do have a large variety of clothes that you can choose from," Paulie said, ushering us to some racks.

I picked out a pair of hiking socks, a pair of black jeans, and a black T-shirt. I decided to go commando rather than wear used boxers or briefs. His outer wear selection was rather more dated. He had leather jackets and trench coats but the leather jackets all look like they belonged in the 70s or 80s and the trench coats were classic models that were a little too close to what the Chief wore for my comfort. I went with a basic black zippered windbreaker.

When Anna stepped out of the changing room I whispered a soft, "wow."

The Penguin was wearing a yellow sundress that actually showed off instead of hiding her curves. She had on a pair of white sneakers with ankle high socks and had a blue denim coat over her arm.

Anna smiled and twirled once in a circle.

"I clean up okay then?"

"You clean up great."

Morpheas leapt up onto a file cabinet near my head.

"I talked to Mom. Just like you thought, every demon and human with any connection to Hell is searching the city for you. They've put spells in place to divert teleportation to a warehouse they have control of. What's worse is that that have people triangulating magic use in the city, so any significant use will send people your way in a hurry. They've also spent a lot of magic to fence in all of New York City and keyed it to both of you. If either of you crosses the border toward the water, Long Island, Westchester or Jersey, they'll know exactly where you did it and be on you in seconds. Hell hasn't used this much power in ages. You must have them scared."

Nick probably wants me before I can pass on his name.

"Our intelligence reveals that they weren't sure if you had managed to get out of Manhattan, otherwise they would've made the circle a lot smaller."

"Thanks but you never mentioned the price." Which is a breach of etiquette because I should know what it would cost me before I got the information in case I wasn't willing to pay.

"I didn't think you'd balk at the price. Bast says if you survive that you need to cover her next visit to Bulfinche's Pub from meal to dessert and drinks."

"Done."

Paulie handed me an envelope with a thousand dollars in it, some prepared chalk, spray paint, and a half dozen burner phones. He sells a lot so they were actually new. He warned me not to use any of them more than once even though he knew I wouldn't.

"Now for the pièce de résistance. Your chariot awaits," Paulie said and went into the back room and came out riding a motor scooter built for two. "I will even throw in helmets at no extra charge."

"Paulie, it's perfect. No self-respecting person would ever go on the run from Hell on a scooter so it'll give us a little camouflage and hide our faces. And let us weave through traffic. Thanks."

"My pleasure. Just be careful and let me know if there is anything else I can do." Morpheas meowed. "That we can do," Paulie corrected.

Anna and I each picked a helmet and put them on.

"I suppose you don't know how to drive a scooter either," she said.

"Nope."

The Penguin laughed and got on the scooter. I walked to the door and opened it and she drove out.

I got on the back. Anna grabbed my hands and wrapped them around her waist.

"Hold on tight."

And I did.

"Family is what we make it."
      -Hex, cursed magi

I stopped in a busy area and texted my home phone one word. *Lockdown Hx.*
I received a reply a moment later.
Done Jv.
I had prepared extra wards for the apartment and building for emergencies. Jeeves would have activated the spell and magically walled off the apartment after warning Crystal, Jake, Moni, and the other tenants in my building to be on alert. My brood was now locked in the apartment. Only Bollywog needed food and I had left a year's supply. I hoped they'd all be okay.

I smashed the phone under my foot and swept the pieces into a sewer grate then climbed back on the scooter behind the penguin.

"Where are we going?" Anna asked.

"Calgary."

"The cemetery in Queens?"

"Yep."

"Why?"

"You'll see."

We headed over the 59th Street Bridge and onto the Brooklyn Queens Expressway, got off in Woodside and went inside the cemetery and hid the scooter in a storage shed.

In the moonlight, we walked arm in arm across the rows of tombstones and the interspersed shade trees, until we came to the grave site I was looking for. As we approached, Anna tried to pull away and walk around it without knowing why, but I lead her onto the grave itself and suddenly a large bright blue sculpted man sitting over the grave appeared. The tombstone was sticking out between his legs.

"This was cloaked?" I nodded. Anna was getting better at probing for magic and she stared at the grave for a moment. "This is a holy place."

"In a way." I motioned to her and we sat together on the grave.

"That statue is tremendous. And I didn't see it until I was right on top of it." Anna wasn't exaggerating. Even sitting, he was over five feet from butt to head.

"I cloaked the grave and have an aversion spell on it so people will avoid it without even knowing they did it. And it's not a statue." I pointed to the word 'meth' written on his forehead.

"A golem like Jeeves?"

I nodded. "His name was Calvin. I created him when I was eight years old out of some kids' clay my mother had bought me. At the time, he was only six inches tall."

"You were eight?"

I shrugged my shoulders. "Like a bird knows how to fly, I knew magic. I kept him hidden for years, all the while he grew. By the time I was fifteen he was this big and he was tired. He had been hurt a few years earlier, defending me from my father's demons."

"Jerome Robinson." Sister Anna was reading the tombstone. Her hands traced over the words 'LOVING HUSBAND AND' then stopped where the word 'FATHER' had been chiseled away. She looked up at me, pain in her eyes. The strange part was, it was my pain. "This is your father's grave?"

"Yes. Nick told you that I first went to Hell to free my father's soul. That much is true. What he left out is what got him there. When my gifts first started manifesting themselves, my parents thought I was delusional and sent me to a counselor. It was Layla, the woman who now owns Plasma. As time went on, Layla and my father began to realize part of what I was. My father was pissed off that I had so much power and he had none. The long and the short of it is, he made a deal with the Devil to get his own power."

"He sold his soul?" asked Anna.

"No, his son's."

"You? How could he?"

"I've asked myself that very question hundreds of times since and I haven't come up with an answer yet. My father brought the demons he summoned into my room while I slept. If his plan had worked, when I woke up I would have been in Hell. It didn't work, thanks to Calvin. My father didn't know he existed. When they tried their hexnapping, he jumped in to save the day. I woke up in time and refused to go."

"Because you refused the demons couldn't take you?"

"My soul, yes. Me, they could hurt or kill. It turns out that parents can only sell their children's souls if the child believes they have to listen or they think that the parent has the power. I knew better."

"So someone who sold their soul could just refuse to give it?"

"Not exactly, but there are loopholes, especially if the person who signed the contract did nothing bad enough to warrant damnation. The thing with Hell is, they always demand collateral on a deal like that. The collateral is always the same: the signer's soul. If the deal goes bad, Hell gets the parent instead. Signing warrants damnation. I banished the demons. They took my father with them."

"After he did that to you, why did you save him?"

"He was my father," I said, realizing how weak an answer it was.

"So his body is buried here?"

"No. It burns in Hell. His spirit isn't here either."

"Then why did you sanctify this place?"

Anna's deductive abilities were growing by leaps and bounds. "I didn't sanctify it exactly. I just protected it from all bad things. It wasn't for my father. It was for Calvin. He was never right after that night. The demons hurt him and the pain stayed. He begged me for years to end him. I couldn't. I made him. I loved him. He was... my..."

"Son?" Anna offered.

I nodded, wiping a tear. "Yes. Calvin wouldn't rub the letter off himself, not without my blessing. I tried to heal him, but all I did was accelerate his growth. One night he tricked me and asked me for a favor. I promised him anything and he called me on it. I had to do what he wanted because I had given my word. We walked here." I grew up in Woodside so it wasn't far.

"Nobody noticed him?"

"I could make people see whatever I wanted back then. When we got here, he thanked me and got into the position he's in now. I rubbed off the 'E' and ended my friend's life. I cried myself to sleep for weeks. To this day, it still hurts to think about it. I used all my power at the time to make sure no one would ever desecrate him or this spot. The side effect of the spell is here we can talk freely, without fear of anyone listening in."

"When you say back then, you mean before you walked away from the magic?"

"Anna, I'm going to be asking you to trust me with your life so I am going to trust you with mine. I need your most solemn oath and promise, on all that you hold sacred that you will never share what I am about to tell you with anyone or anything else."

"I promise."

"I did walk away from the magic. Part of me was afraid of being corrupted, part of me was worried I was going mad. I spent some time in asylums. When I reclaimed my magic I was arrogant, believe it or not." The Penguin smiled at that one. "I thought I knew everything. I butted in during a spat between a couple of old school mages and it didn't go well. Because of me, innocent people were hurt. One of the mages cursed me for it."

"Why?"

"He felt I needed to be taught a lesson in humility and to keep out of matters that don't concern me. His instruction method was to curse me. The basic gist is I can't use magic to interfere in a situation unless I'm asked. The only exception I've found is that my survival instinct can override the curse for self-defense or if someone involves me of their own accord. On top of that, anytime I use magic, it causes me pain. The pain makes me weak. The more powerful the magic, the more extreme the punishment. The only way I can get my strength back on my own is to get sleep and lots of it. Fourteen hours after a rough night isn't unusual for me. Even using amulets or charms isn't pain-free, but making them can drain off some of the excess power."

"Is that what happened when you made my crucifix into a talisman?"

"Yes. That amount of power would cripple me. Sometimes it's not pain. If I use fire, I get a fever. If I stop someone from breathing, I get an asthma attack. Most of the time I just get headaches."

"That explains all the aspirin." Guess I'm not as slick as I thought if she noticed that. "Why not stronger medicine?"

"I'm intimately familiar with medication. I used to be a shrink and a patient. I've prescribed or taken most of them. Aspirin does me the most good with the least side effects. I need to be alert. I also need to hide this information. Were it widely known, my enemies might be able to use it to kill me."

"I will guard your secret with my life. But if you are so powerful, why haven't you broken the curse?"

"I've tried. A feedback loop always knocks me unconscious. I've thought about using a self-propagating spell that would continue even after I black out."

"Why not try it?"

"Let me use an analogy. A normal drinker will pass out when his blood alcohol level reaches a danger level, in effect, saving his life. A drinker who binges too much in a short period, before his body can shut him down, can die."

"You're afraid it will kill you."

"Bingo. There is one other factor a counselor friend of mine thinks is adding to the mix."

"Which is?"

"My fear of power corrupting me is strengthening the curse or weakening my efforts to break it."

"You think the counselor is right?"

"Maybe."

"So if you broke the curse, could you take on Hell?"

"I can take them on now. I would just have a better chance of surviving without the curse."

"Do you think you could break the curse with my help?" Anna asked, fingering her crucifix.

"No."

Anna turned and looked again at the tombstone.

"So your name is Hex Robinson?"

"Not exactly. My given name is Daniel James Robinson. My taken name is Mr. Hex, much like yours is Sister Anna."

"Can I call you Daniel?"

I nodded. "Just don't use it in public, okay?"

"Okay. Let's get down to business. Explain this binding business to me."

"Remember, what I said about those not deserving damnation having more loopholes? I'm hoping Gary hasn't done anything that bad yet but..." Despite what the Chief said, I was hoping I was right instead of him.

"But?"

"If they can get Gary to do something so heinous that the act will damn his soul, they will own him for eternity."

"And you have an idea what that may be?"

"Yes. The most common method is to have the damnee kill a loved one. Usually a lover or parent."

"But Gary's parents are dead."

"Exactly. Who are the closest parent/guardian figures to Gary?" The word guardian clicked.

"Us."

"You got it. He kills us and he's theirs."

"Gary's not evil."

"Not entirely. Not yet."

"What could they give him to make him do that?"

"His parents. Their bodies are no good for reanimation, but Nick could put their spirits into our bodies if Gary does a ritual sacrifice." Then something clicked for me. "Son of a ... That's how Nick is going to get around my safeguards to send his name out if anything happens to me. Outwardly, nothing will happen to me. It will just be Gary's father's spirit in my body. It's brilliant. He gets Gary and gets rid of me in one shot."

"Why compliment him?'

"Because it's true. Luckily, I'm even more brilliant. More modest too." The missing pieces of my plan fell into place. "Here's the part where I ask you to risk your life." I hated to put the Penguin in harm's way, but she was already involved. Nick was going to kill her regardless. Maybe with her help, we could both stay alive and give the Devil Hell, so to speak.

"I just need one more promise."

"Anything."

I explained my plan.

"That's devious, underhanded and treacherous," she said. "And I hate to say, I love it. You really are brilliant."

"And modest," I said.

"Not," quipped Anna.

As I said, her deductive powers were improving.

"What do we do now?"

"I've invested enough power here that a demon could walk right by us and not notice us. We rest and put our plan into action in the morning. We'll be harder to find if we move during rush hour."

"So you want to spend the night together?"

"Desperately, but…"

Anna put a finger on my mouth. "My life has been turned upside down since I met you. And I'm not just talking about all the magic stuff. I mean what's happening between you and me. You know, when I met you, I didn't like you."

"I get that a lot," I said.

"But as I got to know you, I saw what a good man you tried to be. You risk yourself for others for no other reason than it's the right thing to do. I prayed every night for Gary and I included you in my prayers. Then as I started to have feelings for you, I prayed to God for guidance. When you were taken prisoner, I realized that I had more than just an attraction to you. I realized that I love you in a very romantic fashion and I prayed for your safety and for a sign about whether I should leave the order and not take my final vow. That's when Father Kerner showed up and gave me that sign."

"I guess I owe him. I would never have made a move on you. Too many years of Catholic school I guess," I said.

Anna chuckled. "When I rescued you, I got caught up in the moment and the adrenaline. I thought I'd lost you and I just had to kiss you to make sure I'd made the right decision."

She was quiet and I couldn't stand it. "Did you?"

Anna leaned in and kissed me on the cheek. "Yes. But technically to leave the order I have to tell my Mother Superior, not Kerner. And I'm terrified to do that. I ask that you be patient a little bit longer so I can tell her and make it official."

"Whatever you need," I said, touching her cheek with my hand. Then Catholic guilt kicked in, but not about her having been a nun. It was about me being me.

"Anna, I want you to be sure before you do that."

"Why?" All of a sudden, she seemed frightened and hurt. "Don't you feel the same about me?"

"All that and then some. I think you are wonderful and kind and brave and beautiful and lots more. It's not you I'm worried about, it's me."

"An 'it's not you, it's me' speech never ends well," Anna said.

"That's not what I'm saying. I just want you to know what you would be getting with me. I am not a prize. I'm messed up inside. In a lot of ways I'm broken, but I don't let that stop me from doing what I think needs to be done. And if I think I'm right, I will not back down. That might be charming when I'm trying to help people, but not if we have a disagreement. I spend a lot of time recovering from using magic, so we wouldn't have a normal relationship. And if things get serious…"

"I'm leaving my life as a nun. Things are already serious."

I suddenly had a flash of Anna in a wedding dress standing in front of me in a church.

Oh boy. That took a minute to sink in. Anytime I've ever considered getting married I've been against it and moved in the other direction. I wasn't feeling that way now.

I nodded.

"When we get married…"

Anna grinned. "Confident, are we? When, not if? And before our first actual date. You are a fast mover, Mr. Hex."

"Well, first we have to survive what Nick is throwing at us." And even though my flashes can predict the future, it's not set in stone. It was one possible outcome of many. One or both of us could still die. "And I'm not proposing. I just wanted you to know that if it happens, not only do

I come with baggage, but with roommates. You'd be getting an instant family and not the most normal or easiest to deal with. I just want you to be okay with that."

"Your brood are wonderful."

"Yeah, they are. And you need to realize I am overprotective. I will protect you. I will try to leave you out of things that are dangerous, even if you feel I should do otherwise."

"You are involving me in this."

I shook my head. "No, Nick did. I'm just trying to get us both out alive."

"No worries. I'm strong willed and will tell you when you are wrong. Nobody except…" Anna pointed to the night sky and the stars. "… is perfect. All I know is that I'm willing to try to make a relationship with you and I've never felt this way about anyone else."

"I feel the same." I leaned in to kiss her, but it was just a peck on the lips.

"Let me tell Mother Superior first."

I grinned and pulled out a burner phone.

Anna frowned and I grinned.

"Just kidding. I know it's not something that can be said over the phone. And Nick probably has her phone tapped anyway and would trace the call." I scooted so my back was leaning against one of Calvin's knees and opened my arms. "Is this okay?"

Anna scooted over and snuggled in against me. "Yes."

I held her tight and she held onto my arms with her hands and we went to sleep.

"I think God figures I'm a comedian because of that whole if you want to make him laugh tell him your plans thing."
-Hex, cursed magi

I woke up screaming at first light. Well, I screamed and Anna shook me awake.

"Hex, wake up!"

I opened my eyes and visions of horror were replaced with one of beauty.

"Oh sh…" I looked at the concern on Anna's face and changed mid-word. "…crap."

"What's wrong?" she asked.

"I flashed on Gary."

"Is he dead?"

"Much worse. Nick used quantum geography. Years were passing in Hell for days on Earth. Gary's grown and…"

"And what?"

I had to fight not to tremble. Visions of Hell and the screaming of the damned always shake me.

"It's not good. Nick put him in charge of a section of Hell.

"He's surrounded by the damned and they are begging him for his help, mercy, or kindness. Gary is laughing at their misery and mocking them for their weakness. Worse, he's enjoying their pain and adding to it. Our little Gary has grown a sadistic streak that is making the Devil proud." I saw Nick beaming over what he had nurtured like a delighted father.

"Nick's given him power without consequences. In my vision –" I had to force myself not to throw up as I thought about it. "– he skinned a woman without remorse. A demon showed him how to tan her hide into leather and fashion it into a coat. Gary wanted that coat to be uniform. In Hell souls regenerate, so he waited, and watched as the woman's skin grew back. Then he skinned her again. And again. While she was skinless he would take an exposed nerve and twist it between his fingers, inflicting even more agony."

"No, he wouldn't. He couldn't," Anna said weeping.

"But he did. Gary has become a monster. A monster I'm honor bound to try to save."

"Not just you. We," Anna said.

"I don't think even you can turn Gary from his dark, hellish path."

"What if we can't?"

"Then we have to ensure that he doesn't harm and kill innocent people."

"You mean…"

I nodded. "Gary will have to be ended, the monster he's become put down."

"Hex no. Killing is wrong," Anna said, tears streaming down her face.

I wiped a tear away. "It is. But isn't it more wrong not to kill someone who is about to kill or hurt others if that would save the innocents?"

"Gary is an innocent!"

"He was, but the pain made him throw it all away. You don't have to help if you don't want to," I said.

"Then you have no plan. What happens then?"

"I don't know. I try something else."

"And I hide in safety while you risk your life? And maybe get killed instead? No. We go with the plan, but before there is any killing I get to try to reason with him."

Stopping to reason in the middle of a fight is dumb, plain and simple. It works in the movies, but not so much in real life. Still, there was a one in a million shot Anna could pull it off.

"Okay."

I made a quick call without using the phones. Aziel still wasn't answering, so I left the mystic equivalent of a message.

I stood and then reached down to give the Penguin a hand up. From the way she moved, she was as stiff as I felt. We may have been protected, but sleeping on the cold ground wasn't pleasant.

We got on the scooter and I stopped at a food truck for breakfast. I did not like eating anything I didn't prepare myself, so I bought a half dozen raw eggs from the guy and checked them. We drove off a ways and stopped.

"Explain to me why we want to eat raw eggs instead of having them cooked and put on a roll with some bacon and cheese?" Anna said.

"Food can be tampered with and if it's done magically can make you someone's slave. It's more accurate to check food for mystic tampering in its natural form versus after it's been prepared. I checked these eggs and they are safe.

"Safe from magic but what about salmonella?"

"Lesser of the two evils." I cracked an egg on the handlebars and dumped it in my mouth and swallowed.

"Ick."

"But nutritious." I had another.

Anna took one and cracked it, emptied the shell into her mouth and swallowed, making a face the whole time.

After finishing off the raw eggs, we drove back into Manhattan and went back to the Brimmer Theater. I made some preparations with Anna in contact with me the entire time.

When we finished we parked the scooter in an alley a few blocks away from the Brimmer Theater.

"You sure you are okay with this?" I said.

"You mean with you using me as bait? Why wouldn't I be?"

"Nice sarcasm."

"Thanks. Now you are going to be nearby the entire time, right?"

"You will never leave my sight."

Anna pulled me in for a long passionate kiss.

"I thought we were waiting until you told Mother Superior?"

"We are probably about to die, so I figured I was getting one more kiss just in case."

"Works for me. Good luck," I said, stepped back and pulled the cloaking trick I had taught Az.

I disappeared before the Penguin's eyes.

As soon as I did she put a cloaking spell over herself. I had taught her the basics and explained how to make it look like she had not done it well. It was meant to throw off mystic searches, but she could still be seen. It would keep her hidden from any mystic probes done by anyone below master skill level. Nick was far above that.

Anna left the alley and made her way toward the Brimmer. Because it was one of the last places we were seen, it would be under surveillance in case we were dumb enough to go back. Nick would assume I would never be that dumb, but a naïve nun? That he could believe.

Sister Anna went in and walked to the front of the theater, her cloak still in place. I timed my entrance so I didn't make the same mistake the spigh did at Paulie's by moving the door.

Taking out a rosary, she knelt down to pray. And she really did pray.

A hellhole opened behind the penguin. She recognized the stench of the brimstone and turned in time to see a pink demon in a pink tutu step out. Balchain was the demon lord of the dance. Anna went pale. Her fear was believable, mostly because it was real. Anna turned to run, but Nick suddenly appeared to block her path. No hellhole, no skyhole, no nothing. I've never been able to figure out how he transports in and out of a place. Even having been watching for it, I still couldn't.

Anna stopped inches short of crashing into Lucifer. Nick was as calm and cordial as ever. The Devil reached out his hand graciously as if to catch her.

"Don't touch me!" Anna yelled. The memory of their last contact had not been forgotten.

"Very unsocial, Sister..." Nick obviously didn't know about Anna's decision to leave her order. "... but understandable I suppose. It was unfair of me to have done that to you the first time." The apology was done with absolute sincerity, but Anna wasn't buying what he was selling. The Penguin in a sundress turned to run out the back door.

"Don't," Nick warned. Anna stopped. "If you try to leave, Balchain will break your legs."

"Don't have the guts to do your own dirty work, Lucy?" the penguin asked defiantly.

"I know my limitations." Truth is the Devil himself isn't allowed to hurt an innocent physically without clearing it above. There's no problem with him farming out the work though. "Balchain is very skilled in that area. Besides, he enjoys it so. It would be pure torture to deprive him of the simple pleasure of cracking bones."

"I've never imaged a pink tutu as being scary. You've changed my mind." The pink demon nodded his head. "Where's the one with the trench coat and hat?"

"As per our deal, Negral can refuse 'cases' as he calls them. He opted out of coming for you. He has issues with taking the innocent. Balchain is not so morally encumbered. I love the new look. Smart to change it up to hide from me. So Sister, how have you been?" Nick was giving the illusion of a social call and wasn't fooling anyone.

"I've been better. What have you done with Gary?" Anna said.

"You'd be amazed."

"I demand to see him," Anna said.

"You will when the time is right. First, we're going on a little trip."

"Where?"

"To my home."

"No."

"I insist," Nick said, trying to touch her arm. The penguin yanked it away.

"Insist all you like. I'm not going. You have a better chance of getting a snowball fight in your backyard."

"Witty, but misconceived. Hell has all climates, including cold that makes the ice age look tropical by comparison. I love the skiing there. Strap a baby on each foot and away you go. Now move." Nick was actually losing his composure and had raised his voice. Anna held up her crucifix to ward Nick off. Nick tried to pluck it from her hands, but she pulled it away. Nick was not hurt in the least.

"How?"

"The toys of the Nazarene can't hurt me," Nick lied. In Hell, it could have scarred him for eternity. On Earth, he has dispensation to withstand holy objects, at least briefly. Why Heaven would consent to give him that power is beyond me.

Nick extended his elbow as if he were Anna's prom date looking to escort her to the dance floor.

"Nope," the good sister said, planting her butt in one of the theater seats.

The Devil smiled. "You can go willingly or in pieces."

Anna smiled back. "You can't make a good soul enter Hell against her will."

Nick's face dropped. He hadn't expected her to be so well informed. Heh. Score one for the good guys.

"If I don't go willingly, you have no power to make me." And she knew Nick would hesitate before having her hurt physically. Gary might have issues with why his mother's new body had been kneecapped.

"Then I will hurt you. Nobody wants that."

The penguin shrugged.

"Do you enjoy pain, Sister?"

"Not particularly. You can break my bones and kill me, but you can't touch my soul. So in truth, you have no power over me."

"Do you actually believe that?"

The nun's smile infuriated the Devil. "With all my being."

"I will kill Gary, then."

"After all the effort you went through to convert him? I doubt it." Anna and I had the biggest disagreement over how to handle this part of the plan. Anna was selfless enough to offer herself in trade for Gary. I finally managed to convince her that her sacrifice would be pointless, as Gary's own choices got him where he was. This was the only point where

I worried about her cracking. The penguin did not disappoint. She stood strong. Nick switched tactics again.

"I will touch you again and this time it won't be brief." Nick let the threat hang in the air. Anna suppressed a shudder.

"Do your worst." Anna held out her bare hand. Nick looked at it and hesitated. This was not going at all like he expected. He thought Anna would be more easily manipulated.

"Hex taught you how to filter out the darkness, did he?"

"Maybe. Or maybe he taught me how to share the light."

Nick pulled back his hand at that thought. He had no Heavenly dispensation to stop that. It could do some major damage.

"Balchain, secure her to that chair," Nick ordered and the demon of the dance moved to obey.

"Tying me to a chair? Awfully melodramatic, don't you think? What's next? Do we head to the subway so you can tie me to the tracks?" Anna asked.

Balchain slapped her hard across the face. Blood dripped down her chin. I had to stop myself from going after the tutued bastard. If I showed up too early, we'd lose everything.

"I forgive you," she said to the pink demon.

Balchain raising his clenched and clawed hand. "Forgive this."

"Balchain, no," Lucifer said softly. His order was obeyed, albeit reluctantly. "You are right, Sister. Tying you to a chair is too melodramatic. Balchain, put Sister Anna supine on the floor and make sure she can't move."

The demon lord of the dance lifted Anna up, kicking and struggling to the stage and threw her down hard on her back. Using his fist, the pink demon hammered iron shackles, shaped like spiked horseshoes, into the wooden stage floor, immobilizing Anna's ankles, then doing the same to her wrists right next to the crater Zu had made.

"Still in a forgiving mood?" Balchain asked, standing over the nun.

"Not so much really. More of a blessing mood," Anna replied, focusing her power on her crucifix that hung around her neck. Brilliant white light shot out at Balchain and made his pink hide catch fire.

The Devil had to intervene to extinguish the flames and physically restrain the Lord of Hell from ripping the former nun to shreds.

"Balchain, you'd best leave. Send Negral back."

Balchain cradled his scarred face. "And if the Chief refuses?"

"Tell him from me he'd best not," Nick said.

Balchain opened a hellhole and left while the Devil turned his attention back to Sister Anna. "Holy objects will not affect Negral."

"Yet the forgotten god does not seem to want to be a part of your scheme. Why is that, I wonder?" Anna asked. "Maybe he realizes your plan is ill-advised."

The Devil smirked. "Hex has been a bad influence on you, Sister." Nick meant it as an insult. I was rather complimented myself.

"A matter of opinion we disagree on."

"I suppose. I guess the two of you thought splitting up would help keep you hidden from me. Didn't work out so good for you, now did it, Sister? Maybe Hex was merely using you as a distraction so he could get away. Why else would he not make you improve upon such a pitiful cloak? I think you should give him a little payback, don't you? Would you happen to know where the magí is?" Nick asked as pleasant as if asking for directions to the nearest on-ramp.

"If I did I wouldn't tell you," the penguin said.

"Then let's find out for ourselves. Mr. Hex. Mr. Hex. Mr. Hex." By saying my name three times, Nick was trying to summon me and he put a lot of power behind it. There was a very strong pull, but because my nature was human and the ability to be summoned was one I gave myself with a spell in my pre-curse days, I was able to fight it and not go.

Nick knew that and didn't expect it to work. He just wanted to put me on notice, certain that even now, I was scanning the area to learn what was happening.

"I think we can expect Hex within a half hour," Nick said, sitting down in a seat for the long haul.

"Or sooner," I said, doing something dangerous. I body slid five feet and dropped my cloak at the small time. Nick had no idea how I stayed hidden. If he figured it out, I would be easy pickings in the future, if I had one. Nexi automatically take care of little troubles involved in instantaneous transport, like changes in velocity, potential energy and the like.

With body sliding you become intangible and your body slides through space at speeds that can near that of light. It puts a lot more strain on the body and causes much disorientation on stopping. The plus side is it requires less magic so it wouldn't increase my headache too much. You can shield a nexus transport from detection by mages, barring anyone not in the immediate vicinity on either end of it. Sliding makes a lot of mystic noise, like a high-pitched whine. It's almost impossible to hide. I was hoping the noise it made would cover up the cloak I was dropping.

Usually, it takes a moment to accommodate to the new environment, but since it was the same room, it only took a couple of seconds.

"Hex, very prompt of you. I expected a more cautious entrance. Maybe a plan of some sort. This is so unlike you," said Nick.

He was right, so I tried to come across as angry.

"Let her go Nick or…"

"Or you'll what?" Nick asked, pointing at my mouth with a gesture. The Devil struck me mute, so I couldn't speak his true name. Not an unexpected development. He could go after me because I had involved myself in his business and was no longer an innocent. "Too slow, Hex. You're done. I am going to end you or rather have someone else do it." The hellhole shimmered and out walked a forgotten god in a fedora. "Negral, care to do the honors?"

My eyes went wide and I tried to run, but the Chief was on me before I could take four steps. I tried to fight, using a couple of hand hexes, but Negral shrugged them off like I had hit him with a thin plywood board. He wrapped his fingers around my throat and squeezed. Lights began to dance before my eyes. The Chief then grabbed my crotch and squeezed even harder. The grip would have ruptured a testicle if I hadn't managed to get a ward up in time. This one time using magic actually decreased my pain.

This was not going as planned. Nick usually liked to gloat more. I was sure he wanted Gary to kill me, not Negral. I screwed up somewhere and it was going to get the Penguin and me killed.

Negral body slammed me on the stage, knocking the wind out of me and breaking three ribs.

Then the Chief surprised me and whispered in my ear. "C'mon Hex. I don't like you, but you don't deserve to go out like this. The kid's a lost cause, but you can save the nun."

"Negral?" Nick asked confused. Negral must have used his own power to shield his words from the Devil's ears and got caught.

"Some private talk between me and the magí. Any chance I could get some alone time with him?" Negral asked, cracking his knuckles.

Nick smiled. "I appreciate you wanting to settle old scores, but I promised him to Gary. Secure him to the floor."

The Chief then fastened my wrists and ankles to the floor with the same horseshoe spikes Balchain had used on Anna. In fact, Negral spent a little bit extra time on the one on my left hand and I realized that he bent it back and forth enough to compromise the metal's integrity. A good yank and it would crack.

Why the Hell was Negral helping me?

"Gary, you can come in now," Nick said. The hellhole shimmered again and out walked Gary, wearing the coat he'd made out of the damned woman's harvested skin. He was worse than he looked in my visions. He wasn't the same boy we had known. Only days had passed for us, but years had come and gone for him. He was in his late teens, maybe even early twenties. His face had grown hard, his eyes cold. Red fires of fury danced among black shadows in his umbra. His hatred had festered and grown over the death of his parents.

"Like I promised, two fine specimens for us to bring your parents back to life in." Nick handed him a demon blade, a bone knife carved from the leg bone of one of the Fallen, used for thousands of years to commit acts of evil and darkness. "All that remains is for you to do your part."

Gary took the knife, cradled it, practically caressing the thing, a look of demented ecstasy on his face.

"Who's first to go?" Nick asked.

"Wait!" Sister Anna said before Gary could reveal his decision.

"Yes, Sister?" Nick asked.

"I have a last request," Anna said.

Nick was intrigued. "Really? What is it, some taste of sin? A chance to beg for your life?"

"Hardly. Just a few final words."

"Go ahead."

"What I have to say is for your ears only. Please?" The penguin was almost begging.

Nick smiled and walked over to where Anna was nailed to the floor. "Talk to me."

"Come closer," Anna whispered. Nick kneeled and put his ear up against the nun's mouth.

Her words froze him to the very bone. His eyes went wide at the indignity and the fact that I had actually shared the one thing I had that gave me power over him with someone else. The idea of trust was foreign to the Devil and one of his few weaknesses

Nick pointed at Gary and the Chief, immobilizing them.

"What!?" Negral screamed.

Nick stood up and walked a few feet from the nun. I then blinked three times quick. Trapping wards, simple circles on the floor, walls and ceiling, flared to life becoming active and visible. Everyone, even Anna and me, was caught in one.

I blinked four times, shutting off all but three of them.

"Aziel, Aziel, Aziel," Anna said, hoping to summon the angel for backup and it worked.

Aziel appeared uncloaked in the air above us. Anna still couldn't see him, but she could see him rip the shackles off her, then me.

"Angel, I will feast on your heart!" Nick boasted.

"Not happening today," Aziel said, sticking his tongue out. The angel then put his hand on my throat, restoring my voice.

"My Lord," Gary said to Nick. "Why did you do this? Why do you allow us to be held in these weak trappings?" Not all that weak actually. While a normal ward could hold a demon or a god like Negral, they could never contain the Devil. My wards had a special ingredient. The addition of the Devil's true name. Better than secret sauce.

Nick glared up at him. "I did what must be done."

"But for the Satan to obey a lowly nun, it is a disgrace!" Gary said.

"*SILENCE!*" Nick yelled, shaking the entire building even from inside his ward. The display was humbling and terrifying. I forget how powerful the Devil really is. Once, he was the right hand of God and led a rebellion that rocked Heaven to its foundations. Yet, I actually thought I could beat the Devil. Only one thing needed to go wrong and Nick would turn us into primordial soup.

Better make sure nothing went wrong.

It took a moment for me to get control of myself and fight the fear back. This was not the time for self-doubt.

Gary reluctantly obeyed. He had no way of knowing I had told Sister Anna Nick's true name, which gave her power over him, now and forever. Her promise to me involved using it only at my discretion or in self-defense.

I was so frightened I did something I rarely ever do around Nick and his ilk. I asked permission.

"If I may speak?"

Nick's eyes were downcast, his normal façade of civility almost gone. His eyes were burning with the hate of the first of the fallen, but he nodded.

"Is there any written contract between Gary and you or Hell?"

Nick glared at me. The flames of damnation danced in his eyes and for possibly the first time, the Devil wasn't leading the dance. "No."

Nick had been that confident the boy would damn himself. Probably well placed. Time to see if we could change that. I walked over to the ward that held the latest magí.

"Hello, Gary."

"Call me Hellfire." I guess Gary had a chosen a name for himself. I didn't like it.

"Interesting choice," I said.

"What's it to you? You never gave a damn about me."

"Not true. Still better not to give one than to be damned."

"I don't know about that," Gary said.

"I do," the Penguin interjected. "Hello, Gary."

"The name's Hellfire."

"To me, you'll always be Gary. I've missed and worried about you."

"Really, Sister? I don't believe you. All you ever did was lie to me."

"I've never lied to you," Anna said softly.

"Bullshit! Lucifer showed me your sins! You have broken every one of your vows and every commandment."

"I have done nothing of the sort."

"Don't lie to me. I saw it," Gary said.

"Gary, I think you're the one who's been lied to," I said.

"Right, Hex. Sure. I see the light. Now let me out of here and I'll make the world a better place." Still was a sarcastic little son of a pup.

"I think not. Gar – I mean Hellfire, do you really think you're better off in Hell?"

"Hell yes. I rule down there. You couldn't even take down Grundy."

"I took him down. You freed him."

"Liar! You couldn't do it, so you blamed it on me. Negral brought me his head."

"So the Chief nailed him. Doesn't prove any sins on the part of the penguin or myself." Anna elbowed me in the chest, luckily on the opposite side of my broken ribs. I ignored her.

"Gary, one question," Aziel said, floating above me in most of his winged glory. He had healed nicely, but he still had a ways to go. More than a few feathers showed signs of damage. "Did you enjoy torturing Grundy's soul? Did it bring your parents back?"

"What he's here to do will bring his parents back." Nick was trying to change the subject. Why? Anna knew Az must have been talking, but she still couldn't see him. She mouthed the word "Where?" I pointed up. She stared and squinted, but saw nothing.

"That's right!" Gary said.

"At the cost of the lives of Hex and myself?" asked Anna.

"The greater good justifies the means," Gary answered.

"But those you side with have nothing to do with good, whether it be greater or lesser," Anna countered.

"Gary, you still haven't answered my question," Az said. "Did you enjoy torturing Grundy's soul?"

"I never tortured Grundy's soul," Gary said.

I figured out what the angel was getting at.

"Really?" I said, strolling over to where Negral stood trapped and helpless. "Why, oh why, would the Chief just give you Grundy's head and not his soul? Grundy was certainly evil enough. If the Chief killed him, why didn't he harvest his soul and take it to Hell?"

Gary paused, then looked to Negral for an answer. "Why didn't you give him to me?"

"His soul departed his body before I could capture it," Negral lied.

"But he was evil. His soul should have come to Hell and been given to me," Gary said.

Negral looked at Nick. "If it did, I'm sure it would have."

"Which means his soul went elsewhere. He was a necromancer. He could have had a plan in place to put his soul in another body. That means only his body is dead, but Grundy is still on Earth somewhere," I said.

"Hex, don't pollute the boy with your lies," Nick said. Gary twitched at the "boy" moniker. Guess that was one thing that hadn't changed.

"My lies? What about your own? Guess after a while you just can't tell the difference, can you?" I asked.

"Gary, Hex is desperate for you not to kill him. He'd say anything to turn you against me. Don't listen to him," Nick said.

"Yeah, ignore that man behind the curtain," I said.

"Hex, I'm warning you..." Nick threatened.

"Warn away, but frankly I'm sick of your voice." I snapped my fingers and the ward became soundproof. Nick shouted, but we couldn't hear him. It was a beautiful thing, well worth the pain it caused me.

"Hex..." Negral started

With a snap, I cut him off too. Knowing what I knew, I didn't want him to incriminate himself. "You shut up too."

Hell's Detective got so angry his hair burst into an inferno, turning his fedora hat to ashes. "So, Gary, who's lying now?"

Gary turned to Nick for comfort. "Lucifer?"

Nick glared up, a lie on his lips.

"Truth only," Sister Anna ordered. The Devil had to obey. I turned off the mute.

"Gary could have a great destiny. In the face of such greatness, what matter the little details?" Nick said.

"The Devil's in the details," I replied.

Nick shrugged with a smile. "True enough."

"You lied to me?" Gary asked.

"I gave you guidance," Nick said.

"I said truth only," Anna reminded.

"It is the truth," Nick said. "Our ceremony would allow your parents to live again."

"Gary, ask him why you have to do the killing," I said.

"Why?" Gary asked.

"That is my price," Nick said.

"And what would be Gary's price?" Anna asked.

"His soul would be damned."

"And become yours? Along with his power?"

"Of course." Nick smiled.

"So, what do you think of the Devil now?" Anna asked.

"I'm not naïve. I expected as much. It was just the lying that caught me off guard. Lucifer, I want your word Grundy will be caught and his soul be made mine. Deal?" Gary asked.

"Deal, provided you go through with the ceremony as planned," Nick said.

"Deal." Gary was grinning and let loose a barrage of power at the ward, modulating magics against the barrier. The Devil had taught him how to use his offensive power well. I could feel the ward start to buckle. It would have fallen if it wasn't shored up with the Devil's own power via his true name.

"You've lost him, Sister," Nick said. "Accept it and move on."

The penguin stormed over to the Devil and got as far up into his face as she could, without touching his ward. "I haven't lost him yet, deceiver."

"Of course, you haven't," Nick said in a tone one uses on a delusional child. "Such optimism is inspiring."

"We'll see," Anna said. The Devil's mocking laughter filled the auditorium. "Hex, shut him up."

"My pleasure." I snapped my fingers and the Devil's ward became soundproof again.

Anna stood in front of Gary's ward. "Let me in, Hex."

"Not a chance."

"Hex..." The penguin glared at me.

"No. He has a demon blade and the intent to kill you. If you got in front of one of those spells, you'd be vaporized. There wouldn't be enough left of you to fill a shoe. I won't let you commit suicide." Even through the fireworks of magic Gary was throwing out, I could see that his umbra was turning pitch black. Gary had made his decision. Evil was claiming his soul even as we spoke.

"I need to reach him."

"Then do it from out here," I said.

Anna cocked her head at me.

"It's non-negotiable."

"How?" she asked.

I looked at her chest and she got my thought. She lifted her talisman crucifix.

Anna knelt in prayer just in front of Gary, cradling the crucifix in her hands. Her head was bowed and her eyes closed. Az knelt behind her, placed his hands on her shoulder, adding his efforts to hers. The prayers of an angel are a powerful thing. Sister Anna and the crucifix began to glow with a soft, pure light. Az stood wearily, then floated up and away. Anna opened her eyes and raised her head. Lifting the crucifix, she held it out for Gary. The light passed from her, into the crucifix then out toward Gary. It stopped when it reached the ward. I made the alterations so it could pass through and into Gary.

Gary reached out to try to exploit the opening, but in doing so let down his own shields and Anna's light slammed into his soul with the force of a thousand holy sledgehammers.

Gary fell to his knees, fighting the magic and trying to get his personal shields back up, but it was too late. Anna's brightness was inside him and spreading.

Gary screamed as if someone had submerged him in boiling water. Once, the yelling subsided, his eyes went wide, in horror and terror. Gary assumed the fetal position and the sobbing began. It lasted for twenty minutes until the light dimmed and faded.

Sister Anna stood, rubbing her sore knees, exhausted, but cheerful of heart.

"I saved him," Anna said, gripping my arms as tears flowed down her face.

"Maybe. You can lead a man to salvation's gate, but he has to work at opening it," I cautioned and closed the ward back up. The darkness hadn't left his umbra, just been pushed to the side a bit by the light of Sister Anna. Problem was, unless he accepted it and worked to keep it, it would soon be gone.

"Gary?" Sister Anna asked.

"Sister, I'm so sorry," Gary wept.

"It will be okay, Gary," said Anna.

"No, no it won't," Gary said, tearing off his human skin coat and throwing it on the floor. "It will never be okay." He started sobbing again.

"Hex, let me in," Anna ordered.

"Hex, don't," Gary begged.

I turned to Anna and shook my head no.

"Gary, talk to me," Anna pleaded.

"Sister, you made me see the light. Literally. You can't imagine the things I did."

"We can get past that," Anna said.

"I would have killed you. And Hex."

"I forgive you," the penguin said and she meant it. It was more than I could do.

"I don't forgive myself," Gary confessed.

"Why?" Anna asked.

"Because I might still try," he admitted.

"Why?" Anna asked again, truly not understanding.

"It's my nature. I enjoyed doing horrible things. I can see now that it was wrong, but I knew it wasn't right even while I was doing it. I don't know how long this change of heart will last."

"It could last forever," Anna said, trying to convince both herself and Gary of it.

"No, Sister, it can't. Sooner or later, I'll get mad. I'll want to get even and I will. Hex, you were right. Power corrupts," said Gary. This wasn't the right time to bring up the storm bird, Zu.

"I could curse you so you couldn't use your powers," I suggested. Of course, the Devil could probably have lifted the curse inside of hours. The mage who cursed me was a master's master. And the curse wouldn't change the state of his soul. The darkness was steadily eating away at the light the penguin had shared with Gary. He knew the truth. This change of heart wouldn't last long.

"Too little, too late. I'd do what I wanted, with or without power. There is only one solution that will work," Gary said, gazing down at the demon blade in his hands. He was going to use it, just not on its intended victims. There was just enough light left in him to make him want to destroy the darkness forever.

"NO!" Anna and Az screamed in unison. Both started banging on the wall of the ward.

"Let me in!" Anna demanded.

"Hex, let *me* in now. Please," the angel whispered.

I lowered it just enough to let the angel in, but Anna didn't know that.

"Hex, please! I'm begging you!" Anna said.

"Aziel is on it," I said.

"He'll save Gary?" she asked.

"In the only way left," I said.

"What do you mean?"

I did my best to explain. Suicide was a sin. If done for certain reasons, it can be overlooked. With all that Gary had done, committing suicide here and now would be like handing his soul over to Nick. We couldn't let him go free. Gary had become too powerful and when his darkness returned he would find a way to kill us or someone else. He'd spent years torturing and butchering the damned in Hell. The Devil had conditioned him how he should react to get his own way. In the Pit souls regenerate. Real people on Earth not so much. And with the power of a magí that was trained by the Devil, he might know more than me at this point. He would be difficult to stop. It might take years, decades even. People would die in Gary's wake.

Leaving him trapped in the ward for decades, until he died of natural causes, would be torture worthy of the damned. Assuming he didn't figure a way out. A Devil trained magí might eventually figure out the right combination of magics.

And the world would pay if he did.

There was only one humane and safe solution. Az was taking care of it but I could tell it was tearing the angel apart.

Gary sensed what the solution was.

"Aziel, please," Gary begged, as he offered the angel the demon blade. Az knocked it aside and let it tumble to the floor. He took Gary's face in his hands and nodded sadly.

"Thank you," Gary said, embracing the angel. Az reached under his overcoat and took out his soulblade, the fiery sword of the angels. At the moment it was only a hilt. "Will I see my parents?"

"You will, that I promise. They are waiting for you," Az said, kissing Gary on the forehead.

"Goodbye," Gary said simply, turning his head to encompass Anna and me in his farewell.

Az's soul blade flamed to life. Even Anna was able to see it.

"No!" she screamed, beating and pounding at the ward. I pulled her back and held her as she sobbed, trying to make everything better, knowing I never could.

Az cradled Gary with one hand and thrust the fiery sword into his heart with the other. Gary's body convulsed and the fiery sword went out. Az gently lowered him to the floor, then tenderly harvested Gary's soul into his arms. The angel, tears in his eyes, looked at me. I dropped the ward. It had no purpose now. Az flew up to the high ceiling over the stage before doing his golden fade with Gary's spirit in tow.

"Life is never easy, but it beats the alternative."
    -Hex, cursed magí

To say Anna was a turbulent mess of emotions was an understatement. She was having trouble coming to grips with what just happened and looked about ready to rip the Devil's head off his shoulders. Not that she would or could.

"You may still speak only truth," she reminded Nick. "Would you have gotten Gary's soul if he had suicided?"

"Yes," Nick said.

"Could Gary could have rejected the power and lived a good life?"

"No."

Then she asked him a surprise question.

"How do you feel after all this?"

"Disappointed Hex is still alive. Furious you have this power over me. Shamed that Negral witnessed this. Upset over losing my little Hellfire's soul to the angel." That was the part that convinced her. "Happy to have caused you such pain and anguish." That was the part that ticked her off.

"You enjoy pain and anguish?" the penguin asked.

"Yes," the Devil answered.

"Enjoy this." Anna whispered in my ear to adjust the ward. I did. Pure light shot out of her crucifix like a laser and slammed right into the Devil's heart. Nick grabbed his chest and choked down a scream.

"Lock it up, Hex." I put the ward on full and drew a separate one around those that held Nick and the Chief. I used paint instead of chalk. More permanent, less likely to be broken. Next, I hooked up a distraction spell around the entire Brimmer Theater to keep people out by not being aware of the way in.

I waved goodbye to the boys from Hell. I had no qualms keeping them locked up forever or at least long enough to figure a safe way to let them out, although I was still a little out of sorts about the Chief's actions.

First thing's first. I walked Sister Anna back to her convent in the Bowery.

"Do you want me to go in with you?" I asked.

Anna laughed. "I don't know whether or not you are being sweet or insulting that you think I can't talk to Mother Superior without you."

"Sweet. Definitely sweet," I said.

"I still can't get over what happened. There had to be some way…"

I shook my head. "There wasn't. Sometimes there isn't. Sometimes you lose. The trick is to get back up on your feet again and keep going forward," I said.

Anna nodded. "I think I'm going to need a few days to myself for contemplation and prayer, so don't think I'm ignoring you, okay?"

"Sure. Call me when you are ready."

"You're not going to change your mind on me?"

I shook my head. "You?"

"I'm sure. What are you going to do now?"

"Go back and move Gary's body so the police can find it. Then I'm going to visit a leprechaun and Greek god at Bulfinche's Pub to help me write up contracts for Nick and the Chief. Then I'll go back tomorrow and make them an offer."

"After all that, you are going to let Nick out?"

"Probably not, but the Chief tried to help us. It wouldn't be right to leave him in there. I might be able to convince Nick it was his idea."

"Do you want me to go back with you?" Anna asked.

"You being sweet or think I can't do it without you?"

"Neither. I was teasing. I'm not sure what help I would be."

"I couldn't have done this without you," I said.

Anna smiled. "Probably. I'll call you soon."

"I can't wait."

"I love making deals."
   -The Devil

The theater of the damned was undisturbed when I returned.

"Evening, boys," I shouted as I turned off the soundproofing. Nick and the Chief looked cool and collected, relaxed even. It might have fooled me, if the Chief's eyes weren't glowing red and if his hair hadn't burst into flame the moment he saw me. "How're tricks?"

Negral remained silent. Nick was another matter.

"Very good. Haven't had this much time to myself since I fell. Rather enjoying it, more of a vacation than imprisonment really."

The Devil sounded convincing. Nick had conjured up a miniature canopy bed and was dressed in slippers and a blue smoking jacket. He had laid an open book face down on the nightstand. I couldn't make out the title.

"Excellent. Glad you are enjoying your stay at the Mr. Hex Inn. Devils and forgotten gods check-in. The questions remain: Will they check out? Will they try to steal the towels and the soap? Will they remember to tip their room maids?"

Negral did a wonderful imitation of a solar flare erupting.

"Good questions. Answering in reverse order: No, yes and I hope so." the Devil said. "So Hex, what do you want in exchange for our freedom?"

"What makes you think I want something?" I said.

"Everyone wants something, even you, so let's get to the deal," the Devil said.

"So you admit that you can't get out unless I let you out?" Okay, I was gloating but why not? How often did I have the Devil over a barrel?

"For the foreseeable future, yes. So do you want to make a deal? Perhaps play a game? A dozen souls as the stakes for our freedom?" I remained silent. Nick smiled. "A hundred? A thousand?"

"Sorry, Nick, no games. Beating you in a fair fight is only three steps down from impossible."

"You've beaten me before."

"Your games. As far as I was concerned, anything was fair. With me as the game master, I can't play that way. I would have to give you a fair shake, which means I would probably lose. Then you're free and I'm toast. No thanks. Besides, I'm not in the business of souls."

"You can cheat. I don't mind," Nick said grinning.

"Nick, I'm not that stupid."

Negral had a harrumphing noise. I ignored him. Nick shrugged as if making an excuse for the Chief's behavior.

"What if we made it a no-lose situation, all round?" the Devil asked.

One of the rules of the universe is, if something is too good to be true, it probably is. Still... "Go on."

"Regardless of who wins, we each get something."

"Such as?"

"You get my assurances for your safety and that of your Sister Anna. You both go onto the protected list."

"And?"

"I get Negral's freedom," Nick said with a casual hand gesture.

Negral looked a little shocked.

"You will have my and his guarantee that he will not seek revenge on any involved party."

"Ever?" I asked.

"Ever."

"Okay, let's hear your reasoning."

"You can't kill me because of my nature."

"I'd say that's yet to be determined."

The Devil chuckled. "With Negral in Hell, my presence will be made known. I won't have to be there personally. I have vacationed on Earth for extended periods in the past. It will not seem unusual. I have ruled Hell for as long as there has been one, but should I step down, willingly or otherwise, other demons will rise up to take the mantle of Satan." That's actually not his name, but the job title for whoever rules Hell. "We both know their approach would be much more, shall we say, claws on. Because of that, I know you would rather me rule. You've even told others better the Devil you know."

He was right. No reason to say it out loud. "So?"

"You've been raking your brain for a way to get just what I'm offering you. Why not take it?"

"There is always a catch."

"Of course. That's the game part. Are you up for the challenge? In addition to the protected status, you get to ask me a question and ask me a boon. Once both are completed, you must free me. And I will give you a thousand souls just for playing."

A thousand souls freed from Hell? And safety for me and the penguin? It was worth some risk.

"Nick, as far as I know, you've never willingly let a soul go. Who in Hell would?" Negral blushed and his hair went out in a wush. "Why start now?"

"We only have so much room. Overcrowding is getting bad."

"It's getting deep in here."

"Okay, that's not the reason. We both know there is very little I could offer you and almost nothing you would take. Except, perhaps, freedom for souls trapped in eternal damnation. I see you cringe whenever you hear their screams. Their torment tortures you. You're a sucker. I won't even delve into your savior complex. For whatever reason, you waste your time trying to help the less fortunate. Not really much point to it, is there? You help, but what do you get out of it? Do those you help thank you? If they do, do they do it adequately? No, they don't. Do they care about you? Sure, some, but would any do for you what you have done for them?"

My turn to smile. We were standing on familiar ground, but this time the Earth wasn't going to give way under my feet. "Nice try, Nick but I expected something original from you. That may have worked once, but that was years ago. We both know there are people who would lay down their lives for me. I can't ask for more thanks than that."

"But you would never let them do it. Always protecting people. Everyone dies eventually. What's the point?" Nick asked, with the charm of a snake oil salesman.

"I know how they feel and knowing keeps the darkness at bay. That kind of love just burns you, doesn't it?" I countered.

"It does get in the way of some business, but that's not the issue. You give others more than you could ever get back."

"That's debatable."

"Not really. Sure, there are those who might risk harm for you, but do they invite you over for a night of movies and popcorn? No. Why? Maybe part of them fears you, while other portions are envious and jealous of your power. And you never push the socializing. Why? Because no matter how many care for you, there are scores more that hate you and wish you harm. You can't live in a normal house. Without magical protections, your enemies would find and destroy you. You can't even risk accidentally falling asleep without risking an attack in the dreaming. You pay a steep price to help those in need: constant jeopardy. You are in chronic danger, so you never let anyone get too close. When's the last time you had a serious relationship, something more than a fling, with a woman?"

"As opposed to an elephant?" No reason to mention the change in my status with the Penguin.

"Answer the question."

"I couldn't tell you." Best not to fib to the prince of lies.

"I could tell you."

"Don't trouble yourself."

"No trouble. You're one messed up individual. I won't even get into your home situation and those creatures you live with."

The brood was off limits. Nobody messes with my family. I snapped and turned off the sound. Nick realized what happened and stopped speaking. I snapped, turning the mute off.

"Nick, as much as I would love to be psychoanalyzed by the Devil, I am more than qualified to handle that myself. Besides, your sweet talk got old long ago. How about I psychoanalyze you for a while? We can go into the whole problem with divine authority thing. I'll even give you a ten percent discount on my normal rates."

"Another time perhaps. We have a deal?" the Devil asked.

"Pending the contracts, yes."

"Excellent," the Devil said. "I've taken the liberty of drawing up the documents." Nick reached into thin air and plucked out papers. His powers worked fine inside the ward. He had an almost inexhaustible supply of manna.

"So did I." I pulled two contracts out of my inside pocket.

"But how?" the Devil asked. Inside my ward, his view of the world was greatly diminished.

I smiled. When I stopped by Bulfinche's Pub I spoke with a man named Mosie. He's the greatest psychic who ever lived. Makes Garar with his turbaned prophecy gig look like a blind man. Mosie's visions are so powerful that if he doesn't stay drunk, he can't see reality in the normal fashion. The drinking limits the ranges of his visions to mostly hours and days, occasionally weeks. I asked him what the Devil would offer me. He was too drunk to give me any more than the bare basics.

Taking that information, I sat down with Paddy Moran, the leprechaun who owns the joint and the god Hermes. The pair are master tricksters and con artists. The three of us banged out a contract even the Devil couldn't get out of. I then had two others look it over. Jeeves, who despite being made of clay, has a razor-sharp mind and Legba, who is a trickster in the same class as Paddy and Hermes. Jeeves typed it up on his computer and printed it out in duplicate.

"Give me your word not to try anything as we conduct our business involving the contract," I said.

"I give it," the Devil vowed. I made changes in the ward to allow the paper to go inside and come back out. I tossed it in to Nick. The Devil conjured a red leather easy chair, with an end table that came complete with a snifter of brandy.

It was Negral's turn. His hair was again burning bright.

"Your turn, Chief. I want your word, same as your boss, not to try anything," I said.

"What makes you think I will abide by it?" Negral growled.

"You are many things, but you are not an oath breaker," I said. Negral calmed and his hair even went out as he nodded.

"I so swear." I handed Negral his contract. Nick looked up from reading his.

"Why does Negral have his own contract? Your deal is with me," said Nick.

"The Chief is involved. I want him to agree to it in writing," I said.

Nick leisurely reviewed the contract.

"I'm impressed. I doubt that even Jenal could have done better." It was a major compliment. Jenal was quite probably the greatest lawyer on the planet. She had never lost a case and not every one of her cases took place in a courtroom. Rumor has it she even beat Nick more than a few times. I had tried to locate Jenal, but she was unavailable. She was the only one I had any worries of being able to find a hole in that contract, but she would never work for Nick. Jenal prefers the good guys, especially if they're underdogs.

"I have some things I would like changed. Take this gradual acquisition of the thousand souls on your part. I would much prefer the transfer be made immediately and completely," Nick said.

"No," I said. "The contract stays as it is or no deal."

Nick mulled it over. "Fine." The Devil took a tiny nibble out of his right index finger and used the fluid as ink in a pen. Contracts with Hell are usually signed in blood. I used a regular red pen to sign, once Nick passed them back to me. I handed him back his copy.

It wasn't a done deal until Negral signed his. It would basically prevent him from trying to free his boss, directly or through an agent. The penguin and I were also untouchable for eternity. It also gave me one free question that had to be answered truthfully.

"Not touching the nun is fine, but you don't get a free pass," Negral said.

The Devil frowned and stood up. "Chief –"

"Sorry, Nick. Can't do it. I will, however, agree to not seek revenge over this. You do something new, all bets are off," Negral said.

"I won't let you out," I said.

Negral shrugged. "So be it."

"Fine. Stay in there then."

We stood and stared. Negral made a recliner out of fire and sat back in it. He closed his eyes as if taking a nap.

"If Negral stays, we have no deal," Nick pointed out.

I sighed. "Make the change."

Hell's Detective did and we did the signing.

Negral wasn't mincing words today as he tossed me back the contract. "Ask."

"Tell me how to find and safely capture Grundy."

Negral was caught between embarrassment and pleasure at his ignorance.

"I don't know at this moment."

That was that. I had to let him go. I dropped the ward. Negral brought himself up to his full height and bore down on me. I impressed myself by not jumping aside.

The Chief didn't say another word. He nodded at Nick and tried to conjure a hellhole. It didn't work.

"This is a nexus free zone," I said. The new wards wouldn't allow it. Without expression, Negral turned and walked out of the Brimmer Theater. Seconds later, I felt the noise of a hellhole outside.

"Well, Mr. Hex, time for our game, don't you think?" asked the Devil.

"Yes," I answered. The first part of the game was a simple one, older than the Sphinx. I asked a riddle or question of the Devil. It had to have an answer, not something like what the sound of one hand clapping or could God make a rock so heavy he could lift it. If Nick got it right, he was free. Wrong, he stayed trapped.

"And the question is?" the Devil asked. "You want me to tell you where Grundy is and how to capture him?"

"No. I only asked the Chief to get his goat." I knew Negral didn't know or Grundy's soul would already be in Hell, but I had to be sure. And honestly, after his help, I didn't want him trapped in there, but I had to make sure it looked good to Nick. "I found him once, I'll find him again. Your question is a bit more challenging." I took a deep breath. "Tell me how I can end evil on Earth..."

The Devil almost glowed. "Easy..."

"Without destroying it."

"Ah, there's the rub." Nick chuckled. "Hex, you are brilliant."

"Flattery will get you nowhere."

"Are you sure I can't convince you to work for me?"

"Nope."

"A pity. It is the perfect question. If I answer it, I give you the means to banish me from Earth. And get rid of Grundy."

"I can live with that," I said

"I couldn't," the Devil said. "I won't give up Earth."

"So you admit you don't know the answer."

"I didn't say that."

"So you do know it?"

"I didn't say that. I admit nothing. I just won't give you an answer."

"You realize not answering is the same as a wrong answer," I asked.

"Of course. I read the contract."

"Your silence guarantees your continued imprisonment."

"Hex, why do you feel compelled to state the obvious?" the Devil said.

"Just want to eliminate any misunderstandings."

"Then you've done your job. Any other questions?" Nick asked.

"None at the moment."

"Very well. Come back when you're curious and we'll play again."

"That's it?" I said.

"Yes. What were you expecting? Me to rant and rave?"

"Well..."

"Have you ever seen me rant? Or rave?" I admitted I hadn't. "Do you expect me to start now?"

"No," I said.

"Then leave me to my imposed sabbatical."

"Not so quick. I freed Negral. Now for your part of the bargain."

"How could I forget? You are now the proud owner of a thousand souls. Congratulations. What are you planning to do with them?" Nick asked.

"Undecided. Probably free the lot."

The Devil laughed.

"You find that funny?"

"Very. You didn't specify in your contract which souls I was to give you, only that they be human." Actually, I was aware of the oversight. It would be tough to list a thousand souls in one day. To name any specific souls would have given Nick an arguing point in the contract. He might have gotten that clause dropped and then those souls would have suffered more. "I can give you anyone I want. You're worried about evil now? Wait until you see what your life becomes like as the custodian of one thousand of the evilest and twisted souls who have ever lived."

It didn't sound good. "I knew the souls weren't nice people going into this."

"I'm sure you did. You free them and most will come back to Earth to cause havoc. It will be glorious."

"I will find someplace in the afterworlds for them."

"That much evil? Who would take them? Not Heaven. It would ruin the point of having a Hell. True, most death gods would take delight in a thousand fresh souls. What power they would bring! Problem is, the death gods as a whole are not evil. True, some punish it or reward the lack of it. A thousand evil souls to punish. The energy expended in punishment would outweigh the power gained. You'll find no takers."

"We'll see." Nick never made a point without a reason. Time to bait him. "It will still weaken you. It'll be worth it."

"You don't want to be custodian. Take it from me, it's a thankless job."

"You, of course, have another option to offer me."

"Of course. I offer you one soul in exchange for the thousand."

"Seems like a bad trade to me."

"Really? One of something valuable is easily worth a thousand of something worthless."

"And that something is?"

"The soul of your father."

He caught me off guard. Nick still didn't know that I had already freed him, sometime in his future.

"Then we can see what you do with it. Free him or torture him for what he did to you as a child," said Nick, looking at me like a scientist would at a lab rat.

"I think I'll pass," I said.

"On the torture or the trade?"

"Both."

The Devil raised an eyebrow. "Why?"

"Not worth it."

The Devil nodded. "Let me try another tack. I have in my possession a most unique item. An innocent soul."

"Go on."

"Her mother sold her to me, much like your father tried to do to you. Sadly, the daughter never realized what you did and she became mine."

"When?" I demanded.

"Just a few days ago. A pretty little thing with such brown eyes. Only seven years old. Do you want to hear what circle I put her in? What demons have such an innocent plaything, to do with as they please?"

Nick found the right button. "What's her name?" I shouted.

"Broke the famous Hex cool, did I?"

"Her name, damn it!"

"Why? So you can go into Hell and rescue her?"

"Her name. Please," I asked.

"Well since you said please… no."

"What if I gave my word that I wouldn't go in after her?"

"Hmm."

"I need to verify what you say and to do that, I'll need her name."

"Your word that you won't go into Hell after her?"

I nodded. "My word."

"Her name is Gina Martinez."

The same last name as our waitress from lunch. I got an idea where he may have gotten the soul. It killed me to be polite, but I did it anyway. "Thank you."

"So do we have a deal?"

"Let me think on it."

"Okay, but every minute you delay is a minute more that little Gina spends in Hell."

I double-checked that all the wards were set and ran out of there like a bat out of somewhere the Devil would rather be.

"What in blazes is a frenemy?"
    -Negral, Hell's Detective

The basement was abandoned. The boiler had long ago given up the ghost. Debris filled the room and the only light source was the half windows that encircled the walls near the ceiling. Luther had found it for me in his neighborhood. Less than two hours had passed since I left the theater of the damned. Time enough to find Aziel and set up the basement.

A chalk circle was drawn on the floor. Time to get busy. I nodded to Aziel. Time for the summoning to begin.

"Negral. Negral. Negral." At the third mention of his name, the Chief appeared in the circle, still missing his hat. "Hey, Chief."

"What do you want? And what's the angel doing here?" Negral spat, looking down at the ward.

"Az is here because I asked him to be. I have a proposition for you," I said.

"I don't want to hear anything before you let me out."

"But..."

"Our deal was based upon you doing one thing. Freeing me. If I'm not free, deals off."

I erased the chalk line with my foot.

"You're right. I apologize," I said. That surprised him.

"You apologizing? I can't wait to hear this proposition."

"I need your help."

The Chief tilted his head and stared at me. "Why?"

I explained the Gina situation to him.

Negral seemed completely unmoved. "So?"

"I can't go in after her so I want you to get her out," I said.

"You are kidding me. I'm not going to help you," Negral said.

"I want you to help Gina," I said.

"Why would I do that?"

"You've said that your position in Hell is a job, to help you punish the guilty. You claim to hunger for justice. Is an innocent in Hell just?"

"No." Negral was silent a moment. "What would even make you think that I would do anything to change that?"

There was only one way to answer that. "You've done it before."

Negral nodded and glared at Az. "Stupid angels can't keep their mouths shut." Az wasn't there, but even angels gossip. "I had my reasons and a good excuse to explain why to Nick. This time I've got neither. What do you have that could possibly change my mind? You going to let me out of our contract?"

Hell no. I just shook my head.

The angel stepped up to the plate and took a swing. "Please?" Aziel said.

"You are asking me to steal what most would consider the most valuable commodity in all of Hell and all you got is an angel asking nice? Do you know what would happen to me if I got caught or found out?"

"I have some idea," I said.

"You have no idea, you mook. You've seen Hell, but only parts. Those weren't even the worst ones. It's my job to keep order in that chaos, to punish the punishers who get out of line. Those waiting to get a shot at me are legion."

"You've never struck me as a coward," I said.

"There's brave and then there is stupid. I work at being neither. I'll survive longer that way. If that's all, I'll be going," Negral said.

"Wait," I said. "What could we offer you to change your mind? Besides nullifying the contract."

"You willing to trade your soul?" Negral asked.

I wasn't. I was ashamed of it, but that didn't change it.

"I would be willing to put in a favorable recommendation," Aziel said.

"With who?" Negral asked.

Aziel pointed his eyes up. "Might be helpful if you ever have to jump ship."

"It might," agreed the Chief. "I'll consider it if Hex is willing to humble himself."

I started to speak, but Az put his hand over my mouth. "Specifically what?"

"Begging. Groveling. On his belly."

Normally it would never happen. I started to object, but Az looked at me, reminding me of what our real objective was.

Without a single wisecrack, I bent down and crawled on my stomach to him. I begged. I pleaded.

"All those years of you mocking me, pulling your stupid jokes, knowing you were under Nick's protection. You want my help, you make up for all of it. Now. Shine it," he said. The Chief laughed and stuck out his right shoe. I started to use my sleeve. "With your tongue."

I didn't have much choice. Not knowing where his shoes had been, I took one precaution. *"Safe."*

And I licked the damn shoe clean, then the other. My task finished, I stood and walked over to Az, spitting all the way. I was one lick from conjuring a toothbrush.

If Negral didn't do it, I was going to hurt someone. Preferably Negral.

Not trusting myself to speak, I let Az handle things. "Well?"

"I'll see what I can do. Give me three Earth hours. If I'm not back by then, I won't be coming," Negral said.

"You know where Gina is?" I said.

Negral smiled. "No, but I can find out."

"Wait." Az handled him a necklace.

"What's this?" Hell's Detective said.

"Cloaking amulet. Good for two uses. Flip it over for the second time."

"But I'll only need one to get the girl," Negral said.

"The first could keep Nick from finding out it was you. The second is a gift."

Negral tipped his hat and disappeared into a hellhole.

"Think he'll find her?" I asked Az.

"We can only pray," said the angel.

"The innocent should never have to pay for the crimes of the guilty."
   -Negral, Hell's Detective

Four and a half hours later, another hellhole appeared. Negral stepped out, a white glow in tow. It floated timidly, flickering. I would compare the sight to shivering.

"Gina?" I asked. At the mention of her name, Gina began to gain form and looked like a little girl. "My name is Mr. Hex. We are so sorry for what happened to you, but everything is going to be okay now."

"Why did my Mommy do this?" she asked.

"I don't know, but she can't hurt you anymore. This is Aziel. He's an angel," I said.

"Really?" she asked.

"Really," said Aziel. "Are you ready to come with me?"

"Am I going to Heaven?" she asked.

"Yes, Gina," replied Aziel, reaching out his hand to hers.

"Wait," she said, floating over to Negral. *"Thank you."* Gina kissed his check. I think the gesture shocked me more than it did him. Negral just nodded.

Gina floated to me. *"Will you make sure my Mommy can't hurt my little brother and sister, like she did me?"*

"Yes," I said.

"Thanks." With that Gina took the angel's outstretched hand. His wings, now healed, wrapped them up in a golden light that took them off to Heaven.

Negral grunted and made toward the hellhole.

"Hex, this never happened," Negral said, his tone full of menacing.

"Deal," I said. Negral started to leave. "Wait."

Negral spun. "What?"

I put out my hand. "Thank you."

Negral scowled and didn't take my hand. "I didn't do it for you. I did it for the kid."

"I know. I also know you would have done it even if I hadn't humbled myself."

Negral's glare softened for the barest of instants. "I owed you one from the Beltizon zombie demon case. You could have called in your marker. You could have made me owe you a favor in the contract like you did Nick. Why didn't you do it?"

"Your shoes were in need of a shine," I said. Negral crossed his arms.

"You actually held back on me in the theater. Both times. You tried to help me and I treated you poorly. I owed you. If humiliating myself was how you wanted that repaid, I could suck it up. What I want to know is, why did you help me?"

"I don't like you, Hex. Never have, but you stand for something. You are a punk and stubborn to a fault. You won't let common sense enter into following your code of honor. Rather than living in fear of the Devil you stood up to him and beat him at his own games. Something I've never been able to pull off. You help the helpless. I can respect that. Where I work there is not much worth respecting. You deserved better than dying like a dog with the person you were trying to save dying alongside you."

"So what if the Devil caught you?" I asked.

Negral shrugged. "Working for Nick is just buying me time until I have to catch the last train to oblivion. I know I'll have to go someday, but I'd like to put it off as long as possible. Besides Nick and I had it out once already."

This was news to me. "You beat him?"

"Nope, but I survived."

"And you refused to hurt Sister Anna. Why?" I asked.

"She's more impressive than an innocent. She's pure, not because she's young, but because she's fought to stay that way. I've been around a long time. That kind of purity is rare. I wasn't going to help Nick destroy it. That's in spite of the fact that you both are sweet on each other." Negral laughed at the shocked expression on my face. "I am a detective. She deserves better, but you're one lucky guy."

I nodded. "You're all right."

"Don't get all gushy on me," he said.

"I won't, but I did get you something." I held out a Fedora.

"I don't want your gifts. Besides, that hat's not even new," Negral said.

"Before you turn it down, look at this," I said, holding out a picture.

Negral looked at it. "It's Bogie in *The Big Sleep*. So I like his movies. You've made fun of me for this before. Why bring it up at this moment?"

"Look at what he's wearing," I said.

"A Royal Stetson hat. So what?" he said.

"It's not just any hat. It's this hat," I said pointing to Bogie's head.

I watched as the Chief's eyes went wide and I saw a small smile. "How? Why?"

"I know a guy and I called in a favor." A few actually. It didn't come cheap.

"What's the catch? A prank waiting to happen? Hat magically adheres to my head and then turns into a bonnet?"

"No, although I did make one alteration," I said, handing him the hat bottom up. The Chief glared at me. "I put in an asbestos liner and magically treated the rest. It could survive in the sun."

"Your word that this hat is what you say it is, with no tricks?" Negral said.

"My word."

Negral put the hat on and started to look around. I pointed to a nearby wall that sported a cracked mirror and he looked at himself in it. He was pleased. How could I tell? He stopped scowling.

"That was thoughtful."

"It happens," I said.

"We even now?" Negral asked.

"Nope. Not even close."

And the scowl was back again. Negral must have thought I was still holding his markers against him.

"The hat and wiping the Beltizon marker are for trying to help me. I still owe you for Gina. When the time comes that you have to leave Nick's service, I'll help."

"For real?"

I nodded.

"This ain't the start of no kind of friendship, beautiful or otherwise. We're not friends, you know," Negral said.

"Probably never will be," I said. "Just a sappy moment between sworn enemies. Somewhat touching."

"I ain't going to hug you."

"Wouldn't dream of it."

Negral seemed to be struggling with himself but ended up holding out his hand. I moved to shake it, but he pulled it up quickly toward the side of his head. He smiled, then actually shook my hand.

"You know if you don't handle this thing right, there aren't going to be enough hand baskets to clean it all up."

I nodded.

"And Balchain wants to put the nun in his most depraved dance class."

"I figured. But if *you* ever want to go out dancing and need a partner..." I made a made like I was doing the meringue.

Negral dismissed me with a wave and vanished back into a hellhole.

> *"Funerals are for the living. It's rather awkward for the dead to attend."*
> *-Hex, cursed magi*

The triple funeral was a sad occasion. Almost any funeral is. The Penguin and I went together. It seemed like half of Brooklyn had turned out to pay their respects to the slain family. Luther had moved the bodies of Mr. and Mrs. Bending out of his South Bronx hood and into Manhattan, to avoid any police investigation. As a matter of fact, they rode in the trunk of the car he had driven me home in. He put them in the dumpster where the police had found them. A family member was able to recognize Mrs. Bending's body, but the flame-broiled Mr. Bending had to be identified via his dental records. The local papers had carried the story, blaming an unknown serial killer and plastering Gary's face inside the local tabloids, in hopes of finding him.

I put Gary's body in a dumpster in that same part of town. When the police found it, they assumed the same serial killer had gotten the son as well. I used a glamour to give Gary his old face and build back. The coroner was not able to identify the cause of death, as there wasn't a mark on the body. Angel swords don't leave any. He ending up writing it off as coronary failure, surmising that the ordeal of being held captive by the aforementioned serial killer induced a fatal heart attack. Neither Anna nor I felt any need to correct their assumptions.

Luther drove Anna and me to the service. He even attended. Luther is the only vamp I have ever met who is both not weakened in the least by sunlight and can set foot on holy ground without pain or discomfort. I was glad he was on the side of the good guys.

Speaking of angels, Az was in attendance but stayed far enough away so he didn't have to speak to me. I understood. He was still coming to terms with what he had to do. Right and wrong weren't at issue. The fact that it ended this way meant that Az had failed Gary. Most angels didn't take it personally. Az wasn't most angels.

We'd meet at Bulfinche's Pub and hash it out over drinks when he was ready.

The Pendragon was also in attendance. Jason sat next to me, with Anna on my other side. She was sandwiched between Luther and me. Jason's Honor Guard was scattered inconspicuously among the crowd of mourners. I even caught a glimpse of Mikoli in the shadows. The shade returned my quick nod.

The service was a simple one. A reverend said a few nice words in the church and the pallbearers carried all three coffins out to the waiting hearses. Many of Gary's classmates were sobbing and crying. I could tell which ones were faking it and had ulterior motives. First, anyone who went to the funeral was given the day off from school. Second, they wanted to be on TV. A dozen teens made sure they went in front of reporters to be interviewed. I guess grief was news. One girl who was weeping loudly told one reporter that she was Gary's ex-girlfriend. The girl told what a kind and good guy he was. The same lying lass said Gary used to have feelings that he was being followed and it had creeped her out. The girl was lying through her teeth. She hadn't even known Gary well. The reporter made sure to mention the school would have grief counselors on hand. Her comment inspired that station to lead off with a story suggesting the killer had been stalking the family.

The extended family wasn't taking any questions, but that wasn't deterring the journalists from trying. Their grief was real and Anna asked me to intervene, so I caused an illusion that the television cameras had gone dead. It stopped them long enough to run back to their news vans for spares, just enough time for the family to make it to their cars.

Jason had another stretch limo and offered the three of us a ride to the cemetery, which we took. One of his Honor Guard, seeing Luther and his fangs, did a fairly slick job of slipping the Pendragon a cross. Jason did just as good a job giving it back. Luther and I were polite enough to pretend not to notice.

The limousine flipped on its headlights and joined in the funeral procession, one of a long line of cars, each filled with people doing their best to not think about how quickly death can come. Well, maybe not everyone, but I sure was. My fear of death was one of the reasons I first tried to explore the afterlives as a kid and saw my first angel. It wasn't Az. It was my Guardian angel, Raxiel. Truthfully, it wasn't the first time I'd seen Rax but it was the first time she admitted to me that she was an angel. She stopped me before I had gotten very far. The only way I agreed to go back to the mortal plane was by insisting she prove to me that there were afterlives. It wasn't easy. I was a smart alec kid with an answer for everything and she was an angel who played by the rules. Heck, she wasn't even supposed to talk to me. Sadly, Rax and I don't have the closest relationship.

It wasn't that I was afraid of going to Hell or some other bad place. I just needed to know that life wasn't the end of my existence, that some part of me went on. Once Rax convinced me of that, I went home quietly.

Jason's limo was easily the nicest I had ever been in. You could barely notice the armor plating and bulletproof windows. Even had satellite TV.

"Can I offer any of you a drink?" Jason asked, motioning to the well-stocked bar. Most of the bottles had never been opened.

We all declined, but I dry swallowed an aspirin with caffeine. The little stunt with the news cameras had given me a minor headache. Luckily I had spent a few days sleeping.

"Hex, tell me the entire story please," Jason asked. As Jason and Luther are two of the few people on my "trust" list, I obliged.

"You really have the Devil trapped? And freed the Chief?"

I nodded. Both Jason and Luther smiled at the thought.

"Hex, you sometimes amaze me. Can I be of assistance with your prisoner?" Jason asked.

"No. There is no reason to drag you in." There was no known way to kill the Devil. I could destroy his current form with his name, but I wasn't sure if he would somehow be able to survive or reform. Nick was a force of nature. Be easier to kill gravity. And gravity didn't hold grudges for centuries. Nick did. Best to keep other people out of the crossfire. "We can handle it." The Penguin gave me a look of doubt. I gave her a reassuring smile that fell short of accomplishing its goal.

"What are you going to do with him?" Jason asked.

"I don't know yet. He'll keep until I do," I said.

"You have two other bits of unfinished business." Jason meant Grundy and Dartley. "Can I help you with those?"

"Yes, but not now. But soon. Right now, I'm still too wiped." Despite having slept most of the last few days, I wasn't right yet. "Dartley will keep and I need more rest before I think about going after Grundy again. He still has the amulet and is likely in a new body so finding him will be rough." I was hesitant to summon the universe again. Doing that ritual is dangerous, especially in my condition. It would take me most of the next year to feel normal again or least for what passes for normal with me. Performing it anytime soon could very well kill me. Even if it didn't, it wasn't a good idea. I was too weak after the last time and going after Grundy like that almost got Luther and I killed.

"I'll put my people right on it," Jason promised.

"Thanks. In the meantime, could you also track down an Anita Martinez for me as well?"

Jason's network had found the former waitress before we arrived at the cemetery. Funny, when you are speaking of someone in relation to it, it's a cemetery. The rest of the time, it's a graveyard.

Three adjoining gravesites had been picked out for the Bendings and they lined up the mahogany coffins in a row above their final resting places.

The reverend did his best to convince the mourners of several things. One, we shouldn't be sad, the dead had gone to a better place. Two, they would never be gone as long as we remembered them in our hearts. Three, the lives of those present were better off for having known the deceased. He didn't succeed in convincing me on any of the points, but I'm a tougher audience than most.

They were lowered into the ground. First Gary, followed by his mother and finally his father. The crowds left. We stayed longer.

Anna placed a red rose into each grave, silently praying at each one. When she finished, I stepped forward to say my goodbyes with three red roses in hand. I stared into the grave of Gary's dad. The tombstones hadn't been made yet. I laid a rose down on the ground.

"Mr. Bending, I'm sorry I couldn't save you from the monsters. I promise I will find Grundy and make him pay." I stepped over to Gary's mom. "Mrs. Bending, I almost had Grundy. If he hadn't gotten away, you would still be alive." I made no excuses to the dead. The dead don't care about our excuses. "I'm so sorry. I make you the same promise I made your husband. Grundy will pay."

Last, I moved to Gary's grave and laid the last rose down. "Gary, I'm sorry that things turned out like they did. I wish I could have done something that would have helped you make another decision. I didn't think much of your choice, but I admired your final actions. It was the bravest thing you could have done under the circumstances. I don't know where you are now, but it's not Hell so you're ahead of the game. Goodbye."

When we turned and walked away, the gravediggers started filling in the holes.

"Everything is beautiful, especially me."
  -Anita Martinez

I never much cared for LA. It seems like every time I'm in town it's hot and muggy. Forget the fact that everything is too spread out. Most people need a car to get anywhere. Luckily, I don't fit into that category. Good thing too, because being a city boy, I don't own a car. Rarely needed one in New York. And then there's that whole no driver's license issue. I wasn't in California to sightsee. I was here on business. Gina's business.

Anita Martinez had come up in the world very recently. Last week, she was virtually unknown and the Devil's waitress at a lunch. This week she landed a part in a blockbuster film and was rumored to have been offered more than twenty million for the lead, the highest ever paid to a first-time actress. Filming had already begun on a closed set. The talk was Anita was brilliant, her performance Oscar-worthy. Pure magic some were saying. They weren't far from the truth.

I found her alone in her trailer on the movie lot. She was sitting in front of a mirror, combing her long black hair while reciting lines from a script. A frozen daiquiri lay half consumed, melting on the makeup table.

"Yes, can I help you?" she asked, as she caught a glimpse of my reflection in the mirror. She gave me the once over with her eyes. Judging by the way she licked her lips, she liked what she saw.

"Ms. Anita Martinez?" I said.

"Actually, now it's Anita Martin. My stage name," she said, turning to face me. There was seduction in her eyes. I flashed on her. In the past few days, she had enjoyed the intimate company of several men. Apparently, intense sex appeal was in her contract with Nick and she had no qualms about using it. She was a beautiful woman, even without the glamour. Had I not known about her daughter and if it had been before I meet Anna, I might have been tempted. The thought of what she did to Gina made her more repulsive than a leper with oozing sores.

"What can I help you with?" As she stood, a yellow silk robe slid off her shoulders, falling quickly to the ground. Anita made no attempt to grab it. When she turned to face me, she wore a lacy red push up bra, which enhanced cleavage that was already of monumental proportions. Her long legs ended in a pelvis barely covered by a red thong. Anita wiggled her way across to me. I stepped back. The idea of a hunt excited her.

"Don't be frightened. I won't bite, unless you want me to," Anita purred, trying to stroke my shoulder. I grabbed her hand before she could make contact. "Ooh. I like the rough stuff."

"Ms. Martinez, I am here to talk to you regarding your daughter Gina," I said, pushing her hand back to her side. Anita swooned and collapsed into a chair.

"It's horrible, Gina disappearing like that. Next week her picture is going on thousands of milk cartons." The prospect seemed to excite her. "Tomorrow, I will be doing an interview on Good Morning USA to beg for her safe return."

"No need," I said.

"No need? Of course, there's a need. I need to find my baby. Plus, I am going to be publicizing my new film, *The Devil's Own*," she said, obviously in love with the sound of her own voice.

"Appropriate title," I said.

"What do you mean?"

"I found your daughter," I said flatly.

"You did?" she said without skipping a beat, successfully managing not to betray anything. She was a fine actress. "Where is she?" Anita actually appeared to be a frantically worried mother, rather than a devil-dealing monster.

"I left her in the company of an angel," I said.

"An angel!? You killed her!?" she moaned. "You killed my baby? Security!"

She was good, I had to give her that. However, I was better.

"*Soundproof*," I said to the walls. "Scream all you like. It didn't do Gina any good. It won't do you any good."

Anita backed off, acting terrified. She thought she had found the perfect patsy to take the fall for her daughter's disappearance. "So you came here to kill me, too?"

"You're not getting off that easy," I said.

"Where's Gina's body?" she begged, on her knees. "Please tell me, so I can at least bury her."

"You know damn well where her body is. In Hell, where you sent her. Only her body didn't survive." It is possible for a physical form to survive in Hell, but not if its owner is submissive. "Gina is dead, killed by demons. Only her soul has escaped and by now should be in Heaven."

"What are you talking about?" Anita asked, with mocked ignorance.

If the Academy could see only her now.

"I know all about your deal with the Devil. It's time for you to pay the piper."

"Security!" she shouted. "You're crazy!"

"Maybe I am, but at least I never sold my daughter to Hell. Why did you do it? To become a movie star? How pathetic." That got her.

"How dare you mock me!"

"How dare you destroy innocence entrusted to you. You took Gina's future away from her, so I am going to do the same to you," I said. "Your greatest possession is your beauty. You are beautiful no more. *Repulsive forever!*"

Anita waited for something to happen, but she sensed nothing.

"Well, that's it?" she asked, regaining her composure.

"That's it. From now on, everyone who has the misfortune to look upon you only will see the physical manifestation of your grotesque soul," I said.

Anita walked over to the mirror and stared at her reflection. In her eyes, nothing had changed. In her eyes, it never would. "Ha. It didn't work!" she said putting her hands on her hips and turning to me. I half expected her to stick out her tongue and say "Na-na."

"Didn't it?" I said. In answer to my question, her make-up woman knocked and came in the trailer, her back to Anita.

"Ms. Martin?" the woman said. "I have to finish your makeup for the afternoon shoot."

"Doris, I'm glad you're here," Anita said. Doris turned around, took one look and let out a blood-curdling scream. "Doris, relax. It's me." Doris' yells only increased in volume.

"Get away from me!" Doris begged. Anita took a step forward and Doris grabbed her stomach. A moment later she vomited her lunch all over Anita's half-naked body. Still clutching her gut, Doris crawled out of the trailer. Sounds of more hurling on the ground carried inside the trailer.

"My God!" Anita exclaimed, trying to come to grip with what had just happened while wiping vomit off her skin.

"Should have turned to him first. Too late now," I said. Anita turned toward me and fell on her knees in the puddle of former stomach contents.

"Please, don't do this to me!"

"Already done. You are doomed to wander the Earth, forever hiding from others, until the day you die."

Anita grabbed hold of my right leg. "Please, I'm a mother. Think of my three children. What will become of them?"

"You sold one to the Devil. The other two are already back in the custody of James, your ex-husband and their father. He will take care of them."

"But I have official custody!" she intoned as if it made a difference to me.

"Not for long. No court would let children anywhere near a thing like you."

Anita stood and composed herself, cleaning herself off with a towel. She found a ray of light in the darkness. "At least, I still have the twenty million."

"Funny, you should mention that. The money is in escrow, pending your completion of the movie. You can't finish filming, you don't get the money."

"You can't do this to me!"

"Yes, I can." I turned and walked toward the door. "Bye."

"I can't live like this. I'll kill myself," Anita threatened, sounding like a child promising to hold her breath until she turned blue.

"That's your choice, which is more than Gina had. Let me leave you with this one thought. If you kill yourself, where do you think you are going? And do you think they'll be happy that you welshed on your part of the deal?"

"But I didn't!"

"They won't see it that way. Gina's not in Hell," I said. "See ya."

Careful not to step in the pools of vomit, I left the trailer and the sounds of Anita's agonized screams behind me. I didn't look back.

"If at first you don't succeed... Well, that tends to be a problem for other people."

    -The Devil

The next morning, Nick was where I had left him, still reading. Cool as a cucumber, as always. The book was laid down on the table as soon as he saw me.

"Hex, I didn't expect you to take so long. Poor Gina..."

"Is no longer an issue," I said.

"Really?" the Devil answered. Unwilling to appear less than all-knowing, he held back from asking me the how and why. Nor did he insult me by asking if I kept my word.

"In the interest of fairness, just count her toward the thousand you owe me," I said, as I planted my butt in a folding chair and put my feet up on a second.

"You are going to really take the thousand?" Nick asked.

"Looks that way," I said. "But not all at once. I'll take a few at a time, as I can find homes for them."

"These are souls, not puppies. You can't find homes for them."

"Final resting places then."

"Why not all at once?" asked Nick.

"You are right about the fact that I couldn't handle it," I said. The Devil smiled a knowing smile. "You only made the deal for those stakes because of the mess taking care of a thousand souls would make of my life."

"You know I do nothing out of the goodness of my heart."

"True enough."

"When do you want to pick up your first batch?"

"Soon. I'll let you know," I said. Paddy Moran and Hermes had agreed to act as my brokers on this deal, contacting various afterworld deities with my proposal to take a portion of the whole. First on the list was Pluto. He had a river in Hades, the Lethe, which he was insisting the souls drink from. It would cause the souls to forget their lives, letting them start with a fresh slate, like Gary. Worked for me.

"You know I'll have another deal for you on that day," Nick said, as casually as if discussing the weather.

"I kind of figured," I answered.

I stood.

"Later, Nick." I turned to leave.

"Hex," the Devil said.

"Yes?" I answered.

"We still on for lunch next week?"

I sighed. I would have to check up on him anyway. "Sure."

I left the theater of the damned and headed uptown to Bulfinche's Pub. Next week I might be having lunch with the Devil, but today I was having drinks with an angel and a penguin and I didn't want to be late. I might miss happy hour and today that was something I really needed.

"Sometimes what you find at the end of the rainbow is better than a pot of gold."

-Hex, cursed magi

I made my way to Bulfinche's Pub. I needed to relax and it was one of the few places in the world I could.

If you've never been, I recommend it highly. I can't give you directions, but if you are ever in Manhattan and see a rainbow follow it. If you are lucky, you'll end up here.

"So ye have Nick under lock and key?" Paddy Moran whispered to me.

I nodded and sipped a Long Island iced tea. I needed something more after everything that happened. I even told them to run a tab for Bast when she came in to pay off my debt.

"How long can you keep him there?" Murphy, one of the bartenders and the only human one, asked.

"Not too long," Paddy said.

"My wards will hold," I said.

"Tis not your wards I be worried about," Paddy said. "Tis the state of the Pit. Without Nick down there, there will be chaos and we don't need it spilling out onto Earth."

I sighed. The leprechaun was right and I know it. I either had to destroy him or get a deal in place where I could let him go.

"That's a worry for tomorrow. Tonight, I have a date."

"When you called her a penguin, I didn't think you were being literal," Murphy said looking toward the door.

I turned expecting to see Anna in the same dress she was on the run in, but she was in a little red number. When last we spoke the sundress was the only clothes she owned. Crystal was next to her, dressed in penguin suit that looked as if it belonged in an amusement park, although she had a cut out for her face.

"That's my Anna in red. The one in the penguin suit is Crystal."

Paddy rolled his eyes. Although like everyone else he has no memory of Crystal's time as Empress of the world, she'd been to the bar before and left a lasting impression.

I held out my arms for a hug and Crystal waddled in front of Anna to embrace me.

"I love free hugs. And pickled herring. That's cause I'm a penguin.

The Empress Penguin!"

I lifted my eyebrows. "Good girls' day out?"

"The best!" Crystal shouted and then part ran and part waddled to the bar. Paddy casually moved away to allow Murphy to wait on her.

I hugged and kissed Anna. "How'd it go?'

"Bizarrely fun, actually. Crystal wanted to buy me clothes, but I wouldn't let her so she gave me this dress out of her closet. You like?"

"Very much."

Anna had had her talk with her Mother Superior about leaving the order. She'd asked if Anna was sure, then said she was happy for her. Mother offered her a job at the shelter and said she could stay at the convent until she found someplace else to live. The job pays minimum wage, so normally it would be a while until she found a place she could afford.

I offered a solution. I had an empty apartment but Anna refused to take charity, so I am giving her a good deal. Plus, there's a reason I haven't been able to rent it – it's across the hall from Crystal which scares most people off. Anna was okay with that and was moving into it this weekend.

Speaking of Crystal, she was laying across a barstool on her stomach and pretending to swim. Murphy was encouraging her by throwing goldfish crackers into her mouth every time she stood up and clapped her fake flippers.

"I see you found her an outfit," I said.

"You would be amazed how many places in Manhattan sell penguin suits."

"How many are in the Village?"

"About half, but I talked her out of leather. Several times."

Crystal apparently was done swimming and stood up and slapped a fake flipper on the bar.

"A pickled herring smoothie barkeep and don't spare the chocolate and tartar sauce," Crystal said.

"I wouldn't dream of it," Murphy said. "How about we review what you want in it so I make it to perfection?"

"Awesome. Maybe we could add some sardines too?"

"I don't see why not," Murphy said. "Maybe some iceberg lettuce?"

"Yes!" Crystal giggled hilariously and spun in a circle.

"Oh no. This is bad," I said.

Anna tensed up and looked over at the bar. "What is?"

"Murphy found someone who actually likes his jokes. Let me

introduce you." I led Anna toward the bar.

"You know how I got my last penguin costume to stay on?" Murphy said.

"How," said Crystal?

"Iglooed it on."

"You are hilarious!" Crystal laughed so hard she fell to the floor.

"Hey, let me know if you have to run out to the snow bank to get some money to pay for this, all right?"

Crystal started banging her feet and flippers on the floor, tears of laughter flowing down her cheeks.

"I'm so glad that you're happy. You know how I can tell? By your pen-grin."

Paddy came over and put a folded napkin in Murphy's mouth to shut him up, but Crystal kept laughing and in fact rolled away across the room.

Anna and I stepped around the rolling penguin and bellied up to the bar.

"Paddy, Murphy, this is Anna. Anna, this are two of the finest men I've ever met, if you overlook Murphy's attempts to be funny."

"We all do," Paddy said and extended his hand across the bar to shake Anna's. "Tis a pleasure to meet ye lass. Hex hasn't been able to stop talking about ye."

"That's good to hear."

The three of them made small talk when I noticed a blond man in a white trench coat come in the door.

I turned back to the bar. "Paddy, are you okay for that dispensation I asked for earlier?"

The leprechaun nodded. "Consider it my gift to the new couple."

Anna looked confused. "Dispensation for what?"

"Magic only works in Bulfinche's Pub if Paddy gives it his dispensation."

"So you are going to use magic?" Anna said.

"No, I am," came the voice of the bar's guardian angel.

Anna turned and recognized someone she had never actually seen in person before.

"Aziel," Anna said simply. It was not a question. The penguin may never have seen Az before in the waking world, but she recognized him as if she had known him all her life. In a sense, she had. The angel had been watching out for her since before the moment of her birth.

Az nodded, took off his white coat, then unfurled his wings.

The angel took the penguin's hands and they both got misty-eyed.

"I am so sorry about what happened with Gary, but I wanted to thank you for doing your best by him."

Anna was still grieving over what had happened to Gary. She blamed herself for failing the kid. It was a natural reaction. On one level, she failed Gary. We both did, but on a much larger scale, he failed us. It didn't make the pain go away. Didn't even make it any less, but it helped with rationalization, the last refuge of the heavy-hearted. There was nothing I could do to convince her, so I called on someone who could.

"I so sorry that I failed Gary. And failed you," Anna said.

"You failed no one. He failed himself. I thank you for everything you did for him."

The air around Az shimmered in the spectrum of gold.

"Peace be with you," said Heaven's messenger. Az rose up. His golden glow encompassed the Penguin and parts of it hit the rest of us. The glow created a moment of instant understanding in our minds. Az conveyed that Gary had not been ready for or worthy of Heaven, but because of Gary being willing to sacrifice himself to prevent his ascension to power and all the evil that would ensue, Aziel was able to pull some divine strings and got him a second chance.

Gary's soul now rested in the womb of a woman who had just conceived, despite a dozen doctors' assurances that she was infertile. Gary would be viewed as a miracle by his next parents and, like most of the reincarnated, would remember nothing of his previous life. He had a fresh start. Odds are he would not be a magí, so his next life would be normal, if there was such a thing.

No more words needed to be spoken. Aziel gathered up Anna so she floated up into his arms. She, in turn, hugged the angel back. The pair floated up even higher, locked in a comforting embrace. The angel's wings enveloped them, wrapping them in a glowing cocoon. Tears flowed, from both angel and human eyes, mixing together in the hope that their souls might be washed clean.

Maybe it worked. Maybe it didn't. But it did inspire me to do something I rarely do anymore. I prayed to God that it worked for both of them. I was even willing to owe him a favor.

"Not all ends well, but that's no reason not to make the best of it."
-Crystal, former Empress of the world

"What a wonderful place," Anna said. I nodded. That was Bulfinche's Pub in a nutshell.

"I had a wonderful time, Hex."

"Me too."

"Me three!" yelled Crystal from the cab behind us. She was hanging half out of the window, still in her penguin suit.

Anna chuckled.

"Crystal, we're trying to have a private moment here," I said

"That's okay. I don't mind. You aren't offending me."

"Thank you for arranging for me to meet Aziel."

"Getting around the rules is what I do best," I said.

"I better go in," Anna said.

I leaned in for a goodnight kiss. Anna pulled back and grinned.

"We are in front of a convent, you know."

"But not in it, so I think we're okay."

She chuckled and kissed me. It was wonderful but too short.

I watched her go inside. When she opened the door, she revealed a gaggle of nuns who were watching and waiting for her. The others brought her inside, but Mother Superior stepped outside.

"Hello Hex, I am Mother Tina."

"A pleasure, Mother."

"So, you are the one Anna is enamored of."

"Yes, ma'am."

"Anna is very special."

"She is."

"You will treasure her, will you not?"

"Always."

"Good. Trust me, the last thing you want is an angry nun coming after you should you hurt her or break her heart."

"Yes, ma'am."

Mother Tina smiled. "I wish you both all the happiness in the world."

"Thank you, Mother."

Mother Tina went back in and locked the door and I turned to go back to the cab went a man in a black suit jumped out from behind some garbage cans and put a gun in my back.

"No sudden moves, Hex or I shoot."

"Thank you for saving me the trouble of coming to find you, Agent Dartley."

"You blew up Hell's Embassy. And I don't know how you did it, but you got me suspended."

It didn't take much. I just called Uncle Sam and told him what Dartley had done. The head of the DMA called the head of the CIA. Apparently, there was a little more politics to it than that. Sam wanted Dartley arrested and tried, but all that happened is that he was suspended for three months.

"No need to thank me."

"Thank you? I'm going to make you disappear."

I prepared a finger hex to take him out when a woman in a giant penguin suit tackled him to the ground. The pair of them rolled around on the sidewalk and our cab sped off. Dartley managed to end up on top and pointed his gun at Crystal's face.

Before I could step in, a bolt of magic leapt from Crystal's right flipper covered hand and hit Dartley in the face. The man suddenly shrunk and transformed.

Crystal rolled over and reached into the suit that had crumpled to the sidewalk and pulled out a crab.

"That's what you get for messing with the Empress's friends!" she yelled.

I stood there stunned and nervous.

"Crystal, first thank you."

"You are welcome."

"But I thought you lost your powers."

"I did."

"Then how did you turn the evil man into a crab?"

"I found them but I'm not sure how. Every day I check behind the couch and never found them before. But I found them now." She waved her flipper in a mystic hand gesture that should have made the air glow and nothing happened. "Drat. I think I lost them again."

She and I locked eyes and I had no idea if she was lying.

"Nobody hurts the Empress' friends and you Hex are one of my bestest friends."

I nodded. The idea of Crystal with her powers back was terrifying, yet if she had been hiding them, she had refrained from using them before this. Maybe the adrenaline had let her call upon them. Or maybe she was the best actress I'd ever seen.

"Hex, I know your policy on pets." It's simple. I have to approve them. "I won't let Agent Crab out unsupervised. So can I keep him? Or eat him? Or both?"

I bent down and tried to look the horseshoe crab in the eyes, but it was too hard. He had ten. One thing was clear. Dartley was terrified. Being a pet in Crystal's care had to be far more terrifying than anything I would have done to him.

"You wasted your one warning, Dartley." I turned back to Crystal. "Sure. He's all yours."

I picked up the suit. No reason to have it found near the convent.

There were no cabs around.

"I guess we're walking home," I said.

"Excuse me. Be PC. Some of us are waddling home." Crystal ran ahead of me, throwing the crab up in the air, then catching him with her flippers.

PATRICK THOMAS is the author of almost 40 books including the beloved fantasy humor Murphy's Lore series, which includes *Tales From Bulfinche's Pub, Fools' Day, Through The Drinking Glass, Shadow Of The Wolf, Redemption Road, Bartender Of The Gods, Nightcaps* and *Empty Graves* — as well as the future space adventures *Startenders* and *Constellation Prize.*

The Murphy's Lore After Hours spin-offs star the half pixie/ogre Terrorbelle (*Fairy With A Gun, Fairy Rides The Lightning);* the former demon-possessed serial killer Agent Karver of the Department of Mystic Affairs *(Dead To Rites, Rites of Passage);* the cursed magí Hex *(By Darkness Cursed and By Invocation Only);* Vince Argus, the Soul For Hire *(Greatest Hits);* and Negral, a forgotten Sumerian god who works as Hell's Detective *(Lore & Dysorder* and *Bullets & Brimstone).*

Co-Written with John French and Diane Raetz, his Mystic Investigators paranormal mystery series includes *Bullets & Brimstone, From The Shadows* and *Once More Upon A Time. Assassin's Ball,* his first mystery, is also co-written with John French.

He also wrote the steampunk *As The Gears Turn* and the space epic *Exile & Entrance.* He co-edited *New Blood* and *Hear Them Roar* and was an editor for the magazines *Fantastic Stories of the Imagination* and *Pirate Writings.*

Patrick's darkly humorous advice column Dear Cthulhu has been running since 2005 and includes the collections *Have A Dark Day, Good Advice For Bad People, Cthulhu Knows Best, What Would Cthulhu Do?* and *Cthulhu Happens*

His short stories have been featured in over fifty anthologies and more than forty-five print magazines.

A number of his books were part of the props department of the CSI television show and have been spotted on the program. Nightcaps was even thrown at a suspect's head. His urban fantasy Fairy With A Gun had been optioned for film and TV by Laurence Fishburne's Cinema Gypsy Productions. Top Men Productions has turned his Soul For Hire Story, *Act of Contrition*, into a short film.

Please drop by www.patthomas.net or follow him at I_PatrickThomas at Twitter or www.facebook.com/PatrickThomasAuthor to learn more.

No One Is Above The Lore...
Even In Hell
Hell's Detective
LORE & DYSORDER
IT'S NOT EASY BEING HELL'S CHIEF OF POLICE
THE HELL'S DETECTIVE MYSTERIES
PATRICK THOMAS
MYSTIC INVESTIGATORS
BULLETS & BRIMSTONE
Patrick Thomas & John L. French
MURPHY'S LORE
AFTER HOURS
TERROR
GHOSTMAN AND HELL'S DETECTIVE
CASE OF THE MOON MANIA
PATRICK THOMAS / BLAIR WEISS
GHOSTMAN
HELL'S DETECTIVE
DANTE
"Gritty, snappy, very dark
and very funny,"
-J. L. Comeau,
Creature Feature
"Dark... and charming."
-ELLEN DATLOW
The Best Horror of the Year Vol. 4

The Collected Advice Columns Of DEAR CTHULHU Vol. 1
HAVE A Dark DAY
PATRICK THOMAS

The Collected Advice Columns Of DEAR CTHULHU Vol. 2
GOOD ADVICE for BAD PEOPLE
PATRICK THOMAS

Didn't your mother ever tell you to listen to your Elders?
CTHULHU KNOWS BEST
The Collected Advice Columns Of DEAR CTHULHU Vol. 3
PATRICK THOMAS

DEAR CTHULHU
The advice column to END all advice columns

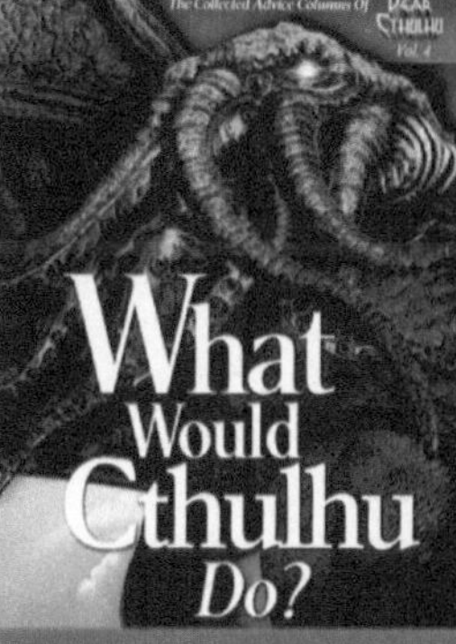

The Collected Advice Columns Of DEAR CTHULHU Vol. 4
What Would Cthulhu Do?
PATRICK THOMAS
The Collected Advice Columns of DEAR CTHULHU Vol. 5
CTHULHU HAPPENS
PATRICK THOMAS

WWW.DEARCTHULHU.COM
WWW.PADWOLF.COM